He grabbed the nape of her neck, forcing her face closer to his. His gaze dipped to her lips. "Once again, Keira, you do not understand the consequences of your actions."

With the heat in his eyes and his body pressed against her, something wildly hot flared in Keira. She was sixteen all over again, mad with desire, reckless and desperate to kiss him. She looked into his glittering eyes and answered breathlessly, "*Aye*, I do."

Critical acclaim for the vividly passionate novels of
Julia London

"London creates magic . . . and leaves her fans begging for more."
—*Romantic Times*

"A triumph of wit and passion."
—*Booklist*

"London's characters come alive on every page and will steal your heart."
—*Atlanta Journal-Constitution*

The Year of Living Scandalously **is also available**
as an eBook

Also by Julia London

JULIA LONDON

The YEAR of LIVING SCANDALOUSLY

Pocket Books

New York   London   Toronto   Sydney

Pocket Books
A Division of Simon & Schuster, Inc.
1230 Avenue of the Americas
New York, NY 10020

This book is a work of fiction. Names, characters, places, and incidents either are products of the author's imagination or are used fictitiously. Any resemblance to actual events or locales or persons, living or dead, is entirely coincidental.

First Pocket Books paperback edition November 2010

POCKET and colophon are registered trademarks of Simon & Schuster, Inc.

For information about special discounts for bulk purchases, please contact Simon & Schuster Special Sales at 1-866-506-1949 or business@simonandschuster.com.

The Simon & Schuster Speakers Bureau can bring authors to your live event. For more information or to book an event contact the Simon & Schuster Speakers Bureau at 1-866-248-3049 or visit our website at www.simonspeakers.com.

Interior design by Jacquelynne Hudson
Cover design by Lisa Litwack
Front cover photo by Barry Marcus

Manufactured in the United States of America

10 9 8 7 6 5 4 3 2 1

ISBN 978-1-4391-7545-3
ISBN 978-1-4391-7549-1 (ebook)

For Jameson, my best and special boy

Prologue

1793
West Sussex, England

Each summer in the village of Hadley Green, the residents looked forward with eager anticipation to two significant events: the first was the week in June in which the vicar put his gout-ridden body into a borrowed coach and took leave of his flock to call upon his aging sister in Shropshire. That was the only week of the year the pulpit could be pried from the vicar's bent hands, and the young, visiting clergyman's delivery of the gospel was markedly more succinct.

The second event was the annual gala at the end of summer given by the Earl of Ashwood. It was a celebration of a good harvest and good tenants, and an opportunity to raise funds for the poor orphans of the St. Bartholomew Parish. It was a day-long festival, replete with enough food and ale to feed the king's army, as well as goods for sale made by the more industrious villagers. There were games for children and adults alike, and a small band that entertained the happy guests who elected to sit under umbrellas at tables festooned with streamers and flowers from the earl's enviable hothouse and gardens. There was a small lake with a pair of boats that young men employed to court young women as they rowed them about.

Traditionally, members of the Quality came down from London to attend the gala and stayed on as the guests of the earl and his lovely—and strikingly younger—wife, Althea Kent, Lady Ashwood. The Quality partook of the crafts and food and ale alongside the residents of Hadley Green, although perhaps less of the crafts and more of the ale. Inevitably, late in the day, the legs of lords and common men were lashed together for three-legged races, the winners promised a kiss from the countess herself.

Given Lady Ashwood's uncommon beauty, most mortal men were keen to try.

It was likewise tradition that when the sun began to slide behind the towering elms, the village residents wobbled home in their carts and their wagons, and the lords and ladies retreated inside the earl's colossal Georgian home to settle in for a night of debauchery.

Those evenings were the stuff of legends. More than one marriage had been threatened by the evening's activities, and more than one marriage made on the heels of compromising events.

In 1793, a torrential late-summer storm ended the outdoor festivities in the early afternoon. The villagers and the orphans were hurried home to meaner shelter than Ashwood, and the earl's illustrious guests were hurried inside to waiting servants who handed them towels and stoked the hearths in their rooms.

A steady rain continued to fall throughout the day, cooling the air and filling the rooms with a damp scent.

The guests, trapped inside like well-groomed beasts, began to seek entertainment. They were modestly diverted by drink, gaming, and flirting through the long stretch of afternoon into evening. But as evening fell, the stakes at the gaming tables grew dangerously higher, as did the number of men and women disappearing from the salon, only to return a half hour later with wigs askew.

Above the gambling and assignations in the darkened rooms of the main floor was a nursery, and in that nursery was Miss Lillian Boudine, Lady Ashwood's ward and niece. Lily was an eight-year-old orphan who had been adopted by Auntie Althea when her parents were taken from her at the tender age of five, both of them succumbing to a wasting fever within a fortnight of each other. One might have hoped that the lord and lady of Ashwood would have changed their ways to accommodate the moppet of a girl, but that was hardly the case. Their soirees and balls and gatherings continued, and Lily grew accustomed to seeing shadowy figures embracing in darkened stairwells, and the sound of doors being shut and locked. She'd heard many feminine giggles and the quiet *hush* of masculine voices. She could detect the scent of women's perfume lingering in the corridors amid the smells of beeswax candles and blazing hearths.

That evening, Lily was relegated to the nursery with Nurse. Nurse had sampled the earl's ale in great quantities, and could not keep her puffy eyes open. She slept noisily in a chair near the hearth.

Lily was rather eager to leave the nursery and have a peek at the adults. She stepped past her sleeping nurse and into the corridor, taking care to shut the door quietly behind her. She ran lightly to the stairwell and hurried down to her perfect hiding place, where she could watch the comings and goings of the adults.

But when she reached the first floor, she found it darker than usual. The rainy weather had led to a shortage of candles, and only two were lit in the long hallway. It was so dark that Lily did not, at first, detect the embracing couple until one of them whispered low. The sound startled her, and Lily quickly stepped behind a console table and crouched down.

She could just make out the shadowy figures through the legs of the console. They were *kissing*. Lily leaned out a little to see better, but in doing so she lost her balance. She caught herself with both hands before tumbling onto the carpet, but panicking, she gasped softly and quickly pushed back, pressing her back to the wall, stifling her breath with one hand.

Several moments passed before Lily dared to look again. She was disappointed to find that the couple had evaporated into the darkness. Lily stood up, carefully looked about, then darted down the corridor toward her hiding place.

But as she reached the top of the very ornate, curving dual staircase that led to the floors below, a hand clamped down on her shoulder. Lily cried out with alarm as she was twirled about and forced to look up into the lovely face of Aunt Althea.

Althea was none too pleased. The ruby of her lips matched the ruby of her velvet gown, and the color in her cheeks was quite high. "What do you think you are doing, Lily?"

"Nothing, Auntie! I meant only to see the ladies' evening gowns!" Lily had used that excuse before with success, but tonight, Althea would not accept it. She put both hands on Lily's shoulders and gave her a gentle shove into the corridor. "Honestly, what am I to do with you, darling? Go back to the nursery! You know very well I am to Scotland on the morrow. I must be able to depend on you to be good whilst I am away."

"I will!" Lily promised earnestly.

"No, Lily, no more of your empty vows," Althea said sternly. "There is nothing that will displease the earl more than your bad behavior, and if he grows weary of you, what will become of you then?" She sank to her knees, so that she could look Lily in the eye. "Your mother, my dear sister, is dead. Another sister is ailing. That leaves only my youngest sister in Ireland to take you in. Do you really want to be *Irish*, Lily? I'll be gone for an age, and when I come back, it had best not be to my husband's complaints and demands that you pack your bags. You really must stop this spying and skulking about!"

Lily felt frightened and guilty. "Yes, Auntie, I promise with all my heart." She was very sincere. She never meant to be bad; it just seemed to happen.

Her aunt softened and smiled, cupping Lily's chin. "My, how you remind me of Maria," she said, speaking of Lily's mother. "She was an imp, just like you. Not as pretty as you, I think, but just as spirited. I miss her so. And I shall miss you desperately." She smiled and kissed Lily's cheek. "Now show me how good you shall be and go back to the nursery and *stay* there." She came to her feet, ran her hand over Lily's crown. "Go before the earl sees you."

Lily ran down the corridor and up the servants' stairs to the second floor. She walked into the nursery and shut the door behind her. Nurse started, but then shifted in her chair and snorted in her sleep. With a roll of her eyes, Lily climbed onto the window seat. It was dark and wet outside; the only light was that which came from the house. She traced a line down the cold, wet pane, leaving a fat trail like that of a snail.

The nursery was never warm. It was far too big for the single fireplace, and Lily was always cold here. She thought it would be lovely if she had a companion, someone to share these interminably long and boring nights.

A movement outside caught her eye. Lily pressed her face to the window and peered out. It was a rider; she could see him trotting past by the light of the house, moving away. Lily suddenly sat up. She knew the rider—or rather, she knew the horse. It was the big gray with black spots on his rump that belonged to Mr. Scott, the woodcarver. Lily had seen him here many times before tonight, as he had crafted the dual staircase that curved up and around the main entry to the first floor.

Why should he be at Ashwood tonight? He was not Quality. What woodcarving would he be doing on the day of the gala? And why was he riding *away* in the rain across the park instead of the main road? Had he not left when the other villagers were instructed to go home?

But ride away he did, disappearing into the dark night.

Lily wrote her name in the condensation on the glass, then realized she was shivering and found her bed.

She was awakened sometime later by a lot of shouting, the cries loud enough to wake even Nurse. "Glory, it must be fire!" Nurse cried, and rushed Lily downstairs—Nurse, in her nightclothes, Lily still in her evening frock—to the main floor.

They were greeted by general bedlam, as the guests were all shouting at one another, and at least one lady was crying. The earl was scowling at the lot of them and Althea was pale.

Nurse nudged a footman and whispered loudly, "What is it, what has happened?"

The footman, an eyewitness to the tumult, was eager to deliver the news. "The Lady Ashwood was playing loo, but the earl refused to give her a purse, for he'd warned her not to carry on, but you know the Lady Ashwood, she did all the same. She lost a bloody fortune. When it came time to pay her debt, she went to fetch the Ashwood jewels to put up as collateral. But they come up missing."

"*What?* The old ones?" Nurse asked, horrified.

Even Lily knew of the Ashwood jewels; everyone knew of them. They were large, priceless rubies, given by King Edward IV to the first Earl of Ashwood for his loyalty during the War of the Roses. The rubies—set in a heavy necklace; in big, teardrop ruby earrings; and the largest in the coronet—were kept under lock and key in the earl's private study.

"Aye, the *old* ones," the footman grimly confirmed.

It was at this moment that Althea spotted Lily and Nurse in the crowd and began moving toward them.

" 'Twas one of them, I'd wager, what with all the carrying on behind closed doors," the footman quickly added, for he, too, saw Althea approaching. "But mark me, Annie, 'twill be one of us who is blamed for it."

"Annie, are you mad? What if the earl sees you?" Althea whispered harshly. She glanced anxiously over her shoulder at the earl, almost as if she feared him. Lily didn't blame her—he seemed very mean. Her aunt looked back at Lily and she smiled thinly. "Go," she said to Annie.

Nurse grabbed Lily's wrist in a painful grip and dragged her up the stairs, but Lily struggled against her, turning back to watch until she could see the adults no more.

The next day dawned bright and blue. There was a lot of commotion around the countess's planned departure for Scotland—everyone knew that she and the earl had argued about the missing jewels until the sun rose.

While the guests were suitably occupied with breakfast or heavy sleep, the servants were assembled in the servants' dining room. Lily had sneaked in through the kitchen and saw her aunt leaning against the sideboard, pale with exhaustion.

The earl was standing between his secretary and solicitor, his neckcloth tied crookedly and his thick brows uncombed. His hands were clasped behind his back as he informed the staff of twenty-four that he would find the thief, and the thief would hang.

The servants watched the three men warily.

The earl's secretary, Mr. Bowman, conducted the interrogation. Lily's governess, Miss Penhurst, so dear to Lily, was shaking. Nurse was crying. When Mr. Bowman asked Miss Penhurst how he might possibly trust her word that she had not taken the jewels when she was sleeping just below the study where they were kept, Lily could bear it no more and rushed forward. The earl tried to shoo her away, but Lily would not go, clasping his hand. "I think I know who took them!"

All eyes turned to her. Lily's knees began to quake. The earl grabbed her elbow, his fingers digging painfully into her flesh. "Is this one of your tales, lass?" he snarled.

Lily shook her head.

"How could you possibly know who took the jewels? Did you see the thief in the act?"

"No, my lord." Her voice was shaking now and her breath had deserted her.

He made a sound of disgust and pushed her away.

"But I saw him riding away," she gasped as tears burned her eyes.

The earl and Mr. Bowman slowly turned to look at her. Aunt Althea stood as still as a statue, staring at her.

"It was the woodcarver. M-Mr. Scott," she added, in case the earl didn't know who the woodcarver was. "I saw him last night, riding away from Ashwood in the park, long after the villagers had gone."

The earl's eyes narrowed.

"It was too late for him to be working," she added.

The earl's black gaze shifted to Aunt Althea. "Working? Working on what?" he asked.

"A repair," Aunt Althea said coolly. "To a wardrobe."

Mr. Bowman eyed Lily skeptically. "How can you be certain it was him, Miss Boudine?"

"It was his horse," Lily said, and instantly feared she was mistaken. "It was the gray, with the black spots around his tail," she said aloud, to convince herself.

"Oh no, darling—" Aunt Althea said, but was silenced by a look from the earl.

And then the earl suddenly smiled at Lily and moved to her side. "Let us have a spot of tea, shall we, Lillian?" he asked, and Lily tried to remember if he'd ever uttered her given name before that moment.

Within hours, Mr. Joseph Scott was taken from his wife and three children to an outbuilding on the Ashwood estate, where he was held until the magistrate could be summoned.

Word spread quickly through Hadley Green and whispers soon followed. Did a thief live among them? Hadn't Mrs. Rollingwood recently reported the theft of her chickens? Hadn't Mr. Clark complained of several bags of flour taken from his dry goods shop? And wasn't it really unsurprising that it was Mr. Scott? Everyone knew his wife was desperately ill, but the doctors in London were not free, were they? And why should he be so silent as to his whereabouts that evening? He said he did not take the jewels, but he would not say where he was the night of the theft. His poor wife was pressed to tell the truth lest they interrogate her children: her husband had not come home until after midnight.

The magistrate, a man with a reputation for swift and stern justice, arrived in Hadley Green within the fortnight. The trial was held in the village commons hall. Mr. Scott, the woodcarver, most likely knew before he was brought before the magistrate that he would be found guilty, for he could not offer a satisfactory answer for his whereabouts on the night the jewels went missing. Nevertheless, a procession of his friends and neighbors tried with all their being to convince the magistrate of his good character. They were followed by a string of witnesses to the events of the night of the crime.

The entire village gathered outside to hear the case of the missing jewels put before the magistrate's bench. Just after noon, two ornate Ashwood coaches appeared: one, for the earl's convenience; as the injured party, he'd attended Mr. Scott's trial all morning. The second carried Lily and the countess, whose trip had been postponed indefinitely. Lily did not know why.

She looked out the coach window at all the people gathered, many of them clamoring for a look inside the coach. "There are so many people," she said nervously.

"Not so many," Althea said reassuringly. "They only seek diversion. They mean no harm. And there won't be so many people inside."

Lily was not convinced of that; she suddenly felt light-headed and clammy. "I don't want to do it, Auntie," she said, shrinking back against the leather squabs. "Can't the earl tell them what I saw?"

"No," her aunt said with a sympathetic smile. "You must tell them in your own voice, darling."

Lily's stomach twisted uncomfortably. "But I don't know what to say!"

"You need only tell the truth," Althea said, then suddenly leaned forward and put her hand on Lily's knee. "But you must be very certain of the truth, Lily. That is the most important thing—you must be certain about what you saw that night. Are you? Are you *quite* certain?"

Lily thought back to what she'd seen. So many things had been said since that night, so many people had come and gone from Ashwood. Still, she'd seen Mr. Scott's horse, and the figures in the hallway. She nodded solemnly. She meant to please Althea, to assure her she could repeat what she'd seen.

But Althea seemed strangely sad. She shifted back, her hands in her lap once more. "Entirely certain, dearest? It was so dark that night, and there were so many people at Ashwood. Are you certain you saw Mr. Scott?"

There *had* been a lot of people about. But Lily felt as if she were the cause of all this ruckus, that the people were gathered here today because of what she'd said, and she didn't want to embarrass Althea or make the earl angry by being afraid to say it now. "I'm certain," she said again.

Her aunt smiled at Lily, but her eyes glistened with tears.

The coach halted; Lily felt the jostling of one of the coachmen climbing down. A moment later, the door swung open, and people crowded in, craning their necks to see inside. Althea reached across the coach, gathered Lily in a hug, and held her tight. "Remember to speak only the truth, love. And don't be afraid—no one wishes you harm." She kissed her cheek and let her go. "Go on, then. Mr. Bowman will see you in."

Lily realized that Althea was sending her in alone. "Aren't you coming, Auntie?"

Her aunt shook her head. "Not this time."

"But you must come!" Lily cried, truly frightened now.

"I cannot," Althea said, and a tear slid down her cheek. "I am so sorry, darling, but my husband . . ." She looked down, and Lily heard something that sounded like a strangled sob. Althea looked up and smiled at Lily. "My sister needs me now and I have been too long delayed. Go on, Lily. It will be over before you know it, and I will come back to you as soon as I can, I promise."

"Miss Boudine!" It was Mr. Bowman, standing at the door of the coach with the curious throng behind him. "Come along, girl, the magistrate is waiting."

Lily looked at Althea, desperate for her aunt's arms. But her aunt smiled and turned her toward the coach door. "You are a brave little girl. You can do anything. Now go."

Lily reluctantly stepped through the opening and was instantly surrounded by footmen who shepherded her through the crowd.

"Let us have a look at the lass!" someone shouted at them, and the bystanders pushed against each other for a better view. The footmen kept moving, guiding Lily into the commons room behind Mr. Bowman.

Inside, it was terribly crowded. Those people who could not find a seat were pressed against the walls. The ceiling was low, making the room seem even more cramped. The footmen had to clear a path through the crush of bodies. Frightened, Lily shifted so close to the Ashwood footman that she could smell the wool of his livery. He clamped his hand on her shoulder, holding tightly, steering her forward.

She was led to the front of the room to stand before a thin, wiry man. He was seated behind a table in his judicial wig and robe. He peered at Lily over the tops of his spectacles, assessing her and frowning as if she were not to his liking. The earl was seated in an ornate chair to the magistrate's right, and to the magistrate's left, in what looked like a hastily constructed box, stood the accused. Mr. Scott's clothes were unkempt and he had the growth of a beard on his face. Lily could smell him—he looked and smelled as if he'd been living in a cave.

She avoided his gaze.

"Come, come," the magistrate said, gesturing for Lily to come closer. Mr. Bowman pushed her forward. The magistrate pointed to the edge of his table, where Lily supposed she was to stand. She was directly across from Mr. Scott, and behind him sat his family. His wife held their youngest child in her lap, and she was weeping. Her daughter sat glumly, and beside her was Mr. Scott's oldest son, Tobin, who stared darkly at Lily.

Lily had seen the Scott family when Mr. Bowman had driven her to Mr. Scott's cottage to identify the horse she'd seen the night of the gala. They'd all spilled out of the cottage to look at her then, and Mrs. Scott's eyes had been red and swollen, just as they were now. Lily was acquainted only with Tobin, as he often accompanied his father to Ashwood to assist him in the construction of the staircase. On a few occasions, Tobin had been sent outside to watch over Lily when Althea desired to speak to Mr. Scott in private.

Tobin was a few years older than Lily, perhaps as old as thirteen, and he'd always been very kind to her. Today, however, his dark brown eyes were staring at her as if he would very much like to strangle her.

"Miss Boudine, do we have your solemn vow that what you will say here today is God's honest truth?" the magistrate asked.

Lily made the mistake of glancing to her right, and saw all the faces peering intently at her. She swallowed hard and nodded.

"Speak!"

"Yes, my lord," she said. Her knees were shaking. She feared she would faint in front of all these people. The earl would be so angry with her—he would make her be Irish. She could feel the old man's gaze boring through her back, just as Tobin's gaze was burning through her front.

"You may proceed," the magistrate said, and suddenly, Mr. Bowman was standing before her.

"Miss Boudine," he said, gazing down at her. "Please tell his lordship what you saw the night of the summer gala."

It was a wonder Lily found her voice at all. She scarcely realized she was speaking. Her voice trembled almost as hard as her knees as she told the magistrate about the shadowy figures in the hallway, the rider on the gray horse with the black spots.

"Have you identified this horse?" the magistrate demanded.

"I . . . I—"

"She has indeed, my lord," Mr. Bowman said smoothly. "She was taken to Mr. Scott's residence two days past and identified the horse on his property as the one she saw that night."

"Is this true?" the magistrate asked Lily.

"Yes, my lord."

Mrs. Scott stifled a sob against her baby's head.

The magistrate peered intently at Lily again. "Do you swear on the Bible that what you have said here today is true?"

She was going to be sick and humiliate herself even worse than she'd already done. "Yes, my lord."

"Very well." The magistrate sat back and gestured to Mr. Bowman. Mr. Bowman in turn looked at the footmen and gave them a curt nod. The next thing Lily knew, she was being whisked from the crowded room and into the earl's coach.

Aunt Althea and her coach were gone.

It was another hour before the earl appeared and took his place in the coach across from Lily for the drive back to Ashwood. He looked at her only once. "You've done well," he said, and turned his attention to the window.

Lily would learn sometime later that after her testimony, Mr. Bowman hypothesized Mr. Scott and a maid at Ashwood were lovers and had worked together to steal the jewels. That Mr. Bowman could not produce the maid did not deter the magistrate; he found Mr. Scott guilty of theft and sentenced him to hang.

In the days that followed, Aunt Althea seemed smaller somehow. Older. She was not the same gay Aunt Althea, and Lily was shocked by it.

It was no secret that Aunt Althea and the earl were at odds. More than once, Lily was awakened in the night by the shouting between them. During the day, Aunt Althea kept Lily close. But she was distracted. There were moments she seemed almost mad to Lily, particularly when she searched Ashwood for the missing jewels.

Lily didn't understand her search. "If Mr. Scott took them, they wouldn't be here, would they?" she asked, confused.

"One never knows," her aunt muttered.

On the day Mr. Scott was hanged for his crime, Miss Penhurst led Lily down to the pond. They rowed about the small lake, gliding serenely among the geese as Mr. Scott met his maker. But Lily was despondent. She believed she had done that to Mr. Scott. She had killed him when she repeated what she'd seen. Miss Penhurst assured Lily that it was not her fault, that Mr. Scott had done something quite wrong and could blame no one but himself. But Lily couldn't help feeling it was all her fault. She couldn't stop seeing the hate in Joblin's eyes.

She tried to speak to Aunt Althea about it, but her aunt refused to discuss it. She said it was tragic and done with and Lily shouldn't think of it, either. Althea stopped playing the pianoforte. She appeared more gaunt with each day, and Lily worried she wasn't eating properly. It was no secret that she and the earl were no longer speaking at all.

At week's end, Aunt Althea made her trip to Scotland after all. Life resumed its rhythm; Lily took her lessons, practiced her drawing, and played with her dolls.

Aunt Althea had been gone almost three weeks when she returned to Ashwood. She was smiling, and said she was very happy to see Lily, that she'd missed her terribly while she was away. But something seemed different to Lily. There was a distance in her aunt's pretty gray eyes.

One day, about a month after she'd come home from Scotland, Aunt Althea walked into the nursery where Lily was doing her lessons, sank down to her knees, and hugged Lily. "I have news," she said brightly. "You are going to Ireland!" She said it as if it were some grand adventure.

"Ireland!" Lily cried, and her heart sank. She would be Irish! "Why, Auntie? Have I done something wrong?"

"No, no, Lily!" she exclaimed as she tucked a strand

of hair behind Lily's ears. "It's just that Lenora is much more able to care for you properly. She has three girls, you know. There is your cousin Keira, and the twins, Molly and Mabe."

Lily had never met them. She didn't want to be with her cousins, she wanted to be with Althea. "No, Auntie, *you* care for me!" Lily said desperately, clinging to her aunt's arm. "Please don't make me be Irish! Please don't send me away!"

"Ah, Lily, dearest, I won't be here to look after you," Althea said. "And I can't leave you alone with the earl, can I?"

"Why won't you be here? Where will you be?" Lily asked frantically. "I could go with you. I could be your companion."

Althea smiled as she cupped Lily's face with both hands and slowly, deliberately, kissed her eyes. "You cannot go where I am going, my love. You can only go to Ireland. No tears, beauty. It is best." She left Lily to sob away her disappointment.

Lily believed she had done this to herself. She had forced Aunt Althea to send her away because she had caused Mr. Scott to hang. It was all her fault.

Her beloved aunt was dead within weeks of her arrival in Ireland. She drowned, they said, a tragic boating accident in the same lake where Lily and Miss Penhurst had floated about one long summer afternoon.

Lily would never forget the nauseating, breath-snatching surge of guilt and remorse she felt when she heard the news. First her mother, then Aunt Althea, and the following year, Aunt Margaret in Scotland. That left only Keira's mother, Lorena.

Lily felt responsible for all of it. Many questions swirled around her eight-year-old brain, questions that followed her into adulthood, questions as to the why and how things had happened, how things might have been different if Althea hadn't sent her to Ireland. If she hadn't gone to Ireland, she might have been with Althea the day she drowned. She might have saved her beloved aunt.

There was another question that burned in Lily's heart, a question that no one had seemed to answer during that tragic turn of events, the question Althea had so desperately tried to answer: Where were the jewels?

One

There was a palpable current of excitement running through everyone at Lisdoon, the Hannigan estate. They'd all been caught up in the frenetic whirl of activity as Lily Boudine prepared to sail for Italy.

Italy!

Her cousin Keira Hannigan could scarcely believe Lily's good fortune. Keira had long dreamed of seeing Italy and places like it; she could envision herself strolling about the piazzas, admiring the art and architecture, and all the Italian gentlemen. But Keira was quite certain she would never leave the western coast of Ireland again now that her parents seemed so determined to see her married.

Lily was going as Mrs. Canavan's paid traveling companion. Mrs. Canavan was traveling in the company of her highly desirable and handsome son, Mr. Conor Canavan. Lily had shrewdly finessed her employment with Mrs. Canavan, for she was determined to engage in a love affair with her son. That Mr. Canavan was not aware that he would be participating in the love affair did not deter Keira's cousin in the least.

Lily was blithely unconcerned. "He esteems me, Keira," she'd said confidently one day as she had examined her flawless complexion in a looking glass. "He'll no doubt be relieved to know that I esteem him, as well. I shouldn't be surprised if he offers for me whilst we are in Italy."

Lily was quite certain of herself, but then again, neither Lily nor Keira were strangers to healthy egos. Keira and Lily were considered remarkably pretty in County Galway and did not want for suitors. Keira's mother said they were cut from the same cloth.

Keira would never forget the first time she laid eyes on Lily fifteen years ago. Keira's mother had warned her to be very kind, for Cousin Lily was a poor orphan. Keira had imagined any orphan would be weakly mannered and dressed in ragged clothes, and that dark circles of ill health would shadow her eyes. She expected an orphan's only possessions to be a dirty, tattered stuffed bear and a wooden bowl.

Lily had been nothing like that. She'd been so exotic, in fact, that Keira was enthralled. She'd been eight to Keira's nine years at the time, spoke with a slight accent to Keira's Irish ears, and wore a frock made of crimson silk. Her hair was black, like Keira's, but silky and long, whereas Keira's was curly. Her eyes were green, like Keira's, but a bit gray, and not the deep green of Ireland, as Keira's father said about her eyes.

Lily had had a very bright smile when she'd stepped out of the carriage and extended her hand to be kissed by

Keira's father. "How do you do," she'd said with a proper curtsy. "I am Lily Boudine."

Keira had thought she was looking at a princess, not an orphan.

Scarcely any time passed before Keira and Lily were fast friends and allies. Fifteen years later, the two women were as close as sisters and truly had their pick of suitors. Lily's pick was Mr. Canavan. Or perhaps more accurately put, Lily's pick this month was Mr. Canavan. She had a tendency to change her mind.

Lily was scheduled to embark on her journey in a matter of days, and Keira and Lily, along with Molly and Mabe, the eighteen-year-old twins, were in the drawing room at Lisdoon, preparing for her months away from home. The room was a large one, with three banks of windows that overlooked the park behind the house. Beyond the park was the sea. One could not see the sea from Lisdoon, but when the windows were open, as they were today, the scent of clean salt air was carried in on a light breeze.

The drawing room was done up in rich gold and red fabrics and thick Belgian carpets. Six-feet-high portraits of Hannigan ancestors graced the walls. Today, however, it had been taken over by fashion plates and dress forms. Bolts of silk, muslin, and brocade, sent all the way from Dublin, spilled over the floral silk settee and the velvet armchairs.

On a sideboard nearby, there was a neglected silver tea service. The water had long gone cold, and the biscuits were left untouched.

Brian Hannigan, the patriarch of this brood, was distressed by all the flummery that had engulfed his draw-.

ing room. "Not right," he complained to his wife, Lenora. "The drawing room is meant to be a place of repose for *everyone*."

"It is only temporary," Lenora assured him, but Brian wasn't at all convinced and had gone to his study to sulk.

Lily—who was the recipient of the gowns being constructed on three of four dress forms—was fortunate to have found a seamstress, Caitrin, of some talent in Galway. She was here at Lisdoon, preparing Lily's wardrobe, and was very adept at copying the latest fashions. Presently, Caitrin was in the corner of the room, finishing a hem on one of Lily's many commissioned gowns. It was a lovely brown morning gown with pale green trim. Keira stood beside Caitrin, admiring it.

Behind her, at a round table in the middle of the room, typically used for gaming or tea, her cousin and sisters were eagerly perusing the latest fashion plates to come from London.

"Here, then, look at this," Lily said excitedly, pointing to one of the plates. Molly and Mabe bent their dark heads over the book to see the plate. "This is the perfect frock for a morning wedding."

Dear Lord, what an imagination she had. "He's not yet made an offer, Lily," Keira reminded her as she examined the sleeve of the morning gown.

"He will," Lily said confidently.

"I think it is lovely," Mabe said dreamily.

"Honestly, I don't know how you can think of such things," Keira said, stepping aside so a footman could carry out the tea service. "Were I you, I could think of nothing but Italy."

"You mean if you were you and *you* were going to Italy," Lily said.

"Really, Keira, wouldn't you be thinking of Mr. Maloney just a wee bit?" Molly asked, smiling slyly at her older sister.

Keira rolled her eyes. "No, I would not. And by the by, Loman Maloney is not the only gentleman in Ireland, if you haven't noticed."

"But he is the only one who seems to want to marry you," Molly said laughingly.

Keira did not want to be reminded of that. Mr. Maloney was a very nice gentleman whose family had made their fortune in shipping. He was pleasant to look at, she supposed, but frankly, he reminded her of all the other very nice gentlemen roaming about Ireland like a herd of sheep. The only difference in Mr. Maloney was that Pappa's opinion of him had, miraculously, improved over the winter, and now he thought Maloney the perfect match for his oldest daughter. Mr. Maloney had taken Pappa's enthusiastic encouragement to heart—he was earnestly pursuing Keira's hand.

Keira was four and twenty. She was well past the age most young women married. She knew that remarks were made around County Galway and beyond about her age and lack of a match. She knew that her reluctance to agree to any match was a cause of great concern for her parents. Yet she couldn't bring herself to settle for someone as steady and predictable as Loman Maloney. She had this feeling, this vibration in her body, that said life was far too short to settle for something so mundane.

Nonetheless, Keira's father was losing patience. He'd

told her not a fortnight ago that if she couldn't settle on a suitor, he most certainly would.

"I think it would be lovely if you and Lily wed on the same day," Mabe said. She was stretched across the table now, her chin propped on her fist. The ribbon that held her long hair back had come undone. "Think of it—a double wedding!"

"With Keira!" Lily laughed. "I should like at least a wee bit of attention on my wedding day, if you please. And besides, Keira will never surrender," she said, and winked at her cousin.

Keira couldn't help but laugh. Lily knew her very well, indeed.

"Lily."

Keira's father startled them all. He was standing in the doorway, his thick legs braced apart, a paper in his hand.

"Aye, Uncle?" Lily asked, coming to her feet. "Were we making too much noise again?"

"Yes. But that is not why I am here. I need to speak to you at once. Come with me, please."

"Why?" Keira asked.

He frowned disapprovingly. "I am speaking to Lily, Keira. Lily, come." He turned and quit the drawing room.

Lily exchanged a look with Keira as she followed Keira's father out.

"Wait here," Keira said to Molly and Mabe, and started after Lily. But Molly and Mabe ignored her command and were quickly on her heels.

In addition to Keira's mother, who was standing before the open windows looking quite pensive, there was a stranger in the book-lined study. He looked as if he'd been riding for a time; dust covered his boots and dirt stained his hands and face. He stood uncomfortably on a carpet square, as if he were afraid to move from it. He nodded his head politely as the women filed in.

"I said *Lily*," Keira's father reminded them, but made no move to clear the room.

"What is it, Uncle?" Lily asked, gazing curiously at the man.

"This is Mr. Hood. He is a hired messenger from Ashwood," Keira's father said. "He's brought a very important message and will return on the morrow with a reply."

"Ashwood," Lily repeated, as if she'd never heard of it, as if the name were new to her.

Brian Hannigan held out the paper to her. "It is quite unexpected news, Lily," he said.

She slowly shifted her gaze from the messenger to peer suspiciously at the paper. She made no move to take it.

"What news?" Keira asked, and leaned over Lily's shoulder to have a look while Molly and Mabe crowded in behind her, trying to see it, as well.

"Molly and Mabe, please do stand back," Keira's mother said. She clasped her hands tightly before her and smiled at Lily. "You have nothing to fear, Lily," she said, and it seemed to Keira as if Lily actually flinched a little at those words.

"No, indeed!" Keira's father boomed. "This paper says that you are the sole heir to Ashwood and rightfully named countess." He grinned. "Lily, do you understand? You are a *countess*!"

The news was stunning. Molly and Mabe squealed with excitement. Keira grasped Lily's shoulders and squeezed them. "A countess, Lily!"

"But how?" Lily asked, clearly confused. "How could I possibly be the countess of Ashwood?"

"I shall tell you." Her father unfolded the vellum he was holding. "This was written by Mr. Theodore Fish, who is the agent for Ashwood," he explained, then scanned the page until he found the lines he wanted. "Aye, here we are." He cleared his throat. "After significant research and consultation with the attorneys in London, it has become apparent that Lillian Boudine is the only surviving heir of Marcus Kent, the late Earl of Ashwood, and as such, inherits the estate of Ashwood outright. Further, the title of countess is legally bestowed if a female is the sole heir, which gives Lillian Boudine the title of Countess of Ashwood and all the responsibilities and entitlements that entails. In the event the female is married, the lands and titles naturally pass to her husband. If, however, she inherits in her own right, they remain hers until her death and pass to the oldest son."

He looked up, his smile beaming.

Molly and Mabe began talking at once, but Lily could only gape at her uncle.

"Lily, are you all right?" Keira's mother asked. "This is wonderful news!"

"She is astounded, Lenora," Keira's father said joyously. "And well you should be, Lily. Think of it—a countess in your own right! Mr. Fish bids you come at once, as there are some matters that require your immediate attention." He held out the letter to her again.

Lily hesitantly took it. "I am . . . I am indeed astounded," she agreed. "But have you forgotten, Uncle? I am leaving for Italy at week's end."

"Italy!" Keira's father scoffed. "You may forget about Italy, lass. Keira will go in your stead. *You* will go to England and assume your rightful place!"

"Italy!" Keira cried. It was so unexpected, a gift that fell into her lap. "Do you mean it, Pappa?"

"Well, aye . . . assuming Mrs. Canavan will have you, aye. I certainly can't send either of them," he said, gesturing loosely at Molly and Mabe.

"Pappa!" Mabe protested.

"I don't believe it!" Keira cried happily. "Lily a countess and me to Italy!"

But Lily said nothing. She stared at Keira's father.

Brian Hannigan looked hopelessly at his wife. "She does not speak," he said, gesturing to Lily. "Why does she not speak? Look at what gold has fallen into her lap, and she stands there like a mute!"

"Brian, please," Keira's mother said, and moved to put her arm around Lily's shoulders. "It is quite a shock, as you can well imagine."

"Does that mean we are kin to a countess?" Molly asked excitedly.

Keira's father grinned. "It does indeed, lass. Come, then, let us take this fine man to the kitchens and feed him well, for he must return at once and tell them the countess is on her way!"

Keira's father and her sisters eagerly showed the man out of the study. She could hear Molly's and Mabe's chatter drifting down the hallway, as they no doubt peppered the poor man with questions. Keira's mind was whirling around the improbable but highly exciting turn of events—her wish had come true! Mr. Maloney would have to wait if he was so intent on marrying her—perhaps she would be gone so long that he would give up and offer for someone else. A cascade of possibilities for freedom began to tumble in her mind.

But when Keira glanced at her cousin, she realized Lily had yet to speak. She was staring at the floor, her face as pale as the white muslin she wore.

"Lily, say something," Keira urged her.

"I don't know what to say," Lily answered.

"I think we should send a note around to Mrs. Canavan straightaway," Keira's mother suggested.

Lily nodded. But she was still staring at the carpet, clearly lost in thought.

Keira knew Lily perhaps better than anyone, and thought her reaction very odd. What woman wouldn't be ecstatic at the news she had been made a countess? Keira didn't believe for one moment that Lily fancied herself so in love with Conor Canavan that she'd not be happy to discover she had acquired a noble title and an estate to govern.

Lily's mood did not improve over the course of the afternoon as more notes were written and more trunks were brought down and Keira's things were packed. Nor at the supper table, when Mabe and Molly questioned Lily tirelessly about Ashwood. It wasn't until everyone had gone to bed that Keira finally found the opportunity to speak to Lily privately, without her sisters hovering about or the servants in and out of their rooms, packing and sorting their belongings.

Keira knocked softly on Lily's door so as not to alert Molly and Mabe, who had rooms next door. "Come," came the soft reply. She quickly stepped inside and shut the door quietly behind her.

Lily's room was dimly lit; only a single candle at her bedside glowed. The windows were open and a cool night breeze rustled the heavy brocade drapes now and again. Lily was sitting on her bed in her sleeping gown, the long tail of her braid hanging over her shoulder. She put aside the unopened book on her lap and leaned back against the down pillows she'd stacked behind her back.

"Are you unwell?" Keira asked as she neared the bed. "You've hardly said a word today."

"I am quite well. But I've been thinking." She gathered her knees up to her chest and patted the bed. "I have an idea."

Keira always enjoyed a good idea, particularly if it was diverting, and eagerly climbed on the bed with Lily, falling onto her side and propping her head in her palm. "What is your idea? That you shall anoint me your lady-in-waiting and host grand balls, aye?" She laughed.

Lily did not laugh. "Hear me out before you refuse me," she said earnestly.

"Refuse you?"

"Keira, I . . . I think you should go to Ashwood. In my stead."

Keira snorted at that absurd suggestion, but Lily's gaze was steady and cool. "*Me?*" Keira exclaimed. "And what would I do there?"

"Mind things," Lily said. "Do whatever it is that someone like me is expected to do until I return from Italy."

"Italy! Oh, Lily," Keira said sympathetically. "I grant you that Mr. Canavan is a handsome man . . . but really you have no idea of his true feelings. And even if he was quite in love with you, surely you must know that he cannot marry a countess."

"I don't know that at all," Lily said coolly. "I do have some idea of his feelings, and I believe that if two people love each other, a title will not stand in their way."

Keira could not believe what she was hearing. "Lily, are you mad? He has not offered!"

Lily leaned forward. She took Keira's hand in her slender fingers. "You know how I have planned for Italy. You know very well what it means to me. I want to go. And besides, I . . . I have wretched memories of Ashwood. I can't bear to face it. Not yet, at least. I really must think things through and prepare myself for it. This is all so sudden, so unexpected. Can you not understand how I need a bit of time to . . ." She fluttered her fingers at her head. "Accept it?"

Keira was hard-pressed to see why any of it was so difficult for Lily to accept. She was a countess now, for heaven's sake! But Keira was reminded of when Lily had first come to Ireland. Keira had heard the story of the night the jewels went missing so many times that occasionally, when the clouds hung low and heavy over Lisdoon at night, and the smell of rain filled the air, she could almost believe she had seen it all with her own eyes.

Lily had had a dramatic flair for recounting the events that had led to her being in Ireland. She'd reenacted the night the jewels went missing so often that Keira had learned some of the parts and had been called upon to perform the part of the earl or the judge.

It was great fun, putting on their dramatic little plays.

But the playacting had abruptly ended when they received word that Aunt Althea had died so tragically and unexpectedly.

Lily never again spoke of the night the jewels went missing. There was nothing that could entice her to relive the experience. Or to speak of Aunt Althea. It was as if she had walled off a part of her past.

"Lily, dearest," Keira said now. "It was so long ago. Surely those memories don't hurt you now."

"It seems only yesterday to me," Lily said softly.

She looked truly pained. Keira loved Lily and couldn't abide to see her so distressed. She tried to imagine herself at Ashwood. "How would I ever do it?" she asked Lily.

"Quite simply. You'll have the letter from Mr. Fish. You will tell them that I have sent you and that you are there to do whatever must be done until I arrive. They cannot dispute it."

Keira pondered that. "Is it a very grand estate?"

"Very," Lily said, leaning forward with hope.

Keira imagined herself strolling about the grounds of a very grand English estate. But then she thought of Italy, of the Italian gentlemen she'd hoped to meet, of the art and the food. "Are there many gentlemen in that particular part of England?"

"Keira!"

"What?" Keira asked innocently. "You hardly expect me to pretend I've entered a nunnery, do you?"

Lily sighed. "No," she said. "I don't know if there are gentlemen. I suppose there are—will you do it, Keira?"

Keira smiled. "Pappa will never allow it—"

"He need not know," Lily said instantly, and at Keira's

startled look, she said, "*No* one in Ireland need know, Keira. Not Pappa. Not Molly and Mabe." She leaned closer still, the tip of her braid touching the bed linens between them. "Not Mr. Maloney."

Now she had Keira's undivided attention.

"We are to meet Mrs. Canavan in Dun Loaghaire to board our ship. We can explain then that there has been a change of plans."

Keira's eyes rounded. Could they really manage it? She looked at the door, slipped off the bed, and hurried across the Aubusson carpet to lock it. A strong gust of wind lifted the drapes; it smelled like rain, and Keira moved to the windows, looking down to assure herself that no one had overheard them before closing them. She fairly leaped onto the bed, settling in beside Lily. "Tell me what I must do. I need only mind the house until you return?"

"Aye, aye," Lily hastily agreed. "Keep things moving along, as it were."

"What things?"

"The things that keep the estate functioning, I suppose. I scarcely know. I would assume you must agree to release funds for food and such things."

That sounded easy enough. "Suppose we do what you suggest," Keira said. "How long before you join me?"

Lily shrugged. "Three months?"

This idea was becoming more and more delicious. It was an adventure, and there was nothing Keira liked better than some adventure to liven up the days. She could do whatever she liked for three long months, with no one at her back urging her to do something entirely different.

"Will you do it?" Lily asked.

Keira sighed. "For you, Lily. For you I will do it because I love you dearly. I have only one small condition," she added sweetly. "I must have the brown morning gown with the green trim."

Lily's eyes narrowed. "*That* is extortion, Kiki."

"*That* is negotiating," Keira countered.

"No." Lily folded her arms and leaned back. "I adore that gown."

On the day Keira arrived at Ashwood, she was wearing the brown gown with the green trim. The letter from Mr. Fish was in her reticule.

She stepped out of the hired coach and looked up at the stunning Georgian mansion. It was the color of sand, with a dozen or more chimneys. The sun glistened against the paned windows and it almost looked as if the mansion were sparkling. *Oh aye*, Keira thought. *This will be my greatest lark yet.*

Two

The auction of Ashwood horseflesh began at precisely two o'clock in the afternoon in the paddock. A recent rain had made everything a wee bit boggy, but the sun was shining brightly, and Declan O'Conner, the Irish Earl of Donnelly, was in fine spirits. He loved the smell of horse, and he figured if there wasn't a little mud involved, it wasn't work.

Declan was a renowned horse breeder in Ireland and England. He'd taken an interest when he was a wee lad, and he'd scarcely been out of short pants when he'd begun to breed racing horses in Ireland. Now, at the age of one and thirty, he bred horses for kings and princes and dukes, and his horses had won some of the most heavily wagered races across England. Recently, he'd been hired by a Danish count to breed a prized broodmare and produce a premier racehorse.

When the Dane's English agents had approached him, Declan had been happy to take the man's money. Not that he needed it; he was a wealthy man in his own right. But the offer had come at a time when Declan was beginning to chafe at the bucolic life in Ireland. It was his curse in life that he'd always had a peculiar ache for the distant—distant lands, distant peoples, and distant lights. He had a strong need to see the world, one that almost matched his need to be near horses.

So Declan had accepted the Dane's challenge. He'd agreed to take possession of and breed the mare in England, where the Dane's agents could see the horse from time to time. He had a small town house in London, but because he needed room for horses, he had let Kitridge Lodge in West Sussex from his good friend the Duke of Darlington. Kitridge, once a Norman castle-cum-hunting-lodge, was too old and outdated to accommodate the slew of servants required to support such an illustrious and large family as the Darlingtons. The rooms were close and dark, the passages narrow and winding, but that suited Declan. He did not need a host of servants or companions. He needed only a place to sleep and eat. The duke had been happy to let it to Declan for as long as he liked.

How long? Declan couldn't say. He never stayed in one place for very long. He'd let the lodge for one year.

Somewhere in that year, however, guilt would drive him back to Ireland as it always did. Declan loved Ireland, of course he did. But he didn't care to be there. An entire world existed beyond her shores, and Ireland seemed so far removed from it. However, his younger sister, Eireanne, was there, along with his maternal grandmother, and he was responsible for them.

Declan's father had died when Declan was only fourteen years of age, leaving him the sprawling family estate of Ballynaheath in County Galway. Declan had not wanted to lose his father, obviously, and he'd not wanted to be earl. He had not wanted to be responsible for Eireanne's happiness, or settle her into a marriage. He loved Eireanne and wanted her to be happy—the idea that he could settle her into a marriage with the wrong man had kept him from pushing any one suitor, and now, unfortunately, a match for Eireanne was hardly a question.

It would seem that Declan had a reputation, even by Irish standards, and there had been some events in his life that had negatively impacted his sister. His grandmother told him that because of his reputation, few Irish men were willing to offer for Eireanne. What she needed, his grandmother said, was to go away for a time. To a school for affluent young women. Specifically, to a school in Lucerne, Switzerland, the Institut Villa Amiels, where affluent young women made the sort of connections that all but guaranteed them a match during the London season.

Declan had thought that an excellent idea and wrote to the school straightaway. Just before he departed for England, he received word they had turned down Eireanne's application.

"You must go on to England, Declan," Eireanne had said sunnily when he gave her the news "You won't be any good to me moping about Ballynaheath, aye?"

She knew him well, knew he was itching to go. "You mustn't fret, Eireanne," he'd said. "That school seems a wee bit priggish, aye? We'll find a better one."

Eireanne had smiled, but she knew as well as Declan that there was not a better school. And there he'd been again, feeling the responsibility for her happiness tether him to Ireland. So he would breed his mare, he would go into London from time to time for society and diversion, and he would return to Ireland to see after Eireanne.

But today, he was looking for a mate for the brood-mare, and the sale of horseflesh from the Ashwood estate was to include some reputable racing horses. He found nothing that would suit him in that regard, but there was one spirited filly he believed he might train for racing; he knew a lady in Hertfordshire who was in the market for a good horse as a gift for her husband.

When the auction was set to begin, the gentlemen were assembled in an area just outside the paddock. Grooms led the horses, one by one, around the paddock in a slow circle as the auctioneer took bids. Most of the horses—two draft horses for pulling coaches, and a pair of geldings—went for nothing more than ten pounds. As gentlemen won their bids, they wandered away from the paddock. So when the filly was brought in with a high step and a spirited toss of her head, there were only five gentlemen left, an estate agent, a pair of grooms, and the auctioneer.

"The opening bid, gentlemen, is ten pounds," the auctioneer announced, and almost instantly, a young buck with a very foppish knot in his neckcloth and shiny new boots tipped his hat.

The bidding quickly escalated from there. Two men dropped out when the bidding passed thirteen pounds. Another was lost at the fifteen-pound mark. That left Declan and the foppish neckcloth with the new boots.

"We've a bid for twenty pounds," the auctioneer said. "Twenty pounds for the filly. Who will give me twenty-two?"

Declan nodded.

"I have twenty-two pounds, gentlemen. Will anyone give me twenty-three?"

The young man looked at Declan as he lifted two fingers indicating he would.

Declan smiled. He would not allow that fine horse to fall into the hands of that fop. There was one thing the young man didn't know—Declan hated to lose more than anything.

"Very well, then, twenty-three pounds," said the auctioneer. "May I have twenty-five?"

Twenty-five pounds was far too much for the horse, but Declan was determined. He nodded. Someone behind him whispered excitedly; a pair of gentlemen turned back to the paddock, as if there were something to see.

The young man's gaze shifted to the filly. He had lace cuffs and the gold fob of his watch was almost offensively shiny. He looked as if he'd walked out of a tailor's shop and headed straight for a horse auction.

"Twenty-eight pounds? Might I have twenty-eight pounds?" the auctioneer asked.

The young buck looked again at Declan, and Declan smiled coldly.

The young man lifted a monogrammed handkerchief to his nose and shook his head.

"Sold, then, to the gentleman for twenty-five pounds," the auctioneer said.

Declan smiled and tipped his hat at the young man.

"Sir, if I may," a man said.

"Aye?" Declan asked, and glanced at the man who appeared beside him. He was the estate's man, small and thin, with a look of business about him. "Congratulations on your winning bid. If I may impose, the countess would like to see you in the green salon."

"The countess," Declan said, and instantly pictured some withered old woman as he put one hand in a glove. "Why is that, Mr. . . . ?"

"Mr. Fish," the man said, with a quick bob of his head. "I am the countess's agent. I could not rightly say, sir, but I believe she is rather attached to the filly."

"Then she should not have offered her for sale," Declan said idly, and nodded at the auctioneer as he passed. "But she did, and I won the bid. What more is there to say?"

Mr. Fish, with his sharp nose and high cheeks, smiled thinly. "Perhaps she would like to impart advice for the care of the horse."

Declan rather imagined she wanted to impart something else entirely. It wouldn't be the first time he'd been summoned into a lady's home under the pretense of business. He pondered that; he hadn't come here for that sort of sport, but he was a man after all. "Is she old?" he asked idly.

"Old?" Mr. Fish asked, clearly confused. "No, sir, she is quite young."

"Comely?"

That caused Mr. Fish to color. His fine-boned hand— Declan supposed it never lifted anything heavier than a pencil—fluttered to his neckcloth as he cleared his throat. "Sir, if I may. The countess has asked you to complete the sale in the green salon."

Declan grinned. "Who am I to say no to a countess, aye? I shall come, Mr. Fish."

"Very good. May I tell her who has bought the filly?"

"Declan O'Conner, Lord Donnelly," he said, and fit his other hand into a glove before he looked up at Fish. "Have the horse delivered to Kitridge Lodge," he said, and began walking toward the house.

He truly expected a plain woman with a plain physical need.

He did not expect an imposter.

It wasn't patently obvious, for the lady behaved in a manner befitting a countess. She didn't do anything to openly spark suspicion, such as neglect to lift her little finger when sipping tea, or curtsy properly. No, Declan knew she was an imposter because he'd known Keira Hannigan all her life, and Keira Hannigan was no countess.

Yet she seemed perfectly at ease pretending to be one.

He had no idea what she was doing in England, much less a small village like Hadley Green. The last he'd seen her—months now, if memory served—she'd been in County Galway (from which they both hailed), and Loman Maloney, whose affluence was matched only by his ambition, was expertly courting her. Keira was a Hannigan, a daughter of an influential, powerful Irish Catholic family known for their horses and their outspoken politics. She was pretty in a way that Declan believed only Irish women were pretty, with black hair, fair skin, and flashing green eyes. She was spirited in the way of the Irish, too, which to Declan meant she was possessed of a good sense of adventure and a clever, if not occasionally sharp, tongue.

What Declan found particularly galling was that Keira did not seem the least bit appalled that he'd discovered her deception in this sleepy little village in England. Quite the contrary. She looked at him daringly, as if she believed he might openly challenge her.

"Lady Ashwood, may I present Lord Donnelly," Mr. Fish said.

After his moment of shock, Declan debated calling her out, but he supposed she would be discovered soon and would suffer accordingly. In the meantime, he had no intention of being drawn into her little game. He'd been drawn into a game of hers years ago, with disastrous consequences. He was here to buy a horse. Nothing more.

"Good afternoon, my lord," she said. Her voice filtered into his consciousness, lodging in that place of the familiar. She moved forward, her dark green riding skirt flaring out around her boots as she moved. She tossed a ridiculously jaunty hat with a gold tassel at the crown onto the settee as she moved past it. She walked in that way beautiful women had of walking: light-footed, with a certain sway in her hip, a pert tilt of her head, a shine in her eyes.

"Lord Donnelly, the Lady Ashwood," Mr. Fish said.

"*Lady* Ashwood, is it?" He might have laughed had he not been so appalled. She smiled pertly.

"Lord Donnelly has bid twenty-five pounds for the filly, madam," Mr. Fish informed her.

"A respectable sum," she said pleasantly. "Although I admit I had hoped she would earn a wee bit more. She's a fine horse. Tea, my lord?"

"Twenty-five pounds is far more than she is worth. And I prefer Irish whiskey," Declan said dryly.

"What luck! We happen to have some on hand. Mr. Fish?"

As Mr. Fish instantly moved to the side cart, Declan

noticed the room. The salon was as impressive as the sandstone Georgian mansion itself. The walls were covered in green and crème silk that matched the heavy draperies. The furnishings were lushly upholstered, the carpet thick, and sunlight streamed in through three pairs of windows that soared all the way to the sculpted crown molding. The ceiling had been painted to resemble a blue summer sky, complete with clouds and sun and fat little redbirds flitting across.

Declan shifted his gaze to Keira, who smiled a bit nervously, a bit brazenly, as Mr. Fish poured three whiskeys. Mr. Fish handed one to Keira, whose upbringing as a good Irish girl made her unafraid of whiskey, unlike the genteel ladies in London's salons.

"Lord Donnelly," Mr. Fish commented amicably as he handed him a whiskey. "Your reputation quite precedes you, sir."

"Apparently, my reputation is alone in that regard," he said, looking pointedly at Keira.

She smiled serenely, pretty as a portrait, completely unruffled. A strand of hair curled against her cheek, starkly black against her creamy skin.

Mr. Fish seemed a little confused by Declan's remark, but being a gentleman, he continued. "We are quite honored that a man of your aptitude in horse breeding is interested in our stock."

"In whose stock?" Declan asked.

Mr. Fish's brows dipped deeper into confusion. "The Lady Ashwood's, of course."

"And does the Lady Ashwood intend to join us?" Declan asked, his gaze still on Keira.

Mr. Fish blinked; Keira laughed and swept forward, smoothing away that errant curl with an anxious flutter of her fingers. "Lord Donnelly is displaying his fine Irish humor, Mr. Fish. Would you be so kind as to excuse us for a moment?"

Startled, Mr. Fish looked at Keira. She smiled a little and lifted her tot of whiskey. "If you'd be so kind," she said again.

"Of course, madam." But he looked entirely perplexed as he put down his tot and strode from the room.

When the door had shut behind him, Keira tossed her whiskey back, then announced breathlessly, "This is not what you think."

"Not what I think? I think you are impersonating an English countess, unless you have made a rather fortuitous match," Declan scoffed.

"No, Declan. This is Ashwood."

"Aye . . . and?"

"And it is Lily's! Haven't you heard?"

He had no idea what she was talking about. "What is Lily's?"

"She inherited Ashwood," Keira said. "Free and clear. Don't tease me, you know that she has."

He had heard the old Earl of Ashwood's estate had passed to a surviving female heir, but certainly Lily Boudine had not once crossed his mind. He didn't know she was associated with Ashwood in any way. "Why in heaven would I know such a thing?" he demanded irritably.

"Honestly," Keira said, just as irritably. "She came from Ashwood. Everyone knows that she did."

"I beg your pardon, I did not. I have not made it my habit to study the family history of Lily Boudine! But what I find remarkable in this illuminating conversation is that you have made no mention of the fact that you are impersonating your very own cousin."

"No!" she cried with a nervous glance at the door. "You are entirely mistaken!"

"Where is Lily?" he demanded incredulously.

Keira sighed. "Italy."

"Do you mean to tell me that your cousin is in Italy and you are parading about as her?"

"I am not parading," she snapped. "I certainly didn't come here with the intent of being the countess, obviously," she said, but Declan saw nothing obvious about that. "She asked me to come and mind things for her, for *she* is now the countess. Aye, aye, I see your look of amazement, and believe me when I tell you it was a surprise to us all, but it is quite true. Whilst Lily is in Italy with Mrs. Canavan, I came here on her behalf. Imagine my great surprise when I arrived and they all believed me to *be* Lily, for apparently our resemblance is much greater than certainly I had ever realized, and really, Declan, it was *their* suggestion."

"Oh, I can imagine," Declan said skeptically. "The devil has a face of an angel, Keira Hannigan."

She frowned darkly. "You have said that before."

"And I will say it again." He couldn't imagine what Keira and Lily were about. He had never thought Keira particularly sensible, but he couldn't believe for a moment Lily would agree to such a ridiculous bit of fraud. "What scheme have the two of you concocted?"

"Must you use the word *scheme*?" she protested. "It is all very simple. Lily had committed her companionship to Mrs. Canavan."

Declan cocked a skeptical brow.

"I came here to mind things until she returns from Italy. But Declan, I never imagined to find things in such disarray! That old earl died and left a financial ruin of Ashwood. You can't imagine the urgency—there was poor old Hannah Hough, for example. Some awful monster of a man was attempting to take her lease and enclose it with his property, and the dear was in danger of being evicted from the only home she's ever known, the very house where she herself was born and raised her three children. Naturally, I had to act."

"By assuming Lily's identity?" Declan asked incredulously.

"Well, I didn't mean to, obviously," Keira said with great exasperation. "But it was imperative that a document be signed by the rightful property owner—the countess—that prohibited the sale or alteration of the lease of that land, or Hannah Hough would lose it all. I had no choice."

He knew Keira was bold, but this was astounding. "Do you not understand that what you have done is unlawful?"

"But it's not," she argued. "When Lily comes to Ashwood, she will set it all to rights. She asked me to mind the place, after all. I have the letter that says she is countess as proof."

"Set it all to rights? People do not appreciate being duped, no matter what Lily asked you to do, no matter what piece of paper you believe you have," he said sternly, and gestured for her to refill his glass. "This is so like you,

Keira," he said angrily. "You act first and think afterward. You don't care who you harm."

Her green eyes widened. Ah, those eyes. They were a man's curse, those eyes. They had lived on in his memory, long past the point of usefulness.

Keira snatched up the decanter of whiskey and refilled his tot. "You're not listening," she said as she refilled his glass. "There was quite a lot to be taken care of, and I have very diligently done that for Lily. Furthermore, I have discovered something so astounding that someone of even *your* incurious nature would want to discover the truth behind it."

"I assure you, I do not," he said, watching her eyes glitter as he drank the whiskey. "By the by, does the venerable Mr. Brian Hannigan know his daughter is masquerading as an English countess? And where is your chaperone? Surely he wouldn't allow you to cavort about England without chaperone."

"That is none of your concern."

"Meaning he does not know," he said easily.

"Why in God's name did I ask you here?" Keira complained, and moved to turn away from him, but Declan caught the wrist of the hand that held the decanter.

"What of Mr. Loman Maloney? Is *he* aware that the object of his great esteem and blissful future is perpetrating an entirely indefensible deception?"

Keira turned a very appealing shade of red. "Mr. Maloney is very busy with his own affairs," she said primly.

"Meaning, I take it, that he believes you to be in Italy, as well."

Keira gave him a small shrug.

Declan shook his head. "Foolish girl," he said, his gaze wandering her face. "I will give you twenty pounds for the filly."

Her brows dipped into a frown. "Mr. Fish said you bid twenty-five."

"He is correct," Declan said as he took in her oval face. "But that was before I knew what you were about. Twenty pounds."

She tilted her head back, knowing full well she was being admired. "Don't be absurd."

"Fifteen," he said, and touched the curl at her cheek with his free hand.

Keira gave him a sly smile. "It was an act of great fortune that I came when I did, Declan. Who was looking after Lily's affairs, I ask you? No one, that's who, until *I* came along."

He moved his hand to the side of her neck. "You must be filled with glee to think that as Maloney and your father believe you to be in Italy, there is no one to keep a proper eye on you, aye?" He smiled at the thought. "It is wedded bliss without the wedding."

Keira's creamy cheeks pinkened even more. "I would *never*, sir."

Declan's smile faded. He lowered his head, so that his lips were only a moment away from hers. "*Never*, Keira?" he asked low.

Her eyes glittered angrily. "Stand back."

Declan did no such thing. "There is an old Irish saying. One should never kindle a fire if one is afraid of being burned."

Her lips parted slightly and her gaze fell to his mouth.

Something stirred inside Declan. "I don't want your advice, my lord," she said silkily. "I want your help."

He looked at her mouth, imagined touching those full lips with his. "You are mad," he said low. "I don't want to help you. I want to turn you over to the English authorities."

"But you won't," she said. "Because that would ruin everything for Lily. Whatever you may think of me, I know you care about Lily."

He couldn't argue that. Lily was the one person to speak up for him at a particularly difficult time in his life, and it galled him that Keira would use that time in his life to buy his silence. She was too bold, too provocative. He splayed his fingers against her jaw and forced her head back. "How is it that you always manage to exasperate me?"

"It is you who are exasperating *me* at present." Her mouth was now directly under his. She expected him to kiss her; he could see it in her half-closed eyes.

"Fifteen pounds," he said.

"I am hardly inclined to sell you the horse now that you have behaved so wretchedly," she said, and her lips curved into a sultry smile.

"Have you considered that if you don't sell me the filly at a fair price, I shall tell the world who you are? Or more aptly, who you are *not*?"

"Not for sale," she said again.

That was Keira Hannigan for you, far too confident for her own good. Her beauty notwithstanding, her impudence in the face of her deceit annoyed Declan to the point he feared what he might do. But he thought of Lily, now the Countess of Ashwood, apparently, and at one time, his only friend. "Don't toy with me, Keira," he said low. "Don't attempt to include me in any of your schemes. And don't expect me to keep your secrets this time," he said.

With one last heated look at her mouth, he turned away from her and walked out of her purloined salon.

Three

Mr. Fish strode in through the door Declan had left open, his thin face made tense with concern. "Is everything in order, madam?"

"Yes, of course!" Keira said, as if it were preposterous to even inquire. "All is well, Mr. Fish."

All was *not* well. She'd created quite a hash of things at Ashwood. She truly never meant to *be* the Countess of Ashwood, but now that she was, things were so bloody well complicated, really, and she'd been rather relieved to see a familiar face in Donnelly. And surprised—dear God, she'd been surprised when she had seen him down at the paddock, so surprised that her heart had stopped and it was a wonder she hadn't tripped over her own feet. But she couldn't very well march down to the paddock and present herself to him without risking discovery when he used her name or openly called out her fraud, so she'd done the one thing only a countess could do: She'd summoned him to her and had prayed for a moment alone before he said something revealing to Mr. Fish.

Declan O'Conner, Lord Donnelly of Ballynaheath, was the most alluring, most enticing, dream-inspiring man Keira had ever known. She'd not have believed it was possible, but he had seemed even more handsome to her when he had strolled into the salon full of confidence, with the scent of horses around him, mud on his boots, and his hair brushing his collar. Rich brown, thick hair, begging for a woman's fingers. His startlingly blue eyes seemed to bore through her. His lips made her mouth water, and she could imagine his hands, broad and strong, stroking her skin.

Keira had found it exceedingly difficult to stand so close to him, to feel his hand on her skin, his mouth only a breath away, and not touch him. But she had not touched him. She knew better than to touch a man like Declan O'Conner. Touching a man as virile as he would only lead to trouble. She'd discovered that long ago.

Declan was an imposing figure, and there was a time she'd been a wee bit frightened of him. He'd always been considered wild, even for County Galway. When he was on the back of a horse, he rode as if he were immortal and had no fear for his neck.

"The only way to truly know a horse is to give it its head," he'd said at a picnic once. "If you fear for your fate on the back of one and tighten the rein, you can't know what the horse is capable of."

At the time, Keira had thought he was rather pompous about it and had ignored his boastful speech. But then he'd put her on a horse that was too wild by half, and when she'd been thrown from it, he had not even bothered to help her to her feet. Fortunately, a pair of gentlemen had rushed to her rescue.

"He bid twenty-five pounds," Mr. Fish said anxiously,

bringing her back to the present. "He honored his bid, did he not?"

This would not go well, Keira guessed. She smiled. "I did not sell him the horse, Mr. Fish."

"Pardon?" Mr. Fish looked confused. "I don't understand. He bid twenty-five pounds for it."

"I don't want to sell to him," she said. "He seems rather dark, does he not?" *Enticingly dark.*

"Dark?"

"Disreputable."

Mr. Fish looked even more confused. "He is an earl, Lady Ashwood—"

"I am painfully aware," she interrupted. "But I did not wish to sell to him. And the rest of the auction, Mr. Fish? How did we fare?"

Mr. Fish pinched his lips together in what she gathered was a supreme effort not to argue. "Not as well as we'd hoped, regrettably. We had bids of two and thirty pounds. The bid for the filly was . . . was crucial for our needs."

A rush of warmth flooded Keira's nape and scalp, but she forced a smile. "No matter!" she said airily. "Once the mill is repaired we will generate more than enough cash to operate Ashwood, will we not?" It had been her idea to rebuild the mill that had sat idle for decades to generate the funds Ashwood needed to pay its expenses. It was a cruel fact that two summers of drought had put many of the tenants behind in their rents, and as a result, Ashwood, the famously luxurious estate, was suffering from a serious lack of available funds to keep things running properly, much less to make the ongoing repairs and renovations an estate this large invariably needed. Mr. Fish had desired to sell unnecessary stock. Keira thought they needed a bigger, bolder plan if they were to survive. If only she knew what to do.

Mr. Fish had not been in favor of opening the mill. "It was closed for the very reason it required more money to operate than it generated," he'd said when Keira first suggested it.

"But that was when it was used solely for Ashwood. Imagine if we allowed all of West Sussex and beyond, allowed anyone who had need of a fine mill, to avail themselves of it for a fee?" she'd suggested. "We could add a granary, too, where they might store their grain."

"Madam, what you suggest is engaging in a trade," he'd said disapprovingly, as if that were tantamount to sentencing herself straight to hell. The English Quality were very peculiar in that regard, she thought. As if engaging in a trade made a person less than human. "It is engaging in our survival," she'd retorted, and in the end, because Mr. Fish believed her to be the countess, he had given in.

Today, he seemed terribly disappointed in her, and she could hardly blame him. Twenty-five pounds would have gone a long way toward providing for various sundries such as candles and oil and wages. "Don't look so despairing," she said cheerfully. "We have many other irons in the fire, Mr. Fish. However, you must excuse me now. I am expected at the orphanage."

Mr. Fish's hollow cheeks reddened. The poor man's plans for righting the listing ship that was Ashwood were altered once again.

It didn't help that Keira really hadn't the slightest idea what she was doing, even with someone as competent as

Mr. Fish to guide her. It wasn't as if Pappa had ever consulted her on the workings of Lisdoon. Oh, but she had put herself in a deep quagmire, and she was sinking fast. She was angry with herself for having lost the sale of the filly.

She strode briskly down the hallway, past portraits and past Chinese Ming vases, past highly polished consoles laden with hothouse flowers. She walked away from the duplicity she faced in the salon, nodded politely to a pair of footmen, smiled at the maid who hastened to get out of her path. She swept up one side of the magnificent dual curving staircase and hurried down the wide corridor to the master suite of rooms.

In the sanctity of her private rooms—pink and white walls and cheerful floral prints in the furnishings and draperies—Keira sank onto a bench at her vanity and rubbed her forehead. She was feeling a slight pain behind her eyes, which was not uncommon these days, what with all the deceit she had to maintain. All right, then, granted, Keira could count herself guilty of some moral lapses in her life, but who among the living hadn't? Yet *this* . . . this had happened in that way things tended to happen to Keira.

It was precisely what she told Declan. When she'd arrived at Ashwood with the letter from Mr. Fish, there was apparently a strong enough resemblance to Lily that fifteen years later, the old butler, Mr. Linford, immediately assumed she *was* Lily.

Keira had tried to correct him, but he was deaf or stubborn—she still wasn't certain which—and he'd insisted she was the countess, and everyone had fawned and seemed so genuinely happy that the countess had returned, and . . . and immediately, that very afternoon, she'd been presented with the problem of Hannah Hough, and Mr. Fish had needed the countess's signature at once just to pay the wages. Honestly, Keira had been so overwhelmed she hadn't known what to do. She only knew that those poor people needed their wages and Hannah Hough's life depended on Lily.

"Do you mean to say that only Lady Ashwood may stop this?" Keira had asked carefully that fateful afternoon.

"Yes, madam. Only *you*! Can you not see why we are so relieved you have come?"

The poor people who depended on Ashwood for their livelihood needed Lily, and Lily had not been there. At the time, Keira's decision to put Lily's name to the paper had seemed remarkably prudent. She had reasoned that she had Lily's approval and, honestly, Lily had requested that Keira mind the estate. Surely she'd had no choice but to save Hannah Hough.

Before Keira knew it, she *was* the countess.

In hindsight, perhaps, it was not the most prudent thing to have done. The lie seemed to grow bigger every day. Keira still believed Lily would come, and together, they would explain to everyone that Keira had done this at Lily's behest.

Then Declan O'Conner, of all people, had appeared.

The man was as maddening as he was attractive. To think she'd fancied herself in love with him once! Granted, she'd been a girl, but *still*. And yes, there was the ghost of the horrible thing that had happened to them, an event so horrifying that even eight years later, every time Keira thought of it, it made her ill.

But she also remembered something else about that

day. She remembered Declan. Vividly. Achingly. That memory of him made her do ridiculous things, such as refuse to take his money for a horse.

It had happened on one of those extraordinarily bright days by a calm sea in Ireland, when sunlight glittered gold and silver on the water's surface. Eireanne O'Conner had invited friends and acquaintances to a picnic at the family's estate of Ballynaheath, the sort of affair for which servants were called upon to haul large pieces of seating and tables to some difficult-to-reach hill, erect large canopies for ladies to lounge beneath, and then stand by in full livery so that the privileged few of County Galway should not want for as much as a berry.

Eireanne hosted the picnics because she'd had little else to occupy her. Her guardian brother was mostly away from Ballynaheath, leaving Eireanne in her grandmother's care, who, although a loving soul, was enjoying her dotage and was often away with her widowed companions.

Yet Eireanne had wanted for nothing. Declan had always allowed his sister whatever her heart desired. Pappa once said it was to assuage his guilt. Keira never understood what he meant by that.

When Declan was at Ballynaheath, everyone knew it. He'd always seemed to her too large for Galway, a sun that was too hot, too intense for the land. One could almost feel the current of excitement that came with him, sparked by the horse racing and weekend gambling at Ballynaheath.

He did not typically attend Eireanne's picnics. Eireanne said they were too tame for her brother. Surely he'd been nowhere to be seen that day, and Keira remembered being disappointed by it.

The setting, up on a hill, had been spectacular, with a stunning view of the sea. Vases of wildflowers graced the pristine white cloths that covered the tables. From the tops of the canopies hung ribbons and more flowers. A court for lawn bowling had been set up, and the gentlemen had discarded their coats and neckcloths in their earnest play. A flautist and a violinist had been brought down from Connemarra.

It was a day for which Keira and Lily, and Keira's friend Eve, had had a plan. They'd hatched it the day before, when the three of them had trekked down to a small lake behind Lisdoon where the Hannigans had lived for two hundred years. They'd carried a picnic basket and three fishing poles. They'd cast their lines carelessly, then ignored them completely as they'd nattered on, gossiping.

The plotting had begun when Eve had confessed her regard for Mr. Brendan, a tall, ginger-haired man only recently come to County Galway. No one seemed to know him very well, save old Mrs. Russell. It was she who introduced him about, even hosting a supper party in his honor. And at that supper party, Mr. Brendan let it be known he'd come to County Galway from County Clare to settle his late mother's property, and when he had his inheritance in hand, he intended to sail to America to make his fortune.

Sailing to America to make one's fortune had sounded very exotic, indeed, and especially to Eve. She'd fancied herself quite in love with him. She talked about him incessantly, about the elegant tilt of his head when he spoke, about his fine, kissable lips.

Keira had understood Eve completely, for she'd had similar thoughts about Declan. She knew it was imprudent—he was wild and seven years older than her sixteen years, but nevertheless, Keira had always felt dangerously intrigued by that man. She'd been fortunate to dance with him at Eireanne's birthday party last spring, and he had gazed down at her with starkly blue eyes and told her she would one day twist men's hearts in knots. She'd then ridden with him that fall on a hunt, and he'd proclaimed her a superb horsewoman.

Granted, there had been an uncomfortable encounter at Lisdoon earlier that summer, when Declan had appeared with Eireanne, and the two of them had disappeared along with Keira's father into the study. Keira was summoned a quarter of an hour later. Eireanne was sitting on a settee, her hands in her lap, her head down. Keira's father was standing behind his desk, and Declan was planted before the windows, his arms crossed, his expression thunderous.

"Keira Rose Hannigan, did you entice Miss O'Conner into Galway for the purpose of meeting a pair of gentlemen?" her father boomed at her.

Keira's gaze had flown to Eireanne as her cheeks flamed. "We . . . we went to purchase gloves, Papa," she stammered.

"And did you take your luncheon at Lough Tarry Tavern with two gentlemen?"

"And Mrs. Flannery!" Keira had cried, thinking she could hardly be faulted for having agreed to the luncheon Mrs. Flannery had arranged. That she hadn't exactly explained her whereabouts to her parents that day hardly seemed a crime to her. She'd always been the adventurous sort, always seeking the experience and ignoring, where she could, the propriety. Nevertheless, her father and Declan had been right angry with her.

And there had been the time Keira had stumbled upon Declan kissing a woman. She'd ridden to Ballynaheath and had seen the two of them behind the stable. She'd been too enthralled to turn away, and Declan had caught her. He'd called it spying. She'd called it an accident.

Keira had never rid her head of that image, or the peculiar, lusty warmth she felt when she imagined Declan doing that to her.

In fact, that kiss was what she was thinking about the afternoon she and Lily and Eve had decided to fish. She lay on the carpet of grass on the riverbank, her ankles crossed, her arms folded behind her head, listening to Eve pine for Mr. Brendan as she imagined Declan kissing her.

"Do you love him?" Lily had pointedly asked of Eve, a slight girl with light brown hair who looked far younger than her sixteen years.

"I do," Eve had said with a girlish giggle.

"Then you must confess it to him before he sails!" Keira had said suddenly, imagining herself confessing love to Declan. She imagined how he would look at her with that devouring gaze, how he would kiss her.

Lily, however, had seemed a little disapproving of Keira's idea. "A lady never declares her feelings for a gentleman until his feelings are known."

"You sound just like Mamma," Keira had said dismissively. Her mother had been forever telling them what to think and how to act. "Whyever not? Perhaps he feels the very same and is afraid to declare his feelings for fear they will not be returned. And besides, gentlemen are quite flattered when ladies esteem them. Eve, it will endear you to him."

"But he is sailing for America," Eve had pointed out.

"Aye, but if he knows you love him, he will send for you when he is *rich*."

Eve had gasped at the possibility, and Lily had frowned thoughtfully.

"And if he spurns you," Keira had continued with much authority, "you will not endure the humiliation . . . because he will have sailed to America."

That had brought a blush to Eve's cheeks. "Never," she'd said softly.

But as that afternoon wore on, the notion that Eve should declare her feelings to Mr. Brendan had become imperative. The three girls had returned to Lisdoon, and together had toiled over a letter to Mr. Brendan, asking that he meet Eve on the shore on the morrow. They had concluded that Eve had "something very dear" to give Mr. Brendan before he sailed. That dear thing was a lock of hair, which had seemed terribly romantic to them.

The fishing poles, long forgotten, had been left behind at the lake. A boy was sent to fetch them and to dispatch the letter to Mrs. Russell's, where he was instructed to wait for a reply from Mr. Brendan.

They'd sequestered themselves in Keira's rooms—mainly to keep out the twins—and paced restlessly.

The boy had returned with a very terse note from Mr. Brendan: *Yes.*

That was it, the sum of Mr. Brendan's response, but it

was enough to elicit squeals so loud from the three girls that Molly had kicked the door in frustration, begging to be let in.

The following afternoon, Keira, Lily, and Eve left the lawn bowling and picnic feast and headed for the cliffs beside the sea. No one thought anything of three girls wanting to pick wildflowers. They followed the path along the river, through an ancient stand of oaks, past meadows thick with late-summer wildflowers, along the edges of windswept moors. When they reached the cliffs where their paths would part, Eve smiled nervously and twirled once more in her best muslin for their approval.

As Eve set off down the path to the beach where she was to meet her love, Keira had been envious of her adventure. But it had been a game to her, a diversion on a summer's day, a childish dream of love.

Keira and Lily had wandered around the top of the cliffs, looking out to the sea, picking wildflowers and arguing about the whereabouts of a gold necklace they both coveted. When Eve failed to return after an hour, Lily was worried. Keira had reasoned that Eve and Mr. Brendan, having declared their love for each other, could not bear to part. Lily convinced Keira that they should walk down to the beach and have a look. Keira would walk up to the river's mouth, in case Eve had missed the turn up to the cliffs. Lily would walk down to the beach. They would meet again at the turn of the path up the cliffs.

Keira had followed the winding path down the cliffs and into dales where the river rushed out to meet the sea. She had not expected to see anyone, least of all Declan, and her heart, her silly young heart, skipped a beat or two when she saw a man in the meadow ahead of her and realized it was him.

Fate. It had to be fate.

How clearly she remembered that day! He was on horseback, naturally, putting a beautiful black horse through its paces. The horse had cantered slowly, the rhythm of its gait smooth and steady. Declan had glided along on the horse's back. His thighs, made thick from years on horseback, were visibly taut in his buckskins as he worked to control the horse's speed with the reins and his body.

He'd looked magnificent to her, a towering exemplification of a man's strength, and Keira's heart had begun to beat rapidly. She'd thought of Eve kissing Mr. Brendan. She'd thought of how she longed to feel Declan's hands on her and his mouth on her skin, and desire had catapulted her into the meadow.

Declan saw her as he turned the horse in a large circle. He had looked at her curiously, as if she were somehow incongruent with the landscape. His deep blue gaze had shifted over her head, to the path behind her, obviously looking for others as he'd reined his horse to a halt. "Keira?" he'd said, looking slightly concerned.

Just the sound of her name on his breath had made her body thrum with desire. Keira had been instantly and hopelessly besotted. She'd kept walking forward, until she was standing a foot or so from the horse.

Declan slid off the horse and swept off his hat, then pushed his hand through hair the color of fall's oak leaves streaked with shades of honey. "Is all well?" he'd asked. "Did someone send for me?"

She shook her head. He'd been so regal, so handsome in a riding coat that fit tightly across broad shoulders. He was a good six inches taller than she. Keira had stood so close she could see the shadow of his beard and imagined the feel of it on her cheek.

"Where are your friends?" he'd asked, looking up the path.

She hadn't answered. She'd stroked the horse's nose. "He's beautiful," she'd said.

Declan had watched her curiously a moment, then had looked back up the path as if he'd expected someone to come and rescue him. "Why are you not at the picnic, lass?"

Keira had shrugged and glanced at him from the corner of her eye. "I can't tell you."

"Can't you?"

"Mmm, no. It's a secret."

"Is it," he'd drawled dubiously. "Does this secret involve Eireanne?"

"No," Keira had said with a smile. "She is at the picnic, of course." She'd stepped closer to Declan and stroked the horse's neck. "What is his name?"

"Fiddler." He considered her a moment, and Keira had wondered what he saw when he looked at her. Did he think her pretty? Did he think of kissing her? Of putting his mouth on her body? "Where are your friends, Keira? Your sisters? You shouldn't be wandering about alone. One never knows who is lurking in these glens."

"You are all I have found lurking," she'd said, and smiled up at him.

His eyes had narrowed suspiciously, but the corner

of his perfect mouth curved up into something of a lazy grin. "Keira Hannigan," he'd muttered as his gaze dipped to her décolletage. "Always into mischief. I suppose it is true what they say—the devil has the face of an angel."

Keira's heart had beat so fast! The horse snorted and tossed his head. Declan reached around her to put his hand on the horse's mane, stilling him. "Easy," he said to the horse, but his eyes were on Keira. "Where are your friends?"

"Occupied."

His gaze wandered the length of her body. "Go back to them." He shifted away from her, toward the horse's body.

A rush of heat filled Keira, a warm, fluid spread that she found very pleasurable. She thought of Eve in Mr. Brendan's embrace. She thought of Declan's mouth, soft and warm on hers, and impulsively put her hand on his.

Declan's smile faded a bit. He looked at her hand on his and leaned back. "Go to the picnic or go home, I care not. You should not be here."

She smiled wantonly, as she had seen her mother smile at her father. "Are you afraid of me?"

His gaze had darkened as it moved down her body. "You are an incautious, foolish lass. Have you any idea how dangerous a bit of flirting can be for a girl as pretty as you? Have a care, Keira."

He thinks me pretty. She'd shifted closer. "I'm not in any danger, am I?"

A thick strand of dark brown hair fell across his brow. His gaze lifted up to her mouth, and Keira had unthinkingly released the breath she was holding. "You have no idea what you are doing," he'd said softly. "Go home."

"I don't want to go home."

He'd surprised her then by catching her at the waist and pulling her close. The horse had whinnied and stepped sideways, away from them . . . or at least Keira thought so. Her gaze had been locked on Declan and his eyes, a cold river of blue. She'd never forgotten the feel of his hand on her waist.

He leaned his head down, his lips just inches from hers. "Think of what you are about. I tell you again—go home."

Keira could scarcely catch her breath. She'd tilted her head back so that she could look up at his eyes. *"No."*

If that had surprised him, he did not show it. His gaze had roamed her face and he'd cocked his head to one side to examine her ear, her cheek. "Are your friends watching from the trees? Is this some sort of jest? A scheme of some sort?"

His voice was low and smooth, stoking whatever it was that Keira was feeling. Passion. Power. Greed. "You think so poorly of me," she'd said. "They are quite occupied, you may trust me. I promise I'll not tell a soul I saw you here if you will promise the same."

He'd smiled dubiously and touched his knuckle to her jaw. Keira suppressed a small gasp. "Where are they?" he murmured.

"I cannot tell you. Trust me."

"Trust." He chuckled. "I do not trust you in the least."

His hand had drifted across the flesh of her bosom. Keira had felt as if she might levitate at any moment, just float out over the meadow, her racing heart keeping her aloft.

Declan had bent his head, put his lips to her ear, and

said, "A wee bit of advice, lass. Don't tempt a grown man, for his appetite is often stronger than his will."

She'd instantly wondered how strong was his will; hers had been incredibly weak in that moment. She was drawn to him, drawn to danger, and she couldn't fight the thing that was building in her. So she'd ignored his warning, risen up on her tiptoes, and touched her lips to his. She'd hovered there, the thrill of it so electrifying that she feared her knees would give out.

I've done it. I've kissed Declan O'Conner.

But if she thought Declan would politely return her kiss, she was wrong, so wrong. He'd very casually licked a slow and sensual path across the seam of her lips. When Keira gasped at the sensation, his tongue had slipped into her mouth, and his grip of her had tightened. It was the most sensual, decadent thing Keira could have imagined. Warmth had burst within her, spreading from her center out to her limbs, climbing up her neck and tingling in her scalp. Declan put his hand to her jaw and angled her head to the right as he delved deeper.

There had been nothing holding Keira aloft but his arm. Her legs had ceased to function; her arms were hanging by her sides.

And then suddenly, too suddenly, he'd lifted his head. "*Goddammit,*" he'd muttered, and let go of her, twirling away from her at the same time he shoved his hand through his hair. As Keira tried to catch her breath, he'd bent down and swept up his hat. When he'd turned back to her, his smoldering gaze drifted over her. "You, Keira Hannigan, are a danger to any breathing man. Go back now. Go to your friends. But go away from me."

Keira had seen the way he'd looked at her, the flicker of desire in his eyes, and for the first time in her young life, she'd understood the power a woman had over a man.

"*Go!*" he'd said sharply.

"You mustn't tell anyone I was here," she'd said breathlessly, her heart still pounding with the exhilaration. "Promise you will say you never saw me."

That had earned her a dark, accusing look. "What are you hiding?"

"Nothing! I swear it!"

"You may be assured I won't tell a bloody soul," he'd snapped, and had thrown himself up on the horse. He didn't look at her as he spurred the horse on. Keira's heart was still pounding, but she turned and ran in the opposite direction, in search of Lily and Eve.

But Eve did not come back from her meeting. They found her several hours later, her face bruised, her clothes bloodied. In a matter of days, Eve had jumped from the cliffs into the sea, ending her life and her shame.

Even now, Keira could not think of that day without being overwhelmed with guilt and regret and sadness. Her deceit then, like now, no matter how innocent she'd believed it to be, had mushroomed. This time, she found herself signing things that ought to have been signed quite some time ago, performing duties that should have been left for Lily, and confronting yet another, not insignificant matter—she'd come to believe that the man Lily had accused of stealing Aunt Althea's jewels was the wrong man entirely. She was thoroughly convinced an innocent man had hanged. If that were true, she feared what Lily would do if she discovered the truth. Eve's death had all but destroyed her; Keira believed that knowing she had had a hand in an innocent man's death would surely destroy her cousin.

A knock at the door startled Keira from her thoughts. "Come," she said.

"Beg your pardon, mu'um," Betts, her lady's maid, said when she entered. "Fresh linens."

"Thank you," Keira said. She shook her head and stood, smiled at Betts. "How did the gown that I gave you fit?" she asked idly as she pulled her gloves on.

Betts blushed. "A bit too large in the bodice, mu'um, but my sister is right handy with a needle and thread. She's envious, in truth—it's beautiful."

"I am so glad it suits you," Keira said. "Tell your sister she may have the next one that doesn't suit me." She winked at Betts on her way out.

In the foyer, Linford met her with her hat and a light wrap. "Thank you, Linford," she said cheerily. "Do you think it will rain?"

"My knee says it will indeed, madam," Linford said, bowing low.

"Good! Lord knows we need it." She put on the bonnet and tied the blue ribbons beneath her chin and walked to the door. Louis, a footman, opened it ahead of her. "Oh! The sweetmeats—"

"In the coach, madam," Louis said.

She smiled gratefully. "What would I do without you, Louis? Thank you."

She continued on to the drive, said hello to Paul, the head coachman.

"G'day, mu'um," he called cheerfully.

"Linford's knee says rain, Paul," she called up to him.

"I'm glad I've got Agnes then," he said, twitching the rein of one horse. "She's as good a mudder as any I've ever seen."

Keira laughed and allowed Louis to hand her into the coach. It began moving along, past a line of elms that marked the road, past green fields where cattle and sheep grazed. They turned onto another road where birds had roosted on top of the stone ruins of an ancient building. They drove past fields where tenants were working, all of whom paused to doff their hats or wave at her.

When they reached the village of Hadley Green, children suddenly appeared beside the coach, running alongside it, calling up to Keira. When the coach slowed to allow a man and his milk cow to pass, Keira opened her reticule, withdrew a few pence, and tossed them out the window. The children scampered for the coins, and one young man, a head taller than the rest, stood up first, his fist clenched around a coin. "Henry Beedle, you must share with your brother this time!" she called out to him as the coach began to move again. "Yes, mu'um!" Henry called up to her, grinning.

Oh, he'd be a charmer, that one. She waved at the children as the coach moved on.

At the gates of St. Bartholomew Orphanage, Sister Rosens, the headmistress, was waiting for Keira. Keira liked Sister Rosens very much. The sister was tall, in the middle of her life, and had been at St. Bartholomew for many years. It was clear she cared for her wards and constantly strove to improve their lot in life. In fact, Sister Rosens had introduced Keira to Lucy Taft. Keira had instantly taken to the nine-year-old. Sister Rosens told her that Lucy was the daughter of the apothecary, who died rather infamously by burning himself while making a combustible tincture of some sort. Her mother died shortly thereafter (some said from heartache, some said from the weight of her debt), the lenders carried their belongings away, and Lucy was deposited at the orphanage. She was sweet and Keira thought she could be trained to a better station in life. Keira and Sister Rosens had agreed that Lucy should come to Ashwood, where she thought to train Lucy personally to one day be a governess or another suitable occupation. As soon as the girl finished her current schoolwork, she would join Keira at Ashwood.

"How do you do, Sister Rosens?" Keira said cheerfully as she stepped from the coach, the box of sweetmeats in hand.

"I do very well, your ladyship. You've brought sweetmeats again! You will spoil the children," she said, eyeing the box.

Keira opened it and grinned as Sister Rosens bent over the box to examine the contents. "Madam, you make it very difficult to honor a vow of austerity," she said.

"Austerity is restricting yourself to only one," Keira said.

Sister Rosens grinned and very delicately selected a confection for herself. "Thank you."

"How do the children fare?" Keira asked as they strolled through the squeaking gate together. There was so much to be done for the orphanage, so many repairs that should be made. All the orphanage's money went to feeding and clothing the children. There was nothing left for repairs.

The livestock pens needed to be rebuilt and there was a leaky roof over the boys' ward. A fire in the chapel two years ago had put Sunday services in the courtyard, or, in inclement weather, the dining room.

"As well as can be expected," Sister Rosens said. "Three siblings were brought to us this week. Their mother died in childbirth and their father had no desire to care for them."

"Oh dear," Keira said. These children were delivered such cruel blows so early in life. This was the first time Keira really appreciated her life of luxury in Ireland. She'd taken it for granted up until now.

She was suddenly jostled by a small pair of arms thrown round her legs. "Lucy, darling! You must have a care," Keira said, dipping down to hug her.

"I'm sorry," Lucy said, and turned her gleaming blue eyes to the box. "What did you bring us?"

"Miss Taft, have your forgotten all your manners?" Sister Rosens asked sternly. "For that, you are allowed the last confection in the box."

Chastened, Lucy bowed her fair head. "Pardon, mu'um," she murmured.

"Here," Keira said. "Take them to the others. And please do be sure that the new children get their fair share. And see there is one left over for you."

"Yes, mu'um," Lucy said, brightening again. She skipped away with the box. Other children playing in the courtyard immediately recognized the box and quickly surrounded Lucy, all anxious for a treat.

Keira and Sister Rosens strolled on, through the gardens the children worked to maintain, past a crumbling old fountain. "By the by, the St. Bartholomew Orphan's Charity Society ladies have persuaded me to host the annual Ashwood summer gala this year, Sister," Keira said. "I understand it's not been held in several years."

"Glory, what welcome news!" Sister Rosens said. "The children have always enjoyed it so. We have twenty-four orphans this year. What a delight for them all!"

"With any luck, we might raise enough funds to repair things here," Keira pointed out.

"God willing." The sister sighed. "There are so many things to do. Here, look at this," she said, and paused at a door to open it. "This was once a nursery, but the leaks in the ceiling have made it impossible to use."

The scent of mildew was quite strong as they walked into the room. In one corner, several larger toys had been placed, presumably for storage. Keira happened to notice a wooden rocking horse. It was hand carved, with the legs kicking up and the horse tossing its head. "That's lovely," she said, nodding at the rocking horse.

Sister Rosens looked, too. "Isn't it? Mr. Scott made several toys for the orphanage. I believe there has never been another craftsman like him."

"Mr. Scott made it?" Keira asked, peering at the horse. She bent down to have a look, running her fingers over the carved mane. "Did you know him, then, Sister?"

"I did."

"What sort of man was he?" Keira asked curiously.

Sister Rosens looked at her. "What sort of man? A good man, madam."

She said it with such conviction that it surprised Keira. "But he was a thief."

"He was so accused and found guilty," she said, "but I never saw that side of him. I know only that with three children of his own, he found time to make toys for our orphans. He was a good and generous man." She gestured to the door.

As Keira walked that way, her questions about Mr. Scott were soaring. Really, where *were* the jewels he was accused of stealing?

Four

In a room above the Grousefeather Tavern in Hadley Green, Declan O'Conner was lying on his back, one arm folded behind his head, watching Penny, the serving girl, look about for her stockings. "Lud, what have we done with 'em this time?" she muttered as she pulled her chemise over her head.

Declan watched the fabric slide over her bare, round rump. "What is your haste?" he asked.

"Did I no' tell you? My brother Johnny's coming home today. He's been gone nigh on a year, milord. I can't wait to lay me eyes on him."

"Where's he been?" Declan asked idly.

"Dunno, exactly. London, I guess. He writ a letter home, and me mum, she had the old vicar read it, and the letter said Johnny's to arrive today on the two o'clock post." She found one stocking, quickly rolled it up and stuck her foot in it, stretching her leg long as she pulled it up. She did the same with the other, then donned her dress, impervious to Declan's study of her body. When she'd finished dressing, she twirled around, pushed her fair hair from her eyes, then bounced onto the bed to kiss him. "Thursday next?" she asked as she bounced off the bed again.

"I'd not miss it."

She smiled. "That's poppycock, luv, and well you know it. One day you'll run off to poke that countess and have yourself a proper time, in a proper bed. I hear she's right pretty."

Declan's good humor faded somewhat. "Not even if she were the last woman in God's creation. You mustn't fret about her."

"How can I not fret, a man as handsome as you? And an earl's man, no less!"

"Not an earl's man. An earl," he corrected her.

Penny frowned. "If you're the earl, then why's it you that do that lord's bidding?"

Declan grinned. Penny embodied what he loved about commoners. Titles, protocol—none of that concerned them. "I am not doing his bidding," he said. "I am breeding a horse for him."

"What's the difference?" Penny asked blithely.

"An important one. Breeding is my hobby, not my occupation."

"Mmm," Penny said, smiling a little skeptically. "Well then! I'm off. Mind you don't tarry, milord. Mrs. Cornish don't like her rooms to be occupied for long in case a proper traveler comes through."

"I won't tarry," he assured her, and watched Penny bounce out the door, tying her hair up in a knot as she hurried out.

Declan took his time dressing, pausing to finish the glass of ale he'd begun before Penny had thrust her hand into his trousers. He tied his neckcloth, combed his fingers through his hair, and pulled on his Hessian boots. He paused to give himself one more look in the looking glass. He had a shadow of a beard. And his hair needed to be cut. He studied his face a moment. He was getting older. Sometimes, he wondered how long he could live like this, always moving, always seeking the next great race. He liked the idea, in a rather casual way, of having children. He thought he would like to have a son to whom he could show the world.

Declan turned away from the mirror and picked up his hat. "That will be enough of your sentimental ruminations for the day," he muttered to himself. Truly, the thought of settling down made him unusually anxious. It was almost as if he could feel the chains settling around his ankles. Eireanne said he was like an old blind goose, running here and there and back again. He smiled, thinking about her. She was a most agreeable sister. She deserved a better brother than he. It pained him that her life had not turned out as she had undoubtedly hoped.

He left the Grousefeather with Eireanne on his mind and walked onto High Street in Hadley Green. It was a warm day, with plenty of sunshine. He thought he might ride to the village of Horsham to have a look at a roan he'd heard about. Very fast and nimble, the old man had said.

Lost in thought about the roan, Declan strolled along so incautiously that when a woman trilled, "My Lord Donnelly!" he made the mistake of glancing in the direction of his name. Mrs. Ogle, one of the more important members of Hadley Green society—meaning, one with wealth—and a well-known scandalmonger, had caught him unawares. Her arm was raised and she was waving furiously at him.

"God help me," Declan muttered, and debated bolting as she hurried toward him, quickly and expertly negotiating a cart full of squawking, caged chickens, one very large mud puddle, and a pair of riders in her haste to reach him.

"How do you do, my lord?" she said breathlessly, pressing a hand to her taxed heart. She wore a lace cap that fashionable women had long ago eschewed, and a Spencer jacket buttoned all the way to her throat.

"I am well, Mrs. Ogle. Thank you. You seem very well, if I may. The very picture of health, and now, having assured myself of it, I must be on my way." He tipped his hat to her.

But Mrs. Ogle would not be put off by his attempt at an abrupt departure, and said, before he could take a step, "Did you, by chance, have the opportunity to attend the sale of horses at Ashwood?"

He could scarcely guess why she would care if he had or had not, and arched a curious brow. "Pardon?"

"The countess is selling a good portion of her stock. Everyone is talking about it."

"Mrs. Ogle, why would you possibly concern yourself with it?"

"Oh, I'm not, I'm not, I assure you," she said, and laughed gaily as she glanced around them. She suddenly leaned in and whispered, "I have it on good authority that the countess is quite unattached."

She said it as if she were imparting some vital piece of news, such as the French had landed on England's shores, or the crown prince had drowned in his ale. Declan leaned forward, too, and squinted at her. "Are you matchmaking, Mrs. Ogle?"

"Well," she said with a laugh and a prim hand at her very

high collar. "I don't claim to be a matchmaker, no, my lord, but I am quite adept at knowing who is good with whom."

"Good day, Mrs. Ogle," he said, and strode forward.

"My lord, please wait! There is news!" she called after him.

Declan groaned heavenward before turning to face her.

"The countess has agreed to host the annual summer gala. It has long been a tradition at Ashwood, one that has been sorely neglected these last few years as the earl's health began to fail him. All of Hadley Green shall be invited, and very influential people from London."

Good God, was there no limit to Keira's bravado? A *gala*? "And that is relevant to me how, precisely?"

"It is a highly regarded affair, my lord, I daresay more highly regarded than anything you might have known in London."

"Preposterous."

"Yes, well, it is nonetheless the perfect opportunity for you to mingle with the Quality whilst you are in our midst," Mrs. Ogle said. "A bachelor might be interested to know there will be many young debutantes in attendance. And the countess, naturally, who, by anyone's measure, is the most desirable of them all."

He desired the so-called countess to go back to Ireland, where she belonged. "Bloody grand for the bachelors, then. I am certain they will have a day of it. But if you are indeed a matchmaker, madam, you surely have ascertained that I rarely court unattached females, for I have found there is generally a sound reason they are unattached. I prefer liaisons with ladies who have already snagged their husbands and require only a bit of diversion."

Mrs. Ogle gasped. Then colored. "Oh! Oh *my,* sir!"

He strode away before she could say another word. Especially about *her.* Keira Hannigan was overly indulged, headstrong, and bloody well dangerous.

She was also beautiful, with sparkling green eyes, and a pert smile that could make the strongest of men weak. Perhaps even worse, she knew very well her appeal to men. Aye, that girl was too bold by half. Impersonating her own cousin! That was enough to earn his disdain, but it was that afternoon at Ballynaheath eight years ago that had made him despise her.

That afternoon still haunted him. She'd unnerved him, made him want her in a way he was unaccustomed to wanting. He had left that meadow hot and hard, feeling her green eyes score an indelible scar across his mind's eye. The softness of her body and the eagerness of her kiss had combined to make him incurably aroused.

He'd been ashamed by his desire. He'd been a young man, only three and twenty, and he'd given in so quickly to her, as if he had no power over his own body. When he'd realized what he was doing, he escaped her, giving Fiddler his head on the ride back to Ballynaheath.

Keira Hannigan had been sixteen years old. What had he done? What madness had invaded him that allowed him to take such liberty with her?

As he'd ridden into the paddock that day, Mr. Cousins, one of the gentlemen in attendance at his sister's picnic, had approached him. "My lord, thank goodness you have come," he'd said. "Have you by chance seen Keira Hannigan, Eve O'Shaugnessy, or Lily Boudine?"

"Why do you ask?" Declan had asked roughly as he

tossed his reins to the stable boy. He'd not wanted to think of her at all.

"They've been gone for a time," Mr. Cousins said. "They've wandered off."

So her friends *had* been close by. Probably watching. She'd made a fool of him, and that had made Declan's mood even darker. "I've not seen them," he'd lied. "But I have no doubt they will make their way home in fine spirits."

"My lord?"

Declan hadn't answered, but strode away.

He did not know that a half hour later, Keira and Lily had returned to the picnic without Eve, because he'd been with Aileen, a scullery maid, in her room belowstairs. He would not know that something was seriously, horribly wrong until several hours later when a tearful Keira Hannigan would report the scheme of sending Eve to Mr. Brendan, and in the course of telling it, admit that she had seen Declan in a meadow down by the river.

He would know when a search party was formed and he'd seen the censure in Mr. Cousin's eyes and in the expression of the men around him, who had obviously heard that Declan had denied seeing any of the girls.

He'd known what they'd believed—that he could have saved Eve, had he owned up to seeing Keira, had he kept his hands off a sixteen-year-old girl and then tried to hide the fact.

The men had found Eve that night. She wouldn't speak, but her appearance spoke for her. Her gown was torn and soiled with blood and dirt. Her hair was undone and wild, and her eyes, God, how her eyes had haunted Declan all these years. So empty. So unfathomably empty, as if the life had been bled from them completely.

The search for Mr. Brendan had been fruitless. The speculation around Galway was that he'd escaped on a ship to America.

Several days later, Eve slipped out of her family home and climbed up to the top of the cliffs of Mohar and jumped. Declan was among the first to find her wet and battered body on the shore where it had washed up.

He left Ireland shortly afterward.

Keira and Lily were sent away to the Institut Villa Amiels in Lucerne for a year.

Curiously, the people in County Galway gradually came to put the blame for Eve's demise at Declan's feet. The girls, they said, were too young and silly to know what they were about, but Declan should have understood that trouble was brewing when he'd happened upon Keira alone. They were right. He'd lived with Eve's death every day. It was part of him now, a weight that bore down on him at odd times, a knife that jabbed at him. Declan believed he deserved their censure.

Lily Boudine, however, did not believe he deserved censure. She had stood up for him more than once, defending him. How could he have known, she'd argued. He was a good man, she'd insisted. The blame, Lily said, belonged solely to her and Keira.

Declan was not a good man, but he would never forget Lily's impassioned insistence that he was.

If Keira regretted what had happened, Declan did not know. She was still as vivacious as ever, still quite esteemed in Ireland.

A few years ago at a Christmas Day feast, Keira caught Declan alone and attempted to speak to him about what had happened that day in the meadow. She was beautiful, too beautiful, especially in the low winter light, where her eyes seemed to shine even brighter than normal. "If I had known," she'd whispered, "if I could have guessed, I would never have . . . have said what I did."

"You mean you would not have lied to me," he'd said flatly.

She frowned. "I cannot express how very sorry I am."

She went on to enumerate the depth of her sorrow, floundering a bit, searching for words. Declan said nothing as she spoke. When she'd finished, he suggested simply that they never speak of it again. And he'd continued to avoid her, the center of his shame and regret.

Until now. Until she suddenly appeared in his life, impersonating her own cousin.

Aye, there would be hell to pay when she was caught at her deception, and she certainly would be, for Keira was also careless. How did she think the English would view her, an Irish Catholic, no less, stealing the identity of a countess? They would think her motives were criminal if not politically sinister, given the struggle for Catholic emancipation in Britain.

He would do well to steer clear of that fiasco and the devil's pretty green eyes.

Five

Keira had tea alone when she returned from the orphanage, which was a rare occurrence given her social calendar. But she was grateful for the chance to think about what Sister Rosens had said about Mr. Scott. She remembered the little rocking horse, so expertly crafted. She suddenly put aside her tea and stood up. A footman instantly opened the door, and Keira walked out of the room, bound for the music room.

It was mere coincidence that had led Keira to question Lily's version of events that Keira knew so well. There had been the letter she found, written by her aunt Althea to her mother and never posted, in which she described a life with the earl as unhappy, and that she sought diversions. Keira had not thought much of it—it was no secret that marriages made for fortunes were often unhappy.

Had she not begun to pretend, and perhaps even believe, that she was a princess in the castle that was Ashwood and therefore deserving of a pianoforte, she never would have questioned it at all.

Keira had been at Ashwood a little over a month when she thought of the pianoforte. She happened to be a rather good pianist, thanks to her mother's insistence on lessons for the better part of Keira's life. *"My darling, no man in his right mind shall ever offer for that impertinent tongue of yours, so I've naught left to depend on but your accomplishments. Again, please."*

Keira thought it odd a house as grand as Ashwood did not have a pianoforte, and inquired of Mr. Fish. "I cannot say, madam. There is no pianoforte."

"Yes, sir, there is," said Mrs. Thorpe, the housekeeper. "Lady Ashwood put it away in the attic after the Incident."

"The Incident" was how the local denizens of Hadley Green referred to Mr. Scott's unfortunate demise. It seemed to Keira that everything that had ever occurred in Hadley Green had happened either Before the Incident or After the Incident.

At Mr. Fish's and Keira's curious looks, Mrs. Thorpe had added, "She bought it for you, milady. Do you not remember it, then?"

"Oh, ah . . . why, yes! I *do* seem to recall . . ."

"I suspect you'll remember it when you see it," Mrs. Thorpe continued. "Such a fancy one, brought all the way from Italy. But once you went away, she couldn't bear the sight of it, she longed for you so, and had it put away in the attic."

Funny, wasn't it, that Lily had never indicated a preference or particular talent for the pianoforte to Keira? All those hours Keira had spent practically chained to the pianoforte, and yet Lily never mentioned one had been brought all the way from Italy for her.

Mr. Fish had then and there instructed the butler, Linford, to have the pianoforte brought down to the music room so that the countess might examine it and see if it was still to her liking.

The pianoforte was indeed to Keira's liking; it was an instrument unlike any she'd ever seen. It was crafted from walnut, and musical scrolls had been carved into the wood. Keira had only to look at it, to lay her fingers on the ivory keys and hear the chords, to know that it was exquisite. Mr. Fish arranged for a man to come down from London to tune it.

Keira had contented herself with playing for her own pleasure for a full fortnight, until one afternoon, a gust of breeze scattered the sheet music she was using. In her haste to stand and catch the pages, she knocked over the bench. When she bent over to right it, she noticed something odd. There was a long marking on the underside. She sat on the floor to have a better look.

She guessed it was the artisan's mark, but on closer inspection, it was an inscription. It was carved beneath the lip of the bench, along one side. *You are the song that plays on in my heart; for A, my love, my life, my heart's only note. Yours for eternity, JS.*

"Oh my," Keira had said, running her fingers over the inscription. She thought it very sweet . . . but then she remembered that Mr. Joseph Scott was a master wood-carver, and he must have been the *JS* who had made the inscription.

Then who was *A*?

The answer dawned so suddenly that Keira had gasped and sat back on her heels. "It cannot be," she'd whispered in awe, peering at the inscription again. Her late aunt, the Countess of Ashwood. *Althea Kent.* The discovery

was completely scandalous, and Keira's imagination bal-
looned with the idea that the man who had stolen Lady
Ashwood's jewels had made her this bench and inscribed
it so beautifully.

"Are you unwell, mu'um?"

A chambermaid had found her on the floor, and Keira
had jammed her finger painfully in her haste to get to her
feet and turn the bench over. "Very well, thank you!" she'd
exclaimed far too adamantly. "Just . . . having a look, that's
all. Time for luncheon already, is it?"

"No, mu'um. It is only eleven o'clock."

"Oh." The maid had begun to dust, and Keira did not
dare look at the bench again with her about. So she tucked it
up neatly under the pianoforte and swept out of the room.

Today, she closed the door behind her and walked to
the pianoforte, staring down at the bench. She sank down
onto her knees and turned it over to look at the inscription again. It was elegantly carved, so beautiful, and the
sentiment so lovely. Mr. Scott had loved Aunt Althea. Keira
righted the bench, took a seat on it, and began to play.

It was such a silly, small thing, really, but the
inscription—or rather, the crime—made no sense to
Keira. A man did not carve a bench and engrave vines and
leaves and flowers down the curving legs and add such a
lovely inscription that professed his love for a woman, and
then steal her jewels.

She wished Althea were still alive to ask, but she'd died
so tragically and so young. Keira had met her only a few
times, but she had lovely memories of her. She thought
Aunt Althea was perhaps the most beautiful of the sisters, particularly in spirit. She was so warm, so alive. Keira

remembered that the most about her—Aunt Althea had loved life. She recalled how she'd tried to entice Keira's mother into a trip to Spain once. Keira's mother would not consider it, given that Molly and Mabe were so young. *"What will you do, Lenora, live your life within these walls? How confining!"* Keira had not known what *confining* meant, but she knew that it must be something wretched if Aunt Althea didn't care for it.

Had Althea loved Mr. Scott? Of course she had—she had accepted his gift of the bench. And then he had stolen from her? *It made no sense.*

Keira was so convinced of it that she managed to gather her courage the next afternoon as she and Mrs. Thorpe reviewed the week's activities at Ashwood. Mrs. Thorpe, with her high collar and tightly bound hair, was the standard of efficiency and did not like to be kept by idle chatter. But Keira stood up as the housekeeper prepared to sweep out of the room and said, "Mrs. Thorpe, please indulge me."

"Yes, madam?"

"Do you think my lady aunt . . . do you know if perhaps . . ." There was no delicate way to say it, and as Keira worried over it, she could sense the housekeeper's impatience. "Did my aunt know Mr. Scott . . . well?"

Mrs. Thorpe blinked big brown cow eyes.

"I beg your pardon," Keira said, and her face flaming, she began to gather her papers.

"No, my lady, I beg *your* pardon. It's just that I've not heard his name mentioned here in fifteen years."

"I should not have mentioned it. But I was so young and I—"

"Indeed, you were just a girl."

"But I've since wondered."

Mrs. Thorpe studied her shrewdly a moment. "I do not have firsthand knowledge," she said carefully. "But I think she must have found him agreeable, for she recommended him with great enthusiasm to Lady Horncastle. He had only completed a section of Lady Horncastle's staircase when . . . well, when he met his destiny. I believe the staircase was never completed."

"Lady Horncastle," Keira said thoughtfully. "Of Rochfield?" she asked, thinking of the old mansion on the downs.

"The very one," Mrs. Thorpe said. "She was her ladyship's friend. Do you not recall her?"

"Only . . . very vaguely," Keira said self-consciously.

"I would think you'd remember her very well. She always brought you sweetmeats. You had such a sweet tooth, then! Ireland must have cured you of that," she said, with a hint of disapproval in her tone. It was a fact that the entire Ashwood population was aghast that Keira did not care for sweets and had politely refused the apple tart presented to her at supper a few evenings past. Apparently, Keira had hurt Cook's feelings.

Keira desired to speak to Lady Horncastle, but as they were not acquaintances, she didn't precisely know how to go about it. As luck would have it, an opportunity presented itself.

The ladies from St. Bartholomew Orphan's Charity Society (or, as the ladies liked to refer to it, the Society) called again about the summer gala. All of Hadley Green was atwitter about the event, and though it was two months away, Keira regularly received notes from the Society with ideas for it. God help her, but she had not wanted to host an event the likes of which the Society ladies described to her, but once again, Keira had been helpless. The orphanage was clearly in dire need of funds. To think of all those children needing Lily's name to build the event! Keira had reasoned that at least Lily would have returned to Ashwood by then. It was the perfect opportunity, Keira told herself. She would plan the event and Lily would have all the credit for it.

On that particularly sunny afternoon, Mrs. Felicity Morton, Mrs. Robina Ogle, and Miss Daria Babcock had called, all wearing a similar gold silk, presumably purchased from the only suitable dress shop in Hadley Green. They'd come as a delegation to discuss the possibility of having a horse race at the gala. Linford served them tea and biscuits in the gazebo while hyacinth danced all around them, the scent of their blooms filling the air.

Keira listened attentively to the ladies' suggestion that a race would be the jewel in the little crown of the gala. They guessed that people would come for miles for the pleasure of wagering on the horses, and that they would raise twice as much as they might expect to merely with games and a kite race.

"I am very fond of horse races," Keira said, to which the ladies twittered with excitement. "I have, in fact, participated in them."

That caused an even greater bit of excitement. "You must race, your ladyship!" cried Miss Babcock.

"I would be pleased to do so, but unfortunately, I am

in the process of reducing the horse stock for winter." That was not even remotely true, but she thought it at least sounded feasible. No need to raise the flag of debt over Ashwood. "I'm afraid there aren't enough horses to field an afternoon of racing."

"Oh, but Lady Horncastle has quite a stock," Mrs. Ogle said. "I had occasion to see her in Mrs. Langley's dress shop and she told me she'd taken delivery of three horses just this month."

"Three!" Mrs. Morton exclaimed. "Why so many, do you suppose?"

"For her son, Lord Horncastle," Miss Babcock said, and leaned forward with the grace and eagerness of a young lady who had something very interesting to tell. She was pretty, Daria Babcock, but Keira suspected she was well aware of it. She reminded Keira of herself in that regard, honestly. There was no sense in pretending it wasn't true for the sake of appearances. The flowers in the salon and the little kitten roaming about Ashwood—all gifts from gentlemen admirers—testified to it. Daria would never want for suitors, either.

"Lord Horncastle finds Rochfield rather tedious and has threatened to move to Town," Daria said. "His mother cannot possibly survive without him and seeks to divert him with a wife, if she can manage it."

Mrs. Morton, who struck Keira as a shrewd woman, narrowed her small eyes on Miss Babcock. "And how do you know this, Daria?"

Miss Babcock shrugged coyly and studied the plate of biscuits from beneath the brim of her summer hat. "I've heard tell."

"Perhaps you might call on her, madam," Mrs. Ogle suggested to Keira. "It is for a good cause, after all."

Keira almost gasped with delight. They had just presented her with the perfect reason to call on Lady Horncastle. "You're right! I must do it straightaway. I shall have Mr. Fish send a note round as soon as possible."

Mrs. Ogle chuckled. "How you do remind me of your lady aunt, Lady Ashwood," she said. "Such a lovely smile, and dancing eyes, just like her. And so generous with your time and influence! She was the soul of generosity, you know."

Keira smiled proudly.

But Mrs. Ogle's smile faded as Linford poured a second cup of tea. "I am so sorry for all that happened, you know," she said.

"Thank you," Keira said. "I have thought quite a lot about her of late." She put down her teacup a moment. "In truth, I have found myself wondering what happened to the Ashwood jewels, as they were never recovered."

"Oh, sold for a grand fortune, I'd wager," Mrs. Morton said.

"It seems odd they were never found after the thief was brought to justice," Keira said carefully.

"Very odd and very tragic," Mrs. Ogle agreed as she stirred honey into her tea. "I shall never forget how shocked and saddened I was to learn that Lady Ashwood had ended her own life over it."

Keira was so startled that she banged her spoon against her teacup, causing them all to jump. "I beg your pardon?" she exclaimed, looking at Mrs. Ogle.

Mrs. Ogle's eyes widened. "You . . . you didn't know, madam? She drowned—"

"Accidentally," Keira said.

Mrs. Morton suddenly leaned forward and put her hand on Keira's arm. "We thought you knew," she said kindly. "It was no secret that Lady Ashwood was terribly unhappy with the earl."

"Aye, but . . . but suicide?" Keira pressed.

Mrs. Morton glared at Mrs. Ogle. "There was a note," Mrs. Ogle said simply.

"A note? What note?"

"They found a note from her in which she confessed that she had taken her own life."

Stunned, Keira could only stare at them. "What else did it say?"

"That, I cannot answer," Mrs. Ogle said. "I suspect no one but the late earl could answer." She picked up her teacup and sipped.

Keira thought of Lily, poor, dear Lily, who would be so distraught to hear it. She would blame herself.

Keira suddenly couldn't wait to speak to Lady Horncastle.

Young Franklin Girard, Lord Horncastle, was precisely the sort of man Declan liked to see sitting across from him at a gaming table. He was green and brash, and had only recently come into his inheritance. Like so many young bucks, he was too impatient for high-stakes wagering, which he proved early in the evening. When he lost quite a lot of money, he refused to stop playing, convinced, as young men often are, that if he had only one more chance, one more hand, he'd win it all back and not be forced to tell his widowed mother of his secret gambling habit.

Those games, as a rule, never ended well for men like Horncastle.

Declan rode out to Rochfield to have a look at the horse he'd won from the young Horncastle. If there was one thing that could be said of West Sussex, it was that it was a beautiful piece of English countryside. The landscape was green and lush, dotted with cows and sheep. As Declan neared Rochfield, he happened to see a lone horse grazing in a meadow with grass up to his knees. It reminded him of the meadow in Ireland where Keira had found him that fateful day. And when he thought of that day, he thought of Eve's empty eyes.

Keira, he thought angrily, she and her brazen deceptions.

At Rochfield, a sulky Horncastle—who had not yet learned the art of losing well—was leaning against the split rails, sullenly watching as the stable master led a pair of black Fell ponies around the paddock. Fell ponies were good, solid workhorses and good jumpers, but not particularly good racers. Nevertheless, Declan made a show of looking over each one.

"Is that all you have?" Declan asked.

"What's wrong with this pair?" Horncastle asked impatiently.

"Are there more?" Declan asked again.

Horncastle shrugged. "A Welsh pony. My mother has him out at present."

A Welsh pony could be made into a good runner. "I'll have a look at the Welsh," Declan said.

"But the Welsh has only just arrived," the stable master said anxiously as he stroked the neck of one Fell.

"There you are, have a look," Horncastle said, nodding toward the pasture beyond the paddock. "Just make quick work of it, will you?"

Declan followed Horncastle's gaze. He spotted three riders, two ladies and a stable boy, trotting back to the paddock. One of the ladies was riding an old workhorse, which labored alongside the Welsh. The Welsh trotted with a high step and toss of her neck, obviously chafing at the restraint. The horse had some excellent lines from what Declan could see, and he liked her spirit.

As the riders neared the paddock, he heard a familiar, lilting laugh and lifted his gaze from the horse's chest to the rider. God in heaven, he should have known there was only one woman who could sit a horse that well.

Keira's green eyes sparkled with her smile as she trotted into the paddock, just as they had that day eight years ago, which, thanks to her, was on his mind once more. She demurely bowed her head. "Good afternoon, my lords."

"Frankie, you didn't tell me we were to expect guests," the other woman said. Declan shifted his gaze to her. She was at least twice Keira's age and wore a lace cap tied tightly around her jowls. The women of Hadley Green were inordinately fond of those caps.

"Mother, may I introduce Lord Donnelly," Horncastle said wearily.

"Lord Donnelly!" his mother exclaimed, and looked at Declan. "Oh! Lord *Donnelly*," she repeated, and managed to slide off her horse without the help of the stable boy who'd rushed forward to help her. "A pleasure to make your acquaintance, my lord. I had heard you'd come to the country. Have you let Kitridge Lodge?"

"I have."

"Oh dear, where are my manners? I should be delighted to introduce you to Lady—"

"No need," Keira said brightly. "I've already had the pleasure of making his lordship's acquaintance."

"A pleasure, was it?" Declan asked.

Keira laughed as if that were a friendly jest. "Lord Donnelly, you know perfectly well that every time we have occasion to meet it is pure delight."

"It is pure something," he agreed. "However, *delight* is not the first word that comes to mind." *Infuriating* was a better word. Lord in heaven, she had gall, parading about as she did. She had no conscience. Or her conscience was discovered after the fact.

He walked to the Welsh, laid his hand on her neck. The horse eyed him curiously. "May I help you down?" Declan asked. "I'd like to have a look at your mount."

"That won't be nec—"

Declan abruptly grasped her by the waist and hauled her down off the pony.

"But thank you," Keira said breathlessly once she was on her feet.

"You might want to stand aside," Declan warned her, and moved to the horse's head. He slipped his fingers under the horse's gum to check her teeth, then pulled down on the bit, forcing the horse to open her mouth. The horse was about two years old, a good age for retraining. Declan stroked the horse's nose, then moved his hand down her neck, to her shoulder and withers. He squatted down, ran both hands down the horse's leg, feeling for any abnormalities.

A movement to his right caught his eye; a pair of small riding boots appeared in his peripheral vision. Declan looked up. "Stand back, if you please."

Keira took one small step back.

"She's been looked after," Horncastle said impatiently.

"What is his lordship doing?" Lady Horncastle demanded from somewhere behind Declan. "Why's he looking at the pony in that manner?"

Declan felt the pony's loin and hips, and checked her back legs, too. The horse snorted and swatted at him with her tail.

"I should like to ride her now," Declan said to Horncastle.

"For heaven's sake," the young man muttered. "Wills,

fetch a saddle." The stable master sighed with resignation—the man knew he was about to lose a good pony.

"I don't understand," Lady Horncastle said.

"Mother, please."

Declan reached under the horse to the cinch and unfastened the sidesaddle Keira had used. Keira was still standing there, watching him curiously, her riding crop in hand. "Taken to English sidesaddles?" he asked idly as he removed the saddle from the back of the Welsh.

"What?" Lady Horncastle asked. "What is that you said, Lord Donnelly?"

"Lord Donnelly is teasing me," Keira said lightly as the stable master appeared with a saddle. He looked, Declan thought, almost teary-eyed.

"Where do you intend to take my horse?" Lady Horncastle bleated behind him.

"For God's sake, Mother, it is not your concern—"

"Not my concern?" the older woman said shrilly. "It is indeed my concern, young man, as those horses belong to me!"

Declan winced for the young Horncastle. Added to his growing list of shortcomings was embarrassing his lady mother before another lord.

"What have you done, Frankie?"

Even Declan couldn't resist Horncastle's response to that and looked over his shoulder. But Horncastle caught his mother by the elbow and twirled her about, marching her up the path to the stables, away from Declan and Keira, where they engaged in a heated argument.

"What have *you* done, my lord?" Keira asked, and playfully nudged him with her boot.

"I'd have a care, were I you, *Countess*. You seem to be everywhere. What are you about, today? Planning a make-believe ball with your make-believe title?"

She frowned reproachfully and glanced slyly at the stable master, who was far more concerned with the horse than her.

"I'll saddle her so that you may take the sorrel and rub her down," Declan suggested to the stable master.

The man stroked the Welsh pony's nose, then reluctantly led the other horse away.

"Why *are* you looking at this horse?" Keira asked curiously. "Lady Horncastle just promised her to me to ride in a charitable race."

"Did she, indeed. I am here on a legitimate endeavor, not to extend an absurd impersonation and to gallivant about on a sidesaddle. When did you turn to sidesaddles?"

"When I came to England," she said. "And I happen to be here for a very good cause, if you must know."

"I mustn't know." Declan tossed the saddle up on the back of the Welsh. "I have no desire to know. I expressly do not want to know."

"I am here for the purpose of charity," she continued stubbornly.

"Hmm," he said indifferently. "I suppose you could use a wee bit of help with heaven above."

"I suppose you'd know something about that," she retorted. Declan cast a withering look at her.

Keira arched a brow as if she dared him to deny it. "I need to speak with you, please."

"No. I am quite firm in my desire not to know what you are about."

"And it pains me to admit that I could use your help," Keira added, as if he hadn't just spoken.

"*No*," he said more forcefully. "I don't want to hear another word."

"*Lady Horncastle knew my late aunt's lover*," she whispered.

Declan paused and sighed heavenward. "I asked you *not* to tell me, aye?"

"But I haven't anyone else to talk to, Declan," she insisted, shifting closer to him as she kept an eye on the Horncastles.

"I hardly care," he said, his gaze on the horse again.

"Whom else might I possibly speak to?"

"Oh, I don't know . . . your parish priest? Your God?"

"Declan, honestly! You know very well I can't do that!" she said, clearly annoyed.

"On my word, lass—"

"You don't understand—my aunt drowned herself," she said low.

He'd thought Keira was wildly exasperating, but he'd never thought her mad until this moment—dangerous and mad. "Please step aside," he said, shifting forward, forcing her to take a step backward. "I want nothing to do with your wild imagination."

"It is not my imagination," she said earnestly. "My aunt drowned herself. Her lover was hanged for a crime he did not commit. I think Lily might have unknowingly had a hand in it all, which will *devastate* her—"

"I won't tell you again," he tried, but Keira laid her hand lightly on his forearm. Declan looked down at her small, gloved hand and remembered another time she had touched his arm. The memory made him feel hot. And angry. So very angry. He would not allow her to drag him into another debacle. "*No*—"

"I am sorry," she said softly. "I am forever sorry. How many times must I apologize?"

She was speaking of another time, another place, of a memory he did not want to recall. "We are speaking of your present deception," he said brusquely. "And I want no part of it."

"Don't you think I know I've made a mess of things?" she doggedly continued. "But I am doing my best, and if only I could find the jewels—"

"Jewels," he scoffed. "Now there are jewels?"

"Jewels, Declan," she said, and glanced at the Horncastles. "Honestly, have you never heard of it?" she asked, speaking low and fast. "They were stolen when Lily lived here as a girl, and she gave testimony that condemned a poor man to the gallows, and I am convinced he was Aunt Althea's lover, not a thief at all, and then Aunt Althea drowned—"

"None of this is my concern," he said, and tried to step around her, but Keira would not move.

"I know you must think I am being selfish, but I give you my word I am not. I should like to know the truth so that I might tell Lily and not have her discover it as I did!"

Declan had to hand it to her—no one could plead quite like she was doing. With those eyes looking at him so beseechingly, the color high in her cheeks . . . He covered her hand with his and leaned forward. Keira's eyes shone with hope. He said, very softly, "*No.*"

She made a sound of unhappiness and yanked her hand free. "You are impossible!"

He snorted. "That is the pot calling the kettle black if ever I've heard it. I am utterly rational. Try and concentrate on what I am telling you, Keira. I will not *help* you again. I'll not keep your secrets, or say I've not seen you if I have—"

"You keep harking back to a terrible misunderstanding that happened eight long years ago when I was only sixteen!"

"It was not a misunderstanding inasmuch as it was a prevarication by you, and it matters not to me if you were sixteen or sixty—"

They were both startled by a loud cry from Lady Horncastle, and when they looked in that direction, they saw Lady Horncastle was hurrying down the path to them.

Keira looked to Declan. "I don't know why I have wasted my breath."

"Neither do I," he agreed, just as an agitated Lady Horncastle reached them.

"Lady Ashwood, you must forgive and excuse me." She put a hand to her throat. "My son has given me the most *distressing* news!" she said breathlessly, and looked at Declan. "You cannot have my horse, my lord! I don't know what you think you and Frankie have agreed, but I have just taken delivery of that pony and I have just this very morning promised Lady Ashwood she might ride her in the races at the summer gala! I will not go back on my word to satisfy my son's ill-made debt!"

"Mother, you will not speak to Lord Donnelly in that manner!" Horncastle exclaimed.

"Madam, you have my sympathy and utmost respect," Declan said, and fit his boot in the stirrup, smiled at Lady Horncastle, and swung up on the pony's back. "You have a keen eye for a superior horse. I mean only to ride her." He abruptly spurred the horse forward, and the pony reacted as Declan hoped—she bolted for the pasture gate, clearing it in one smooth leap. Declan heard Lady Horncastle cry out as he and the pony raced across the green pasture, startling a few cows who had wandered too close to the house.

Ah yes, this pony could be trained to race. Declan could feel the stretch of the horse's muscles as she lengthened her stride, the smooth flow. She would run all day if he let her. Declan eased her up, had her trot and canter, then galloped her once more before turning her around and letting her lope back to the house. The pony snorted, tossed her head, and held her tail high as they trotted back into the paddock, very pleased with her outing.

Inside the paddock, Declan leaped off the horse's back. Keira was leaning against the railing now, her arms crossed, one foot propped by its heel on the bottom railing. She was glaring at him. Lady Horncastle stood on the other side of the railing with one hand pressed against her heart. She was also glaring at him. "You startled me out of my wits, sir!" she chastised him.

"I beg your pardon, madam, but I have learned that is the best way to judge a horse's measure."

"Or a fool's measure, as the case may be," Keira observed.

"You say that as if you know of fools, Miss Han—"

"You could very well have broken your neck!" Lady Horncastle cried.

"Regrettably, he did not," Keira sighed.

And how was it that she had come to believe that *she*

had a right to be appalled with *his* behavior? "No, madam, I did not. I'd not dream of leaving Hadley Green before I see what becomes of you," he snapped, and he suddenly believed he meant it.

Keira glowered at him. He smiled at her.

"What do you mean, what will become of Lady Ashwood?" Lady Horncastle asked.

"In the race," he said smoothly.

"She will do very well on that pony," Lady Horncastle said with great authority.

Declan smiled. "Regrettably, madam, I must collect a debt fairly won from your son." He took the old woman's hand and bowed over it. "I apologize for the inconvenience to you."

Lady Horncastle was clearly disarmed by his pronouncement. "But . . . but what will Lady Ashwood ride?" she cried. "If you take that horse, you take food from the mouths of orphans, my lord!"

"Not at all," he said easily. "If the lady desires to ride this pony, she may bargain with me for the privilege."

"Oh, for the love of God," Keira said irritably. "I will do no such thing!"

"Suit yourself, madam," he said, and tipped his hat to her. "This one will do," he said to Horncastle. "I'll send someone to fetch him. Now then, I've taken enough of your time. I wish you good day, ladies."

As he strode from the paddock to the stable, he was smiling, just a wee bit. He could hardly say if it was because he'd won a supreme Welsh pony on a middling hand of Commerce. Or because Keira Hannigan was so angry with him.

Seven

Lady Horncastle's *nerves* were much improved with a generous serving of wine in her cluttered drawing room. Keira had never seen quite so many knickknacks and trinkets in a home, and under normal circumstances she would have found it amusing to be seated next to a yawning porcelain lion, but she was still quite agitated by Declan's behavior.

Lord Horncastle had stormed upstairs and then stomped about over their heads for what seemed an age before he came rushing down the stairs again, dressed to go out. Keira wished she could stomp about, too.

"One moment, young man!" Lady Horncastle cried.

Keira heard an audible groan before Horncastle appeared in the doorway of the small salon.

Lady Horncastle drew up to her slight height and said sternly, "Do you understand that Lady Ashwood has very generously offered to host a race at the summer gala, the proceeds of which will be donated to the orphanage?"

Her son's gaze flicked over Keira. "She is very generous, indeed," he said tightly. The color had drained from his rosy cheeks and he looked at his mother with the seething indignation of youth. But he wisely bit his tongue, choosing to storm out of the house instead.

Still, Lady Horncastle was not content to leave it at that. She hurried to the window to watch him ride away. "Look how recklessly he rides! Lord, how he tries my patience!"

Keira felt slightly uncomfortable, perhaps because only a few years had passed since she had been the one to march indignantly from her parents' salon.

"You surely recall what a lovely child he was, do you not, Lady Ashwood? He often accompanied me when I called on your aunt. He followed you about like a puppy, didn't he? He was completely besotted with you."

That petulant thing had followed Lily about? Keira forced a smile. "I confess, Lady Horncastle, I was so young, I hardly recall."

"Althea was determined to see the two of you married one day, you know." She giggled like a girl at the notion, and by heaven's grace alone, Keira managed not to choke on her tea.

"Ah, but if only Frankie's father hadn't swallowed that last bite of fish," she said sadly. "That tiny bit of bone choked the life from my husband and robbed my son of the firm hand he has needed to guide him these last few years." She dabbed at her eyes with her napkin. "I've tried. Indeed, the good Lord knows how I've tried. But my son needs a man's hand, wouldn't you agree?"

Keira thought of Loman Maloney, her father's choice for her. Loman would be the perfect male companion for Frankie, as he was very calm and reasonable. Too calm by her measure.

"He allows gentlemen such as Donnelly to influence him too easily," Lady Horncastle said.

Keira snorted. "Donnelly is quite impertinent, isn't he?"

"And reckless!" Lady Horncastle hastened to add.

"Exceedingly," Keira agreed. "He does not seem to care for anyone but himself. I don't care for him at all," she added pertly.

"No, certainly not. You are too refined for that sort. You deserve a far better caliber of acquaintance, Lady Ashwood."

She did indeed. She deserved . . . she didn't want to think what she deserved, and suddenly put her teacup aside, desperate to change the subject. "You have a very interesting staircase. It looks rather like the one at Ashwood."

"It would have been just like the one at Ashwood— on a smaller scale, of course—had the Incident not occurred." Lady Horncastle turned her head stiffly to see the staircase. It curved up one side of the entry onto a landing that had been railed off on the other end where the twin staircase would have met it. It seemed a little off kilter to the discerning eye, but Keira supposed the Rochfield entry was so dark and narrow that it likely was unnoticeable to the casual observer. "Unfortunately, there has never been another woodcarver who could match Mr. Scott's talent."

"Do you remember him?" Keira asked.

"Oh, indeed I do!" Lady Horncastle said, settling back in her chair, her hands resting in her lap. "He was such a handsome fellow. Lovely brown eyes and pale gold hair," she said, touching her lace cap.

"Do you think . . . that perhaps my aunt esteemed him?"

That snapped Lady Horncastle's head around. "*Esteemed*

him? Why in heaven's name would you ask such a thing?"

Heat bled into Keira's cheeks. "I, ah . . . I suppose because I have some vague memories—"

"With all due respect, madam, you cannot possibly have any significant memories of it at all. You were very young at the time. Althea may have been unhappily married to the earl, but she was not an adulteress and you should be ashamed for even suggesting it."

"No, I did not mean to imply—"

"I shall speak plainly," Lady Horncastle carried on. "Mr. Scott was a deceiving man. He was very skilled with his hands and very charming with his words. Althea should not have trusted him, but then again, she was alarmingly trusting of gentlemen in general."

"She trusted him?" Keira asked quickly, seizing on that small bit of information.

"*Trusted* him? I never said such a thing! I hardly know what she thought of him. I only meant to say that she thought he was very good at his work and he was indeed a good craftsman, but *you* know perhaps better than anyone how he deceived her in the end."

One moment, Keira was too young to have remembered. In the next, she was expected to remember very well. "Aye," Keira said, and cast her gaze to the carpet a moment, lest Lady Horncastle see the doubt in her eyes. "He was obviously very gifted. The staircase at Ashwood is quite grand. I think Mr. Scott must have spent quite a lot of time at Ashwood to craft it."

Lady Horncastle's small eyes narrowed shrewdly. "What precisely are you implying?"

"Nothing at all!" Keira said quickly, feigning innocence. "I am merely curious, Lady Horncastle. I've been attempting to reconstruct my rather distant memories."

Lady Horncastle softened at that and even smiled a little. "There is no point in it. Mr. Scott is long since dead, as is your lovely aunt, God rest her soul."

"You are right, of course," Keira said with diffidence. She sipped her tea. She thought about asking Lady Horncastle about her aunt's death, but didn't know precisely how she might. "I suppose Mr. Scott's family is still in Hadley Green?" Keira asked casually.

"Certainly not. How could they remain after that ugly business? Those poor children. There was no work, no one to earn a living, and certainly no decent person would associate with them. Here now, you seem all too curious about an old and ugly business, Lady Ashwood."

"Not at all," Keira said sweetly. "It is as I said, trying to put together faint memories. I have been thinking of my aunt and her tragic death—"

"Don't," Lady Horncastle said abruptly. "It will only distress you. Have I shown you this painting?" Lady Horncastle said, and suddenly rose, walking across the room. "It is a young artist, but he is already quite renowned."

Keira glanced at a rather pedestrian landscape painting on the wall.

"It is Rochfield," Lady Horncastle pointed out, and, as Keira listened to her go on about the origins of that painting, she wondered who else she might ask about Mr. Scott. Certainly no one in her aunt's circle of friends would have dealt with him. Even at Ashwood, the only one who might have spoken with him on more than one occasion would be Linford.

Linford! Keira was amazed she hadn't thought of it before! Of course Linford would have dealt with him.

Her mind on Linford, Keira left Rochfield shortly thereafter, driving a cabriolet with a single horse. Mr. Fish didn't care for it, and warned her that any manner of crime might befall her illustrious person when she was out alone. Keira was not the least bit cowed by his warnings—she couldn't abide the restriction on her movements, she loved her freedom, and she was perfectly at ease in the cabriolet. She rather imagined she would be perfectly at ease in any part of the world. She thrived on new and different experiences, really.

But she was, admittedly, distracted, and therefore did not see the rider until she was almost upon him. His horse leaped off the road, throwing the poor man. Keira careened to a halt and peered around the back of the cabriolet. He had righted himself and was dusting off his trousers.

"I do beg your pardon!" she called out to him. "Are you quite all right?"

"I am unhurt," he said, and grabbed his horse's bridle, easily putting himself in the saddle again. He reined the horse around and came closer to have a look. "I beg your pardon, madam, but you must have a care on these narrow country roads."

"I agree completely," she said, and smiled.

"Perhaps someone should drive you," he suggested, smiling a little, too.

"Drive me?" she echoed. He was handsome, wasn't he, what with his golden hair and blue eyes. "Just because I didn't see you does not render me incapable of driving a wee carriage, sir."

"I would argue that, but then again, I make it a rule never to argue with beguiling ladies."

Keira blushed. She smiled prettily. "What other rules do you have regarding ladies?"

He laughed. "I can hardly divulge that information unless I know the lady."

Still smiling, Keira assessed him. She never said her name, never said aloud that was it Lily Boudine. It seemed as if someone was always on hand to say it for her, and if she didn't say it, then somehow, she wasn't lying. "I never give my name to a gentleman I don't know."

"Then I must introduce myself straightaway. I am Mr. Benedict Sibley."

"Mr. Sibley, good afternoon." She picked up the reins again.

"I beg your pardon, madam, but surely you do not intend to leave without giving me your name? Me, a wounded traveler?"

Keira laughed. "Are you wounded?"

He grinned. "Regrettably, no."

She smiled at him. "Good day, Mr. Sibley," she said, and drove on, glancing back.

He was still sitting beside the road, watching her leave. She laughed to herself and touched the whip to the horse, sending him faster.

There was a mountain of correspondence waiting for Keira when she arrived at Ashwood, and Mr. Sibley was quickly forgotten. There was so much to do—she'd never realized how much work there was in managing an estate! There were menus to be planned and a social calendar to be maintained. There were staffing decisions about who should do what, and how much should be spent on household items. It was little wonder her father was always closeted with his secretary.

Keira would be lost without Mr. Fish. Linford announced him later that afternoon. Keira was busy arranging another batch of hothouse flowers that had arrived, courtesy of one Mr. Anders, a bachelor with thinning hair and bony fingers. Linford had a stack of letters he deposited with the others she had yet to read. "Mr. Fish and another gentleman, madam," he said.

"Thank goodness, a diversion from all of the correspondence," Keira said lightly. "What other gentleman, Linford?"

"I couldn't say, madam. A solicitor, I believe."

"A solicitor. I don't care for solicitors, really. They always want something, like liens against the estate or money for services rendered long before I arrived." She smiled and handed the vase of flowers to Linford.

He took them and started for the door.

"Linford . . . wait," Keira said as he reached the door. There was no time like the present, and she'd never been one to dance delicately around something that interested her. "I was wondering if you recall Mr. Scott."

The elderly gentleman looked entirely befuddled. "Pardon?"

"Mr. Scott," she said again. "He crafted the staircase."

Linford instantly pursed his lips and his ruddy face took on a darker hue.

"I scarcely remember much at all, yet I am very curious to know more about him. I was hoping you could tell me something."

"*Now*, madam?" he asked, glancing at the door. "Mr. Fish—"

"Please, Linford. It will only take a moment."

He shifted his gaze to her again, his lips pressed so tightly together they had all but disappeared. "I don't rightly know what to say," he said slowly. "He was a decent sort."

"Did you think him guilty?"

"It was not for me to say." He looked terribly uncomfortable. "Shall I bring Mr. Fish now?"

Keira smiled. "Yes, please. Thank you."

The old butler wasn't going to tell her more, and it occurred to Keira that no one would, for whatever one might have thought of Mr. Scott, she—or rather, Lily—was the one who'd sent him to the gallows. What could anyone possibly say about Mr. Scott to the person they perceived to be his executioner? That he was a good and decent *innocent* man Lily had sent to an early grave?

Declan, that recalcitrant horse's arse. He was the only one who could help her get to the bottom of it.

But at present, she had a solicitor to meet.

In Ashwood's sweeping study with its tall ceilings and velvet drapes, Keira squared her shoulders in her new white muslin gown with the pale pink sash. Her black hair was bound up with matching pink ribbon, and she wore a strand of pearls at her throat. Mr. Fish entered first. Keira was terribly surprised by the gentleman who followed him in. It was Mr. Sibley.

She could feel the smile curve her lips and glided forward, her hand extended. "Mr. Sibley, how do you do," she said, offering him her hand.

"You've met?" Mr. Fish asked, surprised.

"Accidentally," Keira said.

"The countess unseated me from my horse," Mr. Sibley said, and bent over her hand. But his eyes were on Keira.

Mr. Fish looked aghast by that admission, and Keira could not help but grin. "He assured me he was quite all right, Mr. Fish."

"Lady Ashwood, it is my distinct pleasure to make your formal acquaintance," Sibley said gallantly. "I rather suspected it was you who drove the carriage. But may I say that the rumors of your beauty do not do you justice."

Keira had had too many suitors in her life to be swayed by that bit of flattery. "I wonder if you would be so kind in your remarks had you been harmed?" she said, and gestured to the seating at the hearth. "I do apologize."

"There is no need," Mr. Sibley was quick to assure her.

His eyes, Keira couldn't help but notice, devoured her. Both gentlemen waited for her to be seated before casting out the tails of their coats and sitting opposite her. The kitten Mr. Green had presented Keira with—Blanca, she'd named her—wound her way through Mr. Fish's legs, then rubbed against Mr. Sibley's boot. Both men ignored the cat. Linford stood to one side, prepared to pour tea. Keira gestured for him to begin and said to Mr. Sibley, "You've come down from Town, sir?"

"I have." He could not take his eyes from her. His smile was warm and easy as his gaze flicked over her bosom.

"Did you come down from Town just to see me?" Keira asked coyly.

"I am sorry I did not come sooner," he said. "I have

indeed come to discuss an important matter. My firm has been retained by Count Eberlin."

"Count . . . ?"

"Count Eberlin. He is a Danish count with ties to England."

"And what has Count Eberlin to do with Ashwood?"

"The count has sizable holdings in Denmark. However, he is not on the side of Napoleon, and given the uncertainty on the Continent and the fear of England's engaging France in war, he should like to add holdings here, should the time come that he must leave Denmark . . . for political expediency." He said it in a way that made Keira think it was slightly more nefarious than that.

"He cannot add Ashwood," she said laughingly.

"Of course not. The count has purchased Tiber Park," Mr. Sibley said. "As you are undoubtedly aware, it borders Ashwood to the north."

"Tiber Park!" Keira exclaimed. She knew it very well; it was one of her favorite places to ride. "I am very happy to hear someone has taken that poor old house. It's quite lovely and it is a tragedy that it sits empty. It's falling into disrepair."

"Lord Eberlin intends to begin restoration within the fortnight."

"Oh, that is welcome news!" she said happily. "You may assure his lordship that I am in full support of his restoration." Keira sat back, pleased with herself. If nothing else, Ashwood could be depended on to be a good neighbor.

But when Keira shifted her smile to Mr. Fish, she noticed he was staring intently at Mr. Sibley.

"Did you come here to speak of the restoration to Tiber Park, sir?" he asked stiffly.

"Not entirely," Mr. Sibley said, and smiled at Keira. "The nature of my call, madam, is that in the course of purchasing Tiber Park, it has come to the count's attention that there is some question as to the true boundary between Ashwood and Tiber Park. It has to do with an entailment that has lapsed."

"What has lapsed?" she asked uncertainly. Keira knew of entailments, or the practice of binding up real property for future generations to keep land and its income in a family's holding or trusts for generations. As was the case with her home in Ireland, the family drew on the income from the entail, but was not free to sell the property, as their ancestors had bequeathed it to their heirs.

Mr. Sibley removed a document from his coat pocket. He untied the leather string that held it folded, and laid it out on the table. "I beg your pardon for bringing this matter to your delicate attention, Lady Ashwood. It is not the sort of thing one cares to burden a lady with, but as you are the sole surviving heir, I must."

"Oh, Mr. Sibley. Let me first disabuse you of the notion that I am too delicate to hear what you will say," she said, smiling softly. "Please continue."

"Allow me to summarize the issue. It seems that one hundred acres of the original demesne of Tiber Park was given as a wedding gift to the daughter of the original owner of Tiber Park. She married an Ashwood ancestor. Do you follow?"

"Yes, yes. Do go on."

"The deed and earnings of the acreage followed her

into her marriage and were entailed upon her male heirs. The late Earl of Ashwood, a descendant of hers, was very careful to extend his name and inheritance to any surviving female heirs in the event no male heir survived him, but he neglected to entail that particular one hundred acres to a female heir."

"Meaning?" Keira asked, feeling a small tic of panic strike her heart.

"Meaning that the one hundred acres has been disentailed by his death and lacks a codicil to the original entailment. Therefore, as the acreage was originally the property of Tiber Park, Lord Eberlin intends to petition for the deed to the land to be included with his property."

Keira was dumbfounded. She knew precisely what acreage Mr. Sibley was referring to—it was the most profitable acreage in all of Ashwood's tenancy, the only acres of late to produce a steady income. The lack of hard, ready cash was so dire that she feared the estate would slip into complete shambles without that acreage. She couldn't hand that problem over to Lily on top of her doubts about Mr. Scott and Aunt Althea. She'd promised to mind Ashwood, not destroy it, for heaven's sake. What Mr. Sibley was saying was very serious, and if she had any doubt of that, she had only to look at Mr. Fish's pale face.

"May I ask, do you understand?" Mr. Sibley asked, as if she were a simpleton.

"I understand perfectly well, Mr. Sibley," Keira said sweetly, although her Irish temper was scarcely controlled. She suddenly suspected the "awful man" who was behind the attempt to oust Hannah Hough from her little patch of fertile land was the Danish count. "However . . . I really must disagree. If the property was given as a gift to an Ashwood ancestor, it belongs to Ashwood."

He smiled patiently. "That is one possible interpretation, I agree. But I have done a fair amount of research and believe there is some validity to the count's theory, as well. And now I have come to Hadley Green to continue my research with the parish records."

Keira suddenly came to her feet. "Then we shall wait to hear from you." She smiled as Mr. Fish and Mr. Sibley found their feet, too.

As Mr. Sibley towered over Keira, his gaze slipped down the length of her. "It has been a pleasure to make your acquaintance."

"Oh, but the pleasure has been mine," she said with a soft smile.

That clearly pleased him. He looked at Mr. Fish. "Good day, sir," he said, and strode out of the room.

When he'd gone out, Keira whirled around to her agent. "Does this mean what I think?"

"I believe it does."

"Dear Lord," she said. "The mill, Mr. Fish. We must have the mill functioning very soon if there is even a slim possibility we might lose that acreage."

"The reconstruction has begun," he assured her.

"We must stall him somehow," she suggested. "At least until we can find a solicitor who knows of these things," she said.

"I have already begun to make inquiries," Mr. Fish assured her. "But how shall we stall him?"

"Leave that to me," she said. If there was one thing for which she had a talent, it was persuading a gentleman to do her bidding. "We need just a wee bit of time, Mr. Fish. This cannot possibly be true."

She wished Mr. Fish looked a little more certain of it.

Eight

Mrs. Ogle was having a supper party.

Declan had no intention of attending the meddlesome old woman's soiree, and had scarcely made note of the invitation when he received it. But then he encountered Keira in Hadley Green. She was in the company of some dandy—she gathered men about her like hair ribbons, sorting through them, discarding some, keeping others, and changing often.

It was a small, ridiculous thing, really, and Declan was unhappy with himself for letting her slip under his skin. He'd come out of the Grousefeather Tavern in a buoyant mood, and almost collided with Keira in front of Clark's Dry Goods store. She was wearing a brown gown with green trim and he noted how it complemented her Irish eyes, those accursed, beautiful, expressive eyes, so full of life and mischief. She smiled happily when she saw him in spite of their last pair of meetings. Then again, Keira was not the sort to be ruffled by a few disagreements. "*Dia duit,*" she said, greeting him in the Irish tongue.

"Madam. What brings you into the village? Is there a vacancy in some household you wish to assume?"

"Amusing," she said.

Declan glanced at her companion.

"Oh," she said, as if she just recalled the gentleman was there. "Allow me to introduce Mr. Sibley. Mr. Sibley, Lord Donnelly." To Delcan, she said, "Mr. Sibley is down from London."

As if Declan could possibly care. "Mr. Snibley," he said curtly.

"*Sibley*, my lord," the man said just as curtly. "It is a pleasure to make your acquaintance. I've heard great things said of you."

"Have you?" Declan asked, giving Keira an accusing look.

She gave him one right back. "From Mrs. Ogle," she explained. "She is very pleased to have invited you to her supper. But I told her, likely you will not come, for you prefer horses to people, and that it is said birds of a feather will flock together."

That was it, the small, nonsensical, ridiculous remark that got Declan's back up. She acted as if *he* were somehow in the wrong. "On the contrary," he said. "I should very much like to admire your ever-widening circle of acquaintances."

She wasn't the least bit shamed by that; she smiled broadly. "That will be splendid news indeed for Mrs. Ogle, for now she may count on having Hadley Green's finest at her table."

"I wouldn't go as far as that," he'd said with a meaningful look.

"Oh, come now, my lord. You are indeed a fine dining companion, no matter what others may say," she said with a devilish twinkle in her eye. "We will all look forward to your attendance."

"I assure you, the pleasure will be all mine," Declan snapped.

Keira had the audacity to smile as if he amused her. "Shall we carry on, Mr. Sibley? Mr. Fish will be waiting."

"I was on the verge of suggesting the same," the gentleman said, and thrust his arm out for her hand. "My lord."

"Mr. Snivley."

"*Sibley.*"

"I do beg your pardon," Declan had said, and with his hands clasped behind his back, he bowed and stepped back, allowing them to pass him on the walkway. He watched the sway of Keira's gait, the way she walked beside that man.

He stewed about that chance encounter all the way to Kitridge Lodge. By that point, his good humor had dampened considerably. He summoned his jack of all trades, Mr. Noakes, and had him deliver the favorable reply he hastily dashed off to Mrs. Ogle.

On the appointed evening, however, he regretted that reply. He could suddenly think of nothing worse than Mrs. Ogle trying to match him with one of the rustic young ladies of Hadley Green, all released into society like cows turned out to pasture. He could hear it now— *it is time you married, my lord,* or, his particular favorite, *you need an heir,* as if he were the bull turned out with the cows.

He'd been hearing the same refrain for ten years, but he was not ready for marriage or an heir. Yet here he was, dressed in formal tails and a silky white waistcoat and neckcloth, prepared to endure what could only be an interminable evening, all because Keira Hannigan had aggravated him once again.

When he arrived, the so-called countess had not yet made her appearance, but it would appear that all of Hadley Green had arrived. The guests were piled on top of one another in the cramped drawing room. Someone played the pianoforte very badly at the far end of the room, and the ladies, who sought to review the guests at the same time they showed off their finery, were making things worse by forcing the gentlemen to bump against furnishings to allow them to pass in their turn about the room.

Declan had scarcely sipped his wine before he was subjected to the introduction of three unmarried girls. He sighed. And then he smiled, prepared to make the requisite small talk, for he was the consummate gentleman. And he did enjoy women.

Of the three, he noticed Daria Babcock, a pretty, slight young thing with dark brown eyes and flaxen hair. She was the most intriguing of them all, only in that she did not seem to be trembling with timidity, nor so demure that he could not hear her speak.

"I understand you have let Kitridge Lodge," she said after they had exchanged the usual pleasantries about the summer weather.

"Do you, indeed?"

She smiled a little sheepishly. "There is very little to keep the people of Hadley Green suitably occupied, my lord. We wake up each morning desperate for someone to let a property or sell a horse, all so we might have something to prattle about over tea."

He couldn't help but chuckle at that. "How regrettable you have nothing better to occupy your teas."

"Oh, I think you might be surprised," she said with a sly smile.

Maybe he would. He stepped closer. "Surprise me, then."

But it was at that particular moment Keira made her grand entrance. A sudden whisper swept through the people assembled, and Miss Babcock, distracted, craned her neck toward the door and said eagerly, "I believe the countess has arrived," in a voice full of young reverence.

If the white plume bobbing above the heads of others was Keira, she had indeed arrived. "Now there is someone who might surprise you and give you more than enough to chat about at tea," Declan said wryly.

"Of course!" Miss Babcock readily agreed. "Everyone holds her in very high esteem. She is generous in spirit and in deed. She has a great desire to improve Ashwood and the circumstances of the poor orphans of St. Bartholomew's."

Declan almost choked on a second sip of wine. "She's out to save the orphans, is she?" he said jovially. "She should be so determined to save herself."

"Pardon?"

He smiled. "A jest. Here now, I am keeping you from greeting her. Please excuse me, Miss Babcock." He stepped away before she could think of something to keep him.

Declan downed his wine and signaled to a footman to pour him more. He was cornered by Mrs. Morton, who, naturally, had an unmarried niece who would be visiting later in the month. As Mrs. Morton nattered on about the fine qualities of her niece, Declan caught sight of Keira. She looked, he would admit, very much a countess, one to rival some of the scions of the aristocracy in London. She was resplendent in a gown of white silk and silver trim. She wore an ethereal headdress with a plume that was starkly white against her gleaming black hair. At her breast she wore a large diamond and emerald brooch that refracted light like a small star. She moved around the room, greeting acquaintances, smiling brilliantly, her laugh floating above the chatter and conversations. She was entirely too charming. She always had been.

Most of the men in the room seemed to gravitate to her, openly admiring her and jockeying for her attention. With those looks and what everyone in the room must assume was a fortune at her fingertips, she was a favorite of all.

Keira did not appear to be the slightest bit reticent. He could hear her bright chatter, could see her wax lyrical about God only knew what. It astounded him, really— how did she think she would not be discovered before Lily returned?

This was ridiculous. He should not have come—he was only aggravating himself. Yet he put himself in her path. Keira's eyes sparkled with delight when he did, as if she enjoyed riling him, and she sank into a very deep curtsy, giving him an excellent view of her décolletage. She peeked up at him. "My lord."

He offered his hand to help her up and caught a hint of her perfume. It instantly took him back to a warm, sun-dappled summer afternoon in a meadow in Ireland.

"I did not think you'd come," she said, and withdrew her hand, letting her fingers graze his palm.

"I told you I would."

"Aye, that you did," she said with a careless shrug. "But then again, you seem to revile me." One sculpted brow lifted above the other in silent question.

"Entirely untrue," he assured her as his gaze ambled over her figure. "I haven't thought of you at all."

Keira blinked; her smile deepened. "Really?"

He leaned forward slightly. "Really," he said low. "Miss Babcock tells me you've taken a sudden interest in orphans. What do you intend to do, to use them as your army when authorities land on your door?"

"The children are adorable," she said pertly. "Even *you* would be moved to charity if you saw them. And I believe I have explained myself quite plainly. You must trust that I am doing what is right for Lily's sake."

"Trust? *Trust* is not the word that readily comes to mind when I think of you, lass," he said.

"Aha! There, you see?" She grinned. "You *do* think of me."

"I think you will not like sitting in an English gaol for many years," he said, smiling a little himself.

"How kind. I think of you, too, Declan. I think you are envious."

"*Envious?*" he said incredulously.

"Aye, envious. You are envious that I am well regarded here, and that I am doing well for my dear cousin Lily, far better than you do for—" She suddenly caught herself and shut her mouth.

Declan peered closely at her. "For whom?" he asked,

although he knew very well whom. She meant Eireanne.

"Never mind."

"No, Keira—for *whom*?" he demanded.

"Lady Ashwood? I beg your pardon for the interruption," Mrs. Ogle said, suddenly at Declan's side. "Mrs. Morton's cousin, Mr. Patterson, has come quite a long way ..."

"Yes, of course," Keira said, and gave Declan a murderous smile. "Lord Donnelly."

He bowed his head and watched her walk away before he went in search of another glass of wine.

The wine flowed freely and far longer than was customary for a supper party, and Declan was no stranger to the footmen who circulated throughout the two dozen guests. There was, Declan heard, a slight problem in the kitchen. "Robina hired a cook from London," he overheard one stout lady remark to her companion. "Said she'd cooked for Lord Townsend. But she's scarcely finished the soup!"

Declan sighed and drank more wine. He was introduced to two more young women, one with an impressive chest. The wine was beginning to go to his head and he excused himself in search of fresh air. He wandered out onto the terrace wondering idly if he'd drunk enough wine to fill his boot.

The terrace, unfortunately, was not empty. Keira was there with a small group of admirers. He couldn't hear what she said, but she was speaking with great animation, her hands gracefully sketching a tale as she spoke. Her little group—three gentlemen and two ladies—hung on her every word, laughing gaily.

Her laughter floated directly over his head like a cloud.

He wouldn't be surprised in the least if it opened and doused him. He stared at her across the terrace, insupportably distracted by her. She galled him. Nothing in County Galway had ever been the same after Eve, yet Keira just continued on as if nothing had happened. Her looks, her charm, were a pass to a world that had censured him. Not that he cared—he had his society in London and he was perfectly happy in it. But it galled him all the same. It wasn't right.

Keira happened to turn her head and saw him standing there. Declan swore he saw something—daring—spark in her eyes. It was enough to send him walking straight into the lion's den.

"Good evening, my lord," Keira said, bowing her head when he appeared in their midst. "You've come at the perfect moment, for we were speaking of Michaelmas."

"Michaelmas." Declan could think of nothing particularly interesting about the day.

"Michaelmas," Keira said again, and one of the gentlemen chuckled, as if they had a secret jest. "Mr. Huxley tells me that in Scotland, Michaelmas is a night on which people steal horses."

"Indeed, madam," Mr. Huxley said, laughing. "One may avail himself of the closest horse if one intends to make a pilgrimage. Or so tradition says."

"A pilgrimage to where?" one gentleman asked.

"The public house," another said, and the group laughed.

"The Scots make it a day of horseracing," Declan said to no one in particular.

"Have you raced there?" Keira asked, her eyes sparkling up at him.

Declan wished for wine. "I have."

"I should like to see Scotland one day," she said.

"What of Ireland?" Mr. Huxley asked. "Do the Irish celebrate Michaelmas?"

"In Ireland, one eats goose at Michaelmas," Keira said. "There is a saying: 'he who eats a goose on Michaelmas Day shan't money lack or debts to pay.'"

"And what shall you do here in England on Michaelmas?" Mr. Huxley continued. His gaze, Declan thought, was awfully admiring of her.

"Here?" Keira pretended to think very carefully about that a moment. "A feast of geese," she said. "And then I will steal one of Lord Donnelly's fine horses."

The group laughed. "You best keep your horses locked away, my lord!" one of the gentlemen said.

"I have nothing to fear," he said. "I am sure the lady shall have traveled on by then."

"Where would you have me travel, my lord?" Keira asked gaily, as if they were playing a game.

"I would guess Ireland. Or perhaps some place even farther afield."

"What? And leave us?" Huxley exclaimed.

"Do you see, my lord? Mr. Huxley desires me to stay and steal your horse." She smiled brightly.

The supper bell was rung, thankfully, before anyone could challenge Keira to stay and steal his horse. As the group began to move toward the doors, Keira looked at Declan and gave him an impertinent little smile, as if she were quite pleased with her performance. Declan caught her hand and pulled her back from the group. "One moment, *Countess.*"

"Beg your pardon," she said, trying to pull free. "I am famished."

"Michaelmas?" he said low. "Do you intend to play this absurd game for two months more?"

"For goodness sake," she said, pulling her hand free. "Lily will be here by then. She might very much like a Michaelmas feast."

"Stop this," Declan warned her. "Stop prancing about playing at dress-up and dangling gentlemen from your fingers."

Her eyes widened, and then she beamed at him. "I am not prancing. I am keeping up appearances until Lily comes. And *you* are sounding envious again, Declan."

"For God's sake, don't flatter yourself."

Her smile only deepened. "Well, what am I to think with you skulking about, seeking me out all night?"

"Skulking?" Declan scoffed. "You are deluded. If I wanted you, I would have you in a moment. I do not need to seek you out."

Keira's smile turned to fire. "Just like that? You think I would fall at your bloody feet?" she whispered hotly. "You, sir, will *never* have me—"

He silenced her with a kiss. He didn't know how—one moment she was talking and the next moment he was kissing the ridiculousness right out of her. And Keira—Lord in heaven, the woman made his blood rage. She was neither cowed by the fact that they stood only yards away from dozens of people or that her little charade could be reduced to ashes with a good scandal. She curved into him as if she'd been waiting for him, her mouth opening to his.

Her lips were a confection, soft and tasting of wine. He

touched his tongue to hers, felt her body soften and seem to melt into him.

It knocked Declan completely off balance. His head told him to stop, to step away, to leave this soiree and this village, but his body and his heart told him that it would take a team of twenty to pull him away. His tongue swirled around hers, and with his teeth, he nipped lightly at her plump bottom lip. Desire began to roar in him, wanting more, urging her with his mouth to more.

But it was Keira who stepped back first. She just suddenly faded away from him, ran her finger over her bottom lip as she looked at him, and then smiled as she turned away without a word, walking across the terrace and into the house.

God help me. At any other time, any other place, he would have taken her in hand and shown her what that sort of look might earn her. As it was, he had to follow her into the blasted house and feel that kiss and that look course through him while he sat, unable to act upon it.

The party had all but stampeded into the small dining room, and Declan walked into something of a frenzy as people looked for their name cards. Four footmen in rented wigs and coats tried to help, but it took some doing and a lot of shouting by Mr. and Mrs. Ogle for everyone to find their seat.

Declan was seated next to Mrs. Ogle, who presided at one end of the table, and to his left, Miss Babcock. He had no doubt that Miss Babcock had somehow managed to arrange it, and could see from more than one sour expression that a few mothers had hoped to see their daughters seated next to him.

Miss Babcock's expression was a bit sour, as well, and Declan guessed she had a very good idea of what had just happened on the terrace. Directly across from him sat Keira, who now blithely avoided his gaze, and on her right, Mr. Robert Anders, who, Declan had learned earlier, was the son of a wealthy landed man who would inherit five thousand a year. That sum had undoubtedly earned him the right to sit next to the most sought-after woman in the county. Ah, but if he knew of Keira's deceit, he would take his five thousand and run, Declan was sure of it.

Mr. Sniveling had been given some deference for reasons that escaped Declan—he sat beside Miss Babcock. He did not seem particularly happy with the arrangement, and in the chaos, he tried to engage Keira in conversation across the table, but found that he had to shout to do it.

Like a queen presiding over her table, Mrs. Ogle's face was a wreath of smiles, and she directed her hired help as if they served her every day. Her husband, a dour man with a bulbous nose, made a few welcoming remarks, then invited everyone to sample the quail soup.

Mrs. Ogle lifted her silver spoon, smiled serenely, and dipped it into the bowl before her. Her guests followed suit.

"Lord Donnelly, have you made the acquaintance of Mr. Anders?" Mrs. Ogle asked as she sipped her soup.

"Aye, thank you."

"Lord Donnelly and Lady Ashwood were telling us about the customs surrounding Michaelmas in Ireland," Mr. Anders said.

"Oh! I didn't realize you were so closely acquainted," Mrs. Ogle said to Keira.

"We've known each other for quite some time," Keira offered.

"Some might say too long, eh?" Declan asked, and lifted his wine glass to Keira.

Mrs. Ogle's and Miss Babcock's eyes widened with surprise. Mr. Anders looked aghast. If Declan had leaned up and turned his head to his left, he would not have been the least surprised to see Sniveling drawing a pistol on him.

But Keira laughed. "Indeed, I think some might, my lord."

"How remarkable that you would encounter one another here in Hadley Green," Mr. Anders said.

"It is a small world," Keira agreed.

"One might even say crowded," Declan said.

Beside him, Miss Babcock made a sound that he thought might have been a giggle.

"I can see that Lord Donnelly likes to tease," Mr. Anders said diplomatically.

"Oh, that he does," Keira readily agreed. "We have a nickname for him in Ireland. We call him *Óinseach*, or one who likes to tease." She looked up and smiled at Declan.

A fool, she meant, and Declan couldn't help but chuckle. "Touché."

"On-soch," Mrs. Ogle tried to say and giggled like a girl. "That is very difficult to say, is it not? Very hard on the ears, really. *On-soch*." Miss Babcock tried it, too, with even less success than Mrs. Ogle. It amazed Declan that Ireland could exist so close to England, their histories so inextricably tied, yet in many ways, they were at two ends of the world.

"I've always thought it quite interesting that the old languages still exist in places like Ireland." Mr. Anders was valiantly trying to keep the conversation flowing. "You must tell us of Ireland, Lady Ashwood."

"It's beautiful," she said without hesitation, and put down her spoon. "Particularly in County Galway, where my family lives, as does Lord Donnelly's. My family's estate, Lisdoon, is built in the hills, and it is very green year-round. If one follows the river valley, one comes to the sea, and the Cliffs of Mohar, which are quite impressive. Wouldn't you agree, Lord Donnelly?"

"Quite," he said, and sampled his soup. He could never look at the cliffs now without thinking of Eve. The soup was cold. He picked up his wine again.

"Lisdoon," Sniveling said. "It sounds rather lyrical."

"Lord Donnelly's estate is just north of Lisdoon. You may have heard of it—Ballynaheath."

"Ballynaheath?" Sniveling repeated, and chuckled. "Not quite as lyrical, is it?" Anders and Mrs. Ogle tittered along with him.

"I think it sounds very nice," Miss Babcock said defensively.

Declan smiled at her. "Thank you, Miss Babcock. Only a refined ear would find it so."

"Ballynaheath is beautiful," Keira continued. "His lordship has an exquisite house overlooking the sea. I've forever been a wee bit envious of the setting in the summer. In the winter, however, I think the winds and rain can be rather daunting. Wouldn't you say, my lord?"

He liked the winter days at Ballynaheath. They felt familiar to him. "Not too terribly daunting, no," he said idly. As a boy, he would imagine the cold winds sweeping him along, carrying him off to some exciting place.

"The sea is so captivating, I think," Keira said. "I would stand on the cliffs and watch it for hours. "

Declan flinched inwardly. He'd often wondered how long Eve had stood there, contemplating what she would do. Did she jump quickly? Or did she have to work to find the courage to do it?

"It is ever changing in color and temperament, a living, moving thing. It seems so placid at times, yet it swallows men and vessels whole, and at other times, when it is churning, it tosses its gifts up on shore. My father and I found a chest once, filled with china teacups."

"That's not all it tosses to shore," Declan said, and Keira instantly dropped her gaze to her soup.

"You said your father, Lady Ashwood?" Mrs. Ogle asked curiously. "I thought—"

"My uncle," Keira quickly corrected, and smiled charmingly. "Naturally, he was like a father to me." She carefully avoided Declan's steady gaze. "I do find the sea fascinating."

He had a sudden image of Keira standing on the windswept moors of the Cliffs of Mohar, looking out at the sea, her hair streaming behind her, her gown pressed against her body in the wind. It was a brief, but a frighteningly arousing, image.

"I've not seen the sea since I was a girl." Mrs. Ogle sighed wistfully. "I have often said to Mr. Ogle that a trip to the seaside would be invigorating for us both, and Brighton so near! But he does not like to travel far from home."

"That is a pity," Keira said.

"How fortunate for *you*, Lady Ashwood, that you have enjoyed such opportunity. And to think how all of Hadley Green fretted when you left us!" she said. "We could only guess what savagery awaited you in Ireland. It pleases me to know that you were so warmly received."

Keira stilled. She looked at Mrs. Ogle. "Savagery?"

Mrs. Ogle blithely sipped her soup. "It is often said of Ireland."

"By the English," Declan said, a little coolly. "By those who have never ventured beyond their shire. There is a fascinating world beyond England, full of sights one would never see here."

"Certainly," Mrs. Ogle conceded. "But Lady Ashwood was a child, and even the most beautiful place can seem frightening. That being said, even as a young girl, Lady Ashwood found favor wherever she went," Mrs. Ogle said, and smiled warmly at Keira.

"She does have a remarkable power of persuasion," Declan remarked.

"Oh dear, not very remarkable at all," Keira responded sheepishly.

"No, I must agree with Donnelly," Sniveling chimed in. "I've had occasion to spend time with her ladyship, and indeed, she has persuaded me more than once that I am quite wrong and she is quite right."

Everyone laughed politely at that; Keira smiled charmingly at Sniveling.

"Wait until you've known her for a time," Declan said. "You will be persuaded to more than just her way of thinking."

The polite tittering stopped and an uncomfortable silence settled on that end of the table. Declan thought perhaps he should forgo more wine.

But Keira smiled and continued with her meal. "Best a man in a horse race once and he never forgets it," she said cheerfully.

"A race! You must race him at the summer gala!" Miss Babcock said excitedly.

"I couldn't possibly!" Keira said, laughing. "Lord Donnelly has all the quality racehorses in West Sussex. We have only working horses at Ashwood."

"Lord Donnelly, you must give her one," Miss Babcock said excitedly. "A race would be quite exciting!"

"Oh no, Miss Babcock." Keira laughed. "He'd give me an old nag to ensure his win. I will tell you a secret about Lord Donnelly. He does not care to lose."

Declan had no idea how she could know that about him, but she was right. And he would hate with all his being to lose to her. Then again, he would die a happy man if he bested her. He slowly drained what was left in his wine glass. "I'll give you a horse to ride."

"I believe that is a challenge, madam," Mr. Anders said laughingly.

"It is very much a challenge," Declan said, his gaze steady on Keira.

She returned his gaze, just as steadily. "I don't know . . . shall I trust the mount my opponent would give me?"

"Not if you want to win," Sniveling said with a snort.

"The challenge is not in the horse," Declan said, "but how the horse is ridden. I thought you, of all people, knew that."

"Not entirely true, Donnelly," Anders said. "An old nag will not run as fast as a filly, no matter how well trained the rider."

"Then I shall promise here and now the Welsh pony she covets," Declan said. "You've been on her back, madam. You know she is as good as any horse you will find in Hadley Green."

"I do, indeed," she said, sitting up a bit taller. "If you will promise me the Welsh, I will gladly accept your challenge." She beamed, as if she'd already won.

"I believe it was your challenge," Declan said, and motioned for the footman to pour more wine.

"You are right," she said with a bow of her head. "I suppose I have always been the one to challenge, because I do so enjoy a good challenge. I refuse to shy away from them."

That was met with a laugh from those around them.

Declan laughed, too. Oh, how he would enjoy wiping that smirk from her face. "I, too, enjoy a good challenge," he said. "But I dislike foolish ones."

"Do you mean to say the race for charity is foolish?" Keira asked, clearly delighting in the support she was enjoying from their fellow dinner companions.

"Not at all. That is a challenge I happily and eagerly accept."

"But this is splendid!" Mrs. Ogle crowed, and suddenly banged her spoon against her bowl, gaining everyone's attention. "Lord Donnelly has just challenged Lady Ashwood to a race at the summer gala!" she exclaimed.

A cry of delight went up from the table.

"I understand you wish to support the poor orphans," Declan continued, enjoying the darkening of Keira's cheeks. "Shall we say the loser donates a purse to the orphanage?"

"You have improved on my challenge, haven't you? I cannot possibly refuse," Keira said.

The guests applauded, and more than one called out a promise to add to Keira's purse.

"There, then, you might make a sizable donation to your favorite charity yet," Declan said. "Assuming, of course, you have a purse that these gentlemen may add to?"

Several people laughed.

"I have a purse, my lord," Keira said. "Do *you?*"

"I will match whatever these good people put into yours."

"Then we are agreed."

"Good," he said jovially.

"*Good,*" she said, perhaps a wee bit angrily.

"Oh, here is the venison!" Mrs. Ogle exclaimed with some relief.

The guests' attentions and empty bellies turned to the meal.

After the meal of tepid venison and undercooked vegetables was consumed by some—Declan couldn't manage it—the ladies retired to the drawing room and the gentlemen were served port before rejoining the ladies. Declan helped himself to two. He was still riled from supper. Keira was cleverly beguiling, he'd give her that. All of these people thought she was a bloody heroine.

When the gentlemen rejoined the ladies, a young woman was pressed upon to demonstrate her skill at the pianoforte, and a trio of gentlemen entertained the group with their singing.

Interminable.

Declan had another port and watched Keira smiling and talking to Sniveling. He lost track of her as he had another port, but then spotted her through an open doorway. She was standing in the corridor, her cloak in hand, and Mrs. Ogle fluttering around her like a bird. Snively had donned his hat and cloak, as well.

Declan stood up, strolled in a warm, bleary haze to the front door where Mr. and Mrs. Ogle were seeing Keira out. He stepped into their midst and said to the hired footman, "My cloak."

"Lord Donnelly! Won't you stay awhile longer? We thought to play a game," Mrs. Ogle said.

"Thank you, but it is time that I take my leave." He looked at Keira. "Leaving so soon, Countess? And so many admirers yet."

She gave him what he thought was a very patronizing smile. "I am very fortunate in that regard. Not all of us are so admired."

"Oh, I am sure. I would hazard a guess that being a countess must take its toll on a woman." Declan accepted the cloak the footman handed him. "Perhaps you ought to let someone else give it a go."

"Lord Donnelly, I am beginning to think that something has affected your good humor," Sniveling said curtly.

There was a sharp retort on the tip of Declan's tongue, but he couldn't seem to grasp it. "Meaning?"

"Meaning that it is quite obvious you are envious of others' attentions to the countess."

"*Envious?*" Declan snapped, finding his tongue, which, admittedly, felt a little thick. "If you think I am somehow envious of *you*, sir, you are more delusional than even she. I am quite happy she has turned her smile on you, for I have no use for it. But before you put yourself on the top of her dance card, you might assure yourself that she's not left anyone standing on a cliff wanting to jump."

He knew the moment the words left his mouth that he'd gone too far. Mrs. Ogle confirmed that with a loud gasp. Keira blinked wide green eyes at him, her face pale. She looked wounded, and it gave Declan a peculiar pain behind his eyes.

"Apologize," Sniveling snarled.

"I will not," Declan said tightly, as he tried to understand why he cared that he'd wounded the little deceiver. "Good evening." He did not look at Keira. He strode out of the house, marching down to the drive, barking at a boy to bring his horse.

A half hour later, he reached a darkened Kitridge Lodge. The small, rustic old castle was a dark shadow against the summer's night sky, the only light flickering in a window from a lit hearth inside.

Just last summer, the drafty old lodge had blazed with light and laughter. Declan's good friend Christie, the Duke of Darlington, had come with his wife, the once renowned courtesan Katharine Bergeron. Christie had defied the Prince of Wales and his family to marry her. They'd had a child, a daughter, and Declan had come to meet the new Darlington. He'd envied the warmth at Kitridge Lodge then, the happiness he'd felt within these walls when Christie and Kate and their child were here.

He didn't feel that now. This summer, the lodge was empty and drafty. It felt a little too natural to him at times.

Declan didn't know why that was. Ballynaheath was not empty or drafty, yet for some reason, he knew this feeling like a second skin.

Ah, but Kitridge Lodge was only a temporary refuge, one that he would eventually leave. He always left. His sister, Eireanne, said he was stricken with wanderlust. He didn't know what it was that made him move on; he just knew he'd never found the place that made him feel . . . warm.

Declan handed off his horse to a sleepy lad and strode inside. He stood in the middle of the small foyer with the swords and armor hanging over his head. A headache had sprung up behind his eyes. *Too much wine, far too much wine,* he told himself.

He felt bad, really, physically and in spirit. He didn't think he'd ever regret anything he said to Keira Hannigan, not after what had happened in Ireland between them, and not after he'd discovered her deceit here in Hadley Green. But regret it he did. He'd drunk too much, let his tongue wag ahead of his brain. He kept picturing her speaking of Ireland with that soft Irish lilt, her eyes glittering, her long, tapered fingers fluttering against the stem of her wine glass. And her smile . . . oh, aye, he did regret it.

The pain in his head raged.

He walked into the small receiving salon. Noakes had left a fire in the hearth and it was overly warm in the room. Declan removed his coat and neckcloth, and unbuttoned his waistcoat. He removed his boots and tossed them aside. He filled a tot with Irish whiskey and sat in a chair before the hearth, his feet propped on an ottoman, brooding about the supper party he hadn't wanted to attend in the first place.

He closed his eyes.

He could never forget that afternoon in the Ireland she'd described at supper, a day after which nothing was ever the same. *Admit it,* he thought. *That day changed you.* He'd never again felt quite worthy of happiness. He certainly didn't feel worthy tonight. He'd let those eyes get the best of him.

A pounding on the door brought him up with a start, causing him to slosh his whiskey. *"Cad é sin?"* he muttered sleepily, and finished off his whiskey before making his way to the door.

As he neared the door, it sounded as if someone were using both hands and a boot against it. "I am here!" he shouted irritably, and threw the door open.

A cloud of silver and white rushed past him, sailing into the small foyer and leaving a scent of lavender in its wake. Declan shut the door and turned around as Keira swept the hood of her cloak from her dark head.

"What—"

She slapped him hard across his cheek.

Nine

Declan's head snapped around from the blow of Keira's hand. He stumbled back a step and winced as he touched his fingers to his cheek, then slowly turned his gaze to her.

"You are a horrible, wretched man!" she said angrily.

He said nothing, just stared at her with cool blue eyes. *"Oh!"* She whirled around, passing through the narrow corridor into what looked like a small receiving salon. It was close and overly warm. A cave, she thought. How fitting.

Declan followed her. "Please do come in," he said dryly and casually leaned against the door frame.

Keira yanked the gloves from her hands. "How can you be so cruel?" she demanded hotly.

His gaze darkened, and he looked as if he had something rather heated to say, but his face suddenly fell. "I don't know," he admitted stiffly.

His response surprised Keira, yet she angrily pressed forward. She would not dispute she was doing something wrong, but that did not give him the right to treat her so ill. "You were reprehensible this evening, and for what reason? I've done nothing to you!"

His expression turned thunderous. "Do you truly

expect me to play in your foolish, dangerous game after what happened at Ballynaheath?"

"*A Dhia dhílis!*" she cried, throwing her hands up. "Must you dredge up ancient history?"

"Ancient history?" He laughed harshly. "Eve is *dead,* Keira, or have you forgotten?"

As if she could ever forget. She shook her head, pressed one hand to her abdomen to quell the small wave of nausea at the reminder. "There is not a day that has passed that I do not remember it," she said, her voice shaking. "But God in heaven, Declan, I was sixteen years old!"

"Yes, I am—and I was—acutely aware that you were only sixteen years old. You seem to think that somehow excuses your behavior, then *and* now. Yet it hardly begins to excuse it—then *or* now."

Keira felt a flush of anger and shame rise hot to her face. "All right. But neither does it excuse *your* behavior . . . then or now."

Declan pressed his lips tightly together, glaring at her . . . and then he pushed both hands through his hair with a sigh. "No. It does not." He dropped his hands and moved past her, to the sideboard. She realized that he was only half dressed. She had thought he was remarkably handsome at Mrs. Ogle's in his formal tails, and clearly, most of the women had thought so, too, judging by the way they kept casting looks in his direction. But without his coat and his waistcoat, and his shirt opened at the collar, she could see that he was clearly fit, his shoulders broad and as muscled as his legs. He had the shadow of a beard, and Keira had an image of him standing before her, without a stitch—

She realized he was holding out a tot of whiskey, offering it to her. His deep blue gaze was full of regret and something else, something she recognized—a dull, old pain. It was her constant companion.

Keira took the glass from him and looked away. It was little wonder he reviled her. She was thinking of carnal things as he relived the pain of Eve. Keira had never been able to imagine the horror he must have felt when he'd discovered Eve's broken body washed up on the shore. The image gave sudden rise to hot, angry, impotent tears that Keira quickly swallowed down. She could never escape the memory, the regret, the guilt. She didn't deserve to escape any of it. Despite how it might seem to others, it was such a painful memory for her, one that had held her heart in a vise for eight long years. There was not a day that passed that she didn't think of Eve, didn't imagine the terror Eve must have experienced. Since that day, Keira had developed an almost unnatural need to experience life. Life could disappear in the blink of an eye, and she didn't want to go before she had felt it all, had tasted it, had breathed it in.

She squeezed her eyes shut, pressed her fingers to them. "I will go to my grave regretting a foolish, foolish girl's game," she said softly.

"Let us not think of it," he said, and turned away from her to put the whiskey down his throat.

"How can I not think of it?" Guilt, regret, sadness—it was part of her now, a river running through her that never grew stagnant, that cut deeper and deeper into its trough. If she'd confessed their game when Declan had asked after her friends in the meadow that day, Eve would be alive today, she was certain of it. Keira had believed that in being coy, she was being loyal to Eve. How could she have possibly imagined what would happen?

No matter. She never felt less than completely responsible for it. With a soft moan, Keira sank onto a chair at the same moment she put the tot aside. A rush of memories flooded her mind—of that fateful day, of the days and years that had followed, of the time she'd so clumsily tried to apologize to Declan. "Please stop punishing me," she said low, feeling the millstone of his censure.

"Pardon?"

"Stop punishing me," she said again. "Please, just . . . stop."

"*Punishing* you?" he said with a snort. "What nonsense."

"You know that you do," she said, looking up at him. "You have reviled me ever since that day. Every overture of apology I have made you have rejected."

He shook his head.

"I hardly blame you for it," she said helplessly. "God knows I have reviled myself. I have no excuse but to say I was only sixteen years old and very naïve to the ways of the world, and we were . . . we were diverted by it! Eve wanted . . . she fancied herself in love with him, and honestly, Declan . . ." Keira looked him in the eye. "I was a wee bit in love with you. You know that I was."

He frowned down at his tot, but he did not deny it.

"I was young and foolish and God knows I did not fathom what I was doing." Her voice was full of her own disgust. "Do you think if I had guessed that he would take such cruel advantage of her, I wouldn't have told you straightaway? I never imagined for a moment that anything so horrible could happen!" She pressed her fingers to her temples. "I live with the guilt of it every day. I am sorry, Declan, I am deeply, mortally sorry for it—but I never meant you or Eve or anyone harm."

Declan sighed wearily and sat beside her on the settee. "I know," he said with uncharacteristic softness. "I understand how you feel. Imagine my guilt. I cannot claim to not know what I was about with you. Had I treated you as a gentleman ought, I could have saved her."

Surprised, Keira looked at him. "You?" she said incredulously. "Dear God, it wasn't your fault, Declan." He shrugged and looked away; Keira realized that he must have believed that all along. "No, Declan," she said, and put her hand reassuringly on his knee. "It was not your fault. You would not have saved her, even if we'd never met in the meadow."

"It is done now, Keira," he said. "We both made mistakes. It has no bearing on the present."

It had everything to do with the present, she thought. "I think it does."

He frowned a little and shook his head. "It has no bearing on your deceit at Ashwood. You cannot suggest you are too young and innocent to understand what you are doing," he said, and stood up. He moved to step away, but abruptly turned around and glared down at her. "How can you do it? How can you deceive an entire village, and people who clearly hold you in high esteem?"

She found it difficult enough to do it without being reminded. "I told you, I am doing it for Lily's sake—"

"Lily," he scoffed, and walked to the hearth, his back to her.

"It is true! Ashwood was sinking into financial ruin when I arrived, but there was no mention of it in the letter Lily received. Had there been, I am certain Lily would have come straightaway."

"Why didn't she come?" Declan asked, turning toward her again. "How can she learn she is countess of an estate and not come at once?"

"Ashwood . . . holds dark memories for her, in truth," Keira said. She wasn't certain she had made complete sense of what she thought Lily felt for this place. "She was quite attached to Aunt Althea, and she felt responsible for what happened to Mr. Scott. But she didn't know about the financial problems or the issues with the entail."

Now Declan turned to look at her. "The entail?"

She wished she hadn't mentioned it, and waved her hand dismissively. "An issue regarding the entail of our most profitable one hundred acres. Mr. Fish and I will set it to rights, but the point is, I had no choice but to help her, and as I could only help her by *being* her . . . I did it."

"Keira, lass," Declan said. He squatted down before her, looked her squarely in the eye. "Have you not thought of the repercussions? You are an Irish Catholic, which, for many in England, puts you among the lowest of the low. You are impersonating an English countess. You are committing a crime against the estate of Ashwood, and it hardly matters how well intentioned you are. Nor will Lily's wish alone spare you. England is not a lawless land. You could find yourself in very serious trouble here. Do you not understand it?" he demanded softly.

Keira felt herself flinch a little. "She'll be back before anything happens," she said stubbornly, and wished,

prayed, that it was true. She was not a witless woman—
she understood she could find herself in serious trouble.

Declan shook his head and stood up. "You are playing
a very dangerous game."

"Then help me find the answers I need so that I might
give everything over to Lily the moment she arrives,"
Keira pleaded. "Something happened here, Declan, something that could hurt Lily. My aunt took her own life." He
started to shake his head, but Keira leaned forward. "I am
truly convinced an innocent man died for a crime he did
not commit, and Lily inadvertantly helped it happen with
her testimony. Do you think she can bear that after what
happened to Eve? I cannot let her learn these things as I
did, and she will."

"You don't know that," he said, moving to the hearth.
"You are leaping to conclusions. You are the same impulsive, romantic fool you were eight years ago."

She couldn't blame him for that, but this time, she was
certain and came to her feet. "Did you take note of the
staircase at Ashwood? Did you not admire the intricate
woodwork?"

"What of it?"

"Imagine the time the gentleman must have taken to
craft that amazing staircase. Imagine the hours Mr. Scott
must have spent at Ashwood, in the same house, if not the
same rooms, as Lady Ashwood."

"Keira, honestly—"

"And there is the matter of the pianoforte brought
from Italy for the countess," she said quickly. "It had
been put up in the attic after his death. Can you imagine, Declan, a fine musical instrument put away in a dusty

attic and the countess still very much alive for a time? She couldn't bring herself to touch it, because he had made her the stool, and on the underside of that stool was—"

"My God, your imagination has runneth over, Keira—"

"—a beautiful inscription. It says 'You are the song that plays on in my heart; for A, my love, my life, my heart's only note. Yours for eternity, JS.'" Keira felt breathless repeating it, and watched Declan closely, waiting for understanding to dawn. "The initials," she added hastily. "JS is obviously Joseph Scott, the person who carved the bench. And A is Aunt Althea."

He merely looked at her. "You've crafted a romance, lass."

"How else might it be explained?" she cried with great exasperation.

"I haven't the slightest notion. But let us pretend for a moment that you are right, that Mr. Scott esteemed Lady Ashwood. That does not make him an innocent man. Have you considered his esteem was unrequited? Or perhaps she found comfort in his arms and then scorned him? Perhaps he was merely courting her affection to get close to the jewels. Men have done far worse. There could be any number of reasons that he stole the jewels."

"No, I cannot believe it," Keira said stubbornly. "He *loved* her. He took great care with the things he gave her. And a man who loves a woman as he loved her would never do anything to harm her, I am entirely certain of it!"

"What do you know of love, Keira Hannigan? Does Loman Maloney love you so much? Sniveling?"

She gaped at him, her thoughts scattered by her anger.

"You have never understood what men are capable of,"

he continued angrily. "You are a silly, foolish girl, creating romantic stories to justify your deceitful actions."

"My God. Are you truly so hard-hearted?"

"Now I am hard-hearted because I don't believe your fantasy? I ask you again, Keira—what do you know of love?"

"Perhaps I don't," she said, fighting to maintain her composure. "But I know what I dream love to be, what I believe it to be, what I *hope* it to be. At least I have hope, Declan. At least my thoughts are not as bleak as yours."

For some reason, that made him smile sadly, and he impulsively touched his fingers to her jaw. "Not bleak. Honest."

She jerked her head away from his hand. With a single touch, that unexpected, burning kiss on Mrs. Ogle's terrace was suddenly rushing through her. "You may believe what you like. I still believe an innocent man was hanged and I need help discovering if my doubts are true. No one will speak to me about what happened because they believe I am Lily. They believe I am the one who sent the man to his death and they will not contradict the public memory of it."

"And if, on the slim chance, it is true that an innocent man was hanged, what can you possibly do for him now? There is naught *you* can do at all, Keira, because you are engaged in a rather impressive fraud. The very moment you are caught, you will find yourself in serious trouble. There will be no time or inclination on the part of anyone to clear up a very old hanging. *Dhia,* do you *ever* consider the consequences to your actions?"

She deserved that; she closed her eyes. She couldn't begin to explain how desperately she needed to put this to rights. Eve was dead and nothing could ever change it. Mr. Scott was dead, and while nothing could bring him back, she could at least restore his name to him. She had a feeling Aunt Althea would want that very much.

She opened her eyes and leveled her gaze on Declan. "Have you considered Lily can make amends when she arrives? She can make reparations to the family, she can clear the poor man's name. If he is truly innocent he deserves at least that much."

Declan started to shake his head, but Keira stopped him with a touch to his arm. "You cannot refuse me. I have a bargain you will surely want to make."

His expression changed; his blue eyes looked at her in a way that fluttered in Keira's groin. "What could you possibly have to bargain with me?" he asked evenly.

"I can arrange for Eireanne's acceptance into Institut Villa Amiels."

Declan's eyes flashed.

"I know you've not been successful on her behalf," Keira said. "But I have the proper connections. I could see that it is arranged."

He moved so suddenly that Keira cried out. She whirled around, intending to flee, but Declan caught her. He twisted her about, pushed her up against the back of the settee, his fingers digging into her arms. "Do you know why Eireanne has not been accepted? I have all the money Madame Broussard and her staff could possibly want, yet she denies my sister because of *my* involvement in the death of Eve O'Shaugnessy!"

Keira gasped. She'd never heard that, she'd assumed it was his rakish reputation . . . "What?"

"*Uist*," he said harshly, hushing her in their tongue. "You want a bargain, do you?" he asked, leaning over her, pushing her backward. His eyes were unfathomably dark and hard. "You'll have to do better than that."

"Declan, don't—"

He grabbed the nape of her neck, forcing her face closer to his. His gaze dipped to her lips. "Once again, Keira, you do not understand the consequences of your actions."

With the heat in his eyes, and his body pressed against her, something wildly hot flared in Keira. She was sixteen all over again, mad with desire, reckless and desperate to kiss him. She looked into his glittering eyes and answered breathlessly, "*Aye*, I do."

He bent his head, his lips only a moment from hers. "Bloody fool," he growled, and claimed her mouth, landing full and wet against her lips. He drew her bottom lip between his teeth, and she couldn't breathe, couldn't catch her breath. His tongue dipped into her mouth, parting her lips, sliding over her teeth and into the inferno that was suddenly raging inside her. With her hand she sought his face, her fingers brushing against his jaw and the roughness of an emerging beard, and against the corner of his mouth. This kiss was different; this was a different sort of rage between them. This felt as if it could consume her completely. She *wanted* it to consume her.

Declan slipped his hand inside her cape, over her breast, cupping it, kneading it, his thumb rubbing over the fabric that covered her nipple.

Keira thought she should stop, but she was helpless against the flood of sensation and desire he had stoked in her. He freed the clasp of her cloak and pushed it off her shoulders and dipped down, pressing his mouth to the flesh above her décolletage. She was on a dangerous slope, one in which she'd lost her footing, and she feared that she would slide down with him, going where he took her.

Then without warning, Declan lifted his head and pushed her aside in his haste to move away from her and turned his back. Keira stumbled slightly. His abruptness stunned her; her pulse was racing, her heart still leaping.

"Write the bloody letter for Eireanne," he said gruffly, and glanced over his shoulder at Keira. The glint in his eyes was hard and unyielding.

Keira dragged the back of her hand across her mouth trying to erase the sensation of that hot, sultry kiss as Declan stalked to the sideboard and poured another whiskey. He lifted it up in mock toast. "Well then, Keira, we have our agreement, aye? *Sláinte*."

She didn't care for the way he phrased it. "Declan, I—"

"Don't," he said sharply. "Don't attempt to make this sound any less mercenary than it is. Tell me what you want from me."

Keira swallowed. "I . . . I want to find Mr. Scott's friends. I think—"

"Not necessary," he said curtly. "I don't want to know your every thought, only what I must do."

She bristled. "I want to find Mr. Scott's friends or family and inquire of them."

"Splendid," he said, and drank his whiskey. He put down the tot and glanced at her impatiently. "Is that all?"

Was that all? She couldn't think clearly, not with that angry kiss still simmering in her.

"Well, then, Keira, you may stay and remove your

clothes and allow a better bargain to be made . . . or you may take your leave."

She gasped; then hastily bent down and swept up her cloak. "You must treat me as a countess if we are to succeed."

"Oh," he said, his brows arching. "There are rules of engagement, are there?" He sauntered forward. "Very well, *muirnín*, if I must treat you as a countess . . ." He touched his fingers to her lips and pressed gently.

Muirnín, an Irish endearment, said so sarcastically, stung her.

His finger slipped from her mouth and traced a line down her chin.

Keira stepped back, away from his hand, and fastened her cloak. "I'll send a messenger when I have something we might pursue." She walked across the room, wanting suddenly to be gone.

"By the by, Keira," he said, prompting Keira to pause and look back. "I am curious about one thing. Just how long will Maloney wait? How long will you continue with this absurd charade before you've lost all?"

He was mocking her, and it was more hurtful than she cared to admit. She could scarcely think of Mr. Maloney without feeling a guilty need to avoid him. "*He* is a gentleman and *he* believes I am worth waiting for," she said angrily, and swept out of the room.

She heard his derisive chuckle as she walked to the door of the lodge.

Arse. It infuriated her that all those desperate feelings for him were coursing hotly through her. She felt as if she had just made the devil's bargain, but her incautious heart didn't care. She wanted to live this life.

Ten

Declan was summoned several days later on a warm afternoon as he was receiving delivery of an Austrian horse. He had almost succeeded in putting that night at Kitridge out of his mind, and he had the diversion of the jewel of a horse he'd found in Lancashire a few weeks ago when he'd gone to call on the Earl of Northrop.

Northrop had brought the horse from Austria, where the ever-present threat of war had left the horse's care in shambles. At least Northrop had seen her value, and he had indeed struck a hard bargain with Declan, but Declan would not leave without purchasing the gelding and arranging his care until he could take delivery.

He was as anxious as a child at Christmas when the carriage turned into the gates of Kitridge Lodge, the gelding trotting behind. This, he told himself, is where he found himself on solid ground. He wasn't adrift here, fighting conflicting thoughts and emotions as he had been the last few days. He did not like feeling so unsettled. He liked feeling in control of his surroundings and his work.

Which meant that he did not like the sight of the

ginger-haired boy with the gap-toothed grin from Ashwood who came trotting in behind his horse.

The boy eagerly doffed his dirty cap and thrust a folded piece of vellum at Declan. "From her ladyship, milord," he said.

Declan opened the vellum. It read, *Village green at three o'clock.*

That was all she had written, a bloody summons, as if he had nothing better to do than await her command from on high. He'd conceded, had given in to his desires, and now she thought she might order him about? Declan folded the vellum and stuck it in his pocket. He removed a coin from his purse and handed it to the boy. "Pay very close attention and repeat the message to your lady precisely as I tell you, aye? Are you ready?"

The boy nodded.

"*No.*"

The boy blinked. He looked at the horse, then at Declan again. "No, milord?"

"That's all. Off with you now," he said, and turned to his horse.

A second note arrived later that afternoon, this time in the hands of a footman. "I'm to await your reply, milord," he said.

Declan growled and read the note. *Perhaps you have forgotten your promise. Now the hour has grown too late to continue today, as I am expected to dine at the Mortons' this evening. Might I possibly expect you to honor your word and meet me on the morrow at two o'clock?*

Declan looked at the footman. "A moment," he said, and strode angrily into the lodge, directly to the study, where he penned his response.

Of course I have not forgotten my promise, madam, nor have I forgotten that the proper way a lady should entreat a gentleman to do anything on her behalf is to ask kindly after his help, without tyranny, and to sprinkle her kind request liberally with pleases and thank-yous. I will await you in the village green tomorrow at two o'clock. Do not be late, as I shall not wait, and were I you, I'd bring the letter, which is your end of this abominable bargain.

> *D.*

That evening, as Declan sat down to devour a dinner that Mrs. Noakes had made him, the Ashwood footman reappeared. He delivered his note and did not wait for a reply. *Please,* it said. *And thank you.*

Declan worked very hard to suppress a small smile. He could not do it.

At precisely two o'clock Declan was leaning lazily against a hitching post in the village green when he spotted Keira marching across the green, her gown sweeping a path across the grass behind her. She walked so quickly and so purposefully that the girl hurrying behind her—brought along, presumably, to keep speculation and gossip to a mere din—could scarcely keep up.

At one point, Keira stumbled slightly and righted herself with what sounded like a soft curse. She sailed to a stop before Declan, her eyes narrowed and glinting like tiny emeralds. The girl dragged in behind her, gasping for breath.

"Well! Here we are, my lord," she said saucily.

"Keira."

"May I introduce Lucy Taft?" she said, gesturing to the girl.

"Miss Taft," he said, nodding his head. The girl didn't speak, but looked him up and down.

"Lucy, do be a dear and sit just there a moment, will you?" Keira asked, pointing to a bench.

"Yes, mu'um." Lucy hurried to the bench, collapsing gratefully upon it.

Keira folded her arms tightly across her body, leaned toward Declan and whispered loudly, "I did not intend to injure your tender feelings with a terse note, but I was being cautious. I should think it obvious that discretion as to the nature of our dealing is essential in this matter. The fewer words committed to paper, the better."

"Discretion is essential to you," Declan reminded her. "Not me. Lovely bonnet, by the by."

She colored slightly and put a hand to her overly adorned bonnet. "I couldn't help it. Linford was hovering about, eager to take my note and give it to Wills to be delivered. And it was all for naught as it turns out, for Linford refuses to tell me a thing."

"Tell you what thing?"

"Who Mr. Scott's acquaintances were, of course," she said, glancing over her shoulder at young Lucy. "On my word, he is not the least cooperative! He says 'it is ancient history, my lady, and I daresay that even if I could recall a name or two it would not be useful to you now.' He presumes to know what is useful to me now!"

"He presumes correctly."

"Don't you dare take his side in this!" Keira complained. "I am filled to bursting with aggravation as it is!" The color of her aggravation rose in her cheeks, and she looked, incongruently, quite lovely.

Declan was ashamed of himself. Having had a rather stern chat with himself about the danger to his happiness and sanity that was Keira Hannigan, he was far too easily swayed by a flash of loveliness. The best course was to have this over and done as quickly as possible. "Calm yourself, lass. You're not going about this . . . this busybodyness properly."

"What? What do you mean?" she asked, peering curiously at him.

"I mean that if you want to find something about a man dead fifteen years, you cannot merely walk into a tavern or a drawing room and begin asking questions of whoever happens to be on hand. People's memories are quite short, and that is if they are even inclined to answer."

"Then perhaps you have a better idea," she said flippantly.

Declan smiled. "I'd suggest you find his priest."

Keira frowned uncertainly. "His *priest.*"

"Surely some priest comforted Mr. Scott in his darkest hour. Just as he undoubtedly comforted Mr. Scott's friends and family after his unfortunate demise."

Something clicked and Keira's eyes suddenly fired, followed by a sunny smile. "*Declan!*" she cried. "That's brilliant, truly brilliant . . . it is a wonder I didn't think of it myself!" she said with earnest exuberance.

"A wonder," he drawled. "Well, there you are, then, Keira. You have your next task," he said, and withdrew his pocket watch. He had time to call on Penny yet.

"My next task?" she repeated. "What, you mean *I* should call on the Reverend Tunstill?"

"If he is the one who tends the flock of Hadley Green sheep, aye," Declan said dryly.

"But he's quite old. And *deaf*."

"Then you must speak loudly and clearly. Very well—"

"You aren't leaving," she said quickly.

Not that he wasn't enjoying her high dudgeon. It gave him a rather perverse sense of satisfaction to know that he was not the only one who was feeling entirely discomfited. "I am, indeed. I have an engagement."

"What, at the tavern?" she scoffed.

Oh, she was brazen. He touched his hand to her waist. "Perhaps *you* have a better idea, *muirnín,* aye?"

Keira blushed so furiously that Declan couldn't help chuckle. He enjoyed making her blush, and in spite of all her feminine swagger, it was easy to do.

"You said you would help me," she reminded him.

Declan noticed she had not moved back, but was still standing close. "I haven't all day to devote to your little mystery," he said, and refrained from pointing out that he could be persuaded to devote time to something far more pleasurable.

"That was our agreement. Our agreement was that you would help me in this very regard," she insisted.

"In exchange for a letter benefiting Eireanne. Have you a letter?"

"Pardon?" She glanced at the girl. "I . . . Of course I have the letter!"

She really did not lie very well at all, which made the depth of her deceit even that more breathtaking. "If you have the letter, you will not mind showing it to me," he suggested.

Now she took a step backward. "I will show you the letter after you have spoken to the vicar."

"I daresay *that* was not our agreement, either. You promised the letter for my help."

Keira's fingers toyed with the little pearl dangling from her ear. "Do you doubt my word?" she asked, twisting it.

He casually studied her, letting his gaze wander the length of her fine figure. Her attention to the earring grew a bit more frantic. "Where is it?" he asked.

"With . . . in the carriage."

A beautiful liar. Declan would enjoy exacting his pound of her flesh. "I haven't all day," he said. "Let's be done with it."

"Oh!" Keira said, smiling again, clearly surprised she had won the first small battle. "Well. My carriage is just there. Shall we? Lucy! Come along, dear!"

Eleven

There was a bit of a tiff inside the carriage as to who would enter the vicarage to make the inquiries. Keira, who did not trust Declan's commitment to question the vicar properly, preferred that she and Lucy accompany him inside. But Declan put his big hands on his muscular thighs, leaned across the carriage until his face was only inches from her, and said, "*No.* You have dragged me along to make such inquiries, and by God, I shall make the inquiry without any so-named assistance from you."

Bloody rooster. "Very well," Keira said, and folded her hands on her lap and looked out the window.

But Declan startled her by suddenly catching her chin and turning her face to his, even closer than it had been a moment earlier. "If you think to follow, lass," he said, as his gaze skimmed over her mouth, "you will suffer for it. Are we clear?"

Pompous, bloody rooster. "Go on, then, will you? I'm invited to Foxmoor today and I really can't be late."

"I will remind you that it is hardly *my* desire to be at the vicarage this afternoon, but far be it from me to keep you from your *tea,*" he said, and climbed out.

"Far be it from me," she mimicked under her breath as Lucy's fair head appeared in the open carriage door.

"The gent says I'm to wait inside," she said uncertainly.

"He's not a gent, darling, but an earl. Come in, come in," she urged her, gesturing for her to climb aboard.

The girl settled on the bench and looked around at the interior, wide-eyed. Lucy had come to Ashwood just two days ago. Keira had readied a room for her with a canopied bed and a small easel on which to draw. There were thick rugs, a child-sized table and chairs, and even a miniature tea set. Keira thought it would make Lucy happy, but Lucy had seemed overwhelmed by it. Keira had instantly realized her mistake—everything was new and different, and Lily was unaccustomed to such luxury, and servants, and more than a pair of frocks.

Keira truly hoped she might turn the poor girl's fortune around and make her into a proper governess.

And she supposed that it had occurred to her—after hearing from Daria Babcock of the whispers about the amount of time Keira had spent in Mr. Sibley's company—that she could very well use an escort. Lucy suited Keira perfectly in that regard. At nine years, Lucy was far too young to understand what Keira was about or if she made mistakes in her performance as countess. Ah yes, little Lucy Taft was the perfect chastity wrap for Keira.

They sat for a quarter of an hour, Lucy quietly running her hands over the velvet squabs, Keira staring anxiously out the small carriage window at the wooden door in the stone fence that surrounded the vicarage. She knew firsthand that the vicar could bind one up in a lengthy discourse about mundane things, and worse, he had a tendency to repeat himself. What if Declan didn't understand how to politely turn the old man away from an unintended course in the conversation and steer him back to the question at hand? After all, he wasn't a particularly patient man. Or a civil one.

It seemed as if she'd been waiting for ages, and Keira couldn't bear it another moment. "Come along, Lucy. Let us light some candles in the chapel."

"For who?" Lucy asked.

"Lord Donnelly." Keira opened the door of the carriage. "He is in desperate need of grace from above." She shooed away the coachman who leaped off the back runner to assist her. She shook out her skirts as Lucy tumbled out, and with Lucy's hand firmly in hers, Keira picked up her skirts and marched toward the wooden gate.

"Is he unwell?" Lucy asked as she hurried alongside Keira.

"Who, Donnelly?" Keira said breezily. "Beyond redemption. That is why we must pray for his immortal soul."

She pushed through the wooden gate and into an untended garden in wild summer bloom, a riot of yellow buttercups and pink roses bobbing on leggy limbs in the summer's breeze. Keira marched forward. She had in mind to deposit Lucy in the chapel to light as many candles as she possibly could, while Keira went to find the gentlemen, but before she could reach the chapel, the door of the house swung open and Declan—virile, handsome, towering Declan—emerged, followed closely by a chattering Reverend Tunstill.

Declan frowned darkly at her, but the Reverend Tunstill brightened considerably. "This is a most blessed day, indeed!" he cried with delight. He instantly shuffled around a scowling Declan and took up Keira's hand between his two beefy ones. "Lady Ashwood, it is my great honor to receive you at the vicarage. It is rare that the Countess of Ashwood pays a call to our humble abode. I have been the vicar of this parish for three and forty years, and I can recall two—no, no, I am wrong there, it has been *three*—times that the countess has come to the vicarage. The first time being when I was newly ordained in the year of our Lord seventeen hundred and sixty-five. I was a much younger man then, obviously, but a man of the cloth nonetheless, however I will confess to you that I found her to be quite lovely—"

"Ah . . . pardon, Vicar, but I—" Keira tried as she attempted to dislodge her hand.

"—and charming, naturally, for what countess is less than charming, I ask you, present company very much included."

"My hand, sir," Keira said with a slight wince.

"Pardon?"

"My *hand,*" she said again, tugging to dislodge it from his grasp.

The vicar looked down and laughed. "There, now, do you see? I am so taken with your beauty and charm as undoubtedly all are that I quite forgot I was holding your hand."

Behind him, Declan rolled his eyes.

"Now who have we here, my lady? This fine girl looks familiar to me, but I cannot place her," he said, laying one finger along the side of his nose as he peered at Lucy.

"This is Miss Lucy Taft," Keira said. She could feel Declan's gaze boring through her as she lightly pushed Lucy forward. "She has expressed a desire to light a candle or two."

"Oh my, is someone ill, Miss Taft?" the vicar asked. "Who is it you would light a candle for?"

"Me? But her ladyship said—"

"Lucy, my dear, charity is something that should be enjoyed in the privacy of one's thoughts. It would not do to boast of your intentions."

"Yes, of course, of course," the vicar said. "Listen to the countess, young lady, for she is very wise." To Keira, he added, "I had not one moment earlier remarked to Lord Donnelly that we so rarely see you in our services, madam, and how your attendance would inspire so many others. Lo these forty-odd years, I've noticed a decline in the summer months when thoughts turn to the out-of-doors, but it is important for everyone to remain vigilant of their soul."

"The vicar believes everyone could use a bit of redemption," Declan said to Keira. "And that, by some miracle, you of all people might entice them to receive it."

She gave him a smiling look full of warning.

"Quite right, quite right," the vicar said, rising up to his tiptoes and down again. "It is never too late to bring a wayward soul into the fold and lead them back to the light of Christ our Lord."

"Some walking amongst us now are undoubtedly teetering on the edge of darkness," Declan agreed, his blue eyes locked on Keira.

"Perhaps they have flung themselves into the pit of

darkness entirely," Keira retorted, steadily returning his gaze.

"Oh goodness," the vicar said, and put a hand to his portly belly and laughed. "I daresay we have no need to worry with that in Hadley Green!"

"You might be surprised," Declan said, and the vicar laughed again.

"However I may be of service to you, you need only ask," Keira informed the vicar.

"You are too good, Lady Ashwood!" he said, beaming. "It is a heavenly gift that you have found the means to reopen the mill. You have put many able-bodied men to work, and there is nothing more cleansing to the soul than good, hard work."

That seemed to arouse Declan's interest; he arched a brow in her direction.

Keira smiled smartly in return.

"You remind me so of your late lady aunt. The last time I had opportunity to speak to her was when she received me at Ashwood on a bitterly cold morning. 'Twas the winter of 1802, which you surely will recall was most brutally frigid. Why, I remember that the rain froze midair and stung like nettles against my skin. We had a milk cow, and—"

"Pardon, Vicar, but here is poor little Lucy, waiting so patiently to light her candles."

"Oh yes, oh yes," he said, and put his hand on Lucy's shoulder. "We mustn't keep her from her Christian duty. Come along, girl, let us light your candles." The vicar took her hand, and Lucy glanced pleadingly at Keira as he led her away to the chapel.

When they had disappeared into the darkened opening, Declan swung around to Keira. "I warned you," he said brusquely, and grasped her elbow, wheeling her about and making her walk briskly beside him.

"I came to your rescue," she said, trying to dislodge her elbow. "I know how verbose he might be, and furthermore, I do not recall that you were appointed my lord and master!"

"What in the devil are you about?" he asked, ignoring her. "Do you truly want more speculation and talk about you than already exists in the village?"

"*What?*" Keira asked, startled. "What have you heard?"

"If you believe for even a moment that tongues are not wagging behind closed doors, you are a fool." He pushed open the wooden door in the fence. "*You* are the one who needs rescue," he added gruffly as he hustled her through the gate.

The coachman moved to come down off his bench, but Declan waved him off. He opened the carriage door, put his hands on Keira's waist and lifted her up, dispensing with the need for the step. He told the coachman to wait for the girl, then followed Keira inside, settling on the bench across from her. He idly stretched his arm across the back of the squabs, and his sprawling legs took up all the available legroom in the carriage. He stared at her in a very disapproving manner.

"*Well?*" Keira asked, leaning forward, ignoring his dark look.

"Well what?"

"You know very well what." Keira shifted her legs and her skirts to avoid touching his large, treelike legs. "Did he know of Mr. Scott's acquaintances?"

A sudden and devilishly wicked smile changed Declan's mien. "If you want to hear what that windbag told me, you will seduce it from my lips."

Keira sighed with exasperation . . . but her gaze fell to his enticing mouth.

"*Nicely,*" he said.

She snorted.

One of Declan's thick brows rose above the other. "Ask me nicely . . . just here," he said, and touched a finger to his mouth.

That was the last thing she would do. The very last thing, no matter how sorely tempted she was to taste his lips again. Oh, but that memory had lingered these last few days! She found herself fantasizing about it when she ought to have been thinking about other things, secretly wondering where that kiss might have led had he not been so angry. Ridiculous. She hadn't yet gone *completely* mad. Desire was one thing. Creating scandal with Declan O'Conner was quite another. Had she not promised herself, after becoming Lily, that she would, for once in her bloody life, do the right thing?

"A kiss, Keira," Declan said silkily. "That is the price."

She frowned at the hungry way he looked at her, the confident hint of a smile. *At that mouth.* "For all your talk of my foolishness, you have no decency, sir. You are the sort to extort a woman's virtue from her."

He chuckled and caught her hand. "I am the sort who likes to give pleasure to women," he said, and lazily kissed her palm. "There is a marked difference."

Keira sucked in a shallow breath.

"It's only a kiss," he said lightly. "Your virtue will be

left quite intact . . . unless you ask me with a *please* and a *thank-you* to take it from you."

Keira tried to pull her hand back, but he held it tight. A delicious little shiver raced down her spine. "Are you not the least bothered that you are known as a rogue in every inch of this kingdom and in Ireland?" she asked.

"No."

"I don't want to kiss you, Donnelly," she said. "We don't care for one another, you may recall. Why on earth would I kiss you?" She had to look away from those eyes; there was something far too knowing in them. "I want only your help with this very delicate matter."

He laced his fingers with hers and nudged her with his knee. "Then where is my letter? As I see it, you have only a pair of possibilities if you want to know what I have learned. Either you have the letter to exchange for it, or you give a kiss for it. But the information is not free."

"Bloody, bloody rooster," she whispered incredulously.

Declan laughed low like the rake that he was. "Mere words. I've been called far worse. Where is the letter?"

Keira lifted her chin slightly, and his grip of her fingers tightened. "I've not had proper time—"

"Of course not."

"I've been quite busy!" she insisted, trying to pull her hand free of his once more.

"Aye, opening mills. And yet, it is a feeble excuse." He tugged more forcibly.

"This is extortion," she reminded him, and braced herself with one hand against his chest, for somehow, he had, effortlessly, managed to pull her across the coach to the point that she was practically lying across his lap.

"Call it what you like." His gaze was on her mouth. "But if you want to know the name of Mr. Scott's closest acquaintance, you will kiss me now, before your little sentry returns to save you. If you don't kiss me, I will not tell you, and you will have to bloody well ask the windbag yourself."

Keira wanted to hate him with everything in her being, but she had never felt such potent desire as she did when he calmly delivered his demand, looking at her as if she were water to a dying man. It was impossible to reconcile her voracious desire with the decorum she owed Lily while parading about as her. Not to mention what she owed herself, or her vow to do the right thing, to avoid scandal at all costs.

But she had also made a vow to experience life, to know excitement and daring while she was able. She'd not compromise her virtue for it . . . would she?

Declan, that devil, could see her debate and smiled as if he found it amusing.

"Lady Ashwood!"

Lucy's shout from outside the carriage was enough to decide Keira in the space of a single moment.

She kissed him.

It was meant to be a short peck on the lips, an appeasement—but Declan's ironclad arm went around her back, holding her there as he lazily explored her lips while Lucy banged on the carriage door. Keira struggled against him; he nipped her bottom lip, brushed his palm against her breast, then slowly let her go.

Keira fell breathlessly onto her bench. Declan looked damnably relaxed, but his blue gaze was piercing hers.

Her hat, she noticed, was askew. She had only just righted it when the coachman opened the door and Lucy peered inside.

"Come in, darling," Keira said.

Lucy slowly climbed up and took a seat next to Keira, eyeing Declan warily.

"Hollingbroke," Declan said.

Keira, who was feeling the warmth in her cheeks, looked at Declan. "Pardon?"

"Mr. Edward Hollingbroke was Mr. Scott's oldest and perhaps dearest acquaintance." He smiled a little smugly.

"Oh. The vicar remembered, then, did he?" she asked indifferently, and smiled at Lucy, who was still watching Declan. What a clever girl, Keira thought; she clearly sensed a rake and a reprobate.

"He recalled in excruciating detail," Declan said, and knocked on the carriage wall to signal the driver. "I know all there is to know of Mr. Hollingbroke, from his humble beginnings to his humble occupation today. He lives on the river's edge a mile or two outside the village. He keeps to himself, according to the vicar."

"How interesting," Keira said carefully. "When shall you call on him?"

Declan smiled. "Not me. You. Mr. Hollingbroke is a tenant of Ashwood."

"I should think he would be much better persuaded if *you* asked him, my lord."

"Ah well," Declan said, and shrugged. "You will have to work to convince me of that." And he winked at her, right in front of Lucy.

Keira wisely said nothing, and ignored the playful

nudge of Declan's foot as they rolled along the road back to the village. She engaged Lucy in conversation until they reached the village green. When the carriage halted, Declan opened the carriage door and stepped out.

"Good day, Miss Taft."

"Good day, milord," Lucy said politely. "I hope you are in good health again soon."

Surprised, Declan gave her a puzzled look, but Keira signaled the coachman to shut the carriage door before he could say anything.

Twelve

I shall never understand why things have been left to ruin, Mr. Fish," Keira said one afternoon as they reviewed the books.

"I cannot rightly say, madam. I was not employed with the Ashwood estate until after the earl passed, but I understand that he developed a dislike for spending any money in his last years. We at Ashwood are blessed that you seem determined to see it brought back to life."

She thought of Lily. It seemed with every pound spent on Ashwood, the more anxious Keira felt. She never dreamed of the expense required to keep an estate like Ashwood in operation. *Lily will be here by month's end.* She kept telling herself that. "Isn't it odd," she said idly, "that both Lord and Lady Ashwood drowned?"

"Quite," Mr. Fish agreed.

"What happened to the earl, exactly?" she asked.

"He'd gone out to fish," Mr. Fish said. "And he never returned. I understand the river had been swollen with recent rains, and though they never found his body, they retrieved his mangled pole and his hat, which had snagged on debris downriver. Most here believe that likely he leaned in to take a fish off the hook and fell in. The water was simply running too swiftly for him to extricate himself before he drowned. I was brought on shortly thereafter to see after the finances."

"That is when you sent for Lily," Keira said idly.

"Pardon?"

Keira almost choked at her gaffe. She laughed. "When you sent for me, Mr. Fish."

"Yes, madam."

"I would that I had come two years ago, before things turned as dire as they seem to have done."

"As to that . . . I still believe it is prudent to increase rents," Mr. Fish said.

Keira smiled and shook her head. "You are very tenacious, sir. But I ask you, how will our tenants pay increased rents?"

"They must produce more," he said.

"Is it as easy as that?" she asked, looking up at him. "I don't see how they can simply produce more without a bit of planning. We will rely on the mill. If that should show signs of being profitable, we might build a granary."

"A granary," Mr. Fish echoed dubiously.

"I don't mean to imply straightaway. But if others use our mill, and we find it a profitable endeavor, then why should we not offer a place for them to store their grains, as well?"

"We've not even finished the construction on the old mill. Perhaps we should—"

They were interrupted by the appearance of Linford. "Beg your pardon, madam. Mr. Sibley is calling."

Keira rose from her seat at the desk as Mr. Sibley strode in. "Mr. Sibley," she said, and extended her hand.

He smiled broadly and strode across the room to take it. "Lady Ashwood. How very well you look."

"Thank you."

"Sibley, what brings you to Ashwood today?" Mr. Fish asked.

"Ah," he said, and smiled. "I regret that I must be the one to relay this message, my lady, but Count Eberlin has asked that I advise you that as no agreement concerning the acreage has been reached, he has no alternative open to him other than to bring suit for it."

Keira gasped and looked at a stunned Mr. Fish.

"I do beg your pardon," Mr. Sibley said, wincing unhappily.

It was the worst news. Keira had no idea how these things worked, but she was fairly certain defending a suit against Ashwood would deplete their fragile reserve of funds. She frantically thought of what to do, of what to say.

An idea came to her. She could see from the way that Mr. Sibley was looking at her that he was smitten. She hoped that Mr. Sibley's esteem for her might slow the demise at least until Lily returned. She stepped closer to Sibley. "I don't entirely understand," she said in her softest voice. "Why does the count wish to sue me? It hardly seems an amicable way to resolve our differences."

"He believes he has no choice, madam," Mr. Sibley said. For a brief moment, he allowed his gaze to flick over her. "You have made it plain that you do not agree with his interpretation of the original deed and the specifics of the entail. He seeks to have the land surveyed and the boundaries properly established."

"The boundaries bought and paid for, you mean to say," Mr. Fish said with a derisive snort. "The count's interpretation is incorrect, Mr. Sibley. You yourself agreed that his interpretation seemed incorrect."

"I said it seemed," Mr. Sibley said pleasantly, his gaze still on Keira. "But then again, others disagree. If you are indeed correct, you need not fear his petition."

"I do not fear his petition," Keira said quietly. "I fear that your count seeks to ruin me." She took another step closer to Sibley. "Why would he want to do that?"

Mr. Sibley chuckled as if she were a precocious child. "Madam, nothing could be further from the truth. He hopes to be a good and trustworthy neighbor to you when the renovations to Tiber Park are complete."

"Does he, indeed? You realize, do you not, that I will be forced to increase rents?"

Mr. Sibley at least had the decency to look a bit uncomfortable. "Perhaps if you were to offer a compromise," he suggested.

"A compromise!" she said, as if that were the best idea one might have, and eyed him shrewdly.

"If you would be so kind as to allow Lady Ashwood and myself to confer," Mr. Fish said.

"Naturally. Take whatever time you need. I shall call at another time," he said, and with a nod, he quit the room.

When the door had shut behind him, Keira whirled around to Mr. Fish. *"Augh!"* she cried angrily. "This . . . this *Dane* is making this impossible. He will force me to increase the rents! What of Mrs. Hough? And the Moncrieffs? Little Bill Moncreiff is very ill, do you know?"

"I think it is in the best interests of Ashwood if we

prepare a settlement and present it to him," Mr. Fish suggested.

"What sort of settlement?"

"A financial settlement, whereby Eberlin pays a fair value for the land."

Keira couldn't imagine that they would ever agree to a sum that would replace the lost income from that acreage. "No," she said, shaking her head. "We need a solicitor, Mr. Fish, one who knows everything there is to know about entails and such."

"I agree. However, you will not find that expertise in Hadley Green. We must look in London for it. And if I may be indelicate, we need money for a good solicitor."

"Money, aye, we need money," she said thoughtfully. "Wait here a moment, if you please."

Keira left Mr. Fish and hurried up to her suite of rooms. At the vanity, she opened the top drawer and pulled out a small velvet jewelry box. She sorted through the jewelry contained within it, and withdrew a diamond and emerald brooch. Her father had presented it to her at Lisdoon on the occasion of her twenty-first birthday. Keira would never forget it—the sun was sitting low on the horizon, and the candles had just been lit. She was wearing her favorite blue silk, feeling smartly attired. Her father had leaned over her, kissed the top of her head, and said, "You are the glitter in this old man's eyes, *muirnín*. The happiest of birthdays." He'd presented her with the brooch and Keira had gasped at it. Molly and Mabe and Lily had crowded around her as she held it up to the light.

She loved the brooch. She wore it with all her gowns. She wore it pinned to her wraps to keep the ends from falling, she pinned it to her décolletage on her evening gowns, she had even worn it on a chain to complement a day gown.

It was perhaps her most treasured possession. But it was just a possession. It wasn't a home, like Hannah Hough stood to lose. It wasn't a livelihood as several of her tenants might lose if she lost the acreage.

And it would fetch a nice sum in London.

When she returned to the study, Mr. Fish was standing at the desk. She wordlessly handed him the brooch, and Mr. Fish's eyes rounded. "Madam, this is exquisite. You don't mean to sell it—"

"I do, indeed, Mr. Fish. We need the best solicitor you can find."

The poor man looked dumbfounded. Keira pressed the brooch into his hand and closed his fingers around it. "Now that is settled, shall we go and have a look at the mill? I should like to see what progress they have made," she said, and turned away from Mr. Fish and her brooch.

It was best not to think of it or her family. It was best to think of all that needed to be done.

Thirteen

It was a week before Declan saw Keira again—a full week in which, thankfully, he'd managed to find his footing.

That had been no easy task, for that little devil had managed to lodge herself quite firmly under his skin. He hadn't realized quite how well she'd done it until he'd made the mistake of calling on Penny. In the course of that call, Declan had made a blunder so large that he feared he'd never recover. What he did had never happened in all his life and he hoped to God never would again: He'd said Keira's name as he and Penny had tossed about the sack.

Not that he could really call it tossing about. Bloody hell, it had been a day of new experiences for him in more ways than one, for neither could he . . . toss.

He tried to explain to Penny, but as usual, Penny was quite sanguine about it. "No need to explain, milord," she'd said cheerfully. "It always comes to an end, eh?"

Yes, it always came to an end, but not like that.

The afternoon with Penny had left him feeling quite out of sorts in many ways, not the least of which was his unending uncertainty as to *why* it had happened. He was a robust man—astonishingly robust, thank you—who tended to live in the moment, particularly when it came to women. Certainly he was not in the habit of making love to one woman and thinking of another. Especially *her*, of all the blessed women on this earth.

Declan didn't know what was wrong with him, but he could not seem to shake Keira from his thoughts. He could see her smiling, could hear her laughing. He recalled the way she had of speaking so earnestly about the smallest thing, and her obvious fondness for the foundling she had taken under her wing.

If that wasn't bad enough, he could still feel her small breasts in his hand. And that kiss . . . God help him, she was obviously inexperienced but so bloody eager. It had incited him like a green lad.

So Declan had busied himself with his horses and managed to put Keira out of his mind. He'd brought in Mr. Evans, a renowned farrier, to give his expert opinion on a chestnut's hooves, which Declan suspected were beginning to founder. That could render the horse lame and, at the very least, incapable of racing. He'd mated him with a sorrel mare, the offspring of one of the best racers Declan had ever seen.

They were examining the horse in a meadow. Mr. Evans had the horse's hoof in his lap. "Could very well be foundering," he agreed, and dropped the hoof and straightened up. But instead of speaking about the horse, the man looked past Declan and nodded to something in the distance. "Now that's a beauty, eh, milord?"

Declan followed Mr. Evan's gaze and watched a coach roll to a stop on the road. He didn't know if he'd call the Ashwood coach a beauty, but it was always conspicuous, given the reigning countess's penchant for plumage. With that disastrous afternoon romp with Penny still fresh on his mind and still capable of bringing the prickly warmth of humility to Declan's neck, he said simply, "Pardon me," and began striding toward the coach.

A footman leaped off the back runner and opened the door as Declan strode forward. A parasol appeared in the carriage opening first, popping open into a bright yellow orb that bobbed and weaved as the bearer stepped out of the carriage. It suddenly swung up and over Keira's head, like her own personal sun. She smiled and waved a gloved hand at Declan. She didn't venture far into the field, but stood on the edge, twirling her little sun behind her head as he neared her. "Good afternoon, my lord!" she called cheerfully when he reached the road.

Declan halted before her, his suspicious gaze skimming over her as he removed his work gloves. She was wearing a pale yellow day gown with a green and yellow silk wrap heavily embroidered along the hems, which hung loosely from her arms. Around her neck was a gold cross that dangled above an enticing cleavage. Her hat had a pair of monstrous plumes that dipped and bobbed around her shoulder on a breeze.

She looked, Declan thought, quite ravishing. Like a ripe summer fruit waiting to be plucked and devoured. That he was thinking of summer fruit and Keira in the same moment disturbed him. He unconsciously took a step backward.

"Glorious day, isn't it?" she asked, clearly unruffled by his suspicious gaze.

"What are you doing here? Where is your little chastity belt?"

"I suppose by that remark you mean Lucy Taft. She is at Ashwood today, partaking in her first music lesson. And by the by, I am not *here*," she said, gesturing to the field. "I did not come this way to see *you*. I am on my way to the village." She smiled.

He frowned. "Why do I not believe you?"

"Because you are entirely too suspicious of mankind, Declan. Really, I just happened to see you with your horse and I thought to be courteous. You may ask Louis if you doubt me," she added, gesturing loosely to the footman, who was unaware that he was being called into duty, as he was standing just below the rotund coachman, having a chat.

"Pardon my skepticism, but things are rarely as simple as you'd have me believe," Declan reminded her. "I am waiting uneasily now for the truth to come tumbling from your lovely lips."

"You're far too stiff, Declan."

"Stiff."

"Unyielding. Humorless, as it were. Quite an old fossil—".

"I get your point," he said wryly.

She smiled again and looked past him, over his shoulder. "What is wrong with your horse?"

"He's foundering."

"That sounds perfectly wretched. Is it?"

"You did not stop on the side of the road to inquire after my horse," he said. "Perhaps you should just say what it is you want."

"Oh! I almost forgot," she said, and reached into the little reticule dangling from her wrist. "I have a letter here for you." She withdrew a folded vellum and held it out to him.

Declan took it. "You just happened to see me in this field, and you just happened to have a letter for me, aye? I think the truth is beginning to emerge."

Keira sniffed and looked away.

The letter was addressed to Madame Broussard of the Institut Villa Amiels. He glanced at Keira again. "It is not sealed."

"Isn't it?" she asked, feigning innocence as she leaned over to look. "I must have forgotten."

Declan unfolded the vellum and read it. It was a beautiful letter, a ringing endorsement of Eireanne and a pledge on her behalf.

"Naturally, I had a duplicate sent to the school's greatest benefactor, Mr. Forgionne," Keira added as Declan perused the letter. "He was always rather fond of me. I asked if he would expedite a decision so Eireanne might avoid languishing at Ballynaheath all winter."

Declan slowly folded the letter. It was what he needed for his sister, the thing that might free her from his reputation. "Thank you," he said, and glanced up at Keira. "May I ask, why now?"

"I gave you my word," she said, and smiled sunnily. Declan gazed skeptically at her. "Will you not believe me?" she asked. He shook his head. Keira sighed. "All right. I am in need of your help again."

"I am astonished."

With a roll of her eyes she said, "There is no call for theatrics, Declan. Is it so impossible to believe that I can be your friend and need your help at the same time?"

"Yes."

"Scoff if you like, but we are not animals, sir. We are

humans and capable of many complex yet compatible feelings."

He laughed. How could one woman be so vexing and damnably attractive at once? "Is that the sort of nonsense they are teaching young ladies in private schools these days?"

"Now you sound like my father. It is quite evident to me that men are very plain in their desires and wants and require a bit of practice in cultivating friendships that bear more sophistication than a handshake and a wager."

Now Declan laughed outright, drawing the attention of Keira's men. "I don't need practice, *muirnín*," he said. "I daresay I could teach you a thing or two about compatible and complex feelings," he added, his gaze sliding from her mouth to the small gold cross at her bosom. He could feel the magnet between them, drawing on their heat, pulling them together, and moved closer. "Ask me nicely and I will teach you how to be worthy of Maloney's interminable wait."

She cocked her head to one side to consider him. "I suppose you could, but you won't, will you, for we will never be as much as friends to one another."

"Don't be so certain of that," he said softly. "I've heard tell that my powers of persuasion with women can be rather daunting."

She laughed, but her skin was beginning to flush under his scrutiny. "Perhaps I might persuade you to call on Mr. Hollingbroke instead."

God help him, but he wanted to touch her, to kiss the patch of flushed skin at the hollow of her throat; to see her sleek and naked beneath him. He didn't want to think of Hollingbroke at the moment. "I told you—call on him yourself."

"I did," she said. "I did exactly as you suggested. I asked Mr. Fish where I might find him, and I paid him a call. I even had a perfectly good reason to call, as he has fallen behind in his rent. But he was wretched to me."

"Wretched?"

"He wouldn't come out of his cottage, so I went inside, as he suggested. I was very pleasant, and I didn't even inquire after the rent, but he made it very plain he did not wish to see me, that he found me repugnant and loathsome—"

That tweaked something inside Declan. "Pardon?"

"He said horrible things about me—I mean, about Lily," she added with a slight shake of her head. "He's a hidebound old man, Declan. He said he didn't care if I evicted him, that I'd not find another tenant who would eke as much as a farthing more than he had out of the land, that I was a woman and he'd not speak to a woman about rents and such, and that I had ruined enough lives."

Declan was surprisingly annoyed with Hollingbroke, no matter how right the old man might have been. "Wasn't there anyone with you to defend you? Fish? Your footman?"

"Louis was with me and he did tell Mr. Hollingbroke he was not to speak to me thus, but Declan, I understood him completely. He was indignant for the loss of his friend and thinks that I caused his death. He believes his friend was innocent and wrongly accused, and that I am the one who wrongly accused Mr. Scott. Lily, that is."

"I think it more likely that he is a curmudgeon who has lost his sense of propriety," Declan said. "I'll speak with him."

"Will you?" she asked, her green eyes lighting.

He instantly regretted his words, for Keira's face was at once a lovely wreath of smiles, and he was beginning to fear what he might do for that smile. "I said I would," he said gruffly. He stuffed her letter on Eireanne's behalf in his coat pocket.

"Thank you, Declan," she said gratefully. "When shall we call on him?"

"Not we. Me. I shall pay him a call," he said, throwing up a hand to stop the onslaught of questions he knew would follow.

As he might have predicted, she ignored his hand. "But when? What if . . . what if you were to call on Mr. Hollingbroke on the morrow, and then you could come to Ashwood to buy the horse you liked? Perhaps I was a wee bit hasty in refusing to sell it."

He snorted. "Contrary, you mean to say."

"Come now, when will you call on Mr. Hollingbroke?"

Her eyes were shining. Declan had an insane desire to put his face in her neck and inhale her scent. Keira's smile deepened. She knew, she bloody well knew in that way women had of knowing such things, exactly what effect she was having on him. She was manipulating him, twisting him around like her parasol, and that vexed Declan to no end. "When I have time, I cannot say," he said curtly, and turned away from her, marching back across the field to his horse and farrier.

"Thank you, Lord Donnelly! Oh, and good luck with your horse!" she called after him.

Good luck with his horse? Good luck with his foolish heart.

Fourteen

Mr. Hollingbroke would not come out of his cottage for Declan, either.

With one shoulder propped against the door frame, his arms crossed over his chest, and his hat pulled low over his eyes, Declan sighed impatiently. "Come then, sir, what have you to lose by receiving me?" he called through the weathered wooden door.

"What have I to gain?" Mr. Hollingbroke shouted in return.

It was an excellent question. "Perhaps I can help you out of your predicament," Declan suggested. "It is no secret you are in arrears, sir. Perhaps I can help you find a way to satisfy that debt."

"What's that? You propose to pay the arrears for me?"

Declan wasn't really proposing that at all, but at this point, he thought he'd do just about anything to have this over and done with. "I reckon you won't know until you open this door, aye?"

He heard nothing for one long moment, and had reached the end of his patience. But just as he turned to leave, he heard the scrape of a chair on wooden flooring followed by the uneven gait of someone walking across the room. The door swung open. "Come in."

Mr. Hollingbroke, a stoop-shouldered man, had dirty gray hair and a dirtier, grayer, untrimmed beard. Keira had failed to mention how unkempt the old man was.

Declan ducked his head and stepped across the threshold, pausing a moment so that his eyes could adjust to the darkness and his lungs to the stench of unwashed flesh that permeated the small, two-roomed cottage. "I've cultivated this land nigh on forty years, and ain't never had so many to call," the man said as he walked unevenly toward the hearth. "Now, who the bloody hell are you?"

"Lord Donnelly," Declan responded, extending his hand across the scarred wooden table that separated them.

"Ach," the old man said, waving away Declan's out-stretched hand. "That won't help you. I don't give a damn if you're a lord or a rat catcher."

"Very cordial of you," Declan said dryly, and lowered his hand.

"I didn't invite you here," the old man reproached him. "What are you, the countess's man?"

Declan tried not to bristle at the suggestion. "I have come because I think you might have information I seek." He pulled a small leather pouch from his pocket and tossed it on the wooden table between them. "There should be enough there to satisfy your debt to Ashwood." And then some, Declan reckoned.

Hollingbroke merely glared at the purse. He picked up a jug and poured a dark brown liquid into a tin cup. "That's my private business you've stuck your nose into," he said, and sat on a wooden chair next to the hearth without touching the purse.

"I've not stuck my nose into your private affairs; I couldn't possibly care if you pay your rent or not. I mean only to offer you a deal of sorts—your rents paid in exchange for some information about Mr. Joseph Scott."

Hollingbroke stilled. Then slammed the tin cup on the table. "Did *she* send you?" he demanded. "Is this something to do with her?"

"Who?" Declan asked, momentarily confused.

"The countess, you bloody fool!" the old man shouted. "She come round like she's to do me a favor. She don't even recognize me! She used to ride up here with the countess on her pony and now she pretends as if she never laid eyes on me. She sent you here!"

Declan did not confirm or deny it.

"I don't know you," Hollingbroke said, his eyes narrowing. "Why'd I want to tell you a damn thing?"

Declan was not a man who found it easy to lie, but he had a strange sense of having been in this room, in this conversation before. *Have you seen the girls?* His gut clenched. "Let us say that I am an interested party," he said. "You have a debt you cannot pay as well as information I would like to have."

"Interested party!" he spat. "What, then, she has a noose around your neck, too?"

"Pardon?"

"That woman put a noose around the neck of the only man I ever called friend. She *wronged* him. She wronged us all! And now she comes rolling up in her grand carriage as if she never knew me, as if she never saw my face! You can throw all your coins at me, milord, and it won't make a bit of difference. She won't find another man who can eke out as much as another pence than what I've done on this poor patch of land. The acreage drains poorly. Can't grow more than a bit of grain on it, and what I do grow, the bloody cows graze!"

"Why do you say she put a noose around your friend's neck?" Declan asked. "Did he not put that noose around his own neck by stealing priceless jewels?"

Hollingbroke seemed taken aback a moment. He suddenly pushed to his feet with a snort of indignation. "I won't discuss that with you."

"I suppose you believe he didn't commit the crime because he was Lady Ashwood's lover," Declan said bluntly.

Hollingbroke suddenly came around the table, advancing on Declan with his fist around his tin cup. "I don't know who you are, but you will not sully that man's name any more than she's already done! Joseph Scott was a decent man, on that I would stake my very life! He was not a thief, yet his family has been made to suffer because of her careless accusations. I won't allow you to add to it, by God I won't."

Hollingbroke spoke so adamantly, so passionately, that Declan couldn't help but feel doubt. He eyed the old man, his tattered coat and worn trousers, his grimy neckcloth. "How can you be so certain?" he demanded.

"To hell with you," Hollingbroke said, and turned.

Declan stopped him with a hand to his arm. "If you truly want to see his good name restored, you will tell me. How can you be so certain he did not steal those jewels?"

"Because he was here the night he was supposed to

have stolen them. He had eggs. Eggs! Can you believe it? A thief with priceless jewels under his belt, pausing at this old cottage to bring me eggs from his own coop? He sat in that very chair and discussed the weather, when the rain might let up. Ah yes, I can see your skepticism. You people, think you're so above us all, eh? I had an ulcer on my foot, sir. I couldn't walk for a time. Mr. Scott would come here after his own day of work and till my land. He brought me food from his own larder. He was a Christian man, sir. He did not steal those jewels. If he had, he would not have come here bearing bloody *eggs*."

The eggs didn't prove or disprove anything, nor did Hollingbroke's claims that he was a fine man—he may very well have been engaging in an affair outside the bounds of his marriage, after all. But Declan agreed that Hollingbroke had a point. Wouldn't Scott have been more concerned with hiding the jewels and creating an alibi than delivering eggs? "Did you offer this at his trial?" he asked curiously.

Hollingbroke's expression turned more sour. "I did. And I was laughed at. Your kind, down from London, laughing at the eggs."

Declan could imagine it—this unkempt man, speaking about eggs, and how amusing people of the Quality would find it. Still, Declan was not convinced. "Did Mr. Scott not offer a vigorous defense? Where else was he that evening?"

"He was here for a time," Mr. Hollingbroke said. "And he said so at his trial. But he'd say no more of that night."

"Whyever not?"

Mr. Hollingbroke smiled sourly. "Because he wasn't at

his hearth with his wife and children, sir. You're a chivalrous gentleman—you might guess why he'd not speak. It wouldn't have mattered if he had. On my word, that wretched girl could point her finger at anyone and they'd have believed her lies and fantasies. She sent an innocent man to the gallows, yet she sleeps easy at night."

"I wouldn't know how she sleeps," Declan said. "Is there anyone else who believes as you do?"

Hollingbroke laughed, revealing a pair of missing teeth. "They *all* believe as I do. But they wouldn't admit it at the time, for they feared their own necks, they did."

"Why would they fear their necks? Who were they afraid of?" Declan asked.

Mr. Hollingbroke's smile faded. "Whoever would allow an innocent man to hang."

"Who?" Declan asked again, and Mr. Hollingbroke shrugged. "Come now," Declan said impatiently. "It was fifteen years ago. Surely no one fears telling the truth now, aye?"

"It's not their necks they fear now, sir. It is their shame."

"Shame?"

"For having let an innocent man meet his death. And that's all I'll say on the matter," Hollingbroke said, and sat heavily onto his chair.

"Thank you, sir," Declan said, and opened the door.

"You forgot your coin," Hollingbroke said. "I won't take it for attesting to Scott's honor."

"Then take it to pay your debt," Declan said, and walked out before the old man could stop him.

Fifteen

Keira was a wee bit unwell. She was beginning to stagger under the weight of her deceit, the enormity of it fraying her at the edges. There were days like today that she wondered if being married to Mr. Maloney wouldn't be preferable to the ever-present anxiety she felt.

Earlier that day, the Society ladies had come to call with Mrs. Lorquette and her infant daughter. Mrs. Lorquette wanted the honor of naming her baby Lily, and requested that Keira attend the baby's christening. "I'd be right honored if my baby carried your name, mu'um," Mrs. Lorquette had gushed.

Naturally, Keira had not wanted to refuse the ladies, but she could scarcely look at that beautiful infant without feeling ill. She knew instantly that if she agreed to their request, Mrs. Lorquette could never look at her baby in the same way when the truth came out.

Keira made up an excuse. "By all means, you must use the name if you like," she'd said. "But I fear I will be away from Ashwood that Sunday."

"We could move it," Mrs. Lorquette suggested. "Shall we say the following Sunday?"

"Ah . . . I think that is rather inconvenient, as well," Keira had said with a wince.

The ladies were very disappointed, Mrs. Lorquette seemed hurt, and Keira had moped about since they'd gone. The gravity of what she'd done by assuming Lily's identity beat dully at her temples. She slept poorly, trying to think her way out of her quagmire.

She was furious with herself. Disappointed. How reckless she'd been to do it! Up until this colossal mistake, she'd not appreciated how carefree and simple her life had been. Perhaps it had been *too* simple, as she could not have imagined the responsibilities of a true countess before pretending to be one. Was this what adventure felt like? Was this the feeling of living?

She should have told Lily she could not possibly do as she asked, and gone to Italy with Mrs. Canavan. What in heaven did she think would happen when she came here? How could she not have understood that lies would build upon lies and hurt people? Now she had created a mess so vast and so deep, she didn't know how or even if she could extricate herself from it without harming Lily. Much less herself. Much less little Lily Anna Lorquette. Much, much less Mr. Loman Maloney. He would be appalled if he knew what she'd done here.

Four and twenty years now, and Keira was really not improved over the silly, foolish girl who had kissed Lord Donnelly that sunny Irish afternoon.

The whole thing left Keira determined to end this charade. She didn't know precisely how she would do it, but she would, before anyone else was harmed.

How to end it was weighing on her mind in the green salon that afternoon. She sat staring out the window surrounded by flowers from men who admired her. Lucy was hard at work, sketching flowers in a vase. The girl's talent for art needed much improvement.

"Won't you look?" Lucy asked.

"Hmmm?" Keira asked, looking up. Lucy had turned her easel so that Keira could see her efforts. "I beg your pardon. I've been thinking."

"About what?" Lucy asked curiously.

"About . . . about when I shall be able to return to Ireland," Keira answered truthfully.

"Where is Ireland?" Lucy asked.

"Quite far from Ashwood," Keira admitted.

"Across the Irish Sea," a male voice said behind them.

Lucy gasped with surprise; she and Keira both jerked their gazes to the door.

"Good afternoon, Lord Donnelly," Lucy said, managing her best curtsy yet.

"Good afternoon, Miss Taft," Declan responded. He stood in the door with his hands clasped behind his back, a lock of deliciously dark brown hair dipping over one eye. He was dressed for riding, and his trousers, Keira noticed with a rush of heat to her nape, fit him as well as a glove.

Of all the things that had happened of late, her infatuation with that devil of a man was the last sort of complication she needed. She slowly came to her feet.

"Ah, there you are," Declan said. "It was hard to see you among all these flowers. Linford had his hands full, and I assured him you were expecting me."

He strolled into the room, looking around. Looking

magnificent. She could not recall another man in her life that had the ability to snatch her breath from her as he did, and Keira's witless heart began to beat a little faster. She was suddenly remembering that kiss in the coach and the things he'd said in the meadow while his horse had foundered or flopped, or whatever it was the poor thing was doing. For heaven's sake, Keira could surely conduct a civil conversation with him without imagining all the untoward things she had no business imagining. "Not at all, my lord. Your call is always so . . ."

"Delightful?"

"Unexpected."

He smiled as he walked deeper into the room, pausing to examine Lucy's drawing. "Quite nice, Miss Taft. They are the roses, are they not?"

"No, sir. They are the daffodils and that is a sheep."

"A sheep, is it?" Declan said, looking slightly confused. "Well, you must forgive my lack of an artistic eye, but I admit to being a wee bit confused, what with all the many blessed flowers about."

"Yes, quite a lot come every week," Lucy agreed.

"It would seem all the flowers in England have been cut down because of Lady Ashwood. I imagine there are great swaths of bald land where they once grew."

Lucy giggled.

"Lucy darling," Keira said, and picked up a vase stuffed full of roses. Mr. Anders had indeed gone a wee bit beyond the necessary with his latest offering. "Will you please take these to Mrs. Thorpe? Help her arrange them into different vases. I should like them on every console, and there are quite a lot of them, so you must be patient as you help her."

"Do you mean now?" Lucy asked.

"I do."

Lucy frowned a little. "Yes, mu'um," she said, and reluctantly took the heavy vase from Keira. "I don't know why we must do it. They'll die in the end."

"As we all die in the end, which is why it is very important to live life to the fullest. Thank you, Lucy."

The girl frowned and dipped a curtsy to Declan.

"Good day, Miss Taft," Declan said, and bowed as Lucy, struggling to see over the flowers in the vase, walked past. He turned to Keira when she'd gone. "Did I hear you say you were leaving?" he asked. "Before you have finished creating mayhem and chaos in Hadley Green?"

"My goodness, my lord, you sound almost chagrined," she said with a saucy smile. "I rather thought you'd be pleased."

"I am surprised. You have seemed so determined to remain here and rule over your little kingdom."

"Yes, well, now I am determined to repair the mess I've made and return to Ireland to submit to Mr. Maloney's suit. I shall live quietly as far from society as possible."

He smiled broadly, clearly amused. "Indeed?"

She didn't care for that particular sparkle in his eyes. "Laugh if you will, but you're right about me, Declan. I've caused too much trouble and I vow to never be a bother to anyone again."

He lifted a skeptical brow as he moved toward her. "And what has brought on this sudden change of heart?" he asked, touching her cheek, causing her witless heart to leap. "Have you determined that poor Mr. Maloney has waited long enough?"

Maloney! She certainly didn't want to be reminded of him at present! "No."

"Then perhaps I frighten you," he said, and touched her earlobe. "Perhaps you think that you will succumb to passion and allow me to ravish you, after all."

Keira's face flamed with the truth in that statement. "You flatter yourself. Again."

He smiled a little crookedly and traced a line to her chin. "So how do you intend to repair all the trouble you've caused?"

Keira moved away from the heat of his fingers. "I don't know. I know only that I cannot maintain the lies I've told," she said in all seriousness, and suddenly pressed her fingertips to her temples. "Or the expectations everyone has of me. I never suspected being a countess was so bloody difficult. How do you do it? How do you keep Ballynahcath from consuming you, body and soul?"

He smiled sympathetically, she thought. "I employ excellent men. Tell me . . . has something happened, *muirnin?*"

His question was softly spoken, and Keira had a sudden desire to fling herself into his arms, to have him repair it all for her. Unfortunately, she'd created the mess and only she could put it to rights. "Everything has happened," she said. "It is the gala, which seems to grow bigger and bigger by the day, and I've no idea how I shall pay for it all. And it is Lucy, to whom I am growing quite attached. What will she think of me when she knows the truth? And now, the Society has asked me to attend a christening for a beautiful baby girl with the deepest brown eyes and named for me. She already bears Lily's name, and her mother, her poor dear mother, looked so very hopeful that I would attend her christening and bestow some sort of countess magic on her child," she said with great agitation. "How disappointed she will be to discover my deceit! How will she ever look at her baby and not think of it? And she won't be the only one, will she? I daresay Mrs. Ogle will be bereft and Mrs. Morton not far behind her, as they have made themselves rather indispensable to the countess and her gala—I mean to *me,* of course, but I am not *me,* I am *her,* and I never really intended to be her, especially not the her that would oversee a christening and have a baby named for her, but—but never mind all that," she said, balling one hand into a fist. "It's even worse. This man, this wretched man, wants to steal Ashwood acreage."

"What? How?" Declan asked.

She shook her head. "It is all rather complicated, but he claims that the entail of our most profitable one hundred acres has expired and he has a right to it."

"How does he believe this to be true?" Declan asked.

"Oh, I won't bother you with all the details—the point is that we need a very good solicitor to defend Ashwood from the suit he intends to bring. On my honor, Declan, the state of Ashwood's finances are bad enough without losing any acreage, particularly acreage that is producing."

"I don't understand how he might bring a suit against an Ashwood entail, but I know a solicitor," he said instantly, and took a pencil and paper from the table where Lucy had been painting. "You will not find better in all of London than Mr. Goodwin," he said, jotting something down. He handed her the paper with Mr. Goodwin's name and his address in London.

"Oh," she said, surprised to have her problem resolved so quickly. She looked up and smiled gratefully. "Thank you," she said softly.

Something flickered in Declan's eyes. "I can speak to him if you like," he offered, but Keira instantly shook her head.

"No, thank you, Mr. Fish is well versed on the issue. But Declan, do you not see? For all these reasons, I have come to the conclusion that I must end this travesty and return to Ireland as soon as Lily arrives. It is the only thing I can possibly do after all that I've done."

She expected Declan to say that he'd warned her. But he didn't speak. His stark blue eyes were locked on her, his expression inscrutable. "Have you heard a word I've uttered?" she asked, confused.

"Every last nonsensical one," he assured her.

"Then why do you not speak?" she demanded. "Why do you stand there? This is your opportunity, you know. You may say, 'I told you so, Keira,' or, 'You deserve every bit of your discomfort.'" She whirled away from him. "You should be bringing round a carriage to send me home," she added angrily. "And you'd be right. I deserve every wretched thing."

When Declan didn't speak, she turned around again. "What is the matter with you?"

"I am waiting for you to recall the good you've done. Aye, you should not have gone about it as you have, lass, but that does not change the fact that you have done quite well for Lily. Think of it—you are repairing all that has been left to rot at Ashwood. You have brought attention to the plight of those orphans—what of Miss Taft? Where would that girl be without you? She'd not be painting sheep and daffodils."

Keira shook her head, but Declan touched her arm. "I rode past the mill this morning. There are twenty men working to repair it if there is one. They didn't have that opportunity before you came, Keira. You have done what Lily asked, and I daresay, you've done very well."

As much as Keira wanted to be flattered by his words, she shook her head. "I've only scratched the surface. There is far more to be done."

"You won't accept that you have done good? Then have you forgotten Mr. Scott? Or your aunt's death?"

"No, of course not," she said, and pressed her fingers to her temple again. "I believe he was innocent, Declan. Really, I do. But I've thought long and hard these last few days, and what can be done about it now? The poor man is long dead, and I was foolish to have even brought it up after all these years. Perhaps . . . perhaps Lily need never know."

Declan smiled a bit caustically.

"What would you have me say? Would you have me say you were right again? Very well, you were right, you were *right*."

"Of course I was right," he said, as if that were a foregone conclusion. "Nevertheless, Lily will hear of it in the same manner you have. Do you really want that? I think you are right to tell her all so that she doesn't hear it from strangers. Keira," he said, lacing his fingers in hers, "you are learning things every day. Lily will be here soon enough, and she will appreciate having all the knowledge you will give her. Do it for Lily's sake—she will have enough to endure with the consequences of your deception. Don't add more to her burden than you already have."

Keira could not have been more astonished. "Pardon? I cannot believe my ears, Declan. You've disdained me for it from the moment you saw me here. Now that I want to be truthful, you would have me carry on like this?"

"Honesty would have been my preference, aye. But that was before you let it go for so long. Now you make it impossible to rectify without some sort of criminal charge against you which I fear may be true even with Lily's intervention. And now you've roped me into your scheme and begged me to speak to first the vicar, and then Mr. Hollingbroke. I think we must see it through."

Kate gasped. "You've spoken to Mr. Hollingbroke? What did he say?"

"He said quite a lot, and not much of it something I would repeat in your fair company. But one thing he did avow, and with great animation, was that Mr. Scott was an innocent man."

Keira gaped at him. *It was true!* At last, someone besides herself had said what she knew to be true! But a thought suddenly occurred to Keira, and her eyes narrowed on Declan. "Do I understand that even though I have tried to convince you that Mr. Scott was an innocent man, and you have steadfastly pointed out the error of my thinking, it is the utterings of a deranged old codger with hair coming out of his ears that have caused this sudden change of heart?"

"That is precisely what I am saying. Do you want to hear why?"

"Every word," she said, and sat on the settee.

Declan sat across from her and told Keira everything Mr. Hollingbroke had told him.

As Keira listened to Declan's tale, she could envision it: Mr. Scott riding up to the cottage, a bundle of eggs and perhaps some bread his wife had made. She could see the two men having a tankard of ale, talking about heaven knew what, but passing the hours on that rain-soaked night.

That rain-soaked night.

Keira suddenly shook her head. "Something doesn't make sense," she said. "It was raining that night. Why would Mr. Scott go out in the rain only to deliver eggs? I think Mr. Hollingbroke must remember the wrong evening."

"That is entirely possible," Declan agreed. "But it does not change his rather vociferous belief that Mr. Scott was wrongly accused and wrongly hanged."

"Didn't Mr. Hollingbroke vow it was so during the trial?"

"He did," Declan said. "No one believed him. He's a rather odd little man, after all."

"No one will believe him now," Keira said thoughtfully. This was her moment of vindication, but that notion was erased by the image of Lily Anna Lorquette, and she shook her head. "It is pointless. No one will believe him now." She stood up.

So did Declan. "This isn't a society ball, Keira. You cannot decide to quit simply because you've grown weary of the dancing."

She gave him a withering look. "I am not quitting. I am doing only what I must to keep Ashwood afloat until Lily comes. I can't chase ghosts—Lord knows I've enough to keep me occupied with the gala and the mill, and this wretched suit." She moved, trying to pass him, but Declan caught her arm.

"Let go my arm."

Declan did not let go her arm. Keira tried to escape him, but Declan merely pushed her back against a table and braced his other arm against it, effectively trapping her. "Heed me—I will not allow you to abandon Mr. Scott because it has become uncomfortable for you."

Were it not for his deep blue eyes, Keira would doubt that this was the same man. "What has caused this sudden change in you?" she demanded angrily.

"Lily showed me a great kindness once and I will do the same for her. But moreover, I cannot abide the injustice. I have suffered it myself. I have been wrongly accused of colluding with a sixteen-year-old girl, you may recall. You have turned over this stone, Keira, and now you are going to have to look under it."

"Let me go," Keira demanded. She felt fragile, trapped, so small against his much larger frame, entirely vulnerable to his anger. She felt something else, too, something far more terrifying—a wild shock of pleasure, a thrill so deep that she could scarcely catch her breath. She shoved against him with all her might, but it was like shoving against a tree. He didn't flinch; he certainly didn't move. "You cannot tell me what I will or will not do, Declan!"

His eyes were glittering with determination. "If I cannot appeal to your sense of what is right, then I will force you to do what is right."

She laughed. "Do you believe you can now *force* me to your will?"

"I like to think of it as persuasion," he said with a wicked hint of a smile, and leaned closer to her, forcing her to bend back.

Her pulse was racing dangerously now. "I could scream and the entire house would come down around us. Is that what you want?"

"I want something far more pleasurable," he said, his gaze falling to her lips. "But I will settle for your word."

Keira's face flamed. "*Barbarian,*" she murmured breathlessly.

"If that's the way you'd like it." His gaze was blistering now, inciting her. She felt the hard pulse of ravenous, consuming desire. "I've seen the way you look at me," he murmured. "I know what thoughts clutter that pretty head of yours. You desire me, Keira. You want to feel me between your legs. You *want* me and you are not afraid to let it be known." He put his hand on the small of her back and pressed her backward against the table at the same moment his mouth descended on hers.

Keira made a cry of protest into his mouth. She shoved with both hands against his chest, but Declan grabbed her wrist and easily held it. He was kissing her so thoroughly, so expertly, that her deep desire began to boil. *He is right, so right.*

Declan's hand found her face, his fingers splaying against her jaw, holding her still as he ravaged her lips and mouth. She could feel his arousal pressed against her, could feel the tide of pleasure surging inside her. Pruning scissors toppled off the table, followed by Lily's pencils. She couldn't seem to find the strength to turn her head from his. She was hopelessly lost in smoky arousal and scorching want and didn't trust herself in the least with her own virtue.

Declan made a rough sound deep in his throat, the sound of raw pleasure.

Every lesson, every caution flew out of Keira's head; she eagerly met his tongue, mingled her breath with his, pressed boldly against the evidence of his arousal. His scent—spicy and masculine—spread fire through her veins. When he cupped her face and deepened his kiss, Keira arched against his body, slipped her hands around his waist. Declan responded with another groan and pushed between her thighs.

The pleasure of that kiss, the erotic scent and taste of a virile, robust man, was Keira's undoing. Declan's hand found her breast, his fingers dipping into the bodice of her gown, grazing her skin, sliding over her nipple, and Keira feared she would collapse with want, and worse, would willingly, eagerly, give herself to him.

He dipped down to kiss the swell of her breast above her bodice and she gasped with delight and braced herself against the table. She felt her body softening, spreading, making room for him. His hands drifted down her body and to her hips, squeezing them, pulling her into his body, and pushing back against her with his. Erotic desire became an erotic ache. Her body responded dangerously—she did want to feel him inside her, to feel all the things that would ruin her completely.

Keira might have been ruined that bright afternoon had she not heard voices in the hallway. She gasped, caught his head in her hands and pushed him back.

"Madam?" she heard Mrs. Thorpe say.

"Ignore her," Declan murmured, nipping at her lips.

But Mrs. Thorpe and Lucy were coming, and Keira pushed Declan away and stumbled from the table, dipping down for the pruning scissors and pencils as she went, brushing her hand nervously across her bodice.

Declan stepped behind her, his hands going around her waist, his mouth on her neck. "Come with me to the lodge," he whispered. "Come now. Don't tarry, don't hesitate—"

"*A Dhia dhílis!*" she softly exclaimed, and pushed his hands from her, stepping away, putting as much space as she could between them. She glanced over her shoulder at him, saw the desire swimming in his eyes, the bulge in his trousers. She couldn't speak, couldn't say the things she wanted to say—

"There you are!" Mrs. Thorpe said, appearing in the doorway.

Declan turned away. Keira clutched the shears and the pencils. "Yes! Here I am, Mrs. Thorpe."

"Lucy said his lordship had come. So has Mrs. Ogle, madam," Mrs. Thorpe said. "Shall I bring tea?"

Declan made a sound of disdain; Keira stepped forward. "Has she?"

"Good day, Lady Ashwood." Mrs. Ogle walked into the room behind Mrs. Thorpe.

"Mrs. Ogle! What . . . a surprise," Keira said. Judging by the shocked look on Mrs. Ogle's face, the woman was not oblivious to what had happened in this room only moments earlier, and Keira self-consciously brushed her fingers against her cheek, seeking in vain to brush away the evidence of her desire from her face.

Mrs. Ogle's gaze flicked between Keira and Declan, who turned partially toward her and gave her a curt nod. "I hope I am not intruding," Mrs. Ogle said.

"Yes," Declan responded at the same moment Keira said, "*No!* Not at all, Mrs. Ogle," she said. "Do come in. Yes, Mrs. Thorpe, we should like some tea."

"I really don't want to intrude," Mrs. Ogle said, peering at Declan, her smile thin and suspicious.

"Not at all," Keira assured her. "Lord Donnelly was just leaving."

Declan looked at Keira as if he expected her to send Mrs. Ogle on her way so that they might continue their passionate encounter. Keira very much wanted to do that, but put down her shears and pencils and steered the woman to a seat on the settee. "Keira—"

"Lord Donnelly!" she said with a frantic little laugh, stopping him before he said anything too revealing. "The flowers are truly beautiful. Thank you for coming," she trilled, and smiled sweetly, willing him to go.

He must have read her message, for he slowly bowed and walked out, but not without giving her a very dark and heated look.

Sixteen

Grayson Christopher, the Duke of Darlington—better known as Christie to his family and friends—was surprised when Declan appeared at Darlington House in London. Granted, Declan was known for disappearing from time to time, but he rarely appeared without sending word.

When he did appear at Christie's doorstep, it was in the middle of a summer storm. He was wet and bedraggled, and apologized for appearing so unexpectedly before asking Christie if he had any of the good Irish whiskey Declan had given him during a previous visit.

Of course Christie did, and he and Declan sat in his study—Christie's charming wife, Kate, and his infant daughter Allison had retired. Christie chatted congenially about their mutual friends and his life, but Declan couldn't concentrate. He felt slightly distant, as if his thoughts were not entirely within those four walls.

"May I impose on you?" Declan asked when the hour grew late. "I've let my town house to friends," he said, referring to the small town house he kept in Mayfair.

"Yes, of course," Christie said. "Stay as long as you like, a month, two months—"

"Not as long as that." Declan laughed. "A few nights only."

Christie gave him a curious look. "Then what?"

"Then?" Declan echoed. He had no idea. He laughed. "*Then*," he said with a shake of his head.

"We must have a gathering whilst you are here," Christie said as the two men made their way upstairs for the night.

"No, no, please don't trouble yourself," Declan said quickly.

"It is no trouble, and quite honestly, my wife will be disappointed if we do not," Christie said, and clapped him on the back. "Prepare to be introduced to young ladies desiring a match with an Irish earl."

Saturday evening, Darlington House was host to a little more than one hundred or so guests. The large French doors had been thrown open to the terrace, and paper lanterns had been lit around the large, expansive park. It was a beautiful evening, and everyone seemed to be in fine spirits, including Declan.

The ballroom was filled with beautiful women, chief among them, Miss Nell Adams, the year's most celebrated unmarried woman. Declan had long believed that Miss Nell Adams was the infamous "little bird," as described in the *Times* on-dits, who'd kept Lord Frampton company a year or so ago while his wife had toured the ancient ruins of Italy. The identity of the young lady had been kept quite close, as she was, it was rumored, merely a debutante. She would be completely ruined if her name was ever known, and Frampton certainly would not speak of it. But among the gentlemen of the *ton*, speculation was rife.

Last summer, Declan had, by chance, met Miss Adams

at an assembly and had instantly suspected her, for she was far too easy and even a bit forward in her attentions to him, particularly considering that she was barely out. His suspicions were only heightened now; he'd been invited to dine at the Brockton residence Tuesday evening, as had the Adamses, and Miss Nell Adams had touched Declan's arm and suggested she would welcome a call from him.

Surprised, Declan had given her a pointed look.

"My parents enjoy a walkabout every afternoon. It generally commences at three." She had smiled very wantonly.

Curious, Declan had accepted her offer and called the next day. Miss Adams was quite receptive. She sat next to him on a plush settee, and when the chaperone—an old governess put out to pasture, Declan guessed—turned her back, Miss Adams laid her dainty hand on his thigh then coyly looked up at him through her lashes.

Declan left there thinking he might have had his way with her. But he'd taken nothing more from Miss Adams than a very chaste kiss. He couldn't summon more interest than that. Keira Hannigan had stoked a madness that infuriated him, and now Declan feared he'd lost his mind. He could not escape the fever. That fever was what had driven him to London.

Of course Declan knew Keira was in London. Everyone in Hadley Green knew she was here. When he heard that she'd left, he didn't know why she had, precisely, but he guessed it was to see Mr. Goodwin. And then he'd imagined her being squired about by more London dandies. He'd thought she was a fool, risking so much in London. He truly didn't know why he bothered with the likes of her, but oddly enough, London had suddenly sounded like just the thing. He could pay a call to Darlington, spend a few nights in town with London women who could cure the strange ache he felt.

He did not believe he would see Keira. London was quite big, and as they inhabited different social circles, it was impossible that their paths would cross.

He was almost certain of it.

Declan had had a pair of whiskeys and considered taking Miss Adams by the hand and leading her out to the park behind the house, but as he'd approached her, his eye had been drawn to a single green feather. The feather adorned a black-haired coif, and Declan had stilled. He knew that coif. He knew that slender back and the curve of those hips. He had a sudden image of the pearl buttons on that gown coming undone, one by one, revealing the creamy skin of her back underneath. He could see the green silk sliding off her smooth shoulders, down her body, her back and hips deliciously bare, her black curly hair brushing against her skin.

It was a very stirring image.

Until he realized that their paths had crossed. *Impossible!* It was impossible that she could be here, at Darlington House! How had she managed it?

Declan was instantly moving, making his way through the crowd, following that blasted green feather. He lost sight of it once, then glimpsed the tip of it over a man's shoulder, bobbing as if the bearer were laughing or talking with great animation.

Declan dodged behind one gentleman and around a pair of ladies deep in conversation to reach her. But as he marched forward, he was intercepted by Lord Ettinger, who wanted Declan to join him in the gaming room. By the time Declan could make his excuses, he'd lost her.

He moved through the crowd, watching for her, pausing occasionally to greet an acquaintance who stepped in his path. He found her again when he stepped around a pair of gentlemen. She had just put her hand into Richard Link's palm and started for the dance floor. She happened to turn her head to say something to Link and saw Declan, and her deep green eyes widened with surprise.

"*Dhia duit*," he said.

"Ha! Aha!" Keira stammered and flashed a brief but brilliant smile at Link. "Lord Donnelly!" she said, looking at Declan again. "You . . . you continually surprise me." Her eyes locked on his as she sank into a curtsy.

"The surprise is most definitely mine," Declan assured her, and bowed. Keira's gown fit her far too enticingly. He did not think there was a smoother, more voluptuous bosom in the entire house this evening.

"Donnelly," Mr. Link said, and Declan remembered that Link was standing there, waiting for his dance partner, as the music had begun.

"Mr. Link, good evening. Please pardon the interruption, but Miss—"

"We have known each other for many years," Keira hastily interrupted.

"Oh. I see," Mr. Link said, eyeing Declan.

"I do beg your pardon, Mr. Link, but I . . . I should—I believe Lord Donnelly has important news from home?" she asked, looking hopefully, pleadingly, at Declan.

"No, no news. Not even a wee bit of news. In fact, I

thought you might have news for me. I was not aware you were acquainted with the Duke of Darlington."

Her brows sank. "Didn't you?"

"Not at all."

"Yes. Well," Mr. Link said, looking at Keira, then at Declan. "Clearly there is *some* news that should be exchanged between the two of you. Perhaps another time, Lady Ashwood."

"Mr. Link," she tried, but Mr. Link was already striding away. "Thank you," Keira called after him. Mr. Link turned right, disappearing behind a group. Keira looked murderously at Declan. "I'm in enough trouble as it is without any help from you, if you please."

"How did you manage it?" he asked, glad that Link was gone.

Keira flicked open her fan. "How does anyone manage these things? Did you honestly believe I would come here, uninvited?"

"Quite honestly, Keira, I would believe anything as far as you are concerned."

She gave him a cheeky smile. "I will have you know that the Duchess of Darlington invited Lady Horncastle to this event."

"Lady Horncastle? That old battle-axe is here?" he asked, glancing around them.

Keira stifled a laugh. "Aye, she is." She leaned into him. "She is determined to find her son a suitable match."

"I have no doubt that will progress swimmingly," Declan muttered. Keira giggled behind her fan; she was enchanting. "Now you are in London," he said. "When last I saw you, you were determined to return to Ireland."

She smiled uncertainly, and her cheeks bloomed, perhaps because she was remembering, just as he was, the kiss he'd pressed on her that day. "Mr. Fish and I have come to seek Mr. Goodwin's advice."

He grinned. "Then it would seem that for once, you have taken my very sound advice. There may be hope for you yet."

Keira smiled and graciously bowed her head.

"My humor is now much improved, having been so rudely dismissed from your presence the last we met."

"You were not," she said, smiling.

"I certainly was."

She laughed.

"How does Lady Horncastle enter into it?" he asked idly.

She shrugged and looked across the room. "I needed a place to stay," she said as she scanned the dancers. "Lady Horncastle was more than happy to help me. She saw it as an excuse to scout for potential matches for her son." She smiled sheepishly. "Just as long as she doesn't have me in mind."

Declan smiled. "It's dangerous you being here."

"I know." She sighed. "I really had no choice. And honestly, I am very happy I am," she said, slanting a look at him. "I could never come to London, or to a ball as grand as this as myself, not with all the societal rules as to who associates with whom. Certainly never on the arm of Mr. Maloney," she said with a slight frown. "I want to live, Declan. I want to experience adventure and excitement whilst I am able. As Lily, I can live, at least for a time. I know it is dangerous, but it is so . . . *freeing.*"

Declan understood her. He felt the same way about life. He would much prefer to be out in the world experiencing what life had to offer than to rust away at Ballynaheath, counting sheep and cattle and repairing fence lines. He gazed at Keira as she admired the dancers. It took swagger to do what she did, but it also took a fair amount of courage. "Do you not worry about discovery?" he asked curiously.

She smiled at him and shook her head. "Foolish, aye?"

"Terribly," he agreed. "But only fools discover the world." He gave her a wink. "You must be pleased that you decided not to tuck tail and run."

"Oh, Declan." She sighed sweetly. "What would you have me say? That you were right?"

He smiled lazily and resisted the urge to touch her. "I confess, I never tire of hearing it."

She shook her head with a little laugh, and the sound of it was like a brush of silk across his heart. "Well, there you are, Donnelly. Now tell me—why are *you* in London?"

For you. "Nothing you would find very interesting, I am certain."

"Mmm," she said, eycing him suspiciously.

"Dance, Lady Ashwood?" he asked, holding out his hand.

"*Dhia*, do my ears deceive me?" She smiled as she put her hand in his. "I do believe you are coming around to finding me tolerable."

He curled his fingers around hers. "Nothing of the sort," he lied playfully. "I am merely helping a fellow Irishwoman keep up appearances. A true countess would be holding court on the dance floor."

"My hero," she said with a wink, and allowed him to lead her out onto the dance floor in the same casual manner that he supposed an unsuspecting man strolled off a cliff.

Seventeen

Declan *was an* excellent dancer.

Or perhaps Keira was merely entranced by his easy smile, the crinkle of his eyes in their corners, and the firm way he held her as he twirled her about. It was a waltz, a dance she and her sisters had practiced in the privacy of their rooms. Her father would have perished where he stood had he known any of his daughters were dancing so intimately with a man.

Now Keira understood what her father feared. The dance was intoxicating. They swirled under two massive chandeliers with dozens of beeswax candles, across a polished wood floor, past the French doors where a summer night's breeze swept in to cool them. Declan moved so smoothly, the pressure of his broad hand on the small of her back indicating the direction she would go. He held her other hand aloft in his, and twirled her this way and that. The train of her gown swirled around his leg, and in one corner, he twirled her around and around, forcing her into his body, his leg between hers, his grip on her warm and steady.

Keira had never danced so freely. There were people all about, but she lost awareness of them. She had fallen into a memory of Declan, begun when she was a girl. Yet this was different. This was not a girl's dream she was experiencing. This was something she could feel deep in her marrow, something that swirled and mixed with the desire she felt for him.

When the dance came to its regrettable end, Declan escorted her off the dance floor. She wanted to thank him, but a woman suddenly appeared, her eyes on Declan, her smile vivid. "My Lord Donnelly!" she exclaimed.

Declan gave her a charming, easy smile. "Miss Adams."

From the way that Miss Adams was looking at Declan, Keira could see that she, Keira, was not welcome. She was abruptly reminded that Declan had always moved in a different world than she. He'd always been the reckless, aloof, sought-after earl and Keira had always been the bold, oldest daughter of Brian Hannigan, County Galway's most influential citizen next to Donnelly, made so only because he was a wealthy man. Keira's father had earned his living shipping wool to the Continent to be used in fashioning military uniforms. He used his wealth liberally to influence the political landscape in Ireland.

Keira's family engaged in the sort of pastimes and occupations the English *ton* frowned upon.

Keira was not a countess. She was not from a socially titular family. She would never have had entry into this lush ballroom were it not for her deception. She would never have resided in such fine houses as this—the size and furnishings far grander than anything she'd ever seen in Ireland.

The beautiful woman with the silk gown and flawless complexion and wanton smile speaking to Declan now reminded Keira of that. As Declan turned toward the woman, Keira drifted away from him.

This was not her place. Keira looked around at the opulence and grandeur of Darlington House and realized that in some ways, she'd begun to believe in the lie she had created the day she became Lily.

She spent the rest of the evening milling about, dancing occasionally . . . but none of the dances seemed as magical as the one she'd danced with Declan. She avoided conversation, believing that the less she managed to talk, the safer she was. But it was difficult to stay without company—Lady Horncastle was clearly quite proud of having arrived in the company of a countess, and steadily dragged one poor soul after another to Keira's side. "My Lady Ashwood, you *must* make Lord Dithers's acquaintance!" she trilled, her hand on the ancient viscount's arm.

Keira finally managed to escape Lady Horncastle's attention. She wished to be at some other ball, particularly when, as she wandered through the crowd, she saw Declan dancing with Miss Adams.

Miss Adams looked very happy to be in his arms. Exceedingly happy. Keira had no doubt that all women were so happy to be in his arms. She'd heard about the girl at the Grousefeather. Mrs. Morton talked endlessly about the match she hoped to make for Delcan with Clarissa Pontleroy, the daughter of Mr. Robert Pontleroy, a wealthy landowner in the South Downs. And it was painfully obvious to Keira that Daria Babcock would sink her teeth into Declan like a dog with a bone given the slightest bit of encouragement.

Keira had just asked a footman for a glass of punch

when Declan slipped in beside her and said, "You disappeared."

"I did not. I merely moved aside so all the ladies might have a fair chance to gain your attention."

"Really? I rather thought you abandoned me at the front line of battle and went off to be admired by all the gentlemen in this room."

Keira lifted a brow. "You should marry, Declan. Eireanne would like nothing better than to have the companionship of another woman at Ballynaheath, you know." The footman returned with her punch. "Thank you."

"I don't believe even you would advocate a man marry just to provide his sister with a companion," Declan scoffed, and shook his head at the footman's offer of punch.

Keira shrugged and averted her gaze. "I suppose there are worse reasons to marry. My family seems to believe one should marry for the mere sake of being married."

Declan grinned. "It is society's trap for us all, I'm afraid."

Keira sipped from the punch. It tasted a bit tart; she frowned and looked at the glass.

"It is liberally laced with gin," he said, and chuckled at her gasp of surprise. "You are in London, *muirnín*."

Which was why she needed all her wits about her, she realized, and passed the glass to him. Declan put the glass aside on a nearby table. "Have you seen the park behind the house?"

She shook her head.

"Would you like to see it now?" he asked.

"It's dark."

He winked devilishly. "Don't fret so, lass. I will hold you close to my side and protect you from the monsters that lurk there." He straightened up and offered his arm.

She looked at his proffered arm and thought of him holding her close, of feeling his arms around her, of his mouth on hers . . . "I could use a bit of air," she agreed. She was so foolish. What if they were discovered? What if they weren't?

Keira allowed him to lead her out.

It was much cooler in the park. There were several couples and groups milling about, and laughter drifted above their heads. Declan and Keira strolled down the middle of the lawn in silence, and when they reached a particularly impressive fountain, Declan paused. He stepped away from her, clasping his hands behind his back, and glanced skyward. "Lovely evening."

"It is," she said, looking at him.

Declan suddenly turned to her; his gaze wandered her body. He was admiring her. Keira knew that look; she'd seen it many times in her life. But it had never made her feel so . . . vivid.

"Sibley must be beside himself in your absence," he remarked.

"Who?" she asked with a slender smile. "Do you intend to return to Kitridge Lodge?" she asked. "Or have you decamped for London for an extended time?"

He seemed to ponder that question for a moment. There was something in his expression, she thought, something in his eyes, a glimmer of what she was feeling. "Of course I shall," he said. "I have my horses there."

Perhaps it was the soft light of the torches and the moon. Keira wouldn't call it desire, precisely, but something like longing. "Your horses, of course," she murmured.

He looked down, brushed his hair from his brow. "In truth, I have decided to help you, Keira. I will help you however I can until Lily comes."

Her heart skipped a little "You needn't. I know how you feel about me, and the things I do, especially after Eve—"

"No, Keira. It is not you that I feel so . . ." He shook his head. "My disappointment, my anger, is with myself. I will never be able to forgive myself for it, but that . . . that has been put into its proper perspective." He smiled lopsidedly. "I am far more concerned about your current crime. I cannot leave you to your own devices in good conscience. How would I ever explain to your father that you were in an English gaol?"

She tried to laugh, but an image of herself in some dark, dank cell suddenly loomed in her mind.

"Once Lily comes, Keira, you must promise to seek a new and honest adventure."

Keira's heart fluttered. She had an adventure or two in mind, frankly, and they involved him.

He leaned closer. "In Ireland," he added pointedly.

Keira blinked. "You mean to send me home?"

"Aye. I may jest about it, but what you are doing is criminal. I fear you could be in serious peril if you are discovered."

"Ah, but you will protect me from monsters," she said teasingly, and poked him in the chest.

Declan caught her hand and held it against his chest. "Don't think that. I will help you as I can, but . . . but you know it can be nothing more, aye?"

Her cheeks flamed. "I didn't mean—"

"Listen to me." He wrapped his hand tightly around hers and moved closer. "I share your love of freedom. It is not within me to stay in one place for long. I cannot say how long I shall be at Kitridge Lodge, or even in England. I would not give you false hope, so I am telling you now that I cannot help you beyond Lily's return. Do you understand?"

Taken aback, she could only nod. She truly had never expected more, and certainly not his help. Perhaps it was the suggestion that there would come a day very soon that they would part ways that had her feeling suddenly queasy.

He smiled fondly and touched her neck. "Let us get to the bottom of Mr. Scott's guilt and your aunt's death," he said. "We might start with the records of the trial."

"Yes," she agreed, mentally shaking off her sadness. She forced herself to smile. "The sooner we discover the truth, the sooner I can end this abominable lie."

"Aye, well, one thing at a time," he said, and casually laid his palm against her neck. His gaze locked on hers, and in the moonlight, she could believe there was at least a wee bit of admiration shining there. "We should perhaps be circumspect, aye?" he suggested. "After all, it would not do to have anyone believe there is more to our acquaintance. They might suspect us of conspiracy."

"God forbid," she said with a playful smile. "Such a rumor could ruin my reputation. They might believe I esteem you somehow. Or you me."

He grinned. "Impossible."

"Of course." She smiled. "You reach too far above yourself."

Declan's smile deepened and he pulled her closer. "Ours would be an unhappy union at best," he said, and kissed the corner of her mouth. "You, always defying me."

Keira felt as if she were shining inside. Every touch of his hand, every press of his lips, sent another shock of light through her. "You, ordering me about like a servant," she whispered against his cheek.

"And you, never obeying," he murmured, and kissed her on the lips.

All her inhibitions floated out of her with that kiss. She moved her hands up his chest, to his face and jaw. "This shall be our last kiss," she said.

"What kiss?" he asked as his mouth descended to hers. He angled his head and the kiss, his tongue sweeping into her mouth. His hands moved on her body, up her back, then down again, to her hip. He cupped her face and lifted his head, gazing down at her. "No more," he said, and nipped at her lips. "No more kissing. No touching." He kissed her again.

"Never," Keira said, and giggled when he kissed the grin from her lips.

The sound of voices began to drift into Keira's consciousness, and Declan's, too, for he lifted his head and looked toward the house. "An audience," he muttered, and not happily.

"Perhaps we should return to the ballroom before wagging tongues have plotted our wedding, aye?" Keira whispered, peering into the dark.

"Aye," he said with a sigh. He caressed her back and kissed her once more before leading her out onto the main walk.

As they strolled up the lawn to the house, however, Lady Horncastle and another woman intercepted them. Declan bowed. "Your Grace," he said.

Keira's stomach clenched as she instantly sank into a curtsy.

"Donnelly, there you are," the woman said. "Everyone is talking about you."

"Again?" he asked charmingly.

"Your Grace, may I introduce the Countess of Ashwood?" Lady Horncastle said excitedly. "Lady Ashwood, the dowager Duchess of Darlington."

Keira's stomach fluttered again. The woman was a duchess, and not just any—Darlington was a revered name in England. "Your Grace," she said.

The duchess smiled warmly. "Ah, look at you, darling, all grown up. Lady Horncastle told me Althea's niece was here, and I was delighted! I've not seen you since you were six years or so. It is good to see you grown and well, Lady Ashwood. You must come to London more often! My son Harry has just returned from France—"

"He's a daring sort, to be in France just now," Declan said laughingly, and held out his arm to Keira.

"Some call it the foolish sort," Lady Darlington sniffed.

"Do please give Harry my regards," Declan said. "Ladies." He bowed his head and escorted Keira away.

"Thank you," Keira whispered.

Declan responded by covering her hand with his and lightly squeezing her fingers. It was a simple gesture, but

Keira felt safe with him, almost as if she were protected from her deceit.

As they entered the ballroom, Declan asked, "When do you return to Ashwood?"

"On the morrow."

"Stay."

It was a single word, a small, inelegant word, but perhaps the most beautiful word in the English language. She wanted to stay. "I cannot," she said softly. "I must go back. You advised me not to run from my problems, remember?"

"Upon reflection, I think it is damned poor advice."

She grinned. "When will you return?"

He looked across the room. Keira followed his gaze, saw Miss Adams. "I can't rightly say," he said, and winked at her. "Chin up, Keira, and mind you, don't stand up with all the gentlemen tonight. They'll think you are on the marriage market." He bowed his head. "Good night, *muirnín*."

"Good night, my lord."

She watched him walk away. She had yet to catch her breath, and as she watched him now, as he put his hand on one man's shoulder and the two of them laughed, she tried to draw a full breath. It was impossible. *Oh dear, Keira.* She knew this thing she was feeling. It was intense and devouring, far more so than when she'd been sixteen years. This was full-bodied and robust. Sensual. Consuming.

She still fancied herself in love with him.

Eighteen

Keira did indeed love London, but last night's encounter with the duchess was too much, even for her. Now Keira couldn't help wondering how many others who remembered Lily as a child were lurking about England or standing in ballrooms beside Keira.

So it was with some relief that Keira left London soon after her meeting with Mr. Goodwin. Mr. Goodwin was a jovial, round man with a bulbous nose, who peppered Keira and Mr. Fish with a multitude of questions. At the end of the hour-long meeting, Mr. Goodwin said that he had quite a lot to research and would be in touch soon.

In retrospect, Keira thought the meeting had gone well enough. She was very happy to be back at Ashwood late that evening, and realized, as she bounded up the steps and happily handed her hat to Linford, that she would miss this place very much when she was forced to leave.

Mr. Fish returned from Town the following day. He was very optimistic about the meeting with Mr. Goodwin, as well. "I rather think he will help us," he said. "There really is none better than he, madam."

She would have to thank Donnelly for the name when she saw him again.

Keira spent the next few days tending to the never-ending list of things to do. She also played the pianoforte and tried, in vain, to help Lucy with her art. She was very content to hide away for a time, but inevitably, she was summoned into the village to a meeting about the summer gala.

Oh, the summer gala! Were it not for that, Keira thought she might live quite peacefully. But the ladies of Hadley Green were completely diverted by it, and it seemed that with every passing week, they thought of more things that must be done.

That afternoon, they were all assembled at Mrs. Morton's, who had set up linen-covered tables on her lawn for tea. The tables were laden with china and tea services, freshly baked scones, and flowers. Keira and Lucy sat at Mrs. Morton's table, along with Mrs. Ogle, Miss Babcock, and Lady Horncastle, who looked, Keira thought, a wee bit sour this afternoon.

"Good afternoon, one and all," Keira said gaily as she directed Lucy into a chair. "A glorious day, is it not?"

"Beautiful!" Mrs. Ogle agreed.

"If you find it so, I daresay you have not suffered the trials and tribulations I have suffered," Lady Horncastle sniffed.

"I am very sorry to hear it, madam," Keira said. *Again*, she thought. In London, she'd heard more than enough of Lady Horncastle's trials and tribulations, mainly to do with her son.

"I've had a row with Frankie," Lady Horncastle said, as if Keira had asked. "It has ruined the day entirely!"

"The *whole* day, madam?" Mrs. Morton asked wryly as she casually stirred her tea.

Lady Horncastle ignored that remark and turned to Keira. "You met Miss Reynolds, did you not? Lovely girl with two thousand a year, do you recall? I think her a wonderful match, but my son will not hear of it!" she said, and tossed down her napkin in disgust.

Keira remembered a mousy girl with unflattering teeth. "Won't he?" she asked lightly, and smiled at Lucy.

"Not for a moment!" Lady Horncastle said sharply. "He has his eye on Nell Adams, as does half of London, but I assure you, she will marry Lord Donnelly before the year ends if she marries at all! It's hardly a secret they have become quite attached."

"Miss Adams?" Miss Babcock said, her voice full of disappointment. "But who is she? I've not heard of her."

"Well, you wouldn't, my dear, as she is in Town. Miss Adams is the daughter of a very wealthy man. He makes boats for a living."

"Ships, actually," Mrs. Ogle clarified.

"Ships, boats, I hardly care. He is of the merchant class, and while he has made a rather sizable fortune, it's all been in trade. At least Miss Reynolds may count a baron in her ancestry. You may trust me that if Miss Adams were the king's daughter, she'd not suit Frankie in the least, and besides, she is determined to have Lord Donnelly, and I daresay, he is just as determined to have her."

"Oh," Miss Babcock said. She looked as disappointed as Keira felt.

"I am surprised you didn't take note of it yourself, Lady Ashwood," Lady Horncastle said. "He stood up with Miss Adams three times at the Darlington ball—"

"The Darlington ball?" Miss Babcock said, sounding even more disappointed. "You attended a *Darlington* ball?"

"*Three* times," Lady Horncastle continued. "And he could scarcely take his eyes from her all evening long!"

"My," Mrs. Morton said. "You were quite observant of Lord Donnelly."

"Well, what else could I do, with Frankie flitting about, wanting Miss Adams's attention? To think he fancies himself quite smitten with her! *Lud!*"

"Oh dear, don't look so downcast," Mrs. Ogle said, and Keira instantly straightened her back and smiled . . . and then noticed that Mrs. Ogle was looking at Miss Babcock.

"I'm not in the least!" Miss Babcock said, trying very hard to smile convincingly. "What . . . did you think that I . . . ?" She laughed and waved her hand. "Certainly not!"

Lucy peered curiously at Keira. "Will Lord Donnelly not come round again, then?"

"Of course he shall," Mrs. Morton said, and patted Lucy's hand. "All the gentlemen in Sussex will come round to see her ladyship for she is a delight. But I think we all know where her affections lie, hmm?" she asked, looking slyly around the table.

"Mine!" Keira exclaimed. Was it so obvious? A heat crept up the nape of her neck.

"You are among friends here," Mrs. Morton said. "And besides, I think we would all very much like to see a wedding at Ashwood."

"Pardon?"

"Granted, he is the third son of a viscount, but it is nonetheless a fine family," Mrs. Ogle said proudly, smiling in an identical way to Mrs. Morton. "Your position could do great things for a young man like him."

Keira gaped at her. *"Who?"*

"Why, Mr. Sibley, of course!" Mrs. Ogle said.

"Mr. Sibley!"

"He's quite adoring of you," Mrs. Morton said, smiling brightly.

"That may be, but I am most decidedly not adoring of *him*—"

"Mr. Sibley is an unsuitable match for a countess," Lady Horncastle said with great authority. "He is the *third* son. There will be nothing left for him but a small house and stipend."

"Thank you, Lady Horncastle," Keira said with great relief.

"There's hardly a man within Sussex that is suitable, really. No, my dears, Lady Ashwood may make a match that is quite above us all."

"Have you someone in mind?" Miss Babcock asked sulkily.

"I do, indeed." Lady Horncastle straightened up. "My dear friend the dowager Duchess of Darlington thinks her son Harry—a *viscount*—would fall quite in love with our own Lady Ashwood."

That was met with gasps around the table and a sinking feeling within Keira.

"Do you truly think it possible?" Mrs. Morton all but squealed.

"Not only do I think it possible, I think it is likely imminent."

"I beg your pardon, Lady Horncastle," Keira said

quickly before they marched her up to the chapel to recite her marriage vows, "but I have never so much as met the gentleman."

"A *viscount*, Lady Ashwood!" Mrs. Ogle said excitedly. "What a fortuitous match!"

"Ladies, please," she pleaded. "I have a father and a mother and will thank you not to make a match for me."

Mrs. Ogle's eyes widened.

"What?" Keira asked, looking around.

The ladies all exchanged a look before Mrs. Morton said, "A father and a mother?"

Keira's belly tightened. She was so careless! "My aunt and uncle, naturally. They are like parents to me, and I tend to think of them as such. Really, I should like to end this talk of matches, if you please."

"Oh, I nearly forgot! Have you heard the news?" Miss Babcock said, eager to oblige her. "Dr. Creighton is bringing on an apprentice," she said, and began to babble about the physician's new apprentice.

Keira released a slow breath of relief. But she couldn't help noticing that Mrs. Ogle was looking at her a little strangely.

In the coach on the way home that afternoon, Lucy pulled her nose away from the window and looked at Keira. "Are you going to marry a viscount, mu'um?"

Keira laughed. "No, pet. I've never met the man. Lady Horncastle likes to imagine such things."

Lucy mulled that over for a moment. "I rather thought you'd marry Lord Donnelly," she said matter-of-factly. "I rather hoped it, really."

Keira had, too, once. She smiled and put her arm

around Lucy's shoulders, pulling her into her side. "There is something you should know of Lord Donnelly, sweeting. He is not the marrying sort."

"Why is he not?" Lucy asked curiously.

Keira wished she knew the answer to that. "I don't know."

"I rather like him," Lucy said, pouting.

Keira rested her chin on top of Lily's head.

She rather liked him, too.

Nineteen

A few days after returning to Kitridge Lodge, Declan made good on his promise to help Keira.

He had returned from London a changed man. He'd shaken loose the troubling and misty thoughts of Keira and her Irish eyes, had enjoyed the company of other women—if only on the ballroom floor—and had returned to the countryside to a mare who had successfully mated with the Austrian horse.

When at last he determined it was safe for him to call at Ashwood, he stopped in Hadley Green for a few pints at the Grousefeather, played a few rounds of commerce, and when a particularly bad hand had emptied his pockets, he'd ambled across the village green to the parish offices.

Mrs. Ainsley, a spry, tiny thing, was very happy to see him, particularly after he remarked on her lovely lace collar. "Exquisitely crafted," he observed. "You purchased it in London, no doubt. The Queen's Lace shop, am I right?"

"The Queen's!" she exclaimed, turning a bit red. "No, my lord, I made it myself." She touched it lightly.

"Yourself?" he said, feigning shock. "You are indeed very talented, madam."

Her blush deepened, but she smiled proudly. "Well . . . I suppose I am rather well regarded for my lace."

Soon after, Declan had what he'd come for.

At Ashwood, Linford directed him around to the garden, where he found Keira in a big wide-brimmed gardening hat and apron, cutting roses. Lucy Taft was with her, naturally, making cuttings alongside her.

"Well, well," Keira said when he walked into their midst. "The cat has come home to roost."

"I believe you mean the bird," he said. He glanced at Lucy. "How does the day find you?" he asked Lucy.

"Me? Quite well," Keira said cheerfully, without looking up from her task. "Never better, in fact."

"That is splendid news. But I was inquiring of Miss Taft." Keira looked up. "Oh."

"I am very well, my lord," Lucy said, and curtsied. She peered past Declan. "Did Miss Adams come with you?"

"Lucy!" Keira cried laughingly, and to Declan's curious look, she said, "Lady Horncastle has voiced her opinion far and wide."

"I see," he said, and smiled at Lucy. "She has not."

Lucy looked disappointed.

"You've been gone for a time, Donnelly," Keira said lightly as she returned to cutting roses. "What a fine time you must have had in London."

"It was very pleasurable, indeed," he agreed, and watched as Keira snapped a rose and dropped it on the ground. "How did you find London?"

She dipped down to pick up the rose and tossed it carelessly into her basket. "Passable." She looked at him from the corner of her eye.

"At the very least, you attended a ball. I should think that would have been to a countess's liking."

"Oh, it was lovely," she said, and snapped another rose, and another, and tossed them into her basket.

"Lady Ashwood may very well marry a viscount," Lucy informed him.

"For goodness sakes, Lucy!" Keira exclaimed. "You mustn't repeat a thing Lady Horncastle says. She has a tendency toward delusions."

"A viscount?" Declan asked.

Keira waved her hand dismissively. "Lady Horncastle and Lady Darlington have conspired around Lady Darlington's youngest son, Lord Raley."

Declan couldn't help but snort. He knew Harry, and there wasn't a more dissolute man in all of England.

But his snort of disbelief earned him a dark look from Keira. Her eyes flicked over his face before turning back to her gardening. "And what brings you all the way to Ashwood this afternoon?" she asked idly.

"I thought we might ride into Hadley Green and pay a visit to the parish offices and look up the records we discussed."

"Did you?" She cut more flowers, even though her basket was almost overflowing with them. "What, then, shall we appear on the doorstep of the parish offices and begin to go through centuries of records?" she asked, and snapped another rose, cutting it off too close to the bloom. That one, she tossed onto the path. Lucy picked it up.

"No," he said patiently. "I have done a bit of inquiry with Mrs. Ainsley and found her delighted to make the records of the trial available to me. They've been set aside in a reading room, just waiting to be read."

Keira looked at him fully, her expression cool.

"Are you going to come?" he asked. She didn't answer; she looked at Lucy. So did Declan. "I had in mind to ride," he said.

"Lucy has not yet learned to ride."

As much as he liked the girl, he did not desire her presence today. "I'll have Mr. Noakes join us."

Keira frowned. "Surely he has better things to do than chaperone."

Declan shifted closer to Keira and the pace of her pruning quickened. "If I didn't know better, I'd believe you are avoiding me. And on the heels of having begged me to help you, yet."

"I did *not* beg you to help me. I appealed to your sense of decency. And I am not avoiding you," she said, but the wide brim of her hat was shielding her face from him. "You misjudge me, sir. My thoughts are on far more pressing matters than you."

He didn't believe her. "Very well. Then I shall come round tomorrow and we will ride into Hadley Green and have a look at the trial records."

"All right." She picked up her basket and glanced up at him. "Shall we say one o'clock?"

"That will do."

"Splendid," she said pertly. "Come along, Lucy. It is time for your music lesson."

She said nothing else, but swept past him. Her apron had come undone and one of the ties trailed behind her as she took Lucy in hand and marched from the garden.

Declan stood rooted to the spot until they'd turned the corner and he could see them no more. Only then did he remove his hat and shove a hand through his hair.

Women, bloody women. This was precisely why Declan preferred the company of horses.

He was so annoyed with Keira's less than warm reception of him that he and Mr. Noakes arrived early the following day.

When Keira finally descended from the heavens on that grand staircase, it was in a gray riding habit that hugged her tightly, and a hat identical to Declan's, but with a bouquet of daisies stuck in the band, perched jauntily on her head.

She paused in the entry to don her gloves. Declan looked at her hat, then at her. "Fetching attire."

"Thank you," she said, and leaned forward to have a look at her hat in the mirror.

"Are you ready?"

"Is it one o'clock?" she asked as she tucked a curl behind her ear.

"Ten past."

She turned away from the mirror and looked up at him with glistening green eyes. "Then I am ready." And with that, she walked out the door, to the drive.

Declan followed her. A horse had been brought up from the stables for her, a fine horse that had been rudely offended by having a sidesaddle on its back. With the stable boy's help, Keira put herself on the horse.

She arranged her skirts and fit her feet into the stirrups as Declan and Noakes looked on.

When she was settled, she looked at Declan.

"After you," he said, gesturing to the road.

She set her horse to a trot.

Declan and Noakes exchanged a look, and set out after her.

As Declan guessed, it was an interminably long ride into Hadley Green with Keira bobbing along on a side-saddle, and not because of the time it took them to travel the few miles, but because he was forced to watch her derriere bouncing up and down in that ridiculous saddle. He thought he'd put foolish thoughts from his mind, but here he was, imagining how that derriere might feel to his hand. And it was the flowers in her hatband, as well. Why the flowers annoyed him, Declan could not say. Perhaps because they were so bloody whimsical, so bloody like Keira. Whatever the reason, those two things conspired to put him in an ill temper by the time they reached Hadley Green.

In the village, Keira was off her horse before Declan could tether his. She stood at the door of the offices, waiting for him to open it for her.

"Noakes, you'll stay with the horses, aye?" Declan asked.

"Aye, milord," Noakes said, already reaching in his saddlebag for apples.

Declan strolled to the door of the offices. He looked down at Keira, who was brushing out her skirts. He opened the door and stood back. She swept through, and Declan prayed for patience.

"Lady Ashwood!" Mrs. Ainsley said when Keira stepped inside. "I hadn't expected you!"

"Didn't you?" Keira asked politely, sliding her gaze to

Declan. "Lord Donnelly has something he should like to show me."

"We won't be long," Declan assured Mrs. Ainsley, and with his hand on Keira's back, he ushered her through the door to the reading room. They didn't speak; Keira wandered about the room as Declan removed the leather-bound parish records from a small filing box. She removed her gloves and her hat, then unbuttoned the collar of her habit and the collar of her shirt, so that Declan could see the hollow of her throat.

He looked away from that smooth patch of skin and pushed down any thought of kissing it. "Let's get on with it, shall we?" he said shortly, and slapped open one leather-bound ledger, releasing dust into the air.

Keira waved her hand dramatically as she suffered a small sneezing fit. Declan stoically removed a handker-chief from his pocket and handed it to her. Keira took it without a word, dabbed at her nose, and shoved it back at him. "Thank you," she said hoarsely. "Now then, what is all this?"

"Records. Births, deaths, magisterial proceedings, and the like. Mrs. Ainsley tells me there is one volume that will contain the records of the magistrate's trial. I suggest we find that one and begin to search for the trial."

"Very well," Keira said, and pulled out a chair from the table and sat down. She looked at the contents of the folder Declan had opened. "This appears to be a record of the births," she said, lifting a few of the pages between her thumb and forefinger.

"Then go to the next."

She did as he asked. Within a quarter of an hour, they'd

found the correct ledger. It was rather thick; it would seem that petty crime and neighborly disputes were common in Hadley Green. There were so many of them, in fact, that Keira handed Declan half the stack of pages and they began to look together.

"I found it!" Keira cried a few minutes later. "Look, Declan, it's all here," she said excitedly. "'Proceedings Against Joseph Baron Scott, in the matter of the theft of crown jewels valued at approximately twenty thousand pounds from the Ashwood estate,'" she read aloud.

Declan stood up and came around to where she was sitting, and looked over her shoulder.

"There are pages and pages," she said with dismay.

Declan sat beside her, and together, they scanned the pages of the ledger. The ink had faded and the writing was very tight, presumably done to save paper. They sat close; Declan could feel the heat of Keira's body on his arm. She touched his leg or hand to gain his attention, then leaned closer still to show him an entry or ask clarification of a word.

His head was filled with the scent of perfume.

It was a tedious afternoon.

It was Declan who found the witnesses' testimony. A maid had admitted she'd seen Mr. Scott at Ashwood that afternoon. A stable boy swore he had held Mr. Smith's horse that evening. Lily's testimony, which he and Keira read, their heads bent together, was particularly damning.

There were witnesses to Mr. Scott's character, just as Mr. Hollingbroke had claimed, but none that could vouch for his whereabouts that night. Even his wife was forced to tell the court that he left in the afternoon and did not return until the late evening.

After they'd read through it all, Keira stood up and paced around the table, her hands on the small of her back. "He didn't steal them," she said.

"Something seems not quite right," Declan observed, and looked over the pages that were scattered about the table.

"What do you mean?"

"There is nothing from your aunt. No testimony, no record of her attendance. If they were truly lovers, would she not have attempted to save him?" He looked at Keira. "Why wouldn't she have come to his defense?"

Keira frowned thoughtfully and shook her head. "Perhaps I am wrong. Perhaps they weren't lovers."

"Even so," Declan said, gaining his feet. "I think the magistrate might have asked her if there was any reason Mr. Scott would have had to be at the house that day. It was she, after all, who hired him to do the staircase. Would they not have asked if she'd hired him to do any other work? If she knew of any reason he should be there that night? And they were her jewels that went missing. Why would they not have questioned her?"

"To spare her the unpleasantness of the inquiry?" Keira suggested.

"Spare her discomfort over a man's life?" Declan countered.

"Lily said Aunt Althea left for Scotland to see Aunt Margaret. Perhaps she'd already gone."

"How long was she gone?"

Keira shook her head. "I don't know. I remember that

when Lily arrived in Ireland, the leaves had already turned. It must have been late autumn, and Aunt Althea was the one to have sent her."

Declan picked up the front page of the trial recordings and reviewed the dates. The theft had occurred on the fourteenth of July. Mr. Scott was tried on the twenty-sixth, and was hanged on the thirtieth. He was surprised by how quickly Mr. Smith had been sent to the gallows. "Did she go before his execution? Did she see him hanged?"

"I don't know how we might possibly find out," Keira said.

Declan looked at the papers again. "Mr. Samuel Bowman, the earl's secretary, is how. He prosecuted the crime on behalf of the earl. I shall inquire of him, if he's still alive."

"He is very much alive," Keira said. "Fish has mentioned him more than once." She picked up the papers and put them in the ledger. "I shall ask Mr. Fish where I might find him and make the inquiries. You needn't trouble yourself." She handed the ledger to Declan.

"It is no trouble," Declan assured her as he returned the ledger to the box.

"Aye, well, I would rather you not continue with it," she said tightly.

Declan turned around to look at her, but Keira was busy buttoning her collar. "What is the matter with you?"

"I haven't the slightest idea what you mean. I am fine."

"I know you far better than that, lass," he said. "You are in a pique about something and I haven't the slightest idea what."

Keira sighed heavenward. "I should never have asked

you to compromise yourself to help me," she said. "I appreciate all that you've done, truly, but I . . . I can do whatever else needs be done." She looked at him, her gaze skimming his body. "I don't need you, Declan. I can do what I must. You said you wanted no part of it," she said, looking at him now. "Therefore I am giving you no part of it. Now then, I must take my leave. I promised Lucy I'd take her rowing." She turned away and walked out of the room.

Declan gaped at her. She had essentially removed him from the quest for the truth about Mr. Scott. And while the irony of his annoyance with her for doing so was a little disconcerting, Declan was still very cross with her.

He stalked out behind her, not even pausing to flatter Mrs. Ainsley.

"I am not so easily dismissed, madam," he said, uncaring who heard him.

"I am not dismissing you, my lord, how could I possibly? But I should never have involved you. Will you help me up?"

He marched to where she stood, grabbed her by the waist, and lifted her up, seating her firmly on the sidesaddle. Keira caught the horn and righted her hat and looked down at him. "Thank you. Are you coming?"

"Is that all I am to expect?" he demanded. "A sunny 'thank you, but you may leave me now'?"

"Did you truly want more?"

"Bloody hell—"

"Lord Donnelly, please," she said sweetly. "Mr. Noakes does not desire to hear your protests."

He glared at her, clamped his jaw shut, and spun

around, marching to his horse. If he weren't a gentleman, he'd leave her to bounce home on her own. As it was, he rode past her, intent on staying in front of her. He didn't know why he bothered with her at all, why he'd allowed himself to feel things and think things he'd never thought in his life, or to spend time in London when he had work to do just to rid himself of these thoughts. He'd been taken in by a captivating smile, a fault of his—

He was startled by Keira's appearance on his left. She'd caught up to him on that blasted sidesaddle, and it riled him. He sent his horse trotting faster, but a moment later, he saw her again from the corner of his eye. He turned his head to look at her. She rode like a bloody peacock, her posture erect and her eyes on the road, as if nothing were amiss.

Declan glanced over his shoulder. Noakes was so far behind them now, he'd never catch up. He shifted his gaze to the little peacock again. Did she do this to torment him? He suddenly sent his mount off the road, racing across the meadow, certain he'd be rid of her now. But Keira surprised him; she was indeed a superb horsewoman. Not only did she catch up with him, she passed him. She'd lost her hat, and was bent low over her horse's neck, gripping the horn and the reins, riding recklessly, dangerously. As they approached a stone fence, Declan reined up, certain that Keira would lose her seat.

The horse Keira was riding sailed over the fence, and Keira stayed seated.

Declan's blood fired then. He went after her. His gelding did not disappoint him; once he understood he'd been given his head, the young gelding gained ground on Keira's mare, racing up alongside her. Declan leaned across her gelding's neck and caught the bridle of the mare, pulling both horses up at once. The mare neighed unhappily at him, but Declan held firm, twisting that horse around until she couldn't see.

Only then did she stop.

Declan threw himself off his mount, caught Keira by the waist and hauled her down. She glared up at him, her eyes full of challenge. Declan did the only thing he could. He kissed her. He kissed her hard, his mouth on hers, his tongue in her mouth.

And then he let her go and pushed her back, angry with her recklessness, angry that it had fired his blood and made him want her as desperately as he wanted her now.

Keira stumbled back a few steps. Her chest was rising and falling with each furious breath. She all but bared her teeth at him, threw her crop aside, and marched forward. Declan braced himself to be hit, but Keira surprised him once more. She leaped at him, her arms going around his neck, her legs around his waist, and kissed him back.

She threw him completely off kilter, sent him tumbling head over heels down a dangerous slope in his heart. She also caused him to lose his footing, and down they went, Keira landing squarely on top of him.

The fall did not discomfit her in the least. She merely found his mouth again.

Declan rolled her onto her back in the grass. "You should be locked away in a convent," he snapped.

"It's a wonder you haven't broken your fool neck," she shot back. "Why won't you leave me be?"

"Leave you *be*? I was trying to escape you!"

"Escape me and race back to Miss Adams?" she angrily accused him as she tried to move him off her body.

Declan stilled. And then he pinned her to the ground. "Is that what this is about? You risked your bloody fool neck because you are jealous?"

"I am *not* jealous," she said, struggling again. "I hardly care what you do."

"For your information, Nell Adams is a fortune seeker and a bore."

"I hardly care. Get off me," she said, and shoved again.

"I like women, Keira, I enjoy their fair company. But that does not mean I care any less for you."

If anything, that seemed to infuriate her more. She gave him a mighty shove. "Get *off*!"

"You don't want me to," he growled.

"God in heaven, why won't you just let me *be*?" she cried again.

"Because I cannot!" he roared, and kissed her again, kissed her like he'd never kissed a woman. There was nothing sweet or tender in it, no—that kiss was brimming with fire and unbridled, unfulfilled passion that flamed up in Declan, filling him completely. Her tongue darted between his lips as if she were teasing him. Her body was pressed against his, her breasts against his chest, her leg firmly between his. The scent of her skin and hair, the sweet taste of her mouth and the succulent flesh of her tongue, was wildly intoxicating.

Her hair came undone from its pins and a thick strand drifted between them. Declan wrapped that long strand of hair around his fist and brushed it against his cheek. God help him but he was lost in the feel of her body, in the taste of her skin. They were wild with each other, desire flowing like lightning between them.

He unbuttoned her coat, then her blouse. His hand reached for the globe of her breast, filling his palm with it, and Keira responded feverishly. Her hands ran wildly over him and she shifted beneath him, moving so she could feel more of his body, her fingers brushing lightly against his erection. She wrapped her arms around his neck and pulled herself up to him, devouring his lips.

He shifted again, found the hem of her skirt and pushed it up. She didn't stop him; if anything, she seemed to press harder against him. He stroked her, brushing his fingers against the silky skin of her leg, pausing when he found the soft flesh of her thigh. Keira gasped into his mouth, but her leg fell away, and Declan touched her between her legs.

She made a soft moaning sound as he slipped his fingers into the slit of her sex. She arched her neck, let her head fall back while her body rose up against him. *I am lost.* He put his mouth to the flesh of her open bodice as he stroked her, swirling around the core of her desire, sliding down and slipping inside her. She began to pant; she squeezed her legs shut around his hand, and Declan mouthed the ripe mounds of her breasts, licking and kissing the crevice between them. He could feel her body swell and pulse beneath him, could feel himself spiraling down that golden path of desire, hard and throbbing with the hunger to be inside her.

He wouldn't. For the first time in his adult life, he wouldn't take what he knew he could have. It was different this time, too important, too deep in him. He continued to stroke her, the tempo of his hand quickening in time to her panting. She began to whimper, and buried her face in his shoulder, reaching her climax with a violent shudder. He was also panting, his teeth set against the throbbing of his erection.

A moment passed, and Keira slowly eased away from him. His hand was still between her legs. Her lips were red and slightly swollen from having been thoroughly kissed. They stared at one another for a single moment that seemed, impossibly, more alive than any other moment in Declan's life. He slowly lowered his head and kissed her tenderly as he removed his hand from between her legs.

Keira rolled away from him and found her feet. With her back to him, she shook out her skirts and repaired her bodice. Her hair was full of grass; Declan didn't know how she would explain it. He stood up, tried to help with the grass in her hair, but Keira kept her back to him, kept fidgeting with her clothing.

He didn't know what to say. They'd crossed a boundary, but he wasn't particularly sorry for it. He was still aching from his own unmet need, still burning to be with her. He waited, expecting anger, or, at the very least, accusations. Keira turned her head slightly and glanced at him sidelong over her shoulder.

Declan braced himself.

But when Keira turned around, she was smiling. "Very well, then," she said. "You may call on Mr. Bowman with me."

This woman. He'd never known another like her. At present, he wasn't sure if he should kiss her again or bring her to heel. He put his hands to his waist and lowered his head. "If you are indeed determined to be the death of me, woman, you'll have to work harder than that."

Keira's smile only deepened. She laughed lightly as she began to move toward the horses. "Oh dear," she said airily as she walked past him. "I've lost my hat."

Twenty

Keira was in love. *Love!* Of all the ill-advised, useless things she might feel! What was she to do with herself? It wasn't as if Declan O'Conner would return her feelings—he was a man who avoided attachments at all costs.

When Mr. Noakes presented her with the hat she'd lost in her wild race against Declan, she'd thought of Loman Maloney, and had tried to imagine losing her hat over him. She couldn't picture it. It made her slightly ill to even try.

For a few days, Keira had wandered about her life, working diligently to convince herself that she was not in love, that she was merely infatuated. She sat at the window and stared out at the grounds. She dined with Lucy at luncheon, smiling as the girl talked, but scarcely hearing a word she said. She gardened, she reviewed correspondence, she authorized payments, she played the pianoforte, and she cautioned herself not to become an even bigger fool. She didn't *love* Declan. She couldn't *love* Declan.

But maybe, just maybe, she did. Maybe as ardently as she had eight years ago.

The only thought that seemed to help her take her

mind off Declan was her need to speak to Mr. Bowman. It took some doing getting the man's location out of Mr. Fish, but he'd at last discovered where she might find the aging secretary.

She could hardly wait to see Declan again for any number of reasons, but included among them was the news about Mr. Bowman. She had a slight problem, however, of finding a way to see Declan without raising suspicion or causing talk. It was one thing for him to call on her. It was quite another for her to call on him in the bright light of day.

With every day that passed, she began to wonder why Declan didn't call on her. Surely, after what had happened between them, he would not stay away. Surely something fundamental had changed between them . . . had it not? But Declan didn't come, and Keira began to feel strange. Her thoughts of love turned to doubt.

When Mr. Sibley called, she was in an ill humor. She received him in the music room, where she had been practicing the pianoforte.

"Mr. Sibley," she said when he was announced. "I thought you had returned to London."

"I did," he said, bowing over her hand. "I have returned to prepare the way for Count Eberlin. He shall arrive at Tiber Park by week's end."

"That's nice," Keira had said lightly. Her mind was a thousand miles from Mr. Sibley and the Danish count.

Mr. Sibley leaned over, so that Keira would look at him from her place at the pianoforte. "I will confess, Lady Ashwood, that I have found myself searching for an excuse to be in Hadley Green."

She imagined Declan standing before her now. Her heart had been winging about in the ether with hopes of him, but she realized her mind was firmly planted on terra firma. She knew who Declan was. His reputation—and more than one injured heart—had drifted about Ireland and Ballynaheath for years.

Nevertheless, after what had happened . . .

She realized Mr. Sibley was looking at her strangely. "I am glad you have come," she said out of habit.

"Are you?"

Was she what? She turned her attention to the pianoforte.

Mr. Sibley stood beside the pianoforte, listening to her play. But when Keira hit a sour note, she stopped, laid her hands in her lap a moment. "Do play on," he urged her. "You play so beautifully."

"That is very kind of you to say, sir. Is there some business you would like to discuss?"

"Ah . . . no," he said, smiling a little sheepishly.

She smiled. "I confess I haven't much time today. I am quite involved with the orphans of St. Bartholomew and promised them a crate of oranges this afternoon." She hadn't precisely promised, and Mr. Anders would be dismayed to know what she'd done with his gift of the oranges, but there you had it. She and Lucy had carefully counted them out, delighted to find there was one for every child and even one for the sisters.

"A noble cause," he said as Keira stood and moved toward the door. "If there is any way I might be of assistance to you and the orphanage?"

"Would you?" she asked gratefully.

"Anything. You need only ask."

"That is very kind of you. We could use some kites."

"Kites?"

She laughed. "Can you imagine that I promised them kites? It was very impetuous of me, but it was a favorite pastime of mine as a child and there is that meadow just below the walls of the orphanage. I suggested it and could scarcely believe it—more than half of them have never had the pleasure!"

Mr. Sibley smiled indulgently. "Surely a few kites can be found in Hadley Green."

"One would think," Keira agreed. "But I have yet to find a single kite."

"Well, then," Mr. Sibley said, his chest puffing like bread. "The children must have their kites."

He returned three days later with an armful of kites in all shapes and sizes. He'd purchased them in London, he told her proudly.

"Oh," Keira said. "I never thought . . . I never intended that you should go to *London*—"

"You are all goodness, Lady Ashwood," he'd said admiringly. "It was the least I could do."

Keira graciously thanked him and felt obliged to invite him along. And in truth, she was a wee bit grateful for the diversion. Mr. Sibley's presence kept her thoughts from Declan. It was her own fault, really, for having fallen in love with a rogue.

She loaded Lucy into a coach to take the kites to St. Bartholomew, and Mr. Sibley rode alongside. It was a brilliant afternoon, and an outing that Keira rather desperately needed. It had been a week since she and Declan had tumbled in the grass, one long week of being in love and misery all at once.

With Sister Rosen's help, Keira led the children down to the meadow to fly the kites. There were at least a dozen kites in the air, and the sight of them flying above the treetops brought a handful of curious denizens from the village to see what was happening. Within an hour, more than just the children were flying kites. Some of the villagers and even a few of the sisters were flying kites.

Keira had taken three young boys under her wing, none of them older than four or five. She chose a kite painted blue with yellow flowers. Lucy said it matched her bonnet, which delighted Keira. "I'll have you know that at one time, I was the best kite flyer in all of Ireland," she informed the lads as she lined them up, shoulder to shoulder. "There is a secret to good kite flying. Would you like to hear it?"

The boys nodded.

"The secret," she confided, squatting down beside them, "is to catch the wind in just the right way. And to do that, one must run. Are any of you lads very fast?"

"I am!" the boy in the middle said, his hand shooting up in the air.

"I'm as fast as you," another one said, and the third one, the smallest of the three, merely blinked large brown eyes up at Keira.

"You look very fast," Keira said to him. "I think you must be my helper. And you boys, you must help me keep an eye on the kite. Will you do that? All right then," she said, and handed the string balled around a stick to the smallest boy. She untied the ribbons of her bonnet beneath her chin and tossed it onto the ground before taking her place between two of the boys. "Now then," she said, holding the kite, "on my mark, we shall run as fast as we can, and when we are running fast enough, the wind will catch the kite. You, sir," she said, tapping the smallest boy's shoulder, "you must let the string unwind with the kite, and when we've gone a good distance, we'll hold it aloft and make it do little tricks."

The boy gripped the two ends of the stick in both hands.

"Ready? On the count of three. One. Two. *Three!*" Keira ran; the boys ran after her. She let go the kite, feeding the string as it caught on the breeze and began to rise, calling excitedly to the smallest boy to let the string unwind. When the kite was in the air, she and the boys took turns guiding it. "Move with it!" Keira urged them as the kite dipped and swirled on the afternoon breeze. "And stay clear of the trees!" she shouted after them as they moved away from her, running with the kite, pulling it back then watching it sail off again.

She watched them for a few moments, and when she was satisfied that they knew what they were doing, she turned around.

She almost collided with Declan.

He was holding her bonnet. One corner of his mouth curled up in something of a lazy smile. "I found this and could think of only one person who might have lost it. Again."

Keira could feel her face light with her smile. "I really must do better at keeping them on my head," she said, accepting it from him. She fitted the hat on her head and tied the ends.

"I was looking for you," he said.

Keira was absurdly thrilled to hear it. "How did you know I was here?"

He smiled wryly and glanced up at the dozen kites flying. "I had a hunch."

"Lord Donnelly!"

Keira almost groaned at the sound of Mr. Sibley's voice behind them.

"Did you come to fly kites, my lord?" Sibley asked as he walked into their midst.

"No," Declan said. "Did you, Mr. Snively?"

"Here now, sir—"

"Pardon. Mr. Sibley."

One of the boys cried out before Mr. Sibley could speak, and Keira, shielding her eyes from the sun with her hand, looked in their direction. "Oh dear. Mr. Sibley, their kite has been caught in the tree. Would you mind terribly?"

Mr. Sibley hesitated. He looked at the boys standing helplessly under the tree, staring back at them. He then looked at Declan, and his gaze narrowed slightly. "Perhaps Lord Donnelly—"

"Naturally, I would," Declan said. "But I have injured my knee."

Mr. Sibley looked at his knee. So did Keira. It looked perfectly fine. No doubt to Mr. Sibley, too, who glared at Declan.

"A spill from a horse," Declan offered casually, and shifted his weight, as if daring Sibley to question him as to which knee.

"Then I shall come to the boys' rescue," Mr. Sibley said,

as if announcing he was off to war. He gave Keira a curt nod. "Madam." He began striding in the direction of the boys.

"Intolerable," Declan muttered.

"Mr. Sibley is the one who provided the kites," Keira said. "He has been very kind."

"Has he," Declan drawled. "I thought he'd gone back to London and his little hole there."

Keira studied Declan's impassive face. "He has come back to ready Tiber Park for the arrival of the count." She smiled coyly. "Among other things," she added smugly.

Declan looked at her incuriously.

His lack of concern irked Keira. Had she imagined that afternoon between them? "Mr. Anders has also called. He brought me a crate of oranges."

One of Declan's brows lifted above the other. "You are well favored among bachelors in West Sussex, it would seem."

"Yes. I am."

He mulled that over as his gaze settled on her eyes. "I would congratulate you, but you are doing a fine job of congratulating yourself. I'll leave you to your admirers," he said, and with a tip of his hat he began to walk away.

"Pardon?" she said as he walked. "What? Wait . . . no, please wait, my lord," she said, and hurried in a half skip, half walk to his side.

He kept walking.

"I think you are jealous," she said, pressing him as she hurried to keep up.

He snorted at that. "Don't be absurd."

"You needn't sound so vexed," she said testily. "I rather

thought you'd come around about Mr. Bowman. Mr. Fish has told me where we might find him."

He paused then and looked down at her. "There's a bit of progress. Where is he?"

"Rockingham," Keira said. "I've been thinking how we might call on him—"

"I will call on him."

Keira didn't care for the authoritative way he said it. "Yes, well, I rather thought you would ride along with me."

"Did you, indeed?" he asked amicably. "I thought you might prefer to stay behind and let Mr. Sibley admire you even more. Or eat more oranges that Mr. Anders brings you. I rather imagine you have enough to occupy you."

She gasped with surprise and smiled broadly. "You *are* jealous."

His smile was a little self-conscious. "Wasn't that the point of listing your many admirers?"

Indeed it had been, and her smile deepened with her satisfaction. "At least *they* have called to see how I fare."

"Aha." Declan's gaze swept over her. "We have come to it, have we? If you have encouraged that poor fop's suit to antagonize me, you have treated us both ill."

"Don't be so superior," she said lightly. "I did not encourage his suit and I did not think it unreasonable to think you might be a wee bit envious, given that . . . What we . . . *Everything*." Her face was growing warm, and Declan, damn him, stood calmly and coolly, as if he had this conversation quite frequently. Perhaps he did. Perhaps she was another in a long line of ladies. And she'd been foolish enough to believe—

She gaped at him.

He arched a brow. "Is something amiss?"

"Indeed it is," she said, glaring up at him from beneath her hat. "I think you are a most exasperating man."

"The feeling is entirely mutual," he cheerfully agreed.

"How can you pretend nothing has happened?" she demanded.

He glanced to where the children were flying kites. "Here now, here comes your most ardent admirer," he said, and looked at her again. "Keira, what happened between us was pleasurable for us both. But it is not necessary to attach any more meaning to it than that. I will see Mr. Bowman."

Her breath caught. The remark about her grand schemes aside, she couldn't believe what she was hearing. It seemed so cold and detached, even for Declan. "You don't mean that," she said accusingly. "I don't believe you mean that at all. You're not a tree, devoid of any proper feeling—"

"Mr. Sibley," Declan said, looking past Keira now. "How well you fetched that kite from the tree. You are a fine climber, indeed. Watching you climb that tree leads one to believe you have practiced climbing in all manner of venues."

"By God, Donnelly, it's a small wonder you've not been shot," Mr. Sibley said coldly.

Declan grinned. "I will not argue that. I shall take my leave of you then. Madam," he said to Keira, and strode from their midst.

"Lady Ashwood, shall we return to the kites?" Mr. Sibley asked, touching her elbow.

Sibley was absolutely right—it was little wonder some-one had not shot Declan before now, and if Keira knew a thing about guns, she might do the honor herself. "We shall, Mr. Sibley," she said, and marched alongside him back to the children, imagining all the delicious ways Declan O'Conner could meet his demise.

Twenty-one

He was jealous. Madly jealous. And that surprised Declan. Moreover, it worried him. What had happened to him? For fifteen years, he'd lived comfortably free of entanglements. He'd moved between Ireland and England at will, and before the wars, on the Continent, as well. He had done so without the entanglement of women, something that his friends had not been so fortunate to avoid, and suddenly, he could think of little else but the worst entanglement of them all—Keira Hannigan.

To make matters worse, he had discovered today that while he'd been brooding about her, and trying to shake Keira's ironclad grip on his mind, she was out flying kites and dining on oranges, courtesy of her many admirers. With Snively, for Christ's sake! Did she have no more regard for her future than that? Loman Maloney was a far better choice for her.

The point was, Declan angrily told himself, that if she were going to play loosely with the affections of so many men, she ought to do it with men of a better caliber than Sniveling.

He had no one to blame but himself for his ill state of mind. The unusual mix of innocence and lust for life in

Keira had held him in thrall. He had let his purest, basest instincts take hold of his common sense. It had been a fatal flaw, and the reason he'd stayed away for as long as he could bear it. And while he'd been swept up in the moment—all right, moments, many moments—she was still Keira Hannigan.

If that couldn't put his desire in check, where would this feeling lead? Declan was a man who valued his freedom to roam and breed horses and see his friends when and where he desired. He did not want to be shackled to Ballynaheath all his days. He thought he would give it to Eireanne when she married, and he would make his home in London. He never believed he'd have heirs, not really. But a wife—an Irish countess—would mean he needed a seat, and a place he might call home, and a foundation from which to raise children. Ballynaheath was that. Ballynaheath was his legacy.

Oh, the madness that had swallowed him! He was thinking of *marriage*? Were he ever to see his way to marriage, of all the women in the world, Keira Hannigan would shackle him to Ballynaheath. She would likely be banned from England when the truth was known about this colossal deception, and that was if she could manage to escape greater punishment for her crime. Further, he rather doubted that her idea of clearing the Scott name or contributing to the orphanage or building a mill would have any bearing on how the authorities would perceive her misdeed. She seemed to forget that she was an Irishwoman in England, which was enough to slant the law against her without even benefit of a crime. She was a silly, foolish woman who had no idea how many in England reviled the Irish Catholics. She lived here as she lived in Ireland—boldly. Recklessly.

These were ridiculous, sentimental feelings he was having, and he wondered idly if there was a tincture for it. He would inquire of Widow Cleeney the next time he was in County Galway—she seemed to have a potion to cure anything.

But in the meantime, what did he do with this burning in him?

He rode to Rockingham the following afternoon hoping distance was the cure, as it had been for him when he'd gone to London. He should never have come back from London, and perhaps he wouldn't have, had Christie's youngest brother Harry not arrived on Christie's doorstep.

Now, it was too late.

Rockingham was hardly a village at all. There were a few squat thatched-roof buildings built along a narrow road that housed sundry shops and a blacksmith. That was where Declan inquired after Mr. Samuel Bowman.

"Bowman," the smithy said thoughtfully. "Don't rightly know, milord. But if he lives in these parts, the vicar will know."

The church was a very small affair for England, with a one-room chapel and a raised platform at one end where the pulpit was situated. Declan was fortunate enough to find the vicar inside, polishing the communion pieces. He was a large, cheerful man, with an unruly crop of black hair, who took up most of the space between the pews and the pulpit. "Mr. Samuel Bowman!" he boomed when

Declan introduced himself and inquired after Mr. Bowman, his voice echoing in the cavern of the small church.
Declan guessed he kept his parishioners on the edge of
their seats when he delivered the gospel each Sunday. "Mr.
Bowman never missed a church service until his gout got
the best of him."

"Do you know where I might find him?" Declan asked.

"Well, that depends on your business, my lord. I
wouldn't put a parishioner in harm's way."

"He has nothing to fear from me. I seek some information he may have gleaned from serving the Earl of Ashwood."

The vicar's brows wiggled. "Best not mention the earl,"
he said, and resumed his polishing.

"Whyever not?" Declan asked curiously.

"To hear Mr. Bowman tell it, the Earl of Ashwood
ruined his life."

"You mean the Lady Ashwood—"

"No. The earl," the vicar insisted.

That certainly contradicted what Declan thought he
knew. "How so?"

"You must ask Mr. Bowman that question. In truth,
he never shared his reasons with me, but he has steadfastly refused to atone for any slanderous thing he has
said about the earl." He put down his rag and frowned
thoughtfully. "I best take you round myself."

"I won't trouble you—"

" 'Tis no trouble, my lord! A bit of fresh air is good for
the spirit. And I think you will need some introduction.
Mr. Bowman does not care for strangers."

Splendid, Declan thought wryly. Keira's image suddenly loomed in his mind's eye, and he wished he had a post to kick.

The vicar hummed a hymn on what seemed to Declan to be a very slow ride into the country. Frankly, Declan worried that the vicar's nag—Old Mabel, he called her—would make it as far as the end of the lane, but the horse and the vicar resolutely plodded along.

About a mile from the church, the vicar turned onto a path that led into the woods. It was hardly a road, more of a well-traveled trail. They followed it another mile or so until they came to a modest manor house, which the vicar paused to admire. "It's not as impressive as other houses in this area, but this house has a lot of history in her. Built in the time of Henry VIII's reign and given to Mr. Cromwell's grandniece." He looked at Declan. "Before Cromwell fell into disfavor, of course."

It was apparent that it had been a fine home at one point. It was made of stone, with great columns holding up a portico. But the lawn had gone to seed, and the mortar was crumbling. One of the columns was tilting slightly right.

"I have urged Mr. Bowman to keep it in good repair, for I am an advocate of preserving our past. Yet Mr. Bowman will not hear of it. He does not care for strangers."

"So you keep saying," Declan said.

"Shall we, my lord?" the vicar said, and urged the nag forward.

They had hardly taken a handful of steps when an elderly man appeared in the doorway with a rifle at his shoulder pointed at the two of them.

"Now, then, Mr. Bowman," the vicar said patiently, putting up his hands. "There is no call for that. Put the gun down, please."

"Who is it?" the elderly man rumbled. "Who are you?"

"He doesn't see very well," the vicar said to Declan, and to Mr. Bowman. "I am Vicar Harcourt, whom you know very well. And this is the Earl of Donnelly of Ireland."

Mr. Bowman lowered his gun slightly and peered at Declan. "Ireland? What have I got to do with a mean Irishman?"

"Mr. Bowman! That is hardly charitable," the vicar said sternly. "He cannot help that he is Irish."

Declan gave the vicar a withering look, but the vicar's gaze was trained on Mr. Bowman.

"They're all buggers," Mr. Bowman said spitefully.

With a supreme effort of patience, Declan said, "I won't take more of your time than is absolutely necessary, sir."

"You have no business with me," Mr. Bowman said, but the point of his rifle was now on the ground. "You may as well ride on."

"I think you may very well have information I need, sir," Declan said. "If you will indulge me?"

"Information!" he scoffed. "What sort of information would I have to benefit you?"

Before Declan could respond, a small woman in a lace collar and lace cap appeared on the doorstep. "Samuel!" she said. "Put that gun away and invite the gentlemen in!"

"Don't want them in my house," he argued.

"I will not allow you to treat guests so abominably. Do come in, sirs," she said, and without warning or effort she took the gun from Mr. Bowman and disappeared inside.

The vicar swung down and left his horse untethered, apparently unafraid she would bolt. He walked to Mr. Bowman's side. "Come in, Mr. Bowman."

Declan dismounted and tethered his horse, and with a hand on the gun in his pocket, he warily followed the others inside.

The house was filled with the clutter of a long life. There were books and papers piled on tables in the main drawing room and needleworks in various stages of completion scattered on the settee. Mrs. Bowman shooed a cat off a chair and offered it to Declan, but he thanked her and remained standing. He had a feeling he'd not be long.

Mr. Bowman, however, sat in a chair near the hearth. A cat instantly jumped in his lap and settled in. "Whatever it is you want, you'll not find your answers here," he said to Declan as he stroked the cat. "I won't help you."

"I'll bring tea," Mrs. Bowman said cheerfully.

"Don't bring a bloody thing, Margaret!" Mr. Bowman said, but she was already bustling out the door.

"A bit of honey if you please, Mrs. Bowman," the vicar called after her.

"Well then, get on with it," Mr. Bowman said to Declan as he scratched the cat behind its ears.

"I am here on behalf of a friend," Declan said. "You prosecuted a theft at Ashwood fifteen years ago in the name of the earl—"

"By God, you don't dare come into my house and ask me that!" he thundered.

Declan was surprised by the force of his objection. "I have a very simple question. Why was it that Lady Ashwood did not attend the trial of Mr. Joseph Scott in the matter of her stolen jewels?"

"Oh dear," the vicar muttered.

Mr. Bowman's hand on the cat stilled. The color bled from his face. He suddenly pushed the cat from his lap and struggled to stand. The vicar rushed to his side to help him, but Mr. Bowman slapped his hand away. "You are *vile*," he spat, pointing a finger at Declan. "You have no right!"

"The man was accused of stealing the lady's jewels, yet she did not appear at his trial to testify to that effect," Declan quickly added. "Why was the question not put to her? Was she away from Hadley Green?" Declan pressed.

The color was coming back to Mr. Bowman's face. He was even a bit purple. "You bloody Irishman, you have no idea what you are meddling in!"

"Perhaps we should all sit down," the vicar said.

Declan ignored him and stepped closer to Mr. Bowman. "I think I have an idea. I believe an innocent man hanged, Mr. Bowman, and I believe that you may know something of it."

The old man was shaking. "Get out. Leave at once!"

"I think you should do as he asks, my lord," the vicar said fearfully.

But Declan wasn't leaving without some information. "Why did Lady Ashwood ask you to leave Ashwood after the trial?"

"You reach too far above yourself, you Irish cur! Leave that matter be!"

"Please, please, gentlemen," the vicar pleaded. "Do sit down. We can discuss this like reasonable men—"

"Where was the countess, Mr. Bowman? Why wasn't she there to testify on behalf of her lover?"

Mr. Bowman froze a moment before collapsing into his chair.

"Mr. Bowman! Are you quite all right?" the vicar cried, rushing to aid him.

"I am fine, I am fine," Mr. Bowman said, pushing him away once more. He pressed his fingers into his eyes as if they pained him.

Mrs. Bowman entered the room with a plate of biscuits. "The tea will— Dear God! What has happened? Samuel, are you unwell, darling?"

"I think you should go, my lord," the vicar said firmly. "Mr. Bowman is an old man. He should not be subjected—"

Declan ignored the vicar and abruptly knelt down beside the old man. "Mr. Bowman, I seek to clear an innocent man's name. I wish you no harm, sir, but I should like to know why the countess wasn't present at the trial?"

Mr. Bowman opened his eyes. They were red, with tears or anger, Declan did not know. "She wasn't there. That's all I will tell you."

"Why did Mr. Scott hang so quickly? There were not five days from the time he was found guilty until he was hanged."

"Oh dear," Mrs. Bowman said.

"You are upsetting the lady," the vicar said irritably.

Declan studied Mr. Bowman's face, the sagging skin, the dark circles under his eyes, and the hard set of his mouth. But he saw something else there. He saw guilt. "Mr. Scott was innocent, wasn't he?"

Mr. Bowman glared at Declan and pointed a bony finger at him. "I will warn you again, sir. There are some things in this world that are better left alone. No good can come of your inquiry. Do you understand me? No good can come of it. Now I will thank you to take your leave and never appear at my door again."

Declan suspected that whatever Mr. Bowman knew would go to his grave with him, along with his guilt. He looked at the vicar, and at Mrs. Bowman, who stared at him with fear. "Thank you for your time," he said, and started for the door.

"Sir!"

Declan paused at the door and looked back.

Mr. Bowman was standing again. "There have been times in my life that, against my will, I have been forced to do things in order to protect my family. Do you understand me?"

Declan understood him perfectly. Mr. Bowman had been forced to prosecute an innocent man. He gave him a curt nod.

"You are a bloody fool to open old wounds," Mr. Bowman added acidly.

Perhaps. But Declan could not, in good conscience, leave it now.

Twenty-two

The planning for the gala had begun to consume Keira. She was consulted on every aspect, whether or not she desired it. It seemed as if there were a steady stream of visitors to Ashwood to talk about the arrangement of the tables, or to determine the racecourse, or the number of boats that would be allowed on the small lake. There were never-ending discussions as to the music and food, the crafts and wares. Mrs. Ogle and Mrs. Morton and the ladies from the Society seemed to constantly be at Ashwood, as well as the Reverend Tunstill, who accompanied Sister Rosens from the orphanage. Moreover, Mr. Anders and Mr. Sibley continued to vie for her attention.

Today, Keira and Mr. Graham, the head groundsman, and Mrs. Morton were reviewing the race route on old, yellowed maps of the Ashwood estate.

"We'll stake it down by the gazebo, and then around to the old oak," Mr. Graham said, pointing at a mark on the map. "Surely you remember that old oak, mu'um, do you not?"

"An old oak?" Keira asked, looking at the place he pointed on the map. "I . . . I don't rightly recall, sir," she said, staring at the map.

"Beg your pardon, mu'um," Mr. Graham said instantly. "I rather thought you might. You and Mrs. Thorpe's girl climbed so high you couldn't come down. Took us all of one afternoon to fetch you."

Keira kept her gaze on the map. "Ah yes," she said. She could feel everyone's gaze on her, could feel their curiosity as to why she would not remember something like that.

"Take me!" Lucy cried from somewhere beneath the table. "I should like to see the oak!"

"Lucy, please come out from there," Keira said. "The oak will have to wait. There is far too much to be done for the gala."

"I wish the gala would be over," Lucy said petulantly as she climbed out from under the table, and bumping into Mr. Graham as she did.

Keira sincerely wished the same thing. The gala was only a fortnight away and Lily really should have been home by now. By Keira's calculations, Lily should have arrived last week. She supposed it was weather or something that had prevented her from sailing, but surely Lily would return before the gala. Surely. Keira looked at Lucy. She thought of Sister Rosens, of Mr. Fish. Of Linford and Mrs. Thorpe and a host of others at Ashwood. She considered them friends, if not family. "This course will do, Mr. Graham. Do you not agree, Mrs. Morton?"

"I do," Mrs. Morton agreed.

"Splendid," Keira said, and turned away. She felt a little ill, imagining what all these people would think if she were somehow discovered before Lily returned.

She couldn't think of it. It would drive her mad.

Fortunately, Linford appeared. "A caller, madam," he announced.

"Who is it now, Linford? Mr. Anders?"

"No, mu'um. A gentleman. I have taken the liberty of putting him in the study."

"Always a gentleman," Mrs. Morton said, smiling slyly at Keira. "Shall I finish up with Mr. Graham?"

"Please," Keira said, and thanking Mr. Graham, she followed Linford out and to the study. At the door of the study, Linford opened it and said, "Lord Eberlin, madam."

Eberlin, she thought as she crossed the threshold. Wait . . .

The man who stood in the study was very striking in his appearance, tall and broad shouldered. His eyes were so dark that they looked almost black. He had a thick head of hair the color of honey, a fine pair of lips, a square jaw. He said nothing at first, but stared at her, as if he expected her to speak.

Lord Eberlin. The Danish count, the man who was trying to steal one hundred of Ashwood's best acres. What was it Fish had told her yesterday? Yes, yes, that Mr. Goodwin would call at the end of the week with his preliminary findings. *Stall*, Keira said to herself.

The count was looking at her so closely that Keira felt oddly exposed. "Lord Eberlin. You have come to England at last." She glided forward to offer her hand.

"I have." He hesitated, peering curiously at her face a moment before taking her hand and touching his lips lightly to her knuckles. He let go and stood back. Keira noticed then that he was holding a small bag. "Please forgive my intrusion," he said, his gaze resting coolly on her face. "I have come to Tiber Park and wanted to personally introduce myself to my closest neighbor."

He had an odd accent, one that seemed not quite English or Continental, but somewhere in between. "Welcome," she said, and made her smile as warm as she could manage. "I beg your pardon, my lord, but had I known you would call today, I would have asked my agent, Mr. Fish, to join us."

"My call is purely social," he assured her. His gaze flicked over her, a sort of meandering, stock-taking glance that Keira was accustomed to from gentlemen. But instead of smiling appreciatively as most men were wont to do, he turned away and strolled to the window, still holding the bag, and stood there, looking out.

"Are you looking for something in particular?" she asked, confused by his behavior.

"I am looking at the view," he said. "You have an impressive fountain."

Keira glanced at the window. Three angels trumpeted heavenward, and water spouted from their horns.

"A relatively new addition to the estate," he remarked, and looked at Keira.

His gaze was uncomfortably intent. He did not look at her in the way men looked at her. His gaze was cold, and felt even a wee bit malicious. "I am uncertain of the date it was built," she said.

"Are you?"

How odd. "Have you taken up residence at Tiber Park?" she asked.

His gaze never wavered from hers. "Not as yet, as there is much work to be done. I have taken residence near Uppington Church for a few days."

Splendid. She hoped he would be very comfortable there and would be leaving for it soon. She smiled.

His expression was impassive. "Have you . . . have you thought of Uppington Church since your return to Ashwood?"

"Thought of it? I am not familiar with the church. Is it very near here?"

His jaw bulged slightly, as if he were gritting his teeth. "Very near. Two miles, at most." He watched her, as if he expected her to say more about the church, or to announce that she'd suddenly remembered it. When she did not, he glanced down at the bag he held. "There is a cottage on the river that runs between our properties. Near the old mill." He looked up. "You are to be commended for your work there. It looks as if it will be a fine one."

"That is my hope," Keira said. "You are welcome to bring your grain there to be milled if you'd like. Mr. Fish can give you the particulars."

Eberlin smiled coldly. "Thank you, but there will be no need. I intend to build my own mill."

She blinked. "The mill will be large enough to accommodate both our estates and more."

"Yes, it seems so," he said, nodding. "But I will build my own."

Her heart started to race. She thought she understood him—he wanted to stand in direct competition to Ashwood. "Where?" she asked, knowing the answer.

"Upriver," he said. "On the acreage that will revert to me."

She could not believe his gall. He would come to Ashwood, tell her he was stealing her land and her mill so casually? She laughed lightly and said, "One might think you were in the business of destroying Ashwood, what with your mill and the desire to have that acreage, milord." She smiled. "I am sure that is not your intent."

"You may think whatever you like," he said smoothly.

"I think the acreage is a matter open to interpretation," she said firmly. "You should know that I have hired one of the best solicitors in London. He assures me it is not as easy as you would have me believe." A small lie, but she hardly cared. "And really, my lord, two mills so close?"

He shrugged. "Farmers will have to choose one or the other, won't they?"

Why did he hate Ashwood so? Keira could not catch her breath. He was openly taunting her. "We shall see," she said, just as casually as he spoke. "But the matter can hardly be resolved today. Perhaps another time?"

He made no move to leave. He opened the bag he held. "The cottage near the old mill was, as you know, abandoned some time ago. But I found this."

Keira held her breath. She wouldn't be the least bit surprised if he withdrew a human skull from that bag. But it was a toy horse that had lost two legs. "A toy," she said. "I suppose one of the tenants left it behind."

"I hardly think it a tenant's toy. It was exquisitely crafted. A child's toy belonging to one of your tenants would likely be made of straw and such. I thought you might want it," he said, and held the horse out to her.

"What? The toy?" She didn't trust him, or that horse without its legs. How could he possibly think she would care for such things? "Thank you. I shall give it to the children at St. Bartholomew's."

He slowly lowered his hand. "Very well, then."

She wished he would leave and glanced at the door.

"Well. Thank you for receiving me, Lady Ashwood."

"Of course," she said coolly, and avoided his gaze as she walked to the door.

Eberlin followed her, but at the door, he looked at her again in a very cold and calculating manner. "Madam," he said, and handed her the bag as he walked out.

The moment he was gone, Keira tossed the blasted bag with the broken toy onto a chair. When she was quite certain he was gone, she shut the door and fell back against it, her hands now pressed against her abdomen. She wished desperately for Lily to come.

She did not allow herself to think of what would happen to her when Lily came. But she couldn't bear it if anything more should happen to Ashwood under her stewardship.

Twenty-three

Linford informed Declan that Lady Ashwood was teaching Miss Taft to ride in the park when Declan reached Ashwood. He found Keira leading the small palfrey mare by the bit in a large circle while Lucy clung to the horse's mane.

Declan slowed his horse to a slow walk as he rode into their midst.

"Well, well," Keira said. She smiled as she led the palfrey in a circle around him and his mount. "I thought perhaps you had died."

"Died?" he asked with a wry smile. "Before Lily has come and all is revealed? I couldn't possibly," he said, and dismounted. "Miss Taft, how do you do this fine afternoon?"

"I am learning to ride," she said stiffly. Her color was pale and her grip knuckle-white. The weather was warm, and her face had a dewy look to it. Keira, on the other hand, looked quite fresh in her sky-blue riding habit. A long, thick tail of black hair hung down her back, and she wore an elaborate hat with feathers. Declan couldn't help but wonder after the birds who had lost their plumage to this woman's hats.

"May I come down now?" Lucy asked.

"You've scarcely ridden at all, darling," Keira said.

"Be calm," Declan advised the girl. "The horse won't hurt you."

"It won't do a wee bit of good," Keira said, bringing the little mare to a halt. "It would seem that Lucy is afraid of horses."

"Have you ridden with her?" Declan asked. He'd taught Eireanne to ride by putting her in front of him.

Keira snorted. "I can scarcely manage to remain on that saddle myself."

That caused Declan to grin. If there was one thing he could say about Keira Hannigan, it was that she could sit any horse on any saddle. "Miss Taft, would you like to ride with me? I will show you how to use the reins."

"Yes, please, my lord!" Lucy replied, but in her enthusiasm to get off the horse, she shifted slightly. She gasped and bent fearfully over the horse's neck.

"*Dhia*, she is hopeless," he muttered.

"Completely," Keira agreed.

Declan dismounted and hauled Lucy down from the palfrey. "Allow me," he said gallantly, offering his arm to her when she was on firm ground. "Will you bring the mare?" he asked Keira.

"Gladly," she said, and smiled smartly as she walked past him.

He watched her set her foot into the slipper stirrup and effortlessly pull herself up, and wondered how she managed to look more alluring every time he saw her. She sent the palfrey trotting ahead of Declan and Lucy, her feathers bouncing along with her, and Declan wondered how often Snively or Anders had been around to admire her in his absence.

At the stables, Keira sent Lucy inside.

"Shall I ring for tea?" Lucy asked.

"I think it is too early, dear," Keira said.

"But you always ring for tea when you have callers, mu'um."

"Oh?" Declan said, peering down at the girl. "And have there been a lot of callers to come round for tea?"

"Squads of them," Lucy said matter-of-factly as she studied the fit of her riding habit, yanking on the ends of her coat.

"Oh goodness, Lucy, how you exaggerate!" Keira said laughingly.

"Gentlemen callers?" Declan asked casually.

"Gentlemen and ladies. Her ladyship is very well regarded," Lucy said. "Sister Rosens says she has indomble spirit."

"Indelicate?" Keira asked.

"Indomitable," Declan offered with a chuckle.

Lucy paused; her brow furrowed. "Perhaps," she said uncertainly. "Shall I ring for tea?"

"Oh, very well then," Keira said, and ran her hand over Lucy's crown with a fond smile before sending her on. When Lucy had slipped around the corner of the house, Keira looked at Declan. "A word?" she said, nodding toward the garden. "I prefer not to be seen." She started toward the iron gate.

"Ah. Too many suitors again, aye?" Declan asked as he followed her.

"What?" She swung the gate open, hitting him in the arm when she did.

He put his hand on the gate and deliberately pushed it aside before walking through. "You seem rather agitated, Countess. What has happened now? Has the king come calling?"

"I look agitated, do I?" she asked with feigned surprise. "I can't imagine why, my lord! My only friend all but disappears—"

"I won't say I am distressed to hear Lady Horncastle has gone missing—"

"Not *her*, you ridiculous man—*you*! You are my only friend and you disappeared, and in the meantime, I have been forced to endure the machinations of this entire shire!" she said dramatically, one arm swinging wide toward the shire. "It's been entirely wretched!"

Declan was unable to suppress his smile. "I am quite touched," he said, bowing gallantly. "I think you've missed me."

"For the love of God," Keira snapped, and began to march down the garden path, pausing once to glare at him. "Come, come," she urged him, gesturing with her hand.

There was something in her voice that sounded as if Keira were truly at wits' end. "All right," he said, and put his hand on the small of her back. "Tell me what has happened."

She groaned. "What *hasn't* happened? The Society ladies have a *constant* presence at Ashwood in the planning of the blasted gala, Mr. Fish has been in London, Lord Eberlin has called and presented himself as a very strange man, and now Lady Horncastle has invited Lady Darlington to the gala, as well as her youngest son, with the *express* purpose of making a match! With *me!*" she cried, pointing at herself.

Eberlin? Declan gaped at her. "What did you say?"

"Yes, I agree, it's quite shocking. Apparently, it is Lady Darlington's great desire that I might find love and happiness with—"

"Not that," Declan said, shaking his head. "You said Lord Eberlin. How do you know Eberlin?"

She looked puzzled. "He is the man who purchased Tiber Park."

Declan stared at her in disbelief. "He is also the man who has retained me to breed a champion racehorse."

Keira gasped. "You *know* him?" she cried, grabbing his arm.

"No, no, I've never made his acquaintance," Declan clarified. "I've dealt only with his agent. You never mentioned who purchased the park."

She shrugged. "There was no reason to."

"It is a rather unbelievable coincidence that he is here," Declan said, frowning. "I understood he was coming to England, but not until there was a foal. And I certainly had no idea he'd purchased property."

"He is very odd," Keira agreed, and suddenly rubbed her arms, as if she'd had a chill. "Frighteningly so."

"What do you mean?" Declan demanded.

"I don't know how to explain it, really," she said thoughtfully. "He brought me a broken toy he found in an abandoned cottage."

Declan couldn't help but laugh. "Perhaps he wanted to stand out among all the flowers."

Keira gave him a withering look and began walking again. "Please don't tease me. There was something entirely foreboding about him. He intends to ruin Ashwood."

"You mustn't fret, lass. That sort of gentleman's interests lie elsewhere."

"What sort of gentleman?" she asked curiously.

"The sort who gambles for very high stakes, which, obviously, Eberlin is, as he is determined to have the fastest racehorse in all of Europe. I am curious that he has purchased Tiber Park. I would think his agent might have mentioned it, particularly once he knew that I was letting Kitridge Lodge."

"Not only has he purchased it, but Mr. Sibley tells me a portion of it will open within a fortnight. Really, never mind that—you haven't said a word of the Darlingtons," she complained.

He smiled down at her. "What would you have me say?"

"Declan! Haven't you heard a word I've uttered? Lady Darlington wants to make a match between her son and Lily! That is, *me*."

He laughed.

Keira groaned. "I shall be ruined. You realize that, do you not? They will discover everything and I shall be ruined."

"With Lord Raley, it shall be a race as to which of you is ruined first," Declan said. "Don't fret. Of all the things you must think about, that is the least. I know Harry very well, and he will never marry. He is a miscreant and a source of never-ending concern for his brother, the duke."

Keira sighed. She cocked her head and studied him.

"For all your lack of feeling, sir, you do know how to calm me." He was surprised by that, but even more surprised when she reached up and brushed her fingers across the stubble of a beard he'd not touched for a few days. The touch jolted him; every fiber was suddenly thrumming.

"Where have you been, Declan?" she asked softly.

Keeping away from you, muirnín. "Did you not receive my note?" he asked, clasping his hands tightly at his back to keep them from her. "I called on Mr. Bowman, as I said."

She nodded. "But what took you so long?"

He felt uncomfortable, as he had no good answer for that. "I had to find him," he said vaguely. "Afterward, I wanted to review the record of the trial once more."

"What did you find?"

"In him? Nothing but guilt."

"Guilt." Keira winced. "What did he say?"

Declan couldn't look at those eyes and not think of the things he'd like to do with her. He put his hand to her elbow and guided her to walk. "Mr. Bowman refused to speak of it—any of it. In fact, he warned me from looking into the matter. But I strongly sensed something was there, something he intended to keep hidden. Mr. Bowman knows why an innocent man was accused, was tried and hanged. Unfortunately, he will not speak of it."

"Perhaps I might speak to him," Keira suggested.

"I think not. He made it quite clear he will not speak of it, and he does not care for callers. He meets them at the door with a gun."

"A gun! Then what are we to do?" Keira asked with obvious frustration.

"There must be someone who will speak of it besides

Hollingbroke," Declan suggested. "A servant, or someone from the village. Someone who knows what happened."

"Someone, but who? I am running out of time. Lily should have been home by now."

"Everything will be all right, Keira," he tried to assure her.

Keira made a clucking sound. "How easy it is for you to say, Declan. You cannot feel the weight of my deceit."

"Perhaps not, but I have indeed felt the weight of deceit," he reminded her, and Keira guiltily lowered her gaze. "You put yourself in this untenable position, and now you must see it through. That means you must keep breathing, one breath at a time."

She shook her head.

Declan touched her hand. "Keira, look at me." She paused to look at him warily. "You know as well as I that you must go on."

She nodded, then turned away, walking to a bench and sinking heavily onto it.

For all of Keira's foolishness, Declan knew she had never bargained for this. She seemed genuinely perplexed and contrite. He squatted down before her. "You can bear a few more days of it, lass. You're Irish, remember? You can do it for Lily's sake, because I know you'd not want to hand her an unmitigated mess when she returns to Ashwood."

"Yes, but Lily would understand if I—"

Declan stopped her by catching her chin and forcing her to look at him again. "For once in your blessed life, think about the consequences of what you do. Think of the children who will benefit from the summer gala.

Think of all the residents of Hadley Green who have worked to craft wares to be sold to benefit those children. Think of the men who are now employed, thanks to your idea of rebuilding the mill, and of the tenants of Ashwood whose livelihoods are protected from harm with you here and whose livelihoods would surely be derailed if your deception were discovered before Lily was here to set it all to rights. Think of Lucy, think of Mr. Scott's children, who have lived all these years without a father, and the one father they did have called a thief. Don't they deserve the truth?"

Keira's shoulders sagged. She closed her eyes, but said nothing.

"You cannot forget that so many depend on you," he said softly, and touched her cheek.

She opened her eyes then, and Declan could feel that powerful river's current flowing between them. "All right," she said softly.

He could see the emotional strain in the lines of her face and the set of her jaw. Declan would never have believed it, but he felt sorrow for her, felt a strong desire to help her, protect her. He could not help himself; he kissed her. She made a small sound when he did, one that sounded like relief and hope all at once. Declan rose up, pulling her up with him, kissing her deeply. His body was quick to respond; desire was thrumming in him, hardening him, drowning out everything else. He wanted to taste her skin, to feel her beneath him. "Come to the lodge," he said into her ear as he kissed her neck. "Come to me tonight," he insisted as his hands slipped over her body.

"I'll be ruined," she whispered hoarsely.

"You're already ruined, *muirnín*. You want to live, to experience life, aye? Then come to me."

"*No*," she said weakly.

Declan caught her hand and brought it to his mouth, kissing her fingers. "You want to come—I can see it in you," he said, and brushed his knuckles across her cheek.

Keira moved her face from his hand. "You see what you want to see."

"Then tell me what I see," he said, dipping down to peer in her eyes. "Tell me."

"Can you not see it plainly?" she moaned. "Do you recall that afternoon in Ireland?"

He faltered. "You know I do."

"I fancied you," she said. "It wasn't as impetuous as you think. I fancied you, and I had hoped for that moment. I still do. I still hope for the moment you fancy me as I fancy you."

He didn't know what to say to that. He was treading on dangerous ground here, but he couldn't promise her more than what he was offering. Which, he realized, was a rather shallow offer. He wanted her, but it had to be her choice. He cupped her face, traced a line along her jaw.

Keira pushed his hand down. "But I am not a doxy. Perhaps this would be a good time to remind me once more of the consequences of my actions," she said, and brushed past him as she started up the path.

Having his words tossed back at him stung. Declan was beginning to understand that, for the first time in his adult life, he had no idea what he was doing with a woman. He wanted her, but he was afraid to have her completely. He watched her walk briskly away, her hair swinging across the middle of her back. He did not call her back. She was right, of course—he was the height of hypocrisy.

Aye, but Declan had never in his life desired someone as completely as he desired that exasperating woman. What exactly he was going to do about that was very unclear to him, and he'd never been so bloody unclear about a thing.

Twenty-four

Keira's heart was beating like a drum as she ran up the steps into the entrance of Ashwood. She pushed open the double doors with both hands and strode through, tossing her hat onto a console, her riding gloves right behind them.

Declan O'Conner was killing her. *Killing* her. If he wasn't stoking unimaginable desire in her, making her want all the things she should not, could not want, he was urging her to think of the consequences, to understand that what she'd done had dire effects on others' lives.

As if she didn't know that. As if she didn't wake up with that thought and go to sleep with it eating away at her.

Keira looked at herself in the mirror above the console. She was so bloody ignorant! Declan was right—she never thought of consequences. She hadn't eight years ago, and she hadn't when she stepped out of the carriage at Ashwood for the first time. She'd never meant so many things to happen.

"Lady Ashwood, I rang for tea," Lucy said, appearing on Keira's right.

She wondered how long the girl had been there while she'd been burning inside and had failed to realize it.

"Oh yes, tea," Keira said. "Thank you, darling, but I don't think Lord Donnelly will be coming in." Thank the saints for that, at least. She didn't trust herself with him in the least.

"Not for him, mu'um. For Mr. Fish and the other man."

Keira paused in the smoothing of her hair and turned to look at Lucy. "Mr. Fish is here?"

Lucy nodded. "Should I not have sent for tea?"

"No, no, you were right to do it," Keira said, and put her hand on Lucy's shoulder. "I will make you a countess yet," she said, and earned a broad smile from the lass. "I think you have some lessons, do you not? Go and find Mrs. Thorpe, and I shall see you before supper."

"Yes, mu'um," Lucy said, and skipped off toward Mr. Scott's staircase.

Keira looked at herself in the mirror again. She could feel Declan's lips on her skin, could almost see the imprint of his mouth on her cheek. She smoothed her hair again, took a deep breath, and walked to the green salon.

Mr. Fish and Mr. Goodwin stood instantly when Keira walked into the room. "Mr. Fish," she said. "Mr. Goodwin, what a surprise."

Mr. Goodwin bowed. "A pleasure to see you once again, Lady Ashwood."

"Thank you." She gestured toward the settee. She was hardly in a mood to discuss Eberlin's suit at the moment. "Tea should be along shortly," she said absently.

"Thank you kindly, but I must return to London as soon as possible," Mr. Goodwin said. "I have news that I think you should hear."

"Oh? Please do be seated, Mr. Goodwin," Keira said, and sat on the edge of a chair.

"I'll be honest, madam. It is not particularly good news," Mr. Goodwin said as he took the seat she indicated. Mr. Fish remained standing. "I have come to Hadley Green to review the parish records to see if I might find anything to contradict what I have found thus far. Unfortunately, my research suggests the entail of the acreage in question is just as Mr. Sibley described it to you. Legally, it should revert to the owner of Tiber Park. There is no provision for you to inherit it."

Keira didn't speak at first; she was too stunned. Her mind began to race around the improbability, the repercussions of it. "Surely you must be wrong," she said at last, and slowly gained her feet. Mr. Goodwin stood, too. "I can't believe this," she said, looking at him. "I've never heard of such a thing!"

"I wish it were not true, madam, but that is the law and there is precedence for it. As I said, I intend to review the parish records with the hope of finding something that might contradict it, perhaps a provision that was made in the last few years, but I am not hopeful. Therefore, I think it best if you bargain with the owners of Tiber Park. At the very least, perhaps you might reach a settlement to compensate in some way for the loss of the acreage. I should be happy to—"

"No, I won't bargain."

She said it quickly, without thought. She would not sell Lily's land, and certainly not to a man who, for reasons she could not understand, sought to destroy Ashwood.

"Madam, if I may," Mr. Fish said. "Now that we have

been presented with the legal truth, why should you not seek a fair trade for the land?"

"There is no fair trade," Keira said briskly. "And none will be forthcoming, of that I am convinced. I've met Lord Eberlin, Mr. Fish. He will not bargain. He will as soon bring Ashwood down."

Mr. Fish looked perplexed and, Keira thought, a little impatient. "Has he said as much?"

"He has not, but I know that I am right, sir. There is something disturbingly wrong about Lord Eberlin, and I would not bargain with him even if I were at liberty to do so."

"But . . . but you *are* at liberty to do so," Mr. Fish argued.

"I am not," she said low. She wanted to tell him, dear God, she wanted to tell him the truth. What would he do, without Lily here to vouch for her? "You must trust me on this, Mr. Fish."

Mr. Fish seemed stunned. He glanced at Goodwin as a footman appeared at the door, carrying a tea service. Keira allowed the footman to pass and then walked to the door. "Mr. Goodwin, do please look at the parish records. I shall hope and pray that you find something that will help us there. Good day," she said, and quit the room.

Her mind was racing. She would not sell or bargain with that man.

Something told her she better push for the granary, for Ashwood would need all the income it could generate.

Feeling an uncharacteristic restlessness, Declan spent the late afternoon at Kitridge Lodge with a tankard of ale in one hand and a gun in the other, shooting at targets he set up along a fence. His only companion was Mr. Noakes, whom Declan dispatched to pick up one of two buckets he'd shot and set it up on the fence rails again.

"You undoubtedly think you've a mad Irishman on your hands," Declan remarked to the stoic caretaker as he took aim with one eye loosely closed. "You'd be right." He fired, missing the bucket completely. "But not because I am Irish."

Noakes wisely did not question him on that.

It was because Declan didn't know what he was doing. Keira's distress—even though she had brought it on herself—disturbed him. He wanted to somehow protect her from what was coming. It was a very primal need, he thought, one he'd never really had in quite this way.

And what, exactly, did it mean that he was having these thoughts and feelings at all, and for Keira, of all people? There were not two people more ill suited for one another. Hadn't that always been true? Wasn't it true yet? Keira Hannigan had caused him trouble for years. But this was different. It felt different, it tasted different. Yet it was still trouble.

Declan didn't know the answers to his questions. He could only wish that Lily would bloody well get to England.

The shooting and the ale did nothing to ease him, so Declan spent a restless evening, as well. He made a valiant effort to read, but he wasn't much of a reader, really, and his thoughts kept interrupting the words that explained the history of the Nordic peoples. At some point, Declan fell asleep in his chair; he awoke when the book slid off his lap and with a pain in his neck.

He blamed that on Keira, too.

The next day, after working with his horses, he thought of Penny. He'd not seen her in a few weeks, and it occurred to him that he might ease some of his restlessness in a most pleasurable way.

Penny was happy to see him; she smiled broadly and sashayed across the room to greet him. "An ale, milord?"

"An ale will not quench my thirst," he said, his gaze lingering on her bosom.

Penny smiled wantonly and leaned over, her breasts inches from Declan's face. "There is an empty room at the end of the hall," she said softly.

Declan grinned. "Bring ale," he said, and made his way through the crowded tables and chairs, mounting the stairs to the rooms above.

When Penny appeared a quarter of an hour later with a pair of tankards, Declan was sitting at the table, his feet propped on another chair. He invited Penny to have a seat at the table with him. She looked at him curiously, but gladly sat. "Oh, but it feels quite nice to be off me feet." She sighed, and draped her arms loosely across her belly, then looked at him, and then the bed, expectantly.

Declan smiled at his old lover. He'd been rash to come; he should have known he couldn't summon any desire to bed her. Honestly, he felt nothing but a friendly fondness for her. His thoughts were consumed with a raven-haired, green-eyed devil. "How is your brother?" he asked, sipping his ale.

"Me brother?"

"James?"

"Johnny, you mean. Oh, he's gone again, milord. He

scarcely spent a fortnight in my mother's home before he was gone again." She laced her fingers behind her head and stretched. "He's always wandered, that one. When he was a wee lad, 'twas up to me to mind him, and I was forever chasing that lad here and there and pulling him home again. Seemed like he wanted to run away."

Declan knew that feeling. He'd had it from the time he was a young man. When his father had died, leaving Declan the earldom, he had not wanted the responsibility, or to be chained to Ballynaheath all his days. Even then, he'd feared he'd never be allowed to leave Ireland for very long.

"That's his way of living, in truth," Penny said. "He's not happy if he's not seeing the world and something new with it every day."

Declan understood that deeper than anyone would ever know. "You've lived in Hadley Green all your life?" he asked Penny curiously.

"And me mum before me and her mum before her," Penny said proudly.

A thought suddenly occurred to Declan and he leaned forward. "You were here, then, when Mr. Scott was hanged."

"Oh, aye, I was indeed," she said. "I was only a girl, mind you, but it was a big to-do. Pappa, he saw him hanged and brought us all a confection. They sold them right there at the gallows."

"What did they say about him? About Mr. Scott?"

Penny shrugged. "That he was a bloody thief," she said unequivocally, and began to massage one knee. "He stole the countess's jewels."

"He was accused of it, yes, but the jewels were never recovered."

"Well now, they say he buried them somewhere in these parts." She chuckled. "Johnny and I, we dug up half of Sussex looking for them."

"Was there never any mention of his innocence?" Declan asked.

"Lud, no!" Penny scoffed. "Oh, aye, Louis says so, but Louis was little more than a lad himself. What's he know about it, eh?"

"Louis?"

Penny smiled sheepishly. "A footman at Ashwood. He comes round now and again. What . . . you thought I pined for only you, did you, milord?" she teased him.

Declan smiled. "What did Louis tell you?"

"Oh, I don't rightly remember," she said with a flick of her wrist. "Just that unlucky chap fell on his pitchfork because of it."

What unlucky chap? Declan put his tankard down. "What do you mean?"

"I don't rightly know, milord. Louis said once that an Ashwood chap died for talking too much. I don't remember aught else he said. Louis and me, we weren't exactly chatting it up."

A servant at Ashwood had the answer they'd been seeking all along. They'd assumed, when Linford and Mrs. Thorpe would not speak of it, that no one would. "This is important, Penny. Why did Louis tell you that?"

"Oh, it was a trifling thing," she said. "We were laughing about digging around for those bloody jewels, we were. Everyone round here dug for them. Everyone dreamed of being rich. Louis said the only man at Ashwood to say he'd not believe it of Mr. Scott was found lying stuck on a pitchfork one day. Took a right nasty tumble, I'd say."

Declan suddenly stood up.

"Where are ye going, milord?"

"I must speak with Louis," he said, and reached for his coin purse. "He's still a footman at Ashwood?"

"Aye, he is—but speak with Louis? About that old man?" Penny scoffed. "That was a long time ago, gov'na. Come here, now. I've got something ye might like a bit better than that."

Declan tossed a few coins on the table, leaned over, and kissed the top of Penny's head. "Thank you, Penny. You always know just what to say." He winked at her as he went out.

"If that doesn't take the bloody cake," she said after him, and picked up the coins, shoving them down in her ample cleavage.

Linford answered Declan's rap on the door at Ashwood. He bowed his old head and said, "Her ladyship is having tea with the ladies from the Society, my lord. Shall I inform her you have come?"

"Actually, I should like first to speak with Louis. Is he about?"

"Louis?" Linford said, frowning slightly. "May I ask, my lord, has Louis done something to offend?"

"Not in the least. But I think he might answer a question that has been on my mind."

"Perhaps I might answer it, as well," Linford offered.

"I think not, Linford. It is Louis I must see."

Linford didn't seem to particularly like that, but he gave Declan a curt nod all the same. "If you would be so good as to wait in the reception room, my lord?"

"Thank you," Declan said, and strode past the old butler.

He'd waited only a few minutes before Louis entered with a wary expression. He looked to be about Declan's age, which would have put him at the age of sixteen or seventeen the year Mr. Scott was hanged. Louis's gaze darted about the room, almost as if he expected someone to leap out at him. "My lord?"

Declan moved past the footman and shut the door, then turned to face him. Louis looked rather anxious now. "I shall make this brief, sir," Declan said. "What do you know of Mr. Scott's demise?"

The footman looked at him blankly. "My lord?"

"Mr. Scott, Mr. Joseph Scott. He hanged some fifteen years ago for stealing the countess's jewels."

The color bled from Louis's face. He looked to the door. "Not a thing, my lord. On my honor, not a thing. I was a lad then, ignorant of many things. I beg your pardon, but I am attending the countess." He tried to reach the door, but Declan stepped in front of him. "Look here. I do not seek to bring you trouble. But I believe an innocent man was hanged for the crime."

"I'd know nothing of that," Louis said again, and attempted to step around Declan.

This time, Declan stopped him by putting his hand to his chest and pushing him back. "I do not think I am the only one who believes he was innocent, Louis. I think there are many others who believe it, as well. But unfortunately, memories are short in Hadley Green, so when Penny told me you shared my skepticism, I thought we should have a bit of a chat. I want only to know why you believe him innocent."

Louis glanced down at Declan's hand on his chest. "I beg of you, sir, I've been at Ashwood eighteen years. If I lose my position, I'll have nowhere to go. My old mum is sick and she depends on me for her keep."

Declan dropped his hand. "You won't lose your position, I give you my word. And if you do, I'll personally find a post for you. Tell me what you know."

"Nothing," Louis said. "God as my witness, I don't know a thing."

"You said something different to Penny."

His face colored and he glanced down. "Penny ought to keep her mouth shut," he muttered.

"Tell me," Declan insisted again.

Louis sighed with resignation and made a helpless gesture with his hand. "No one here believed Mr. Scott took those jewels, aye. And . . . and Mr. Caufield, he tried to tell the old earl in a proper way that it wasn't Mr. Scott, that he'd seen the Lady Ashwood and Mr. Scott in the gardens on more than one occasion, but then Mr. Caufield, they found him a few days later with a pitchfork stuck in his chest. Ain't no one going to say they believe Mr. Scott was innocent after that."

It seemed so simple now that Declan was hearing what Louis had to say. The countess had had an affair, and when the earl found out, he punished the poor man by accusing him of theft. But *murder*? "What makes you believe Mr. Caufield's death was not a tragic accident?"

Louis groaned and looked at the door again. "You know as well as I do, milord, that when a man's been a stable master all his blessed life, he wouldn't leave a pitchfork lying about—much less trip and fall right on top of it, eh?"

God in heaven. "If what you imply is true, then why didn't the countess save the man from false accusations? Why didn't she attend his trial, or at the very least, produce the jewels to prove his innocence?"

He shrugged. "They say he threatened her," Louis said. "She and the earl had a terrible row the night the jewels went missing. Even the scullery maids could hear it, three floors down."

"He threatened her? With what?" Declan asked, and tried to imagine what sort of threat would keep a woman from saving her lover from the gallows.

"I don't know, milord," he said with a shake of his head. "It was so long ago, aye? Whatever it was, it was too late for Mr. Scott. I remember she said that very thing to Captain Corbett the morning she sent Miss Boudine to Ireland. I overheard her say it on the drive as I helped the lass into the coach. She said, 'I hanged him myself. There was naught I could do.' I'll never forget it, for it sent a chill through me bones."

Stunned, Declan stared at Louis. Althea Kent knew. She knew Scott had been wrongly accused and did not intervene. Had she taken her own life out of guilt? "Where might I find Captain Corbett?"

"That, sir, I could not tell you. He was a friend to the Lady Ashwood, and come down from London to take the girl away. He always came down from Town. I know, because he would hire a London coach to bring him."

Declan nodded. He reached into his purse and fished out a crown for Louis. "You have been most helpful."

Louis hesitantly took the coin and looked at it. "I have your word, sir, that I'll not lose my post?"

"You have my word," Declan assured him, and Louis slipped the crown into his waistcoat. "Now if you would be so kind as to tell your lady I have come to call."

"Aye, milord." Louis walked to the door and moved to open it.

"One other question," Declan said, drawing the footman's attention back to him once more. "Why did Lady Ashwood send Miss Boudine to Ireland?"

Louis shrugged. "I wouldn't know, sir. I'd guess the lass knew too much about the countess and her lovers. Perhaps you might ask her, eh?"

Twenty-five

Keira was mildly alarmed when Louis leaned over her shoulder and whispered in her ear that the Earl of Donnelly was waiting to see her. She nodded and smiled at Lady Horncastle, who was sitting directly across from her and going on excitedly about the prospect of making a match between Keira and Lady Darlington's youngest son.

"He has at least fifteen thousand a year," she said from her seat at the table on the terrace, where they were having tea. Below them, in the gardens, work had begun on the tent that would be erected for the gala, which was a mere four days away.

"He is considered quite the catch by all who have knowledge of these things," she said as she looked sagely around at the assembled group, which included Mrs. Morton, Mrs. Ogle, and Miss Babcock. "It is a very nice feather in your cap to have him so very interested in *you*, Lady Ashwood."

"The only interest in me is on the part of his mother," Keira said dryly.

"But my dear, that is the way things are *done*," Lady Horncastle insisted as she held out her cup for a footman to pour tea. "The gentlemen tell their mothers, who arrange for the introductions to be made."

"Mr. Sibley does not depend on his mother," Mrs. Morton observed.

"Nor does Mr. Anders," Miss Babcock added.

"Really!" Lady Horncastle said with the great exasperation of one being contradicted. "None of you understand how these things are done among the Quality as I do!"

Keira wasn't certain Lady Horncastle understood at all. She couldn't imagine Declan needing his grandmother to make his introductions for him. She rather imagined that women sought introduction to him.

"I thought I understood Lady Darlington's son was engaged to be married to a debutante," Mrs. Morton said.

"Excuse me, ladies," Keira politely interrupted. "There is a small matter I must attend to."

The ladies quickly gained their feet. "You refer to Lord Merrick, her second son," Lady Horncastle said to Mrs. Morton as Keira walked away and they resumed their seats. "To a debutante from Scotland, of all places! I've heard they think nothing of going unbathed in the north . . ."

With Louis on her heels, Keira walked quickly to the reception room. Louis opened the door ahead of her, and she saw Declan standing at the windows, peering out. She marveled that every time she saw him, a little bit more of her breath was snatched away. He looked so very handsome standing there, his dark hair brushing his collar, his coat fitting so tightly across his shoulders. He turned around as she entered and smiled in a most tender fashion, as if he were happy to see her, and her heart melted a wee bit.

She heard Louis shut the door behind her.

"The Society ladies are here."

"Dear God, not the Society ladies," he said with mock alarm.

"For heaven's sake, Declan, they are making matches for me left and right, and if they see *you* here, that will toss them all into matrimonial hysteria."

He laughed.

"It is not the least bit amusing," she warned him, walking deeper into the room. "You have no idea how difficult it is to bear their constant attentions while pretending to be someone I am not. But I must hurry back before they wonder where I've gone. Why did you come?"

"To see you."

There went another wee bit of her heart, melting away like butter, and she smiled a little.

"Don't smile at me like that, lass. I am not one of your many doe-eyed suitors," he said.

Her smile deepened. "I have thought you many things, my lord . . . but never a doe-eyed suitor," she said softly.

They gazed at one another a long moment. Declan's gaze slipped to her mouth and Keira's blood began to heat. "If you do not intend to court me, then what brings you here today?" she asked.

"I have news," he said. "I think we can prove Mr. Scott was innocent if we speak with Captain Corbett. Then we may turn our attention to finding the jewels, which, if my assumptions are correct, are likely in this house."

Surprised, Keira blinked. "Pardon? *Here?*"

Declan told her what he had discovered. Keira listened in rapt silence, slipping down onto a chair as she tried to absorb it. She could imagine it—that rainy night, Lily seeing Aunt Althea and Mr. Scott together. Mr. Scott fleeing before they were discovered . . . but not with the jewels. Joseph Scott had lost his life for Aunt Althea. His family had lost a husband and father to Mr. Scott and Althea's illicit affair. Mr. Caufield lost his life, as well. And Lily . . . Lily had unwittingly set the wheels in motion. How would she ever bear it?

"Do you recall Captain Corbett?" Declan asked her. "He is the man who escorted Lily to Ireland."

Keira was still trying to absorb the truth. It felt as if everything at Ashwood were held together with spider's silk, and something as small as the swipe of a finger would bring it all tumbling down. She began to shake her head. She didn't recall Corbett—but then an image suddenly loomed in her mind of a barrel-chested man with a stovepipe hat helping Lily out of the coach. Keira *did* remember him—he'd stayed a day or two before returning to England, a jovial man with a very long and loud laugh. "Yes, of course. Captain Corbett."

Declan was suddenly standing close. "If we speak to Captain Corbett, we will have what we need to clear Mr. Scott's name."

The jewels, the jewels . . . "If the jewels are indeed here at Ashwood, then I need not worry so about Lord Eberlin stealing Lily's land. They could be the security she needs."

"Aye. Have you had any word from her?"

"I look for her every day," Keira said. "She said at three months she'd return, and three months have come and gone now. But Declan, how will we find Captain Corbett? We don't know where he is."

"He is likely in London, according to Louis. I could go and look for him and return in a day or two."

"You cannot *leave*, Declan. The gala is but four days away."

"I'll return in time for it," he said impatiently. He was staring at her, his eyes a fathomless blue, and she couldn't begin to guess what thoughts were swimming in them. "I will leave at dawn. But I cannot sit idly by knowing what I do about Mr. Scott and not use it to see him free."

"But how will you find Captain Corbett?" Keira asked again.

"I will ask about. Make inquiries in those places a gentleman of his stature might frequent." His eyes wandered the length of her. "I should go," he said. "If I am to be away, there is much I must do." He lifted his gaze to hers again; he looked as if he meant to say something more, but he pressed his lips together and walked to the door. He paused there and turned to look at her. "I will be back just as soon as I can," he said, and walked out.

Keira stood rooted, staring at the place he'd just been. She was afraid of being alone when Lily arrived and her deception was made known to everyone. God, how her deception had scored her; she was no longer the person she'd been.

Keira grasped the back of a chair, her fingers digging into the silk covering, her knees all at once feeling weak. She didn't want any of the things she had taken—the name, the title, and this beautiful house. If she could, she would walk away this moment, walk all the way home, where she would lie down and dream of the man and the life she could never have. *God in heaven, where is Lily?*

The faint sound of feminine laughter reached her. Keira swallowed hard, then made herself walk to rejoin them.

The day passed very quickly. Keira walked the grounds with Mr. Fish at her side, examining the structures that the groundsmen were erecting for the gala. She smiled and nodded, said yes to a variety of things, then wondered absently what she'd agreed to. She needed to think, she desperately wanted to escape and think. How could she possibly search for the jewels without drawing attention to herself?

It hardly mattered; she had no time to look, as there was so much to be done. It wasn't until the hour before supper was served, when Keira was playing the pianoforte while Lucy practiced her letters, that she could even think about them. She wondered where she would hide jewels in this house.

In the middle of a piece Keira particularly loved, one that made her think of Ireland and green, verdant hills, and soaring cliffs and a crashing sea, she abruptly stopped playing.

Lucy looked up from her slate.

Keira stood from the bench and went down on her knees.

"Mu'um?" Lucy asked as she put aside her slate and chalk.

Keira turned the bench over and ran her fingers along the inscription. *You are the song that plays on in my heart; for A, my love, my life, my heart's only note. Yours for eternity, JS.* Tears blurred her vision as she imagined the painstaking effort to carve this into the bench for the woman he loved.

"Is something wrong?" Lucy asked.

Keira turned the bench right-side up and took Lucy's hand, guiding her to sit on the bench. "Lucy, darling, there is something I want you always to remember," she said. "One must always stand up for what is right, no matter how uncomfortable that may be."

Lucy looked confused.

"Promise me this, that if you remember nothing else of me, you will remember that whatever I did, I did for love. Will you remember that?"

Lucy gasped. "Are you going to die?"

Keira laughed and grabbed the girl in a hug. "No, darling! At least I will not die today." She reared back, clutching Lucy by the shoulders. "I want you to know that, aye? Now go and finish your letters. I must speak to Mrs. Thorpe."

A bewildered Lucy slipped down from the bench and walked back to her slate, glancing back over her shoulder at Keira. Keira smiled as happily as she might. "Is that a look of worry I see, lass? You mustn't! All is well."

If Lucy knew Keira lied, she did not show it.

Keira found Mrs. Thorpe in the stores, making note of the laundered linens. "Madam!" she exclaimed, and quickly put down her pencil and paper. "Did you ring? I did not hear the bell—"

"No, I didn't ring," Keira said, and idly ran her fingers over a stack of folded bedsheets. "I beg your pardon, Mrs. Thorpe, but if I may, I would like to ask you something."

"Of course." Mrs. Thorpe said it as if she were about to be asked a favor she did not want to grant.

"Do you recall Captain Corbett?" Keira asked sheepishly. "He took me to Ireland."

"I remember him very well indeed, mu'um," Mrs. Thorpe said stoically. "He was a friend to your lady aunt."

"A dear friend," Keira agreed, hoping to high heaven that was true. "I was wondering, what do you suppose happened to him?"

"Happened to him? Nothing that I am aware."

"Would you, perchance, happen to know where he is?"

Mrs. Thorpe stacked her hands against her abdomen. "I wouldn't know, Lady Ashwood. I would suppose he is in London yet, but I am not personally acquainted with Captain Corbett."

"He was a frequent visitor to Ashwood?"

Mrs. Thorpe said nothing for a long moment. "Surely you remember, Lady Ashwood. Do you not recall how many hours he spent with you, playing chess? I believe he taught you the game."

Chess? Keira couldn't recall a single instance she'd seen Lily play chess! "Of course I do," she lied. "Which is why I should like to assure myself he is in good health. But I haven't the slightest notion where to look."

Mrs. Thorpe shrewdly considered her, and for a slender moment Keira feared the housekeeper knew the truth. "I suspect he still resides in Cheapside," she said. "At the very least, someone there would know what had become of him."

"Cheapside," Keira repeated.

"Yes, madam, Cheapside is what I recall. Is there

aught else?" Mrs. Thorpe picked up her paper and pencil again.

"Yes. I have quite a lot to keep me occupied on the morrow. Please do see to it that Lucy completes her lessons."

Mrs. Thorpe stiffened almost imperceptibly. "As you wish," she said a little curtly.

Keira could hardly blame Mrs. Thorpe's curt response. The woman simply didn't want the responsibility of Lucy heaped on top of her many other responsibilities. *Poor Lucy!* What would become of the girl if Keira were discovered? She had to make some provision for the girl straightaway. Now. Because tonight, she would go to Kitridge Lodge and tell Declan to look in Cheapside. It had to be tonight, because Keira had made up her mind. She had a strong sense that her world would disappear sooner rather than later.

Twenty-six

The *sound of* someone banging on his door filtered up the stairs, down the corridor, and into Declan's suite where he was preparing for bed. What time was it, then? "Bloody hell," he muttered.

The banging continued as he pulled on his buckskins and a shirt. He started down the stairs, running his fingers through his hair. He glanced at the mantel clock. It was ten o'clock. He mentally ran through the gambling he'd done of late, determined he had no outstanding debts. Nevertheless, he took up his pistol, and with that in hand, he strode to the front door as the banging started up again.

"Bloody hell, I hear you!" he shouted, and yanked the door open. He blinked at the fluffy little blossom pointed right at him. Beneath it—and the man's riding hat onto which it was pinned—stood Keira. She was dressed in a riding habit and was tapping a crop against her skirt.

Keira glanced at the pistol, then at him. "Expecting someone?"

"Expecting no one at all." He propped his arm against the edge of the door, leaning into it. "What in the bloody blazes are you doing here at this hour? Did you *ride* here?" he asked, peering past her.

"It is a full moon," she said, and touched the tip of her riding crop against his leg. "I have come to tell you that Captain Corbett resided in Cheapside all those years ago. And I have come . . . to tell you that you were right." Her gaze slid down, to the open vee of his shirt.

"You needn't have come all this way to tell me something so painfully obvious, but now that you've gone to the trouble, you may as well tell me what I am right about this time."

She sighed. "You were right that I . . . I am a wee bit afraid," she admitted.

"Well then." He casually admired her body. "What precisely do you fear?"

"I should think it obvious," she said, and tapped him again with her crop.

Declan caught the crop with his hand. "Nothing is ever obvious where you are concerned, Keira Hannigan. What do you fear?"

"*You*," she whispered, and stared at him with those Irish eyes.

He could feel that ocean-deep stirring in him, that absolute need to be with this woman in the most intimate way. He grinned. "I am the last person you should fear. I rather imagine you could persuade me to slay dragons." He let go her crop, and took hold of her wrist. "You have absolutely nothing to fear from me," he said, and pulled her forward, across the threshold. "On the contrary." He shut the door with his foot and dropped his pistol on a console. "It is I who should fear you."

"*Me?*" She laughed.

He took the crop from her hand and tossed it on the

floor. "Most definitely you," he said, and caught her by the waist, pulling her into his chest. He kissed her before she could speak, kissed her before he allowed his fear of coming too close to love to persuade him otherwise. "But don't ever fear me," he said, and kissed her neck as he removed her hat and tossed it onto a chair.

He pulled a pin out of her hair, then another, and dropped them as he pushed her back onto the first step of a winding staircase. "If you must fear," he whispered into her ear, "fear ennui." He kissed her cheek, her mouth. Keira did not resist him; she put her arms around his neck, held her head to one side as he ravaged her neck and pulled her hair down to hang loose around her shoulders. He guided her up the stairs with one hand around her waist. "Fear propriety," he said, and with his free hand, he pulled the gloves from her hands, dropping them on the stairs as he went.

At the top of the stairs, he pushed her against the wall and deftly undid the buttons of her riding coat. "Fear the stifling rules of society," he said low as he pushed the coat from her shoulders. "Fear the English, fear children with sticks, fear green horses," he added for good measure as he undid the buttons of her blouse and pulled the shirt ends from her skirt. He pushed the blouse open and cupped her breasts through her chemise, squeezing them, steadying his breath. "Fear all of that . . . but never fear me."

Keira's lips parted; Declan grabbed her up against him, lifting her off her feet, and walked into his bedchamber, pausing to shut and latch the door behind him. He moved her onto the bed, then went down on one knee before her, slipped his hand under her skirt to stroke her calf.

He gazed up at her shining green eyes. "This will be only if you want it, Keira. It must be for no other reason than that, aye?"

She braced her hands on either side of her knees, and as he moved his hand up her leg, she whispered, *"Aye."*

That word, so softly spoken, so freeing, was Declan's undoing. She was indeed a woman after his heart. She was Irish, she was bold, she was heart-stoppingly alluring. He watched her eyes as he removed her boot and stocking, then the other. She observed him almost curiously as he removed the second stocking and boot and slid his hand up over her knee before reaching to undo the ribbon of her chemise. He watched the silk ends float open, then carefully pushed the fabric aside and gazed admiringly at her small, firm breasts. He'd never been so powerfully attracted to a woman, never so hotly aroused as he felt himself in that moment.

He stood up and moved over her, one knee to the bed, one hand bracing himself against it, forcing her onto her back, straddling her, holding himself above her as he took her in. *"Ta tu go haliann,"* he whispered, telling her she was beautiful in the language that meant something only to them in this sleepy village in England.

Her smile was instant and softly seductive, a smile that had Declan fighting his own wild desire before he'd even begun. Her lips moved over his like water. Her touch was light, but there was a gentle eagerness in it, as well, sending little shocks through him every place she touched him. He slipped his tongue into her mouth, and Keira sighed with deep pleasure. The sound incited him, drifting through the curtain of his consciousness, sinking down into his groin.

He rolled onto his side, pulling her with him, and found the fastening of her skirt. When he had it off her, he rolled onto his back, guiding her to straddle him, so that he might help her off with the chemise. Keira excited him; she didn't flinch when he lifted her arms, didn't shy away when he pulled the chemise over her head. She remained straddled on his groin, where the force of his desire was fully evident. She was bare to him now, her nipples dark and erect against the creamy white of her skin, her abdomen flat and smooth, her neck long and elegant. Thick, silky black curls spilled around her shoulders, and those eyes, those Irish eyes, shone down on him.

It was almost incomprehensible to him that he could feel desire like this for this woman, of all women. He cupped her breasts and lifted up to take them in his mouth. Keira pulled at his shirt, and he helped her discard it. Her hands stroked his chest and he suckled her breasts, every touch driving him closer to madness. Her fingers skated over his nipples, inflaming him while she feathered his face with light kisses.

Declan abruptly put her on her back again, and stood up, watching her as he removed his trousers. Her lips parted when she saw him erect, but she showed no maidenly angst and neither did she shyly look away. She was fearless, more than any woman he'd ever known, and that alone made him love her.

That was the thing, he realized, that had made him so bloody restless of late. He understood it now as it coursed through him. He loved her. For the first time in his life, Declan knew what that feeling was, what it felt like to truly love a woman.

He laid himself gently on her, and began the assault of her skin and senses. His hunger beat steadily, growing stronger, pushing against him, seeking escape. He lavished her with his hands and mouth, slipping his hand between her legs, feeling the damp warmth between them, the pulse of her body in the valley of her sex. His kisses grew more urgent; he was delving deeper, plumbing her depths, and Keira was responding with little gasps and moans of pleasure, with her hands, with her mouth.

He squeezed her hip, hiked her leg up to his waist. He wanted to taste the dampness of her, and dipped his head down, between her legs. Keira gasped loudly and bucked against him. He held her hips firmly; she dragged her fingers through his hair as he licked her, delving deep within her, swirling around her core.

"*Declan,*" Keira said, her voice deep and husky. "Dear God, what are you doing to me?"

He could not know that she meant the question sincerely. Keira was completely submerged in the pool of longing, floating along beneath him, quivering with every touch of his mouth or his hands. She had never guessed that this could be so pleasurable and decadent at once. She felt the pull of her body, dragging her down into that pool of desire and want and pleasure, but she boiled beneath the surface. "You make me desperate," she said as her fingers dug into his hair. "I think I could very well perish."

He moaned and sucked at her skin. The sensation was astounding. She was falling and soaring at once, her release so violent that she shuddered.

She was still flying away when Declan moved up and settled in between her legs, one broad hand on her thigh, holding it up. "I cannot touch you like this and not have all of you."

The thirst for her was very clear in his eyes, in the set of his mouth, in his ragged breathing. Keira responded by arching her back against him and pushing her bare breast into his palm. He growled low, stroked her hair and her face, and sank deeper in between her legs. She could feel his erection against her wet skin, could feel her body adjusting and opening to him as he pressed gently against her.

Declan brushed the pad of his thumb across her nipple, and it felt as if fire rushed through her body. He kissed her breast, teased her nipple with his tongue, and Keira dug her fingers into his shoulders and held tight. She closed her eyes, felt herself floating again, adrift in a sea of erotic sensation.

"You're radiant," he said, and kissed her shoulder. "Beautiful." He pushed against her, slowly and gently entering her body, pausing when he met her barrier, and then kissing her tenderly before impaling her. Keira gasped at the lush sensation of having him so deep inside her, mixed with such pain. Her legs fell apart when he began to move. He slid deep inside her with a guttural sound of pleasure. He buried his face in her breasts, laced his fingers with hers and held her hand tightly as he moved, slowly and carefully.

She felt tenderhearted toward Declan, but anxious, too. It was almost too gentle, too caring. Her defenses, her sense of propriety, her fears, had been shattered the moment he entered her, and now she would have all of him. She began to move with him, wanting to feel him deeper, feel him harder, feel him melt into her, become part of her.

"*Keira,*" he muttered raggedly as she lifted her breasts to his mouth and moved with him. With a moan, he slipped his hand under her back, lifting her up as he began to move more ardently. Keira arched into his body, feeling another explosion beginning to build in her.

Declan shifted his weight; his stroke and pace lengthened as he reached for her core. He began to move with the urgency that she felt, thrusting deep inside her. Keira strained to meet him and find that release once more. Now Declan was past the point of gentle, tender strokes, he was swimming in the current they'd created, the fast flooding waters of desire carrying them on.

And then he began to stroke her, his fingers dancing on her sex as his body moved inside her. Release came to her in one long wave. She cried out, clawed at the sheets, lifted herself to him as she felt him convulse inside of her.

A few moments later, she felt his breath warm on her neck, the pounding of his heart against her breast. His fingers were tangled in her hair, his palm pressed against her cheek.

The experience was liberating. It set Keira's heart free, her imagination soaring. She felt above the earth, above her deceit. She wanted nothing but to feel his hard body beside her, to marvel at how a man could corral his strength and send her soaring as he'd just done and yet not harm her. She felt a bond to him that could never be broken, not by words, not by time, not by another being.

She twisted in his arms so that she was facing him. Declan pushed her hair away from her face. A smile played at the corners of his mouth as he rolled onto his back. Keira went with him. "You look like a fat cat who has had too much milk," he said, caressing her back. "Are you all right?" he asked, his voice softer.

"Perfect," she said, and rested her chin on his chest.

He stroked her cheek with his knuckle. "Have you, by chance, ever called on Widow Cleeney?"

"Widow Cleeney!" She laughed. Widow Cleeney lived alone in the woods between Ballynaheath and Lisdoon. She had a few goats and a pair of mean Irish wolfhounds that kept most strangers from her door, and touted herself a healer.

"Aye, Widow Cleeney," Declan said, eyeing her suspiciously. "My father once told me that she wasn't above using black arts in her remedies, and I'll be damned if I don't feel a wee bit bewitched at present."

Keira giggled and kissed his chest.

"Aye, laugh if you will," he scoffed. "There you are, all warm and rosy in my bed. I should put you on your pony and send you home, but I feel utterly bewitched and a slave to your schemes."

"Good," Keira said, and lightly bit his nipple.

"God help me." He sighed, and ran his hand over her crown, kissing the top of it, as if they were lovers.

Lovers, Keira thought. It had such a delicious, exciting ring to it.

Twenty-seven

They lounged lazily in Declan's bed before a roaring fire he'd built at the hearth. Keira was still flushed from that extraordinary experience, and thoroughly besotted with Declan. She wanted to study his face and his hands, and to feel his lips on her again. As it was, she could scarcely take her eyes from him. She could scarcely keep what was undoubtedly a silly smile from her face.

Declan indulged her endless list of questions. She asked him what he would do when he was finished with his work at Kitridge Lodge. He said he would like to see Africa.

"Africa," she said dreamily. "That's exciting."

He traced a lazy path up her back. "It would be a rather mean existence. The luxuries we have here do not exist there."

"I wouldn't care," Keira said. "I would love to see it one day. And Italy," she added, thinking that she would be there now had things not turned out as they had.

"Italy, eh?" he said.

"My mother and father honeymooned there and I have always longed to go."

"It is grand," he agreed.

Keira touched his bottom lip. "Do you ever miss Ireland?"

He seemed to think about that for a moment. "Some of it," he said. "Mostly, I miss Eireanne when I'm away."

"I've always been very fond of Eireanne," Keira announced.

Declan smiled and pushed her hair from her face. "And she has always been fond of you. However, there have been times that I have been less fond of your friendship."

Keira smiled. "I don't blame you," she said, and kissed his chest.

"You've changed, *muirnín.*"

"Have I?" she asked, surprised.

He nodded as he smoothed her hair and moved it over her shoulder. "You think beyond yourself now, of others. You are a remarkably good countess."

She grinned. "How heartening it is to know that your opinion of me has improved so," she said teasingly. "Perhaps I might impose on you to convince my father I have changed."

"Well now," he said as he wrapped his arms around her and pulled her close to kiss her. "I can hardly work miracles."

They talked about Ireland, and Keira listed the things she missed: her family, naturally, and the ceilidhs, or folk festivals, that were generally held in the summer.

Declan groaned. "There is no greater bother, to my thinking."

"Naturally *you* would say that, as you have been so generous as to host them. But as a mere guest, I find the stories and the dancing and the vats of Irish whiskey delightful."

"I will admit that a vat of Irish whiskey does hold a certain appeal," he agreed.

"Come now, you must miss something besides Eireanne," Keira pressed.

He thought about that for a moment as he stroked her hair. "The hunting. There is no finer hunting than at Ballynaheath."

She thought that curious, as he was so rarely at Ballynaheath. It puzzled her as to why. Ballynaheath was such a grand estate, an old castle that had been soundly and artfully renovated through the years. It sat on a thousand wooded acres with sweeping views of the sea, and Keira had always thought it a bit mystical. She would think that anyone would be happy to settle there and call it home. "Why have you never married?" she asked bluntly.

He arched a brow. "Pardon?"

She held his palm up, matching her hand to his. "You can hardly blame me for inquiring, can you? It's the way of the world. One inherits a title, and an estate, and one marries and produces heirs."

"Lord strike me if there is a woman who does not wonder about my lack of a wife," he said with a weary chuckle.

"Don't you want an heir?"

He looked her in the eyes as he intertwined his fingers with hers. "Do you want to know the truth?"

"I do."

"I honestly don't care."

She gasped at that. "I cannot understand how you'd not care about something so very important," she said.

"What of your legacy? Your name? Your title? How can you not *care*?"

He laughed again at her shock. "Perhaps that was a poor choice of words," he admitted, "but producing the obligatory heir is not what inspires me. Freedom inspires me. The world inspires me. Like you, *muirnín,* I want to live my life and I don't care to give it up for marriage and heirs and the responsibilities that accompany that."

Keira was surprised. "You make it sound as if you would forgo all pleasure on this earth for the sake of being married."

"Not all pleasure," he said with a wanton wink. "But if I married, I would need to provide a wife with a proper home. My home is Ballynaheath. It is as far removed from life as anything I know. Frankly, I'd rather Eireanne have it."

"But Eireanne will marry and have her own home one day," Keira pointed out. At least, she hoped that was true.

"Yes, let us suppose that Eireanne attends school with your help, and then at the frighteningly ripe age of three and twenty, is presented during the Season in London. Perhaps some gentleman will look past the whispers and offer for her, and she will marry. Then what? I will be left with a drafty old castle. No, I prefer my vagabond life. I desire above all else to be free to go where there are horses, and friends, and good food and better wine, and to see the world at will."

He was very poetic. Keira had never known anyone like Declan, anyone who had not wanted the things they'd all been taught to want since their earliest memories.

"Tell me the truth about Maloney," he said. "Do you esteem him?"

She gave him a withering look. "No. At least not in that way. Loman is a very kind man. And he is rich."

Declan chuckled. "And therein lies the foundation of a successful marriage."

"Not entirely. He can be rather tedious. And he does not care for great adventure. He is the sort to seek his hearth."

Declan smiled sympathetically and stroked her hair. "I was very earnest when I told you to fear propriety and society," he said softly. "They stifle you if you allow it. Live, Keira, live to the fullest extent you might before you are shackled to some hearth by marriage and children."

Keira didn't want to think of that now. She didn't want to think about society or propriety. She wanted only to think of Declan and this singular, extraordinary moment in her life.

Something had happened to Declan tonight. Coming together with Keira had been quite moving to him; he was amazed and alarmed by how moving. He'd tried to ignore the feeling, but it was impossible; whether it was the irrepressible joviality in her chatter, or the shining Irish eyes, or the mere sight of a beautiful woman, he had not been able to put down the feelings he was having. Strange, heartrending feelings. For a woman who had the capacity to drive him quite mad.

At one in the morning, he had made her get out of the bed and dress, silencing her weak protests with a kiss. "There is enough talk as it is," he said, feeling that need to protect her even more strongly now. "And I want an early start to London."

He insisted on accompanying her home. At the Ash-wood stables, Declan shooed away a sleepy stable boy and helped Keira stable the horse. As they walked outside, she looked up at him once more. "Safe journey, Declan."

He smiled. "Promise me you'll not fret so, lass. Lily will come soon enough and this will be over. You will return to Ireland in peace."

"So you keep mentioning," she said archly.

"Should I remind you that not two days ago, that is what you desired above all else?" He stepped behind her, put his arms around her middle, and kissed her neck.

"I said a good many things a few days ago," she said.

"Be strong," he murmured, and left a soft, lingering kiss on her lips. He stepped away then, tipped his hat, and started for his horse.

"Declan."

He paused and looked back at her.

She smiled, and there it was again, that peculiar feeling of love in his heart.

"It was . . . magnificent."

He thought of several things he might say, but he moved back to her, put his arm around her shoulders there in the moonlight at Ashwood, and kissed her As she always did, Keira returned his kiss with verve. But she pushed away from him after a moment. "Go on, then," she said, and still smiling, she walked away from him, disappearing into the night as she headed to the mansion.

He left Ashwood thinking of the way Keira had come to him tonight, knowing very well what would happen if she did, and the courage it must have taken to do it. He imagined making love to her in the moonlight, of pulling her off her horse and taking her in the sweet grass, letting her lusty breathing fill his lungs, feeling her body tight around his.

He had taken something very dear from her tonight, and the fact that he had taken her virtue left him feeling things he'd never in his life felt, things that were foreign and mystifying and somehow felt threatening to his independence.

Declan was not a fool—he didn't want Keira to leave Ashwood. He wanted her to remain here, to give him the pleasure of initiating her in the many different ways of love. But he was a practical man and he knew that whatever he was feeling could never be more. It was the cruelest of ironies that Keira's gross deception had brought them together, but that deception would keep them apart. She would be in Ireland, and he would not.

He would miss her when she was gone, more than he could possibly say.

Twenty-eight

At Ashwood the next morning, Keira marveled at how every-thing seemed the same when she had changed so pro-foundly. It seemed almost surreal to her now that she had given up her virtue, then confessed her love to a man she would never have.

It all reminded her of her mother's warning. *Mind you, have a care with your person, my darlings, for the whole of you is the most valuable thing you offer a husband. If you misuse your body, no decent man will have you, and you will remain with your father and me and knit stockings for the rest of your life,* her mother used to warn them.

Had it been worth the risk? Yes. Oh, yes. *Yes.*

She wondered about Declan, and he remained at the edge of her mind, but she had too many things to do to keep idly dreaming. There was a stack of correspon-dence, Lucy was desperate to be entertained, and a small crisis having to do with the racecourse had occurred, in which a part of it had been washed away by a late-morning rain.

The following day, her night with Declan seemed almost a remote dream. The constant pressure of the gala, the anxiety of her deception, and the incessant waiting for

Lily, and for the moment this would all end, left her with no appetite.

That afternoon, as the finishing touches were being put on the tents on the lawn, the racecourse was being rerouted, the boxing ring set up in one of the stables, and Lucy had been suitably occupied with music lessons, Sibley called.

He strode into the salon with a warm smile on his face. "Countess," he said, bowing low over her hand. "On my word you are lovelier each time I see you."

He always said such predictable things, she thought. *Don't look at me as if I am one of your doe-eyed suitors,* she heard Declan say. She scarcely heard another word Sibley said, her thoughts were so full of Declan. But she realized as he chatted amicably about the gala that he was truly smitten with her, and she'd done nothing to discourage him or Mr. Anders. Keira wanted to bury her face in her hands. She had experienced so many marvelous, wondrous things, done things she would never have believed she was capable of doing. But in many ways, she was still very thoughtless, and she didn't like that about herself.

The rest of the day flew by with a swirl of visitors and workmen. Keira crawled into bed at half past midnight and was up with the dawn's first light the following morning. It was the day before the gala, and there were a million things to be done, and Declan had not returned from London. She needed him and his strength, his wry humor.

The ladies from the Society arrived just after luncheon to oversee the setting up of booths and activities. Keira was among them, overseeing the placement of the puppet stage, which had to be moved when it was discovered that a flock of birds had taken up residence in a tree underneath which people would be seated.

She and one of the groundsmen had determined the best next location when Louis found her. "Beggin' your pardon, madam, but Mr. Fish is here with a pair of gentlemen. He bids you come straightaway."

"Gentlemen? What gentlemen?" she asked suspiciously.

"Mr. Sibley and Lord Eberlin."

Keira's pulse leaped. Today of all days! But there was nothing to be done for it; she couldn't avoid it. Fortunately, she had the excuse of having too much to oversee to tarry with a prolonged discussion. "A package has come for you, as well," Louis said.

"A package?"

"Aye, mu'um. Come just now."

The package, which looked like a hatbox, was in the foyer. A note was attached to it, the seal unmarked. Keira opened the note.

I have not forgotten your challenge of a race. If the Welsh pony is ridden properly, she might be capable of beating my gelding. I shall bring her around this afternoon to ensure your dainty sidesaddle will fit her. As for the hat, I saw it in London and thought it so madly ridiculous that it would suit no one quite as well as you, given your unusual taste in bonnets. I think you might look rather comely in it.

D.

An irrepressible grin instantly spread across Keira's face. She folded the letter and put it in her pocket, then opened the box. It was a garden hat with a wide brim and red silk flowers. She'd never been more delighted with a gift, and eagerly took it out of the box to admire it.

He thought of me.

"They are in the green salon, mu'um," Louis said from somewhere behind her.

Keira reluctantly put the hat down and followed Louis to the green salon. She felt as if she were walking into an icehouse. Mr. Fish was within with Lord Eberlin and Mr. Sibley. "Gentlemen," she said, and looked directly at Fish. "I wasn't expecting you."

"I beg your pardon, Lady Ashwood, but Lord Eberlin was rather insistent that we discuss things straightaway."

Straightaway, did he? She shifted her gaze to Eberlin, who coolly regarded her. "How may I help you, my lord?"

His dark gaze bored through hers. "I noticed the preparations for the summer gala are all but complete. It looks to be quite the event."

"That is my hope. The orphanage at St. Bartholomew's is in desperate need of renovation."

"You may depend on a sizable donation from me," he said.

There was something in the way he looked at Keira that was uncomfortable. Was it anger? "Thank you," she said. "How may I be of service, my lord?"

"I assume the gala will follow the pattern of the past?" he asked, ignoring her question. "Frivolity will abound into the early-morning hours?"

He said it in a way that sounded almost malevolent.

"It is a celebration, sir," Keira said. "You may call it frivolity, but it is indeed a festival."

"Indeed," he drawled.

She didn't care for his tone or his expression. "I really must return—"

"Forgive the intrusion. I had hoped we would resolve our differences before now."

Keira glanced at Mr. Fish whose expression was inscrutable. "I am not certain that is possible."

"Not possible? Then what are we to do in regard to our hundred acres, Lady Ashwood?"

She bristled at the condescension in his voice. "If you mean the Ashwood property you are trying to pilfer, I suggest *we* do nothing."

Now Eberlin smirked. "As you have been advised by your solicitor, that acreage does not rightfully belong to Ashwood. It belongs to me. However, I understand your reluctance to part with the profits, and I have come to make a fair offer for your loss."

She suspected Mr. Fish was behind this. "There is no fair offer that you can make for land that is mine, for I don't believe you have a legal claim to it." She could see Mr. Fish frown and look down at his feet, but she hardly cared.

Eberlin stepped closer to her, his gaze piercing hers. "I don't think you want to see this matter resolved in a court of law, madam."

Keira's fear and intense dislike of this man emboldened her. "I have nothing to fear from a court of law, sir. You are trying to usurp my property and I believe any court would agree with me."

"Do you." It was a statement, not a question.

"I do."

His eyes narrowed. "Might we have a private word, Lady Ashwood?"

Mr. Fish abruptly looked up and gave her a cautious look.

"Why? So that you might attempt to intimidate me? I have nothing to say to you that cannot be said in front of Mr. Fish or Mr. Sibley."

His gaze darkened. "But I have something to say to you that I am certain you will not appreciate hearing in front of these two fine gentlemen."

The back of Keira's neck prickled. She couldn't begin to guess what he might possibly have to say to her, but he was looking at her with cold intent.

"Lady Ashwood, I would not recommend it," Mr. Fish murmured.

"And I suggest that you will regret it if you do not," Eberlin said easily.

Now Mr. Fish looked at him strangely, and even Mr. Sibley seemed surprised. Keira's stomach turned acid with trepidation. What could he possibly know? He couldn't know the truth—he'd only just come from Denmark. "I will regret nothing, sir," she said coldly. "But if speaking with you privately will bring this to an end, I will do so." She looked at Mr. Fish, at his suddenly worried expression, and said, "Please go, Mr. Fish. I will be quite all right."

"As you wish," Mr. Fish said, his voice clipped. He looked entirely unhappy as he quit the room, but not as unhappy as Mr. Sibley, who had yet to meet Keira's gaze.

When the door closed behind them, Keira folded her

arms tightly across her chest and looked coolly at Lord Eberlin. "Whatever you must say, I pray you say it quickly. I have much work to do before the gala tomorrow, and as I do not intend to hand over even a blade of grass belonging to Ashwood without a fight. Therefore, it would seem to me that there is nothing left for us to say."

"You are very cocksure for a woman who is practicing the art of great deception," he said smoothly.

Keira felt the blood drain from her face. "I have no idea what you mean! You overstep your bounds, sir—"

"Save your feigned indignation for someone who believes your charade. I don't know who you are," he said, casually moving forward, his eyes dark and foreboding. "But clearly, you are not Lily Boudine."

"That is absurd!" She prayed that her knees did not betray the truth. "I will not listen to your slander. I will have my footmen remove you immediately. You are no longer welcome here, sir!"

"You won't have me removed because you are not Lily Boudine. I don't know what you are about and I hardly care. But I think you will hand over the acreage in exchange for my silence, or face a few questions by authorities who will not take kindly to your stealing a title and an estate. What do you hope to gain from it? Marriage? The Ashwood wealth?"

She forced a laugh that sounded hollow to her. "If you think to frighten me with absurd accusations, you will be disappointed. No one will believe such rubbish! You are an outsider, my lord, and you are attempting to cause trouble for the purpose of stealing land from Ashwood."

Eberlin's gaze was cold and hard as it moved over her.

"I was prepared to make you a fair offer. But now I think I'd rather enjoy seeing a few questions put to you."

Her heart was pounding. She wouldn't be surprised if he could see it against the muslin of her gown.

"However, I will give you one last chance. I will have the papers drawn up that transfer the acreage free and clear to Tiber Park. You will sign them. Or you will face the authorities. It is your choice . . . whoever you are."

"This is absurd. You are not welcome at Ashwood, sir," Keira snapped. She couldn't bear to look at him another moment. She couldn't breathe. She could scarcely feel her legs, yet somehow, she managed to walk to the door. Somehow, she managed to open it. "Good day, sir," she said, and looked straight ahead.

He did not move straightaway, but when he did, he slowly moved forward, pausing at the threshold to stare down at Keira before walking down the carpeted hallway.

She turned away and grabbed the back of a chair, thinking she might be sick.

"Lady Ashwood!" Mr. Fish exclaimed when he entered the room moments later. "What has happened? Are you unwell? Here now, let me fetch you some water." He tried to take her elbow, but Keira suddenly straightened.

"I beg your pardon, sir. I did not break my fast this morning—"

"You should eat something," he said, and strode to the door. "You there!" he shouted at someone. "Bring Linford at once!"

"Mr. Fish, it's not necessary—"

"You are very pale, madam," he said. "You look very unwell."

She allowed him to help her to a seat while frantically thinking how she might escape Mr. Fish. She had to think, she had to *think*.

"Linford, there you are," Mr. Fish said as the butler walked in. "Lady Ashwood has taken ill. She has not eaten. Bring her something—bread, or some cheese if you have it. And tea."

"At once," Linford said, and hurried out.

Mr. Fish flipped the tails of his coat and sat across from Keira, his face full of concern. "What did he say to cause you such distress?"

She had to find her bearings, and tried with a flick of her wrist to seem entirely unaffected. "What you might expect. He wants the acreage."

"That's all?" Mr. Fish asked skeptically.

"He, ah . . ." She looked down at her lap and thought desperately how to explain her near collapse. "His offer was not what one might expect to hear in polite society." She glanced up at Mr. Fish.

The man looked entirely scandalized. He stared at her, his eyes wide, and then suddenly clamped his jaw shut and stood. "Outrageous," he said. "I will not stand for it."

"Mr. Fish! Please do not trouble yourself. I am not easily intimidated."

"As a gentleman and your agent, Lady Ashwood, I cannot stand idly by while he insults you!"

"I beg of you, please let it be," she said, feeling ill again. The lies and deceptions—they were too much, too heavy, too suffocating. "We might deal with it after the gala, shall we? In less than twenty-four hours, scores of people will arrive on the grounds of Ashwood and I can think of little else but that at present."

"Yes, but I could speak to him—"

"I would that you do not. Please, Mr. Fish. Let it be."

He looked as if he wanted to argue. But he pressed his lips together and glanced to the window in what Keira thought was a supreme effort to contain himself. "Very well," he said tightly, as a maid appeared with a serving tray. "If that is what you wish," he added in a voice that clearly relayed his disagreement.

"For the moment, it is."

"I shall let my displeasure be known when the suit is taken before a court of law," Mr. Fish said tightly. "I assure you, a judge will not look favorably on his harassment of you."

A judge. Keira hadn't really thought that far ahead. She imagined him making his accusations against her, before a judge. Before witnesses, before all the people of Ashwood and Hadley Green she had come to care about. She suppressed a shudder.

"I will leave you to eat something, Lady Ashwood," Mr. Fish said. "You must keep up your strength." He nodded curtly and walked briskly out of the room.

Keira thanked the maid and looked at the plate of bread, cheese, and grapes. She didn't want food. She wanted whiskey, anything that could dull the gnawing fear in her belly and the brutal pain behind her eyes.

Twenty-nine

Declan did not find Keira at the mansion; the footman who responded to his rap on the door said he'd last seen her walking with Miss Taft.

He walked across the grounds looking for her. Tents and temporary gazebos had been erected for the gala, and long tables filled the tents, presumably for the goods and wares that would be sold to raise funds for the orphanage. In addition, a small stage had been erected for plays and puppet shows. There was a platform for musicians, and tables and chairs were set up under the towering oak trees. There was a badminton court, a lawn-bowling court, and of course, in the meadow below the lake, a quarter-mile racecourse. The grounds had been meticulously prepared for the event. The grass was clipped low, flowers bloomed in any direction a person looked, and birdhouses set out in the trees provided a musical background.

Declan was proud of Keira. This summer gala was an extraordinary undertaking for a young woman, and she had done an exemplary job of putting it together, particularly given the unusual circumstances. It looked to be a splendid affair.

Declan spotted Keira with Lucy in a rowboat on the

lake. Keira was wearing the hat he'd sent her, and that pleased him enormously. He had no idea why he'd done it, especially given his ambivalence about carrying this infatuation any further than he already had. But he'd seen it in a shop window and had known instantly that there was no other woman who could wear it as well as she.

It occurred to Declan, as he stood on the edge of the lake, that he wanted to make Keira happy with the gift, that he wanted to see that sparkling smile and those brilliant eyes full of gratitude. Today, seeing her in it, looking as fresh as an Irish rose, he was glad he'd purchased the hat for her.

Lucy was the first to see him, and waved so enthusiastically that she almost tipped the boat. Keira exclaimed with panic as she reached for Lucy and pulled her down to her seat. There was a bit of a delay as the two of them worked to get their rowing in a rhythm, but then Lucy lost her oar, which necessitated that they row in a circle for a moment until Lucy could reach it. At last, they made their way to shore.

"We've been rowing!" Lucy excitedly declared.

"Yes, Miss Taft. I saw you," Declan said, and reached down to pull the boat up through the reeds.

"We rowed all the way across," she continued breathlessly as Declan lifted her out of the boat and put her onto dry ground. "It took ages, and my arms hurt, but it was quite fun. Lady Ashwood said that if we were to win the boat races on the morrow, we must row all that way."

"Did she?" Declan peered curiously at Keira as he held out his hand to help her out of the boat. Her smile was as bright and sunny as it had ever been, but he noted the worry around her eyes.

"I will do the boat races, and the egg races, and the three-legged races," Lucy announced, holding up her fingers as she enumerated her events. "Louis said he would race the three-legs with me, and he has very long legs, so I suspect we shall win. What are you going to do, my lord?"

"Me? Oh . . . I thought I might enjoy a horse race."

"He thinks he shall best me, Lucy," Keira said lightly.

"But . . . but you are faster, mu'um," Lucy said.

Keira laughed. "Good girl."

"We shall see who is faster on the morrow, shall we?" Declan said. "If you'd like to see the horses, Miss Taft, they are in the stable now."

Lucy gasped. She looked at Keira. "May I?"

"If you will promise you will not be a bother to Mr. Jepsen."

"I promise!"

"Off you go, then," Keira said.

Lucy started running toward the stables, her gold hair streaming behind her.

"The boat races?" Declan asked, as he examined the hat. "I had no idea you were so versatile."

"Pardon?" she asked absently, and looked back at the boats. "Oh, that. I decided only this morning. Declan, how can I thank you for that hat? I adore it."

He smiled. "It suits you." But Keira was not really listening to him—she was squinting after Lucy. "Keira? You don't seem yourself."

"I am certain it appears so, because you are looking at a doomed woman," she said, turning her gaze back to him.

"Pardon?"

She nodded.

"You are hardly doomed, *muirnín*."

"Oh, but I am," she said emphatically. "That wretched Eberlin called today." She glanced over her shoulder, as if she expected someone might be listening, then whispered, "He *knows*, Declan."

"Knows? Knows what?"

"About me," she said. "He knows about *me*."

That was impossible. Declan shook his head.

"Yes, yes, I know what you must be thinking, for I thought it, too. How could he possibly know it? He's a stranger here! He's only just come to England! How could he possibly know what no one else in England knows, save you?" She closed her eyes as if the mere suggestion pained her.

Declan took her by the elbow and forced her to walk along at a leisurely pace. "You must be mistaken. Why do you think he knows?"

"Because he told me quite unequivocally. He came to make an offer for the acres he would steal from Ashwood, and naturally, I refused him. I cannot assume Lily's rightful role and then sell the land out from under her, and particularly that acreage, can I? And when I said no, he insisted on a private word, and he . . . he said he knows I am not Lily Boudine, and if I don't now give him the acreage free and clear, he will turn me over to the authorities. Therefore, I am utterly doomed, for I will not give Lily's land to him!"

Declan was stunned. He stopped and forced Keira to look at him. "When did this happen?"

"Not two hours ago." She groaned. "God knows I deserve this calamity. It is of my own making! I should never—"

"Keira, think," Declan interrupted. "How could he possibly know it? It isn't possible. He has bluffed you."

"Aye, I thought so, too. But he clearly suspects me."

Declan wondered what Eberlin could possibly know. Could he be guessing? Declan started walking again, leading Keira with him. "Where did you leave it with Eberlin?"

"I hardly know! I denied it, of course, and gave him no quarter. He said that he would give me one last chance to give him the acreage, and he would draw up the papers to that effect. But if I did not sign them, he would tell the authorities I am not Lily Boudine."

This presented a much larger problem than anything Declan might have imagined. Up until this moment, his greatest worry was how Lily might ever take her rightful role—but this!

"Heaven help me . . . I know that I have become a great burden to you, and on my word, I have tried diligently to think of how I might repair what I have done without your help, I truly have. But Declan," Keira said, "I am at a loss to know what to do now."

"Ah, *muirnín*, you've had a wretched pair of days, have you not?" He put his arm around her waist and pulled her in close as they walked. "Let us be reasonable about this. Eberlin has no proof you are not who you say you are, and any English authority would take your word over his. Now then, he said he would draw up papers for you to sign, is that it?"

She nodded.

"That should take at least a week, I'd wager. That will give us enough time."

"Time? Time for what?" she asked.

"I have news from London," he said. "Corbett is indeed living in Cheapside. However, at present, he is in the country, and his butler informs me that he will attend your gala on the morrow."

Keira blinked. "He'll be *here*? Lady Horncastle must have extended the invitation. I think she has invited the whole of London," she said a little petulantly.

"But this is advantageous, Keira. We may speak with Corbett and hopefully have what we need to instigate a full inquiry into Mr. Scott's hanging. At that point, you may return to Ireland. You could be gone at week's end. Eberlin cannot take the acreage without you, and he could hardly accuse you in your absence."

"To Ireland?" she repeated softly.

Declan squeezed her waist. "Do not fear Eberlin. He wants the land. If he thinks he will have it, he will leave well enough alone. You must give him reason to believe you will sign whatever agreement he draws up. That will give us the time we need."

They had come to the gazebo at the far end of the little lake. It had been decorated with paper lanterns and paper flowers, and chairs around a table had been set up. Declan led Keira inside and she stood at the railing, looking out at the lake. Her shoulders were stooped, he noticed, and her face hidden from him by the wide brim of her hat.

Declan was fairly certain he'd do anything to take this burden from her. She could be vexing, yes, but he'd come to appreciate that there was also something enormously appealing about her fearlessness for living.

He touched her arm. Keira looked up; her brilliant green eyes were swimming with doubt. "It will be all right," he said softly. Keira frowned doubtfully and shook her head, but he cupped her chin and forced her to look at him. "It will be all right," he said again, and bent his head to kiss the corner of her mouth. "Everything will be all right," he assured her again, and kissed the single tear that slid slowly down her cheek. "You have heart, Keira, you always have. Have heart now." He kissed her on the mouth.

Keira seemed to sag into him, her mouth opening beneath his, her arms encircling his waist tightly, clinging to him. As always, her ardent response robbed Declan of rational thought. The slightest bit of good sense and the smallest shred of decorum drained from him. The warm summer air seemed to crackle around them, and he felt that insatiable need for her building in him again.

He lifted his head and gazed down at her. Her eyes were glistening, her lips wet from his kiss. He had an enormous desire to have her there, in the gazebo, just like this.

But her precarious situation was not far from his mind, and he looked back toward the house. "Come then, *muirnín,*" he said, taking her hand. "Let us see the gala through for the sake of those orphans, aye?"

With a sigh, she nodded. "You have my word, sir, that should I escape this calamity with my head on my shoulders, I shall never be a bother to you again."

He appreciated her resolve, but that vow did not comfort him in the least. He thought a life without at least a little bother might be tiresome.

Thirty

On the morning of the gala, Keira expected to wake to gloomy skies, but the sun was shining and it was a cloudless summer day. She expected that no one would come, but they did. Squads of them. In wagons, in ornate coaches, on horseback, on foot. She expected some disaster to happen, but there was none.

She dressed for the day in cool cream muslin and silk, and wore the hat Declan had sent to her from London. She pinned fresh flowers to the crown and walked out to a gala.

Keira wandered through the crafts tent and made some purchases for her family. For Molly and Mabe, linen wraps embroidered in red silk. For her mother, a lace collar and cuffs. She found a leather knife sheath for her father.

She visited all the games that were being waged across the grounds. Keira particularly liked the archery contest, and attracted quite a crowd when she was called upon to demonstrate her skill. Keira had very little skill, however, something to which Lord Frampton could attest, as she very nearly pierced him with an arrow, much to the delight of the crowd. She played lawn bowling, she watched a bit of boxing, and she served as the master of ceremonies for the egg race.

The people of Hadley Green were a jubilant crowd; their laughter and raucous cries filled the summer air, along with the scent of roasted mutton and ale, which flowed freely from several barrels set around the grounds. Keira joined the Society ladies for luncheon on the terrace, where they dined on foods for a softer palate, including roasted chicken and finger potatoes.

But what pleased Keira the most that day was that the children of St. Bartholomew's Orphanage had the grandest time of all, and little Lucy Taft delighted in playing hostess to them. They followed her around like geese, from badminton, to lawn bowling, to fishing on the lake and petting the horses. Their laughter seemed to lift above that of the adults.

She paused often to speak to those who had come. All complimented her on a successful gala. She saw Declan twice—both times in the company of Daria Babcock. Miss Babcock was holding a long-stemmed rose, which Keira knew was the prize given for lawn bowling. She saw Mr. Sibley and Mr. Anders more often, as each sought to escort her about.

Quite a lot of people had come down from London, courtesy of Lady Horncastle, but to Keira's considerable relief, Lady Darlington and her son were not in attendance after all. "Lord Raley has taken ill," Lady Horncastle said. "A fever from his journey to the West Indies. Deplorable conditions there, I understand. Lady Darlington naturally stayed in London to look after her son."

"The West Indies?" Mrs. Morton said curiously. "But I thought you said he'd come from Spain."

"I don't recall saying anything of the sort," Lady Horn-castle argued.

In spite of the lovely day she was having, a part of Keira waited anxiously for some axe, somewhere, to fall. But nothing fell.

With ale in hand, Sister Rosens told her the goods and wares were selling at a brisk pace, and the wagering on games was quite good. She said that some mysterious benefactor had sent around one hundred pounds to the orphanage. "It will help us to repair the well," she'd said, her eyes glowing with delight.

In the late afternoon were the races. In the three-legged race, Keira cheered louder than anyone for Lucy and Louis, but they suffered an unfortunate fall near the finish line and lost. They were redeemed, however, in the boat races—Louis took Keira's place, and sailed, so to speak, to victory with Lucy.

The last event of the afternoon was the highly touted, much anticipated horse race. It seemed as if all of England had heard of the wager between Keira and Declan, and had bet accordingly.

There were five riders in all, and their mounts were led from the paddock, one by one, to a chorus of cheers from the crowd. Declan appeared by Keira's side just as his gray gelding was led through the crowd. "Hang on tightly to your sidesaddle, madam, for I intend to win," he said amicably.

"Then I wish you luck, my lord. You will need it," she said as the Welsh pony was led from the paddock. She had a full saddle on her back. Declan arched a questioning brow at Keira; she winked at him and moved away.

Lord Horncastle, who, for reasons Keira never did understand, had become the master of this ceremony, and stood up on the second rung of the fence, demanding everyone's attention. "Ladies and gentlemen," he said, bowing as low as he might from his precarious perch, "the prize event of the day is about to commence. Lord Donnelly has wagered against Lady Ashwood, in which he will match and double every pound that is pledged in the event of her victory, and Lady Ashwood, being a lady of high caliber and superior breeding, has made the same agreement. To date, forty-two pounds and eighteen pence have been wagered on Lady Ashwood's victory. A mere seven and thirty pounds have been wagered on Lord Donnelly."

"What of the horse? What horse does she ride?" someone shouted from the crowd.

"The horse, sir, is one from my very stable," Lord Horncastle said.

"Lost from your stable, you mean," someone said, and the crowd laughed.

Lord Horncastle, who'd had a few tankards that day, gave a patronizing smile, as if he'd given the horse to Declan rather than lost it over a hand of cards. "I can vouch that she is as good a racing horse as you might find in England. Lady Ashwood has every advantage. We must leave the rest to her."

All eyes turned to Keira. She playfully curtsied and removed her hat. "Rest assured that I am an adequate rider," she said cheerfully, and smiled at Declan. "I have a very fine feeling, my lord, that I shall win today."

The crowd cheered her and playfully jeered Declan,

who doffed his hat and bowed low. "It is a coincidence of a celestial nature, then, my lady, that I, too, should feel very fine today. I think *I* shall win."

The crowd roared with delight. Declan gestured grandly to the horses. Keira tossed her hat aside and walked to the Welsh pony. A murmur ran through the crowd as the groom bent over and cupped his hands to help her up, Keira put her right foot into his hand, gathered her skirt, and when lifted up, she straddled the horse. She smiled at them and primly adjusted her skirts so that only the top of her stockings showed. "I grant you, it is scandalous," she said to the stunned looks of the women and the roar of approval from the men. "But it is for an excellent cause." She could see Lucy's happy smile.

"Another scandal?" Declan teased her in a low voice.

"I've spent part of a year living scandalously. I will at least leave the orphanage well endowed."

Declan grinned approvingly. "A worthy opponent," he said, and walked to his horse, vaulting himself up onto the saddle. "Are you at the ready, then?"

"Aye, completely." She wheeled her horse around toward the start line, as did Declan and the other three gentlemen.

Lord Horncastle had brought a red scarf for the occasion, and made a show of it to the crowd along the fence. The jeering and cheering continued as they lined their horses at the mark. Mr. Wilson, taking his place beside Keira, wished her luck.

"And to you, sir," she said jauntily. Several gentlemen in the crowd called their encouragement to Keira, but even more women called out to Declan.

She slanted a glance at him. "Ride well, but you will not catch me."

He chuckled at that. "You have great confidence in your ability, but I have a wee bit in mine, as well."

"Under ordinary circumstances, I would believe you had the advantage," she said, to which Declan kindly nodded his head. "But today, I have the advantage."

"Pray tell, what is that?" he asked as Horncastle called for them to set.

"Determination," she said, and before Declan could speak, Horncastle threw down the scarf and shouted *Go.*

Keira was off with a roar of the crowd. She held nothing in the reins, but gave that pony her head and bent low over her neck. She felt as if she were fleeing Eberlin and her fate, fleeing the deceit she had inflicted on this parish. She would ride to Ireland like this if she could, to the safety of her parents' house, as far away from the frivolous, silly girl she'd been as she could possibly go.

But the other riders were on her heels. She rounded the first bend, dug her heels into the pony's flanks, and the pony burst forward. Keira leaned down, lying as flat against the pony's neck as she could without losing balance. She managed to dip her head and look back—the other riders had faded, but Declan was coming up on her flank.

She could hear the crowd cheering, could see the next bend in the course. "*Ha!*" she cried, and slapped the horse's rump with her crop.

As she rounded the curve, Declan pulled closer. She caught a glimpse of him riding smoothly on the back of that gelding, as if he had not yet begun to race. But Keira was not inexperienced, either. Her father always said she'd been born to the saddle, and today she intended to prove it. She suddenly reined right, intentionally bumping the gelding and knocking him off his pace as they reached the flat part of the course.

Keira dug in her heels and used her crop once more. The pony bore down and edged ahead of the gelding. They rode like that, neck and neck, until the course began to turn back to the finish line. Keira had the inside track, and as they turned the corner, she nudged the pony just outside her lane, cutting a bit off her course. The pony veered onto grass, and Keira shouted again, urging her forward and faster. Her hair had come undone from its pins. Her skirt was flying up around her knees. If felt as if she would tumble off with every jolt, and it required every bit of her strength to hang on.

She was turning back to the finish line, racing head-long into chaos and revelation and the consequences of what she'd done, and the only thing she could do was win. She could at least do this one thing right.

But Declan was not a man who would give up a race. He was riding so close she could hear his gelding's labored breath; he was gaining on her, overtaking the lead at the quarter of the track. But that little Welsh pony was like Keira—she would not allow the bigger gelding to win, not this time. The horse stretched long beneath Keira; she felt the horse's muscles tense and release, tense and release, as she hurtled over the earth.

She wasn't certain who had won when they thundered across the finish line. She didn't know until she pulled the pony up and wheeled her around, and Declan—a beam-ing Declan—bowed low over his horse's neck to her.

The crowd was roaring her name. Declan moved his horse to her side and looked at her with an expression of pride and admiration. "Well done, *muirnín*," he said. "Very well done."

"I won?" she asked breathlessly.

He grinned. "By a nose."

She laughed and rubbed the pony's neck as she caught her breath.

She'd *won*.

At the conclusion of that race, Declan felt something strange in his chest, almost as if his heart were swelling. With pride. With something deeper.

He'd been impressed with the Welsh pony's performance. She was fast as fire and had been unwilling to give any ground to the gelding. But what had given him the strange sensation was Keira's ride. She'd astounded him. She was a fearless, flawless rider, unafraid to take risks and absolutely hell-bent on winning. He had greatly admired her pluck—she rode better than most experienced men he knew. His admiration was helped along by the fact that, at the finish line, her cheeks had the rosy hue of her exertion, her hair was wild and tangled from the ride, and her eyes were glittering with excitement. He was more than happy to match her purse and add to it. The orphanage had been the recipient of one hundred pounds from the race alone.

He wanted to speak to her, to tell her how proud he was of her race, but Keira had been swallowed up by an adoring crowd and whisked away.

Someone handed Declan an ale, and he gratefully drank it down. He wandered through the crowd, accepting the congratulations on a race well run. His thoughts turned to another task—finding Captain Corbett.

Anders had been good enough to point the captain out earlier in the day. He was round and had a thick head of gray hair that was second only to the thickness of his moustache. He had a booming laugh that could be heard across the grounds.

As the families and villagers began to leave the gala late in the afternoon, and preparations were made for the evening revelry, Declan saw Corbett again. He was sitting under a tree, his hat on his knee. An empty tankard lay on its side beside him. He looked as if he'd had a very festive day.

Declan caught a passing footman and took two cups of ale from him, then strolled to where Corbett was sitting. "Good evening," he said.

"Good evening, sir!" Corbett said happily, his eyes on the pair of ales Declan held. "May I congratulate you on a race well run."

"Thank you," Declan said. "Earl of Donnelly, at your service."

"I know very well who you are," Corbett said jovially. "I am Captain Corbett, formerly of the high seas, but in these last few years, of Londontown." He spoke as if his tongue had been loosened by ale.

"I know who you are, as well," Declan said congenially, and squatted down next to him to offer more ale.

Corbett took it with a gracious nod and drank thirstily.

"I should like a word," Declan said.

"With me? We are not acquainted, are we, my lord?"

"We are not acquainted, no. But we perhaps have common acquaintances."

"Oh?"

"Lady Ashwood, for one."

"Aha!" The captain's blue eyes crinkled. "I'll confess, I've not spoken to our lovely hostess. She's been a little bird today, flitting here and there. Between you and me, she's rather frightening with a bow and arrow." He laughed. "I rather feared she'd not recall me at all, for she was such a tiny thing when last I laid eyes on her."

"Speaking of which, Captain . . . there is a delicate matter I should like to broach with you."

Corbett looked surprised. Then appalled. "Has this to do with money? I know I've enjoyed more gaming tables than I ought to have done, but I pay my debts."

That made Declan smile, and he shook his head. "It has to do with what happened here at Ashwood fifteen years ago."

Corbett frowned thoughtfully.

"Mr. Joseph Scott in particular."

Corbett's thick brows sank. "I know nothing—"

"I know that he did not steal the countess's jewels," Declan said. Corbett watched Declan warily, but he did not deny it. "He was Lady Ashwood's lover, but he was not a thief," Declan said.

Corbett lifted a brow. He drank down the ale and put the cup aside. "You seem to have a very firm opinion."

"It is the opinions of others who were here that have given me cause to believe it is true."

Corbett nodded as if that did not surprise him. "It is water under the bridge, my lord. It happened fifteen years ago by your count. It hardly matters now, does it?"

Declan was slightly taken aback. "I would hasten to

disagree, sir. It matters to Mr. Scott's family and to his name, even now. I thought perhaps you might know the truth. After all, the countess entrusted you to escort Lily to Ireland."

"*Ach*, it was necessary that she go," he said with a flick of his wrist. "She was constantly under the earl's feet."

"Was that the reason?" Declan asked. "Or was she sent to Ireland because she knew, perhaps without even fully realizing it, of the affair between the countess and the woodcarver?"

Corbett scowled at him. "What do you want from me?"

"I hope that you can give me the missing pieces of the puzzle. Why didn't she save him from the gallows? Why did she end her life?"

"You ask quite a lot," Corbett said shortly.

"But you were a friend to Lady Ashwood. Why did she not speak out on behalf of her lover?" Declan asked.

"She had no choice," Corbett said. "The earl held her at Ashwood rather against her will. He would not allow her visitors, he would not allow her to speak."

"Could she not have sent a note to the magistrate?" Declan asked.

Corbett looked at him as if he were daft. "Let me assure you that Althea Kent was a brave woman. She could have sent a note to the magistrate, and she would have had no shortage of willing messengers. But she was quite miserable in her union with the earl, and I daresay any woman might have been. He was a powerful, wealthy man, but he was cold and cruel. She did not send a note to the magistrate because she feared he would act on his greatest threat, and send that beautiful child, her ward, to a London poorhouse if Althea dared to speak. And he'd have done it, too, without as much as a twinge of conscience."

Stunned, Declan stared at the man. "But . . . if Mr. Scott did not take the jewels, where are they?"

"Who could say?" Corbett said with a shrug. "A servant took them, I'd wager. They were quite valuable. Althea looked for them herself. She tore Ashwood beam to pier, searching for them, to prove they'd not been stolen before Mr. Scott hanged. But she never found them." Corbett sighed and downed the rest of his ale. "I've not had cause to think of this ugly business in many years," he said.

Declan signaled for a footman, handed him Mr. Corbett's empty tankard, and accepted a full one in exchange.

"It is important that I know one more thing, sir. The countess . . . she has begun to question what truly happened then, but she was quite attached to her aunt. Did Lady Ashwood take her own life?"

Corbett shook his head. "That's one theory. They say she left a note for the earl, but I don't know that anyone saw it." He looked at Declan. "But there are others who say the lady was a strong swimmer. I don't know if she was, but I do not believe Althea Kent would take her own life."

Now Declan was stunned into near speechlessness. "So much death and tragedy over a love affair? Affairs like this among the Quality happen all the time."

"The earl was an unforgiving man," Corbett said. "There now, you have your answer. What do you intend to do with it?"

"Exonerate Mr. Scott," Declan said solemnly. And

hopefully explain to Lily what may truly have happened to her beloved aunt.

Corbett nodded. "Fair enough. With the earl gone, no one has reason to fear the truth any longer, I suppose. Now sir, if you please, I should like to make the Countess's acquaintance again."

"Come," Declan said, and rose up, offering his hand to the captain to help him up, as well.

They walked to the terrace behind the house, where tables had been set with candles and flowers for dining. Keira had repaired her appearance and had donned a gown the color of the Irish mist. Her hair was combed and pulled back from her face, but fell down her back. She smiled when she saw Declan and he felt instantly lighter. "There you are, my worthy opponent," she said with a grand curtsy. "Did you hear? More than one hundred pounds were donated as a result of our race."

"It is owed all to you."

"I had great inspiration," she teased, and turned her smile to Corbett.

"Madam, may I present Captain Corbett."

Declan saw a shade of trepidation flick across her eyes; but Keira had become the consummate actress. "Captain! What a pleasure to see you again!" she exclaimed, and took his hand in both of hers. "It's been quite a long time, has it not?"

"Ah, madam, look at you now, all grown up," Corbett said with genuine fondness. "I always knew you'd be a beauty. Your eyes are a bit greener than I remember and your hair curly now . . ." He peered closely at Keira. "But yet as lovely as you were fifteen long years ago."

"Thank you kindly," Keira said.

"You've kept up with your chess, have you?" Corbett asked jovially.

"Ah . . . not as much as I would have liked," she said, tucking a lock of hair behind her ear.

"Come and indulge an old man with tales of your adventures," he said, steering Keira away.

Keira glanced pleadingly over her shoulder; Declan winked at her. She responded with a slight roll of her eyes, then turned her smile to Captain Corbett as if he were the most important man in the room.

Declan was certain of one thing—no one would ever believe that woman wasn't a countess, no matter what Eberlin thought he knew.

He didn't see her again until the late-night hours. The dancing was in full swing now, fueled by the copious amounts of ale that had been consumed all day and into the night.

Standing on the edge of the terrace, Declan happened to catch a glimpse of the blue silk Keira had donned for the evening behind the evergreens on the terrace. He peeked between them; Keira was leaning with her back against the wall, her eyes closed.

"I remember finding you and Lily with Eireanne behind some potted plants at Ballynaheath during a Christmas ball."

She opened her eyes and smiled wryly. "Do you refer to the one ball held at Ballynaheath in the last one hundred years?"

"In the last ten," he corrected her.

"I remember it well. I was fourteen years old."

"Fourteen years and already plotting the fate of Lily and . . . what was that boy's name?"

"Ciaran Dougal," Keira said with a weary grin. "Do you recall him? He was only a wee bit older than we were and could think of nothing but sailing the seas like his father and his grandfather. I can't now recall why we were so thoroughly convinced he'd be a good match for Lily. I think perhaps it had to do with his lovely eyes."

Declan smiled.

"But you ruined everything, you know," she said, frowning playfully. "To think that Lily might be married to a sea captain today had you not interfered when you did."

"When next I see her, I will apologize on bended knee for having ruined her chance at happiness."

Keira laughed softly and yawned again.

"You're exhausted. You should go to bed."

"I don't dare," she said with a shake of her head. "Not until every last guest has left. But I would not object to a wee bit of airing."

Declan wanted to wrap his arms around her. He wanted to put her to bed himself, lose himself in her arms. "Allow me," he said, and offered his arm. He led her off the terrace and onto the lawn.

They ambled past empty tents and tables, past an ale barrel that had been tipped onto its side. They walked across the lawn bowling area, where the balls still lay as they had at the conclusion of a game.

"I am proud of you, lass," Declan said. "What you managed to accomplish here today is as astonishing as it is commendable. You should be proud of what you've done for the orphanage."

Keira shook her head and looked down at her feet. "There were so many others involved."

"No, you. None of this was possible without you, and no one can ever take it from you."

She smiled a little sheepishly. "Thank you. I suppose I am a wee bit proud of myself. I wish only that I might have done it without deception."

"Aye," Declan said. They strolled a little farther, toward the lake, where the rush torches were beginning to burn low.

"Did you have opportunity to speak to Captain Corbett?" Keira asked. "I did not dare—I feared he would discover me if I asked questions."

"I did," Declan said, and quietly filled Keira in on what Captain Corbett had told him about the reasons her aunt had not spoken out for Mr. Scott, and the suspicions surrounding her death. Keira listened in stunned silence. By the time he'd finished, they'd reached the gazebo.

"*Dhia,*" she whispered. "I don't know what to say." She looked out over the lake. "Poor Lily," she said softly. "She'll find the truth so distressing."

"Aye," Declan agreed. "I would very much like to know where the jewels are."

"Will you continue to look for them?" Keira asked.

Declan glanced out at the darkened lawn a moment. "I suppose I will," he said, and realized in that moment that he would. "Joseph Scott deserves it. So does your aunt. It seems the least I can do, particularly as I shall be at Kitridge Lodge for several more months with a pregnant mare." He would need something to fill the days and hours that he would be missing Keira. "And you won't be here to distract me with your galas and your hats," he said with a bit of a smile.

Keira smiled sadly. "I don't want to go, Declan. I want to help you find the jewels. I want to put everything to rights. If only I . . ." She stopped herself from saying more.

"Ah, Keira," he said. He put his hand on her waist, drew her to him, and kissed her tenderly. It was a sad kiss, he thought, the sort of kiss two lovers shared when parting.

He did love her. That was the peculiar thing he'd been feeling, that strange weight in the very center of him. He loved Keira Hannigan unlike anything or anyone he'd loved before, and he wished, on that starry summer night, that he knew what he was to do with it, how he was supposed to accommodate the knowledge of it in the landscape of his restless soul.

He cupped her face, studying it in the dim light, his gaze moving over her delicate features, trying to keep the image of her and her Irish eyes as bright and real in his mind as she was to him now. "I will miss you, *muirnín.*" He would miss her like he would miss breathing.

Keira wrapped her hand around his wrist. "I will miss you more," she whispered, and with a quiet sigh, she closed her eyes.

Declan kissed her softly, but a harder desire quickly took hold. She was warm and soft in his hands, and he realized that very soon, he'd not see her again at Ashwood, would not have those Irish eyes sparkling back at him. He would not be touching her like this again.

He thrust his fingers into the thick tail of hair at her back and deepened his kiss. She smelled like lavender. He moved his mouth to the lobe of her ear, then her neck, and the soft indentation of her throat, where he could feel her pulse beating wildly beneath his lips. He dug his fingers into her hip and bent down to her bosom, his mouth on the swell of flesh above her décolletage. Above him, Keira gasped with pleasure, fanning the fire of desire that had suddenly engulfed Declan.

He groaned with the ache to be inside her, and impulsively grabbed her by the waist and twirled her around, depositing her on the bench that lined the interior of the gazebo as he went down on one knee before her.

"And what do you think you're about?" Keira asked with a lilt in her voice. "Do you not see there are guests everywhere?"

"Guests who are well into their cups and more concerned about their own amorous encounters," he said, and slipped her satin slipper off her foot. He held her leg in his hand and kissed her ankle, stocking and all.

Keira giggled. "Have a care with my shoe, sir!"

"What shoe?" he asked, and moved his mouth up her leg, to the inside of her knee, pushing the skirt of her gown up as he went.

"Declan O'Conner, you are leading me down a path of debauchery," Keira said as she braced her hands against his shoulders.

"You don't seem to mind." He nipped at her leg just above her stocking, then lifted his head, and put his hand against the inside of her thigh. "Do you want me to stop?" he asked silkily.

Keira's playful smile disappeared; she drew a slow, steadying breath. "We will be discovered," she whispered.

"Not if you remain very quiet," he said with a wink, and slipped his hand between the slit of her drawers to feel the springy curls that covered her sex.

"*Oh*," she moaned.

He moved his fingers deeper into the wet folds. He would go to hell for this, for lusting after her so, but Declan didn't care. He was hard, and the only thing he cared about was giving her pleasure and watching her take it. She was warm and wet, and he stroked her mercilessly, his fingers glancing against her sensitive core, sliding slow and long and back again. With each stroke of her flesh, with each of her sighs that reached his ears, he throbbed with want in every vein.

He imagined moving inside her, feeling the stroke of her body on him. He withdrew his hand and gathered the yards of silk of her gown and pushed it up, over her knees, so that her drawers and stockings were revealed to him.

Keira's breathing instantly turned quicker; her fingers curled around the edge of the bench as if she were fighting to keep her seat.

It was unbearable for Declan. He reached for her waist, dragging her closer to him, then put his fingers in the slit of her drawers and ripped them wide open.

"*Declan!*" Keira whispered.

"*Sssh,*" he warned her, and silenced her with a long, passionate kiss that left her gasping for breath before he moved once more between her legs.

Her scent instantly aroused him to madness.

He touched his tongue to the springy curls and Keira hissed in an effort to keep quiet. Then he touched his mouth to her and she caught a cry of pleasure in her throat. "Heaven help me," she groaned as he delved into her with his tongue.

Nothing could have aroused him more than her faint plea, and with a growl, Declan began to explore her flesh with his mouth, feasting on her flesh, his body awash in her scent.

When he drew the core of her desire in between his teeth and lips, her fingers sank into his hair, and holding fistfuls of it, she writhed, pressing up to meet him, then sinking away when she couldn't bear the pleasure he gave her. He had no intention of letting her escape it and grasped her hips, holding her firmly against him, pushing her to the edge, and then losing himself as she fell headlong over it, stifling her groans of pleasure, clawing at the bench, while at the same time rising up to meet him again.

And then she lay still, completely spent. Declan kissed her thighs, and then her knees, then sat back on his heels as he tried to catch his breath. He pulled a handkerchief from his pocket and wiped his mouth before using it to clean her.

Keira slowly righted herself then pushed her gown down. Her green eyes were dark, her hair a tangled mess. She stared at him for a long moment, her affection for him quite evident in her lazy, satisfied smile. "You are a wicked man, Declan. *Diabhal.*"

"Thank you," he said with a smile. He pulled himself up and sat beside her on the bench. Keira cupped his face in her hands and kissed him until he was laughing, then settled back, leaning into him.

He laced his fingers with hers. They said nothing, just

let the cool night air sweep over them. A sound of laughter reached them, and Declan sighed. He turned his head to look at Keira. "Your guests will wonder where you've gone."

"Round the bend," she said.

Declan rather thought he'd gone round with her.

Thirty-one

Keira hadn't wanted to leave the gazebo. She had wanted the night to last forever. But she dutifully bound her hair at her nape, shook out her skirts, and allowed Declan to adjust her bodice. They started back, hand in hand. "I think I shall take up archery when I return to Ireland," Keira said lightly. "I rather like it, don't you?"

Declan didn't answer, but dropped her hand. She noticed he was looking up the darkened path. She followed his gaze and saw Linford running toward them. *Running.* Wide-eyed, Keira looked at Declan. He looked like she felt—a little ill. "God save me," she whispered.

"Madam," Linford said, wheezing for breath, "please do come straightaway."

"What is it, Linford? What has happened?"

"You must come."

Keira's heart began to race. She knew what had happened—Eberlin had made good on his threat. He'd brought the authorities, and now she would have to beg them to believe her. They hurried after Linford, but at the edge of the lawn, he turned into the garden. "Through the servant's entrance," he said.

Keira looked at Declan. *"Eberlin,"* she whispered.

Declan nodded. "Go with Linford. I'll find out what is happening."

"Do come, madam," Linford said, and reaching the house before her, he held the door of the servant's entrance open. Keira smiled anxiously at Linford as she passed, but he did not quite meet her gaze.

Oh God. Dear God. She felt as if she were walking to the gallows as she moved down the hall. Her belly churned and her palms dampened. She clasped her hands together, pressed them tightly to her abdomen. Everything had gone so perfectly. She should have known the magic of the day would not last.

"In the receiving salon," Linford said.

Keira had no idea how she did it, how she managed to move one foot in front of the other, to make herself walk down that long corridor to the front of the house and the receiving salon. At the door, she paused a moment to draw a shallow breath. She lifted her chin; this might be the moment of reckoning for her, but she would meet it with as much dignity as she could muster, in spite of her enormous lie.

She walked through the door and her breath caught in her throat. It was not Eberlin who stood in that room; it was Lily. Lily with her black silky hair and sea-green eyes, who so closely resembled Keira . . . but then again, not.

"Kiki!" Lily cried and grabbed Keira in a tight embrace.

Keira felt dangerously close to collapsing with relief. "I thought you would never come," she said into Lily's neck.

"I know, dearest, I am terribly late. But foul weather made it impossible to sail." She suddenly reared back and grabbed Keira by the shoulders. "What has happened here?"

Keira's gaze flew to Linford. And Louis, who was looking at Lily as if he'd seen a ghost. "Leave us," Keira said softly.

Neither man moved. "Please," Keira pleaded.

Linford bowed his head and stepped out. Louis did, too, but his step was slower. He looked at Keira with a mixture of confusion and perhaps a little disdain. When she heard the door close behind her, Keira smiled tremulously at her cousin. "Oh Lily . . . there is so much to tell you, I don't know where to begin."

"At the beginning," Lily said, pulling her down onto a settee with her. "I don't understand what is going on here. Linford took one look at me and seemed ill. He summoned Mrs. Thorpe from her bed, and the poor woman could not speak. They looked at me as if seeing a ghost. Only the footman would say it. He said, beg your pardon, mu'um, but we already have Lily Boudine. She is the countess. Imagine my great surprise, Keira!"

"I know, it's—"

"I thought, perhaps you'd not come to Ashwood after all, and I said, I am the countess, I am Lily," Lily continued breathlessly. "I said to Mrs. Thorpe, do you not remember me? You taught me how to braid my hair. But she didn't answer and I realized that something was terribly, terribly wrong. And it dawned on me then and there that you *had* come, and for some reason, they all believed you to be *me*."

"Aye," Keira said, and clasped Lily's hand. "I will tell you everything."

"Oh no," Lily said, peering closely at Keira. "Oh *no*, Keira!" She suddenly surged out of her seat and walked to the window, then whirled around to her cousin. "Of all the stupid, reckless things!" she said. "Why would you do it? How could you not see the chaos it would cause?" she cried.

"Because of Hannah Hough," Keira said, finding her feet as she swallowed down unshed tears of relief. "I never meant this to happen, Lily. What I'd not give to go back and do it all again! But I cannot. I can only tell you that I thought I was doing what you asked me to do."

"Be *me*? I never asked you to be me, Keira," Lily said incredulously. "What in the bloody blazes are we to do now?"

Keira lost her heart then. She couldn't carry her deceit another step, and she collapsed with it, sinking like a rock onto her knees, her skirts pooling around her. All the frustration and fear and regret brought their full weight down on her shoulders.

"Keira!" Lily cried with alarm, and rushed to her, falling down on her knees beside her. She threw her arms around Keira and hugged her tight. "Oh my," she said, her voice softer. "What has happened?"

Keira told her everything. How the resemblance between them, aided by fifteen years, had been rather convincing, and how they had all mistaken her for Lily. She told her how she had never meant to do what she had, but there was the problem of Hannah Hough who would lose her home if the countess did not do something, and the wages that needed to be paid, and the gala, and the mysterious Danish count who was attempting to steal one hundred acres and had threatened her, and why she had never told anyone the truth.

"Oh Kiki . . . you should have gone back to Ireland," Lily sighed. "Staying here only made it worse."

"I couldn't," Keira said woefully. "I couldn't leave them all, and I couldn't leave Ashwood to sink into ruin. And there was Mr. Scott."

Lily blanched at the mention of his name. "Mr. Scott," she repeated, as if she didn't trust herself to say it. She sank back onto her heels. "What could that man have to do with anything?"

Keira groaned. She closed her eyes a moment, then found her feet. She offered her hand to Lily and helped her up to the settee. "I have some distressing news," she said. "Mr. Scott did not steal the jewels."

Lily stared blankly at her.

"Declan and I have discovered the truth," Keira added.

"Declan? Declan who?"

"Donnelly," she said with a wince.

Lily came off the settee again.

"I know what you are thinking," Keira exclaimed. "It is the strangest of coincidences that he should be here breeding horses, at Kitridge Lodge of all things! I had no idea he was here, on my honor, I did not, Lily. He . . . he just appeared one day. He'd come to see the horses we'd put up for sale."

"The horses?" Lily cried, and put her hands to her head as if it pained her. "What has any of that to do with Mr. Scott?"

"Mr. Scott didn't steal the jewelry from Aunt Althea— he was her lover."

Lily gaped at her. "That is impossible," she said angrily. "You have created quite a fantasy—"

"I haven't," Keira insisted and stood up. She grabbed Lily's hand. "You will believe me when you see what I will show you."

She pulled Lily out of the receiving room and down the corridor, past a surprised maid and two wary footmen. In the music room, Keira lit a candelabra and pulled Lucy to the pianoforte. "Do you remember this?" she asked, pointing at the instrument.

"Of course I do. It was Althea's."

"Everyone here believes Althea had it made for you," Keira said. She handed Lily the candelabra and turned the bench over. "Look there, Lily. Look at the inscription."

Lily at first didn't seem to even see it, so Keira grabbed her hand once more and pulled her down to her knees and held the light close. Lily leaned over, squinting at the inscription. She read it, sat back on her heels, and then leaned forward to read it again. "I don't understand," she said. "I don't understand."

"Oh Lily," Keira said sadly. "Mr. Scott didn't steal the jewels. Aunt Althea did not drown accidentally. She took her own life. Or someone else took it from her."

Lily paled; she gaped at Keira. Then her eyes narrowed. "I don't understand what you're about, but that is *not* true," she said angrily.

Keira grabbed her hands and held them with her own. "It is true, darling," she said solemnly, and told Lily all that she knew. With each breath, Lily sank deeper onto her heels, her eyes fixed on Keira.

A quarter of an hour later, Keira stepped outside the

music room and summoned a footman. "Please fetch Lord Donnelly for me," she said. "Tell him . . ." She glanced over her shoulder to Lily, who was still sitting on the floor, staring at the carpet in disbelief. "Tell him Lily Boudine has come home to Ashwood."

Thirty-two

Declan knew before the footman told him that Lily had come home; the rumors were already sweeping through the late-night crowd. He'd heard that something was quite wrong about Lady Ashwood, and when a woman explained that there were two of them, one appearing on the drive just as others were leaving, he knew.

Declan found Lily and Keira sitting on a settee facing each other in the green salon. The moment Lily saw him, she surged to her feet. "My lord," she said softly, and hurried across the room to shut the door behind him. As she did, Keira slowly stood. Her eyes, full of shock and trepidation, locked on Declan's.

"I would ask after you and yours, but I think Keira's predicament demands our immediate attention," Lily said as she swept by him. Her arms were folded, the color in her cheeks high. She was pretty like Keira, but in a softer way. The color of her eyes wasn't as striking, or her nose as pert. There was indeed a strong resemblance between them, which of course Declan had known, yet there was no mistaking them. Declan supposed that the moment some of the longtime servants saw Lily, they knew their mistake.

"Aye," he said. "The guests are aware that something is amiss."

"Dear God," Lily said helplessly.

"Lily," Declan said, moving forward, grasping her hand. "Keira did something so lacking in judgment that she may never recover from it."

"I beg your pardon!" Keira exclaimed.

"But it is done," he said, ignoring Keira. "And while she was wrong to have done it, she has made the best of it and has done some very fine things in your name. She has kept Ashwood safe for the time being from some serious challenges to the property. She has put men to work rebuilding the old mill and has made plans to mill grain for profit. She has taken the orphanage under her wing and helped raise funds to renovate St. Bartholomew's. And she has begun repair to Ashwood. She has been extraordinary in your stead, but now, it is time to acknowledge the truth and send her back to Ireland before anyone can make trouble for either of you."

"And leave me to clean up this mess?" Lily asked, and removed her hand from his.

"Keira has committed a crime in assuming your identity," he explained. "I am uncertain that you can give her complete protection from English law."

Both women looked at him then, their green eyes wide.

"I assure you that the common Englishman will find it an egregious act for an Irish Catholic woman to impersonate an English countess, no matter how good her intentions. They will assume her reasons for doing so were not because she is a foolish girl, but because she sought some personal or political gain."

"But she had my permission to do what she must," Lily pointed out.

"So you say," he said. "There is no proof of that."

"Then I will write a letter now," Lily said, looking to the writing table.

"The question will surely be asked why, if she had such a letter, did she not present it ere now?"

Keira and Lily exchanged a troubling look.

"I suggest we go now and announce to whoever is still assembled here tonight that the rightful countess is here. Keira and I will leave for Ireland on the morrow."

"You?" Keira asked.

Declan looked at her beautiful face. "You must leave straightaway, and I cannot leave you to travel alone. We'll ride."

"But what of your horses? And your commission to produce a foal?" Keira asked.

Yes, what of his commitments? He'd hardly thought this through. The only thing he knew was that he could not leave Keira to fend for herself. When this revelation had come to him, he couldn't say. He only knew that, looking at her now, he would accept no other scenario. "I shall have to rely on Noakes to see to it in my absence." He looked at Lily. "And you must put your trust in Mr. Fish and rely on him. He will guide you through the days that follow."

"Mr. Fish?" Lily repeated, and shook her head, pressing her fingers to her temples. "I cannot believe this is happening." Her hands were shaking, Declan noticed.

"I will fetch Mr. Fish," Declan said. "I will ask that Linford prepare the guests for an announcement," he added, and left the two young women staring at each other uncertainly.

Mr. Fish was stunned. He stood in the receiving salon, his gaze alternating back and forth between Keira and Lily, as if he couldn't make sense of it. Keira could scarcely look at him, she felt so guilty.

"I cannot apologize to you enough," Keira said. "I never meant to deceive anyone so completely, but especially you, Mr. Fish. You have been my friend and my advisor, and . . . and Ashwood would be ruined had it not been for you."

Mr. Fish swallowed hard and clasped his hands tightly behind his back. "I cannot say that I understand your deception," he said stiffly. "Or that I don't feel sorely duped."

It pained Keira to hear that, but she bit her lip and nodded her head. She deserved his disdain, if not his complete censure.

"I don't know what to say beyond that," he said.

Declan gave Keira a brief, reassuring smile, but Keira was not soothed. She despised herself for having hurt Mr. Fish as she clearly had done. "I understand, sir. It is my great hope that one day you will see your way to forgiving me—"

Mr. Fish snorted.

Keira winced. "But until that day comes, it is my most ardent hope that you will not fault Lily for it. She is completely blameless, and she needs your help now more than ever."

Mr. Fish glanced at Lily, his expression cool. "I agree that she does indeed need my help."

"Then . . . then will you stay on, sir?" Lily asked carefully.

Mr. Fish pressed his lips together as he considered her. "For a time, madam," he agreed. "For a time."

Lily sighed with relief. "I cannot thank you enough."

"Well," Mr. Fish said briskly. "His lordship suggests we inform your guests. I agree that it must be done in the name of all that is decent, for these people have put their trust in . . . Miss Hannigan."

Keira thought she would be ill as she watched Mr. Fish stride out. She realized then that she was gripping the back of the chair so hard, her fingers ached.

"Come then," Lily said, holding out her hand to Keira. "Let us have this over and done. It's gone on far too long."

Keira could only nod. Lily put her arm around Keira's shoulders and forced her to walk. Declan opened the door for them, and as they passed, he touched her hand. "Chin up, lass," he said to her.

With their arms around each other's waist, Keira and Lily walked out onto the terrace, Declan behind them. He took his place next to Mr. Fish, who had indeed assembled the remaining guests. Keira glanced up; clouds were beginning to drift across the landscape of stars, swallowing them up as they lazily drifted along. She wished one would swallow her up now. She could hear the whispers below them, the gasps as people moved closer and saw Keira and Lily together.

Declan stepped forward. "I will tell them—"

"No," Keira said. "It must be me." She closed her eyes a moment to gather her resolve, then let her arm fall from its anchor around Lily's waist and stepped forward, standing alone at the top step of the terrace. "Thank you all for coming today," she said, in a voice that surprised her with its strength, and looked out at a sea of familiar faces. There were the Society ladies and their spouses. There was Sister Rosens, who was still holding a tankard and had laughed today as Keira had never seen her laugh. There was Benedict Sibley, his gaze as admiring as ever. There were new friends, as well, such as Captain Corbett, whom she had discovered was a delightful curmudgeon. There were a few members of the household staff, such as the footmen and Linford and even Mrs. Thorpe. All of them looked up at her, their expressions confused and curious.

"Thank you," she said again. "We raised more than four hundred pounds for the orphanage today."

That earned a round of polite applause, but it was clear the orphanage had long been forgotten. Every gaze was riveted on her. "And now," Keira said, her knees trembling, "I would like to introduce the true Countess of Ashwood, Lily Boudine." She gestured to Lily; a murmur rose in the crowd as people turned to each other and asked that someone repeat what Keira had said, for surely there was some mistake.

Lily stepped forward and slipped her hand into Keira's and gave it a gentle squeeze.

"You may have noticed our resemblance. I am . . . I am actually Lady Ashwood's cousin, Keira Hannigan," Keira said, a little shakily.

There were more gasps, and the murmuring grew louder. Just below Keira stood Mrs. Ogle, who was staring at her, slack-jawed.

"It is a . . . a rather funny thing," Keira said. "When we received news that Lily had inherited the estate and the title as the sole surviving heir of the late earl, she was committed to travel to Italy. She asked me to come and mind things for her until she would be able to assume her rightful place, which, naturally, I could not refuse to do. But when I arrived, I was mistaken for her . . ."

Keira hesitated. *No, no,* this was all wrong. There had to be a better way to tell them. She looked at Mr. Sibley, whose expression had changed to disbelief and, she feared, disgust.

"Go on!" a woman called up. "Don't leave us dangling!"

Lily squeezed Keira's hand again, and Keira cleared her throat. "I was mistaken for my cousin, and I meant to tell you all, I did, but there was the rather urgent matter of Hannah Hough, which required the countess's intervention, and . . . and it seemed to me that Ashwood needed its countess."

Her gaze fell upon Lady Horncastle, who looked enraged. And Sister Rosens—oh God, how disappointed her expression!

"I must emphasize that Lady Ashwood did not ask me to . . . to *be* her," Keira tried to clarify. "She is entirely blameless in this as she did not know—"

"I asked her to come and mind things," Lily said, her voice bright and clear. "She had my full support to do whatever was necessary."

There was more murmuring, the sound of confusion growing louder. And there was anger. Daria Babcock, the sweet young miss Keira had befriended, was smirking now. Mrs. Morton had Mrs. Ogle's ear and was talking quickly, her expression angry, her hands moving. Mr. Anders put down his tankard and turned away, pushing his way through the crowd. Keira was at least thankful that Lucy was in bed now and did not have to hear this.

"I wanted you all to hear the truth from me," Keira said. "But now Lady Ashwood has come home, and I am no longer needed here. So I will thank you all for your . . . your friendship and kindness to me and ask that you give Lady Ashwood your allegiance," Keira said. Tears began to fill her throat. She didn't think she could say another word and looked at Lily. Lily smiled and nodded to the door behind them. Keira bowed her head and began to walk that way.

"*Liar!*" someone shouted at her. Keira gulped down a swell of nausea. She did not see Declan move, but she heard him.

"See here!" he said loudly and firmly.

Keira gasped and whirled around. Declan was standing at the edge of the terrace, his legs braced apart. "Before you condemn, remember the good she has done for you all!" he thundered. "The orphanage has been greatly benefited, and had it not been for her efforts here today, I daresay they would not have benefited quite so handsomely, aye? Many of you have been put to work building a new mill. She has made sure your wages were paid and your rents not increased. So before you judge her, remember what she has done for Ashwood and for you."

He turned away from them, his blue eyes dark. He moved to usher Lily and Keira inside, and someone shouted, "Bloody pogue! Go back to Ireland!"

Declan clenched his jaw and sent the ladies into the

house ahead of him as the angry shouts from the crowd grew louder.

"I will send them on their way," Mr. Fish said crisply, and stepped out again, leaving Declan, Lily, and Keira alone. Declan looked at Keira. "You're a brave woman," he said. "I'll be back in the morning. Be prepared to ride. Lily, welcome home," he said, and began striding down the corridor.

Keira watched him walk away. She'd never seen him look like that, had never seen his expression so determined.

Lily moved, pulling Keira with her. They hurried down the carpeted hallways and up to the pink and cream rooms Keira had called home all these months. Lily walked across the threshold and looked around her. "I spent hours in this suite with Aunt Althea," she said wistfully.

"What was she like?" Keira asked as she closed the door behind them. "I have so many questions about her now."

"Beautiful," Lily said sadly. "A princess. I wanted to be just like her." She sank onto the chaise before the hearth as Keira began to gather a few things. "I can't believe her own life ended so tragically. How alone she must have felt! How afraid! Tell me again," Lily said. "Tell me everything."

Keira told her everything again. They talked until the early-morning hours, until Lily had exhausted all her questions.

"It took you so long to come back," Keira said when Lily grew quiet. "Was the reason Mr. Canavan?"

Lily smiled sheepishly. "No. Mr. Canavan was not as exciting as I thought he'd be," she said with a wan smile. "It was truly foul weather and . . . and I was reluctant to come back here, Keira. There are so many pieces of my memory that are missing, yet I have strange, uncomfortable feelings about this place. Especially now, after what you've told me about Althea. I don't know what to think at all."

She lay down on the bed and stared up at the canopy. Keira lay down beside her. "I think it is a lovely place, Lily I hope you find your peace with it."

They talked until they both slipped into sleep.

But Keira's sleep was restless. She woke before dawn and finished putting her things together, then waited for Lily to wake.

When Lily at last opened her eyes, she saw Keira sitting on the chaise, watching her. "Keira? What time is it?"

"Half past seven," Keira said. "Lily, there is one last thing I must tell you. There is a girl named Lucy Taft . . ."

Lucy was in the nursery eating her breakfast under the watchful eye of a maid, who looked at Keira with disgust when she entered.

Lucy, however, seemed her usual, cheerful self. "Good morning, mu'um," she said, which Keira considered an excellent sign. She had not heard of last night's chaos.

"Betts, will you please excuse us?" Keira asked the maid.

The maid stood and walked out of the room without a word.

Lucy, obviously sensing something was wrong, lowered her spoon and stared at Keira. Keira knelt next to Lucy and took her hand. Tears had already flooded her vision. "Darling, there is something I must tell you."

"What is it?" Lucy asked, her voice trembling. She did not seem to notice Lily standing at the threshold.

"Something has happened," Keira said. "Something in Ireland, actually, and I . . ." She didn't know how to say it. "I must return to Ireland."

"Ireland?" Lucy said. Her chin began to tremble, and Keira's eyes welled. "But when?"

"Now, darling. Today."

"*Today?*" Lucy cried, and began to sob. "Why?"

Keira grabbed her and held her close. "I am so very sorry!" she whispered. "It's rather a long story, and one that you would not possibly understand. I haven't much time, dearest, but I want you to remember what I told you. Do you remember?"

Lucy hiccupped on a sob and nodded.

Keira cupped Lucy's face, smoothed her hair back, and kissed her cheek. "Whatever you might hear said of me, you must always remember that I meant no harm. Remember that I meant only to . . ." There were no words that could explain to a nine-year-old girl what was in Keira's heart. "I meant only to live, Lucy," she said simply. "There is nothing more I can say for myself than that. I wanted to live, to taste freedom, to be and do all those things that I will never be and do again. And in the course of it, I found you! I adore you, lass, don't ever believe otherwise."

"Then why can't I go with you?" Lucy begged as tears streamed down her cheeks. "I promise I shall be good. I shall do whatever you ask."

Keira's heart broke. Lucy was another consequence of her impetuous, impulsive actions. She'd thought she was doing the girl a world of good by taking her from the orphanage, but now she realized she'd only hurt her. She embraced Lucy as the girl cried, swallowing back her own tears. "You cannot go with me, darling, not this time," she said, stroking Lucy's fair head, but Lucy was inconsolable.

"Here now," Keira said softly. "I need you here! I have a very important favor to ask you. My cousin has come. She will be the countess now! But she doesn't know a soul at Ashwood and she will need a dear friend. Will you be her friend, darling? Will you be someone to whom she can talk?"

"No, mu'um! I want to go with you!" Lucy cried.

"Oh Lucy, I would give my world to take you with me, but I cannot. And Lily needs you so. She needs you more than either of you know."

Lily suddenly appeared, sinking down beside them. "Lucy, I am so very happy to make your acquaintance," Lily said, smiling.

Lucy sniffed and stared ruefully at Lily. "She looks very much like you, mu'um," she said curiously to Keira.

"She's prettier," Keira admitted, and smiled at Lily. There were tears glistening in her cousin's eyes. "And she will adore you as I do, I suspect." She kissed Lucy once more and stood up, leaving Lily to console Lucy as she silently went out, her heart crumbling a little more with each step.

Thirty-three

If he'd spared even a moment to think, Declan surely would have convinced himself that it was madness to do what he was about to do. Yet mad he must be, for he could not turn his back on Keira now. She was rather firmly lodged in his heart. He loved her, and he was concerned for her safety. So he'd gathered his things and had packed the saddlebags.

He was ready when Mr. and Mrs. Noakes arrived to work.

Mr. Noakes was stunned by Declan's request that he look after Declan's horses until he could return. "Are you unwell, my lord?" he asked.

"No, but I am needed in Ireland. I expect to return before winter."

Mr. Noakes seemed bewildered, but accepted that explanation. He promised Declan his horses would be properly attended until he could return. Declan had no doubt of that, but he felt wretched for leaving them, particularly his pregnant mare. He'd never left his horses behind. Never.

He saddled the gelding and tethered the Welsh pony to his mount. With one last look at the horses in the stables, Declan rode to Ashwood.

It was only a quarter past nine in the morning when he arrived. Linford greeted him coolly, and Louis looked him directly in the eye, his expression challenging. It would seem that once again, he was considered guilty through his association with Keira. He was, however, surprisingly unbothered by it this time. He just wanted to get Keira out of here.

He found Keira, Lily, and Mr. Fish in the salon. They were a solemn trio, and all three stood when he entered the room.

"My lord," Mr. Fish said.

"Eberlin has summoned the constable," Keira said. She looked almost frantic.

Declan looked at Mr. Fish. "Is this true?"

"It is. I received word from a friend of mine this morning. Eberlin has sent a messenger to the constable to report that an extraordinary crime has been perpetrated here."

"Word travels very fast in Hadley Green," Declan mused. "How long until the constable will come?"

"A day at most," Mr. Fish said.

Declan looked at Keira. "A day's head start will be enough. I doubt the constable will pursue us if Lady Ashwood does not wish to pursue it. But let us be safe," he said, and handed some clothes he'd gathered at Kitridge to Keira.

"What's this?" Keira asked.

"You will travel faster and lighter as a man."

Keira looked at Lily, who nodded. "Come, Keira. There is no time to debate it."

The ladies returned a short time later with Keira dressed in buckskins that were tightly belted and tucked into a pair of riding boots, yet she looked to be swimming in them. The riding coat and waistcoat were just as ill fitting, but Declan was satisfied that they hid her feminine curves. The greatcoat swallowed her whole. He removed a knife from his boot and cut the sleeves and hem of the greatcoat.

"There, now," he said, standing back. "You look like a sickly boy."

"Please!" Keira protested.

"Her hair," Lily said, and helped Keira wrap it up and tuck it under a hat. Lily tied a neckcloth around her neck so that it would thicken the appearance of her slender neck.

"Do I still look like a sickly boy?" Keira asked.

"Aye. But more importantly, you do not look like a woman," Declan said. "Say your farewells, lass. We must be away."

He stood aside as she hugged her cousin. "I am so very sorry, Lily," she said. "And Eberlin—"

"Don't fret," Lily said, and put on a smile for her cousin. "I shall deal with him," she said firmly, and Declan had the distinct feeling she would do precisely that.

Keira looked at Mr. Fish. "Good-bye, Mr. Fish."

He nodded, his expression stoic.

"Come, Keira," Declan said. "We'll go out the servants' entrance."

With one last look at Lily, Keira followed him. They walked outside where the horses were waiting. Declan smiled reassuringly at Keira, and touched her face, pushing a curl from her temple. She was beautiful to him. An Irish princess. He regretted what she'd done, but he could no longer believe he would change a moment of it. It was another private admission that made his heart reel. He was leaving his horses for this woman. It was a painful transition, this business of love, but he supposed there truly was no joy without pain. "Let's go," he said, and helped her up onto the pony's back.

They started up the private road that led into the Ashwood forest. Keira rode like a man—silently, with her head down, her focus on the road ahead. They rode until the sun was high overhead, then paused to eat something and water the horses. "How long to the sea?" Keira asked.

"If we can cover fifty miles each day without unduly tiring the horses, we should reach Pembroke in three days."

They continued on until night began to fall and Keira complained of hunger. Declan found a suitable campsite beside a stream. Keira helped herself off the horse and set about gathering as much firewood as she could see in the small space around them while Declan watered the horses. He hobbled them, and left them to graze while he built a fire from the wood she'd dragged to the spot on the stream. Once the fire was burning, Declan threw down the bedrolls, laying them side by side. He eased himself down beside her and arranged the saddlebags to make a pillow of sorts, then held out his hand to Keira, helping her down.

She lay on her side, staring morosely into the fire.

Declan was bone weary, but he was aware of her body next to his, the curves beneath the greatcoat, skin as soft as butter, and hair that smelled like springtime. He wanted to pull her into his arms, but Keira seemed lost in her thoughts.

Declan closed his eyes, drifting into a shallow sleep. At the far edges of his consciousness, he could hear the occasional snort of the horses, the crackle of the fire, and . . . and an odd sound that roused him from a deeper sleep. He lay there with his eyes closed until he realized what he was hearing. Keira was quietly crying.

He opened his eyes and listened to the sound of her tears for a few moments before rolling onto his side and slipping his arm around her belly, pulling her to his body. "Don't cry, *muirnín*. Everything will be all right," he murmured.

"I've made such a horrible mess of things," she said woefully.

"Aye, you have indeed."

"Don't agree with me," she said tearfully. "That's the absolute worst thing you might do."

Declan smiled in the night and stroked her hair. In the fire's waning light, he could see it black against his hand, as smooth as satin. "Come here, you foolish girl," he said, and moved her hair aside to kiss her nape.

"If you had the slightest bit of sense at all, you would leave me here and let the wolves feed on me."

"There's not enough of you to make much of a meal."

"I didn't intend to feed them all winter," she said, and twisted around, so that she was facing him. She touched his brow, her fingers sliding down his cheek, to his mouth. "Why are you doing this?" she asked quietly. "You could have left me to face the consequences. I am fully prepared to do so."

He couldn't help but smile at that. "That's welcome news. Keira Hannigan at last understands there are consequences to her actions."

"This is madness, you know, riding across England like a pair of outlaws."

It was interesting, he thought, that even in the dimmest light, he could still see the green in her eyes. "Think of it as your last adventure," he suggested. "I wouldn't be surprised if your father sent you off to a convent after this."

Keira winced. "That would be the kindest thing he might do to me," she said, and smiled a little lopsidedly as she traced a finger across his bottom lip. "Do you know what I think?"

"I can't begin to imagine."

"Then I shall tell you. I know I am a fool . . . but I think you might be an even bigger fool than me."

Declan grinned. "Why is that?"

"Because you are here with me now."

Her smile, her eyes, everything about her beckoned him. He touched his lips to hers, and as he knew she would, Keira kissed him back with all the anticipation he felt in him.

Her mouth set him aflame, and her body, pressed against the length of his, was excruciatingly pleasurable. It didn't seem to matter that they were under a canvas of stars, in the backwoods of England—the intensity between them was as if they were two people who starved for what only the other could give. Declan rolled her onto her back and came over her, slipping his hand into the coat, finding the shirt, and roughly undoing the opening as he kissed the hollow of her throat. He slipped his hand into the shirt and filled his hand with the soft pliancy of her breast. He could feel the contraction of Keira's sigh of pleasure under his lips.

He was mad for her, completely mad. The desire swallowed him, submerged him in the taste and scent of her. Keira moaned softly as she arched into the palm of his hand. The horses shifted; a log fell from the fire, and Declan felt as if he were drifting in a carnal dream, a dream in which his heart beat with life for the first time in thirty-one years. His heart was beating for Keira.

He took her breast in his mouth.

Her hands were inside his coat, then slipping inside his shirt, her fingernails raking up his chest. She was panting lightly, and, in something of a lust-filled daze, Declan cupped her face with his hand and lifted up, seeking her mouth with his. Keira moved against him in a way that was purely woman, slow and smooth and soft, as he sucked and nibbled her body. His desire swelled in every vein, his heart swelled with each of her little gasps of pleasure, flooding Declan with emotions that were new to him. He wanted her with breathless desperation, and when he maneuvered the buckskins down her legs and slid into her body, he gritted his teeth against the cry that was in his throat, the words that were on the tip of his tongue.

Love. I feel love. I love you.

Keira's leg rose up his side, pressing against his ribs, urging him deeper. She cupped his face in her hands, kissed his mouth and his eyes as he moved inside her. He moved her with his body and his hands, moved her until the wave began to build in her. When Keira cried out into the night, he lost himself within her.

It was exquisite.

Moments later—maybe minutes, maybe hours, maybe days, Declan didn't know—Keira stirred and pressed her face into his neck. He was lying on his back, gazing up at the summer night's stars.

"There is one thing I shall never regret," Keira said, and nibbled his ear. "I shall never regret you."

"That sentiment is entirely mutual," he said, and kissed the top of her head.

"I love you yet," she whispered.

Surprised, Declan reared back a little to look at her.

Keira smiled sheepishly and nodded. "I loved you that day in the meadow, and I still love you. I rather think I always shall."

Declan didn't know how to respond. A million thoughts raced through his mind, not the least of which was that he loved her, too.

"For heaven's sake, don't look so astounded," Keira said. "You know very well that I do. I suppose I am like all the other females in Ireland, all desperate for the attention of the Earl of Donnelly."

"You are . . . you are nothing like the other females in Ireland," he assured her.

"Have a care, sir—that sounded dangerously close to admiration."

"It is far more than admiration," he said, and stroked her hair. "I love you, too, lass."

Keira blinked. Her eyes widened. She came up on her elbows and grinned down at him. "What a strange dream I seem to be having."

He smiled. "You have vexed me, exasperated me, and scandalized me, yet I shall always hold you very dear in my heart."

She gazed at him a long moment before lowering her

head. "That, sir, is the sweetest thing anyone has ever said to me." She put her hand on his chest, directly over his heart, and closed her eyes.

Declan closed his eyes, too. The morning would come soon enough, and reality along with it.

They rode all day every day, stopping only to rest and water the horses. Keira ached all over; her legs felt like gravy when she stepped off the horse and she barely had the strength to lift her arms. It was remarkable to her that Declan always seemed so . . . strong.

The soreness notwithstanding, or the fact that she was fleeing England like a common criminal, Keira began to think these days riding through England were the grandest days of her life. She'd never felt so free. She was free of buttons and bows and hairpins. She was free of society and ladies desiring to marry her off to their sons. She was free to be exactly who she liked to be, and it was wonderful.

They rode until Keira complained she was entirely too filthy to even bear it herself. Declan had grinned at that, his gaze skimming her unkempt hair and dirtied shirt. "I think you are the most alluring I have ever seen you," he said with a wink. But that night, he found a small lake, and under a starlit sky, they braved the cold waters and swam. Together. Without a stitch of clothing. If Keira thought Declan had shown her heights of sensuality before, she was pleasantly surprised to find there were new heights.

Keira had made the decisions that had changed her life, and there was nothing to be done but live it. Furthermore, she didn't want to think about it all now. There would be plenty of time for thinking later. Declan would be disappointed if he knew how much she didn't care of the consequences of what she was doing now. But it was different this time—this time, she was acutely aware of them, but she'd made a conscious choice to be with Declan. Keira had one chance at this extraordinary bit of happiness, and damn it all to hell if she didn't take it.

When they arrived at Pembroke in the early evening of the third day, they'd missed the ferry that would carry passengers and livestock across the Irish Sea and were forced to wait for the following day's ferry. Declan arranged lodging for them under the name of Mr. Sibley and his son, the younger Mr. Sibley. They laughed at that and called each other Sibley. Declan also requested a hot bath be drawn for the younger Mr. Sibley, and surprised Keira with it.

She exclaimed over the hot bath that was brought up, and quickly stripped the clothes she'd worn for the last several days from her body and stepped into it, sighing with pleasure as she melted into the waters. "I think I've never had a better gift, Mr. Sibley," she said.

"Neither have I," Declan said, and kissed her before urging her to sit up so that he could wash her hair. Keira closed her eyes and submerged herself in the luxurious sensation of it. When he'd finished, he removed his clothes and fit into the small tub with her, her back at his chest. He methodically bathed her shoulders, kneading them as he did, then moved to her breasts, and her abdomen. His hand slipped in between her legs, and he massaged her there, too, until she was moaning with pleasure.

When she had floated back to that little room above a noisy street in Pembroke, she turned about in that tub and straddled him as he'd taught her to do, sliding down on him, watching his eyes glaze with pleasure. He kept his eyes on her face as she moved on him. His hands roamed her body, and he kissed her here and there, but mostly he watched her, stroking her hair away from her face so that he could see her until his own desire made it impossible for him to see any longer.

He gathered her in his arms then, surging up to meet her, his grip strong, his breath hot on her skin. He exploded hot and hard in her, shuddering with the force of it.

They remained there until the water turned cool, then ordered a meal and wine, and slept holding one another.

It was the last time they would come together. When they crossed into Ireland the next day, something changed between them. Keira didn't know why that was, but in some place inside her, she understood it.

The adventure was coming to an end.

Thirty-four

They reached the village of Galway three days after setting foot on Irish soil at Wexford. The summer was beginning to wane; Declan noticed the days were shorter and the nights cooler. He felt as if at the end of their journey there would be no sun left.

A small hole in his chest was growing larger as they neared home. He was not so obtuse that he didn't know what that hole was. What that hole meant to him was another matter altogether. There were still glaring problems as far as Keira was concerned—the crime she had committed in England for one, but that would be overcome eventually. There was something else, however, that could not be overcome: Declan's desire to be free.

He didn't have the slightest idea how to go about reconciling his love for Keira with his need to be free. It was something that had been with him from his birth, and he couldn't give up that piece of himself.

They stopped in Galway and he entered the dress shop to buy Keira a gown. It delighted Mrs. MacDougal to no end. "For your sister, then?" she asked cheerfully as she wrapped up the gray muslin.

"You are blessed with an astute nature, madam," he

said with a wink. Let her think what she wanted about the gown. He turned to leave her dress shop, but happened to see a bonnet with quite a lot of frippery on it. "I'll take that as well," he said, reaching for his purse again.

"The bonnet!" Mrs. MacDougal exclaimed. "That's right sweet of you, milord, if you don't mind me saying. It's been sitting in my window for months and months. Ah, but Eireanne will look lovely in it, will she not?"

"It is very nice," he said vaguely, and minutes later, with gown and hat in hand, he left the shop and rode back to the woods, where Keira was waiting.

She thanked him politely for the clothes, but he noticed that she scarcely looked at them. He used a saddle blanket draped from a tree limb to give her some privacy to change. When she'd dressed, she handed him the clothes she had lived in these many days. He stuffed them in a saddlebag and stood back to admire her. "You look lovely. No one will suspect you are the younger Mr. Sibley."

She grinned and looked down at the gown. "It is lovely. And the bonnet!" she exclaimed. "If I didn't know you quite as I do, I'd think you'd gone a wee bit soft for bonnets."

He'd gone soft, all right, but it wasn't for bonnets. He took Keira's hand and kissed her palm. "So we have come to the end of our journey, have we?"

"We have come to the end of this journey, aye. But something tells me I have only just begun my own journey."

He arched a brow. "That's a tantalizing thing to say, Mr. Sibley. What, pray tell, do you mean by it?"

She shrugged. "I am a different person now. What,

are you surprised? Something in me is quite different. I can feel it. Right here," she said, pressing her hand to the middle of her torso.

Oh, but he felt it, too.

She sighed and fitted the bonnet on her head. "I will be glad to have this ordeal behind me." She tied the velvet ribbons under her chin and held out her arms. "How do I look?"

Declan's heart lurched a little. "You look like an angel, *muirnín.*"

She laughed. "The devil has the face of an angel, aye?" she said, harking back to the first days he'd encountered her at Ashwood.

"Aye," he said simply. He would never forget it, not a single moment of it.

She looked at him as if there were something she would say. He could see the sadness that rimmed her eyes, mixed with a worldliness that he'd never really seen in her. He thought she might ask him what the future held, but she did not. "Well then, let's do go on," she said, and turned away from him. "Pappa will want all the hours left in the day to speak very sternly with me."

She could pretend to be at ease with it, but she wouldn't look him directly in the eye. Declan himself was deeply conflicted; it seemed like a moment was approaching when he had to make some life-altering decisions, and God as his witness, he was at a loss to know what to do.

Keira said nothing as they rode for Lisdoon, but when they reached the cliffs just miles from her home, Keira suddenly reined to a stop.

Declan was surprised by it, and wheeled the gelding around, but Keira had already thrown herself off the Welsh and was striding toward the cliff edge. Declan's heart seized. *"Keira!"* he shouted, and vaulted off his horse. He ran after her, catching her before she reached the edge. "What are you doing? Are you all right?"

"I am quite all right," Keira said, shaking him off. "Honestly, Declan, did you think I meant to jump? No, I did not mean to alarm you. I meant only . . . I am sad. So very sad. That's all." She looked out at the sea a moment, and then doubled over.

"Oh love—"

Keira put her hand out, keeping him from her. "I told you I won't regret it, and I mean that, I never will," she said resolutely, forcing herself up. "Not so much as a moment of the time I have spent with you, even those moments you were perfectly wretched to me."

"Keira—"

"I will miss you very much, Declan." She stood up and looked at him expectantly.

He swallowed. He straightened the tie of her bonnet. He ran his palm down her arm. "I will miss you, as well." He wanted to say more, but God help him if he knew how to express what he was feeling.

She gaped at him. "Is that truly all you can say? How can you let me go, Declan? How can you pretend as if nothing has happened between us?"

"Oh God, Keira," he said and reached for her, but Keira jerked out of his reach. He felt that hole in his chest open a little wider. "I will always love you, Keira Hannigan. Hats and all. But I don't know how to change who I am."

Keira looked as if he'd just slapped her. She nodded

slowly, then looked out to the sea. "I would never ask you to be anything other than who you are," she said quietly. "Not me, of all people."

Her expression was heartbreakingly sad, and Declan reached for her once more, but Keira moved away from his hand. "Don't," she said, low. "Please don't. It is time we both got on with our lives, aye?" She began walking away, toward the horses.

"Keira!" he said.

"No need to soothe my feelings," she said lightly. "We are in Ireland now, and we have our separate lives and families. We always knew we would, did we not?" She twirled around and walked backward, facing him. "I shall always love you, Declan! But it truly is time we go our separate ways." She twirled about again and walked on, leaving him to stand there, looking after her.

He watched her mount the mare with the ease of a horsewoman and glance back at him. "Are you coming?"

He slowly strode forward, his gaze narrowed on her, his suspicions high.

Keira did not look at him for the rest of the ride into Lisdoon

At the door of the Lisdoon mansion, there was a great hue and cry from Keira's family. They hustled her in, their arms around her, and her father pounded Declan on the back to thank him for escorting her home from Wexford, where the two of them said they'd met quite by accident.

"Where are your trunks?" Mabe asked.

"They'll be along," Keira said easily, and smiled at Declan as her family tried to pull her farther inside.

"Thank you so very much, my lord. Please do not trouble yourself any further. I am sure Eireanne is anxious to see you safely returned."

Declan was standing in the foyer with her father, his gaze boring through her. Keira had thought her battered heart had completely broken, but she had discovered today that it had not yet been smashed to pieces. Not until this very moment. She kept her bright smile, hiding behind it, using it as her shield.

Molly and Mabe and Keira's mother ushered her into the salon. Her mother, Keira noticed, was obviously very happy to see Keira, but kept looking at her suspiciously.

"What did you love best about Italy?" Molly asked in the salon.

"Oh, the art," Keira said.

"There's my girl," her father boomed as he walked into the salon. He was alone. Keira's heart wrenched; that meant Declan was gone. He was gone, out of her life. It was truly over.

Keira's father grabbed her up and twirled her around. "Well, they fed you well in Italy, aye?" he asked, and laughed roundly along with Molly and Mabe.

"I've seen that hat," Keira's mother said shrewdly. "It has been in Mrs. MacDougal's window for an age."

"Oh, aye . . . yes," Keira said, and touched the hat.

"Why do you have it?"

"I fancied it," she said as innocently as she could.

"What art?" Molly asked excitedly. "Did you see the Sistine Chapel?"

"Umm . . . no," Keira said. "It was closed for renovation."

"The chapel?" her mother asked.

"Aye," Keira said, avoiding her gaze.

"Why are you wearing your boots with that gown?" Mabe asked, looking at Keira's feet.

"Where did you say your trunks were?" her mother asked.

Keira could feel the heat crawling up her nape. Her father looked so happy to see her, and Molly and Mabe were desperate for news and tales of Italy. But her mother, God bless her eyes, her mother had always known when something was amiss.

"Well?" her mother asked as she brushed Keira's hair back from her temple.

"They . . . they are not here," Keira said carefully.

"Ach, don't fret, lass. I'll send a boy for them," her father said jovially. "So good to have you home. I don't think I can let you from my sight again!"

"Your color is very high, Keira. Are you unwell?" her mother asked, and pressed her palm to Keira's forehead.

"I'm fine, I'm . . ." She closed her eyes. She was in love, she was desperate, she was sad, she was so many, many things that she had never been in Ireland, that she didn't know how to tell her family all that she was now. She opened her eyes. "I'm different."

Mabe snorted. Molly looked a little envious. Her father laughed and poured wee drams of whiskey for them all. But Keira's mother kept her gaze steady on her. "How so?"

"Well, that . . . that is rather an interesting story," Keira said, and shook her head at the dram her father offered her. She sank onto the silk-covered settee and looked out the big windows at the forest. "One that I don't think you will care for, actually."

Her father's smile faded. Her mother sighed and sank onto the settee next to her. Molly and Mabe gaped with excitement.

"My darling girl," her mother said. "What have you done?"

"Steady yourself, Mamma," Keira said, "because I have done an extraordinarily stupid thing. More than one, actually. One might say scores of stupid things."

"Do you mean more than all the stupid things you've done in Ireland?" Mabe asked, her voice full of awe.

"I do, indeed," Keira said, and told her family about her extraordinary adventure, beginning with the day the letter from Ashwood had come for Lily several months ago.

Thirty-five

A few days after Declan returned home, Eireanne had received her letter inviting her to attend the Institut Villa Amiels. She was beside herself with excitement and so concerned about what she might wear that Declan was compelled to take her to Dublin to be outfitted for her first trip abroad.

For once, it suited him to spend a fortnight doing little more than signing his name to bank drafts. He'd done nothing but sulk since arriving at Ballynahcath. Keira's abrupt dismissal had stung him, and he had convinced himself she had done him a courtesy by it, for just when he thought he'd lost his heart to the woman, he was reminded that he did well enough without her. So he turned his focus forward, to his horses, and to planning his return to Kitridge Lodge just as soon as Eireanne's schooling was settled and the travel arrangements made.

In Dublin, Eireanne and Declan's grandmother went out every evening to the theater or opera. Declan wandered about between two gentlemen's clubs, but he was not interested in gaming. He was not interested in women. The only thing that held any interest for him at all seemed to be good Irish whiskey. It helped him to silence the thoughts in his head and dull the strange throbbing in his chest. Declan simply did not feel himself, and after a fortnight, he was beginning to wonder if he ever would feel himself again.

By the time he and his family returned to Ballynaheath, he'd made up his mind. He was returning to England straightaway, to his pregnant mare and his horses. That's where he belonged. Not here, brooding—and he was brooding, as much as it pained him to admit it—for the most foolish woman on God's green earth.

Declan was so disgusted with himself that he took an uncharacteristic walk around the extensive grounds of Ballynaheath. More accurately, he had marched out of his study and onto his lawn in something of a restless pique, but once there, he realized he didn't really know where to go. So he wandered aimlessly, trying to recall the last time he'd walked Ballynaheath.

What he found was breathtaking. He walked past beautiful vistas of the sea, and through thick, mossy green woods. Perhaps that was what he found most enchanting— the estate was beautifully green. All of Ireland was green, but his estate seemed particularly so, and the color of it in late summer reminded him of Keira's eyes.

Declan announced that evening that he was leaving Ballynaheath in a fortnight.

Eireanne sighed and put down her fork. "Really, Declan, I am beginning to believe you are English."

"I am as Irish as you, pet, but I have a pregnant mare at Kitridge Lodge that requires my attention. Besides which, you will be departing for school soon. What reason have I to stay here?"

"That doesn't make your grandmother feel particularly loved," his grandmother said with a sniff.

Declan reached for her hand and squeezed it. "If you think for even a moment that I am not aware of your friendship with Mr. Barney, you are mistaken. The less I am about, the more you can devote your attention to him."

His grandmother chuckled. "I am but an old woman in want of companionship, and your presence will not influence my social calendar, my lord. I am hardly concerned with either my virtue or your care and feeding, as you have proven perfectly capable of seeing after it yourself," she said. "When might we see you home again?"

"I can't very well say," he said honestly. "There seems so little for me here at present."

"There is more here than you know," his grandmother said as she pushed herself from her seat to stand, waving off the footman who hurried forward to help her. "And you would see it with your own eyes if you would only bother to look about you, my lord. Now then, good night, my dears. I have promised Mr. Barney a round of whist this evening."

"Good night, Grandmamma," Eireanne said. She rose from the table, too. "I beg your pardon, Declan, but I've so much to do before I go." She kissed his cheek as she went out, leaving Declan alone in the dining room.

Could they not see he needed their company this evening? Of course not. He was so rarely in their company, they could not possibly understand that he needed them more than ever.

He repaired to the study and, predictably, thought

about Keira. He wondered if Maloney had been round to see her, if the planning for their wedding was under way, which Keira would be wise to do before word filtered back from England. "Bah," he said to himself, and put his glass aside.

Now even whiskey annoyed him.

By week's end, he determined he would pay a call to her before he left. He couldn't see what purpose it would serve, other than to torment him, but away he went, trotting to Lisdoon on his gelding.

Keira, the butler said, was indisposed.

"Tell her to dispose herself," he said to the man. "Tell her Lord Donnelly would like a word."

The butler returned a few minutes later with two footmen. "Begging your pardon, my lord, but the lady is indisposed. She bids you come another time."

If Declan hadn't been so irate, he feared he might have sunk down into despondence right there on the steps at Lisdoon. As it was, he hoped to find a bunny or two to kick.

By the end of the following week, he could no longer mope and ride about Ballynaheath. He had no society. His friendships were few and it seemed that most everyone was away before the autumn rains set in. He had nothing but empty hours. One afternoon, he had his saddlebags brought out so that he might fill them, and found the clothes Keira had worn on their journey. He'd forgotten he'd stuffed them in one.

He held the shirt to his face and breathed in her scent. He removed the buckskins and the waistcoat and tucked them in his bureau, but he put the shirt back in his saddlebags.

On Saturday morning, the day of Eireanne's departure, Declan and his grandmother saw her out, waiting as her trunks were loaded onto the coach. "Remember that you are expected at Christmas," he warned Eireanne.

"Of course!" she said brightly. It was good to see Eireanne's smile; she was clearly excited about this turn in her life, and Declan was excited for her. "You are leaving on the morrow?" she asked Declan.

"Aye." He glanced back at the monolith of a castle that was Ballynaheath. "It will be quite tiresome without you about, I fear, and no other society to divert me."

"There are the Hannigans," his grandmother offered.

"Oh yes, Molly and Mabe are such a delight, and now Keira," Eireanne said as she straightened her gloves. "But as Keira has cried off from Maloney, she may not care for society just now."

Declan stilled. "Pardon?"

"Mmm?" Eireanne said absently, holding out her hand to admire her new silk gloves.

"You said Keira had cried off."

"Aye. Haven't you heard? She was all but engaged to Loman Maloney, but then she went to Italy, and when she came back, she cried off."

"That is poor form, if you ask me," Declan's grandmother said. "And really, she can do no better than Mr. Maloney."

Eireanne laughed. "Maybe she fancies an Italian."

"Yes, well, don't you get any ideas about Italians," Declan said, and opened the door of his coach. Eireanne beamed as she put her arms around him and kissed him farewell. She said farewell to her grandmother, and she and Declan watched Eireanne's coach roll away. Eireanne hung out the window waving until the coach turned a corner and she could see them no more.

"The gelding," Declan said to a waiting groom.

"Where are you off to?" Declan's grandmother asked.

"I have a bit of unfinished business," he said coolly. She'd cried off from Maloney? Was she mad? Was *he*?

When Declan reached Lisdoon, he threw himself off the horse before he'd even come to a halt and took the steps two at a time up to the door. He pounded with his fist. There was a wee contretemps when the butler informed Declan that Miss Hannigan was not taking callers.

"She will bloody well take this call," Declan said, and pushed past him and a footman, shouting her name.

Keira appeared on the landing above, leaning over the stone balustrade, her sisters beside her. "Declan!" she cried. "What on earth?"

She looked beautiful in a gown the color of roses, breathtakingly beautiful. "Come down here," he commanded her, pointing to the ground at his feet. "Come down at once and I will not make this call any more of a theatrical drama than it already is."

"I don't think it is possible to make it any more dramatic."

He glared at her. He could hardly restrain himself from lunging up the stairs. "Come down, Keira. At once."

"Now what have you done?" Molly asked her sister.

"What is this about?" Mr. Hannigan thundered, appearing in the foyer where Declan stood, his napkin still tucked into his collar. "Donnelly! What in hell's name are you about?"

"I would like a word with your daughter," Declan said, his gaze still on Keira.

"That is not possible," Mr. Hannigan said, and waved his arm at his daughters. "All of you, go back to your rooms! You are not allowed callers—any of you!"

"What have *I* done?" Mabe cried.

"I will see her," Declan said to Hannigan.

"Now see here, Donnelly—"

"Pappa, please." Keira started marching down the stairs, her gaze glittering, her gown trailing behind her. "I will speak with his lordship and make certain he understands that no one calls at Lisdoon in such a brutish manner."

"Don't play countess with me, lass," Declan warned her.

"I am not playing anything with you," Keira said smartly as she sailed to a halt before him, her eyes blazing. "If you have something to say to me, sir, you may say it like a gentleman."

"Very well," he agreed. "Shall I say it *here*?" he asked, gesturing to the space around them.

Keira's eyes narrowed. She pointed to a room directly to her right. "The sunroom," she said, and with a toss of her head, she marched on to the sunroom. Declan and Mr. Hannigan followed her.

In the sunroom, Keira shooed her father away. "You may stand just outside if you like, Pappa, but you must allow that only I can impress upon Lord Donnelly that his behavior is insupportable!"

"We'll not tolerate it, Donnelly!" Hannigan shouted as Keira closed the door.

She twirled about and folded her arms. "Why are you here?" she demanded. "Shouldn't you be in Africa or some such place?"

"Why did you cry off from Maloney?" he shot back.

One of Keira's brows rose. "I beg your pardon, but that is none of your concern."

"Ah," he snapped. "You blithely made your life my concern whilst in England, but once in Ireland, my shoulders are no longer needed, aye? No, Keira, I will not accept that. Why did you cry off from Maloney? You know very well that once news of what happened at Ashwood reaches Ireland, no proper Irishman will offer."

"Please do not presume to tell me who I shall marry," Keira said haughtily.

"Bloody hell if there isn't something amiss here," Declan said, advancing on her. "A scheme of some sort, and I will know what it is." He stood so close that Keira had to tilt her head back to glare him in the eye.

"Just because I sought your help once does not mean that I need or want to seek it again."

She was so exasperatingly beautiful. Declan grabbed her shoulders. "What are you about, Keira?"

"Do you *really* want the truth?"

"Aye!"

Her gaze suddenly softened and fell to his mouth. "I am with child."

She said it so softly that Declan wasn't certain she'd even said it. He gaped at her. A million emotions—surprise, fear, *elation*—began to swirl through him at once. "The devil you say," he said tightly.

"It's true," she said. "I cried off because I am with

child." A lone tear slipped out of her eye and slid down her cheek.

The news knocked Declan almost to his knees. He let go of Keira and whirled away, his hand on his head, trying to absorb it. His heart and his thoughts raced madly. He turned back to her, peering at her. "Why?" he managed, and grabbed her arm, pulling her close. "Why didn't you tell me?"

"Because you would do the proper thing and be forever tied to me," she said, and abruptly pushed him away with both hands to his chest.

Declan was rooted to his spot. He would be a father. A *father*! Pride and love rose up in him along with his ire. Keira had tried to keep the news of his baby from him. He didn't know whether to strangle her or hug her. "Did you think I wouldn't discover it?" he asked her incredulously.

"I thought you would be in Africa," she said over her shoulder. "And then it would be too late."

"Too late!" In two strides, Declan caught Keira by the shoulders and forced her around. "What right do you have to keep this from me?" he demanded. "I am to be a father, and you would keep that from me? How long have you known?"

"I . . . I didn't know I was with child until you'd gone, on my honor," she said earnestly. "And I didn't send you a note because . . . because I don't want to be your obligation, Declan! God in heaven, I don't want to be the thing that tethers you to Ballynaheath. Don't you know that? If there is one thing in life I want, it is to be free. I can never have that, but *you* can, and you are the only person I know who understands it. I would not take that from you. I would not see the resentment build in you, year after year after year. So go, please just go. No one knows and I will never tell a soul."

"Jesus, Keira—" He took her face in his hands. "Do you know that I have thought of little else but you? Do you know that I have ached for you and despised you for setting me free? I was leaving Ireland, Keira. I was on my way to England when I heard the news—God save me," he said, thinking of how close he had come to losing this woman and his child. "A more foolish girl I've never known." He kissed her temple, her cheek, her mouth again. He kissed her with love, with pride, with the lightness of spirit that came with a new beginning.

Keira's hands wrapped around his wrists, clinging to him. "Who is the fool, Declan? You want life and adventure. You will come to despise me for forcing you to settle when you want to soar."

He brushed his palm roughly over her head. "Did it ever occur to you that with the right woman, I would not soar alone? Think of it, *muirnín.* There are places in this world just waiting to be explored. Foods to be eaten, strange drinks to be sampled. We could do that—you and I and our brood could do that," he said, and rested his hand against her abdomen.

Her eyes widened with surprise. A smile slowly began to form on her lips. "Do you truly mean it?"

"I have never meant anything so ardently in my life. I love you, Keira Hannigan. And I know now that there is no life, there is no adventure, without you."

"Oh, Declan, you cannot imagine how happy that makes me." She sighed, and pressed her forehead to his and laughed. "But you do realize that makes you an even bigger fool than me, aye?"

That might be, but he was a very happy fool. He kissed her again, only deeper, his body waking to the possibility of seeing this woman each morning, to the life they could have, to the happiness that could be his.

Thirty-six

It took two days for the constable to arrive, and when he did, he questioned Lily endlessly, but at last conceded that there wasn't much he could do about Keira's deception within the bounds of the law, not with Keira gone from Ashwood and Lily unwilling to pursue the matter further.

Lily hoped that would be the end of it, but it was not. She found it quite daunting to be countess of such a grand estate, particularly when there were so many hard feelings about what Keira had done. She knew she was viewed with suspicion. Mrs. Morton told her that there were many in Hadley Green who believed she and Keira had concocted the scheme for some nefarious reason. That they could not name the nefarious reason did not keep tongues from wagging and speculating.

The only person who seemed to accept Lily without question was little Lucy Taft. But the poor girl pined for Keira. Lily's heart went out to the girl—she'd once pined for Althea.

Declan was right about Mr. Fish—he was there to guide her through the morass of business and legal issues facing

Ashwood. Declan was also right about Keira—the more Lily learned, the more she understood what a remarkable job Keira had done in her stead. She hoped she could do as well for Ashwood.

The toughest hours were when the day had closed and Lily was left to wander about Ashwood alone. It was a strange sensation to see the estate through adult eyes. Although the mansion was quite impressive in size, it didn't seem as large to her as it had as a child. And there were rooms she'd thought were in one wing of the house when they were in another.

Over the course of the first fortnight, Lily wandered the house, looking into all the rooms, recalling some things, some events, and wondering about others, constantly struggling with an incomplete memory.

Moreover, she'd not slept well since she'd come—what Keira had told her about her aunt and Mr. Scott burdened her. The news that Aunt Althea may have taken her own life was devastating. Lily could not help but feel, in part, responsible for it. Had she known Althea and Mr. Scott were having an affair? She tried to put together the bits and pieces of her memory to form a picture, but there were too many holes, leaving many troubling questions that disturbed her. But perhaps none more than the one that had always plagued her: if Aunt Althea and Mr. Scott were indeed lovers, and Mr. Scott had not stolen the jewels . . . then what had happened to those jewels?

After almost a month of being at Ashwood alone, Lily was elated to receive a pair of letters from Ireland. The first was from Molly, who wrote with scads of exclamation marks and underlined words that Keira's pregnancy was perhaps the greatest scandal Galway had ever known. Molly wrote as if Lily somehow had heard this news about Keira, which of course she had not, and she was shocked and scandalized to hear it. But she was not terribly surprised. Lily knew her spirited cousin very well and knew that caution had never been one of her more admirable qualities.

The second letter was from Keira, likewise filled with underlined words and exclamation points, all about Declan O'Conner. They had married quickly, obviously, and remained blissfully ensconced at Ballynaheath, away from scandal, and planning an adventure to Africa after the baby was born the following year. Declan wanted to find some Arabian horses to breed, and Keira wanted to see a camel. It seemed impossible to Lily that the two of them had fallen in love, what with their history, but she supposed stranger things had happened.

Keira was also concerned for Lily. She apologized profusely for the mess she'd left, and warned her again to keep her distance from Eberlin. She reminded Lily that he somehow suspected the truth about her, and had, according to Keira, the eyes of the devil.

But for the most part, Keira's letter was filled with happiness. Lily did not begrudge Keira that happiness in the least, but it did feel a wee bit unfair that she'd been left at Ashwood to repair all the damage Keira had caused while Keira planned for a child and a marriage with someone she loved.

It made Lily realize how lonely she was. She longed for her cousins, longed for anyone she could call friend.

It was no help that the Danish count Eberlin seemed

bent on destroying Ashwood. She had yet to meet the man, but nevertheless, he'd begun construction on a mill upriver from the Ashwood mill. Lily had recently received a summons to appear in court concerning the acreage in question. With Mr. Fish's and Mr. Goodwin's help, she was prepared to battle for what was rightfully hers, but it was daunting to face so many challenges without someone to lean on.

Autumn was setting in one rainy afternoon when Linford announced she had a caller.

She looked at the calling card, saw the name and recoiled: Eberlin. Her first thought was to refuse to see him. Her second thought was to demand why he was so intent on destroying Ashwood. "Send him in, please," she said, and stood, smoothing her wine-colored gown.

She clasped her hands tightly before her. When Eberlin strode in, she was taken aback by his appearance. She didn't know what she'd expected—something more like a gnome, in all honesty—but she had not expected this strong, handsome man with piercing dark brown eyes and wavy golden-brown hair. He was tall and broad shouldered, his jaw square. There was something vaguely familiar about him, too.

"Madam," he said, bowing deep.

He had an odd accent, one that she could not quite place. "Lord Eberlin," she said stiffly. "What brings you to Ashwood this dreary day?"

He moved closer, his eyes boring through hers. "I thought it was time."

"Time for what?"

One dark brow rose above the other. "Is it not obvious?"

Lily blinked. Keira was right—he was an odd man with a hard gaze. "Obvious? On the contrary, my lord, there is nothing obvious about your call or the ill will you hold for Ashwood." He stepped closer, studying her face. Lily's pulse fluttered and she was thankful for the footman who stood at the door. Something was so disturbingly familiar about Eberlin . . . but what?

"You are as beautiful as I knew you would be," he said as his gaze casually wandered her body, lingering on her décolletage, on her mouth. "Perhaps even more."

She felt strangely exposed and said stiffly, "I beg your pardon."

He lifted his molasses-brown gaze to hers, piercing hers. "Do you truly not know who I am? Or are you as adept at playing dangerous games like your cousin?"

A tiny flicker of trepidation forced Lily one step back. "I've only just met you, sir."

He smiled. In any other circumstance, she might have thought it an easy, handsome smile, but there was something rather sinister about it that made Lily's blood run cold. "Perhaps this will jog your memory. I am Tobin. Do you recall me now?"

Lily gasped. Her pulse began to race. She did indeed know him now, knew that he was Tobin Scott, the son of Joseph Scott. She'd not seen him since the day of the trial when he'd stared daggers at her. She had not recognized the boy as a man. "Tobin," she said softly. "*Tobin* . . . I can scarcely believe it is you."

"Surprised, are you?"

Astounded. "Yes," she said. "I never knew . . . I never knew where you'd gone."

He smirked a little. "Here and there."

"And your name, Eberlin—"

"Ah, yes. That title derives from an estate I own in Denmark."

"Denmark? But how—"

"And now I have returned to Hadley Green and Tiber Park with but one goal in mind. Would you like to know what that goal is?"

Lily blinked. She wasn't sure she wanted to know.

He smiled again, and impulsively touched her cheek. Lily flinched, and Tobin paused, his fingers on her skin, casually tracing a line from her cheek to her mouth. "To destroy Ashwood," he said softly.

Lily gasped and jerked away from his hand.

"Be forewarned that I will not rest until I have," he added smoothly. He let his gaze flick over her once more, then turned and strode from the room without another word, leaving Lily to gape after him in shock.